I0575280

William John Robertson

A century of French verse

Brief biographical and critical notices of thirty-three French poets

William John Robertson

A century of French verse
Brief biographical and critical notices of thirty-three French poets

ISBN/EAN: 9783744722896

Printed in Europe, USA, Canada, Australia, Japan

Cover: Foto ©Raphael Reischuk / pixelio.de

More available books at **www.hansebooks.com**

A CENTURY OF
FRENCH VERSE:

Brief biographical and critical notices of thirty-three French poets of the nineteenth century with experimental translations from their poems.

⚜ ⚜ ⚜

WILLIAM JOHN ROBERTSON.

⚜

LONDON:

A. D. INNES & CO.

BEDFORD STREET.

1895.

THIS VOLUME

IS

DEDICATED

WITH AFFECTION AND GRATITUDE

TO

DANIEL FERGUSON RAMSAY

AND

ARCHIBALD EDWARD BUCHANAN BROWN.

Contents.

CONTENTS

CONTENTS

Ballade against such as speak ill
of France.

MAY he be met by monsters spouting fire,
  As Jason was, in quest o' the fleece of gold ;
Or to a beast be, like Belshazzar's sire,
    Seven years transformed, and won in field and
    fold;
Or dree such dolorous loss and sore despight
As erst the Trojans wreaked for Helen's flight ;
  Or swallowëd be, like Tantalus of old
And Proserpine, in Pluto's pool obscene ;
  Be worse than Job in grievous sufferance,
Or held as thrall in Dædalus' demesne,
  That wisheth evil to the realm of France !

Four months may he sit singing in a mire,
  As bittern doth his head i' the marish hold ;
Or led in harness, like a beast of hire,
  Be to the Grand Turk eke for silver sold ;
Or thrice ten years, like Magdalen naked quite,
In cloth of wool ne linen cloth be dight ;
  Be, like Narcissus, drenched in waters cold,
Like Absalom hung by the hair the boughs between,
  Fordone as Judas was for malfeasance,
Or in worse case than Simon Magus seen,
  That wisheth evil to the realm of France !

His wealth, so might Octavian's time be nigher,
  Should molten flow in's body as a mould;
Or like Saint-Victor's were his penance dire,
  To be between the moving millstones rolled;
Or by the waves engulfed in sorer plight
Than Jonah lodged in whale's maw day and night;
  Banished be he, nor Phœbus' sheen behold,
Nor Juno's boon, nor solace of Love's queen;
  And by great God be doomed to foul mischance,
As King Sardanapalus was, I ween;
  That wisheth evil to the realm of France!

ENVOY.

Prince, may the troop of Eolus swoop him clean
Where Glaucus reigneth in his forest green,
  Forlorn of peace and hopeful countenance;
For he deserves no goodly thing to glean
  That wisheth evil to the realm of France!

Ballade contre les mesdisans de la France.

FRANÇOIS VILLON.

xiv

Introduction.

When Ralph Waldo Emerson disposed, in one summary and emphatic line, of

> 'France, where poet never grew'

he was apparently convinced that she could claim no representative singer whose name might be fitly placed along with the five starry names of Homer, Dante, Shakespeare, Swedenborg and Goethe. It is not unlikely that the American sage, with his puritanical prejudice against 'amorous poetry' and his instinctive dislike to 'sad poetry', had preconceived the existence of certain uncongenial elements in French verse, for even in Goethe's *Faust* he found something that was 'too Parisian'. And it is probable, also, that he was better acquainted with French writers of the so-called classical period than with the lyrical voices of the present century. His denial of a poet to France, regarded as the utterance of personal feeling, might therefore be dismissed as unworthy of serious consideration were it not likewise the laconic expression of a widely-diffused opinion. Nevertheless there must be many lovers of verse who think that the name of Victor Hugo would have completed the circle of supreme poets more appropriately than that of the Swedish visionary. Tennyson denoted a truer appreciation of Victor Hugo's place in literature when he apostrophised the

> '. . . . . . Bard whose fame-lit laurels glance,
> 'Darkening the wreaths of all that would advance,
> 'Beyond our strait, their claim to be *his* peer'.

And Swinburne may be forgiven some excess of enthusiasm, if any excess there be, in that splendid *Birthday
Ode* which proclaims how

' The mightiest soul put mortal raiment on
' That came forth singing ever in man's ears
' Of all souls with us '. . . .

But, even if Victor Hugo had never existed, it would
surely be a rash thing to assert that ' poet never grew '
in the country which produced Villon and Ronsard in her
archaic age, Malherbe and Regnier during the period of
formal development, André Chénier in the blackest days
of her intellectual eclipse, and Lamartine, Musset, Banville,
Baudelaire and Leconte de Lisle as representatives of
the modern movement which has been made illustrious
by so many men of genius.   Unless, indeed, an appeal
from blind prepossession to blazing evidence is lost upon
those who willingly believe that no good thing can come
out of Nazareth !
    The oracular judgments of great men are by no means
least among the curiosities of literature.   Within half a
century of Jean-Jacques Rousseau's confident prediction
that such a thing as French music could never be, France
gave birth to Hector Berlioz, the supreme master of
modern orchestration and perhaps the most poetical of
all composers ; in less than another half-century she had
conquered Europe with her brilliant operas. . . . ' Equally
' a want of books and men ' was the reproach of Wordsworth to a revolution which produced Lazare Carnot and
Lazare Hoche, and from which has since proceeded the
most ample and splendid literary movement ever known.
. . . According to Voltaire the dramatic art was in its
infancy in England in the days of Shakespeare.   And yet

out of the mouths of these Elizabethan babes and suck-
lings human speech was perfected.

    ✱   ✱   ✱   ✱   ✱   ✱

Although French poetry in the nineteenth century has
exercised a large influence on the lyrical literature of
Italy and Russia, it must be confessed that it has generally
met with grudging recognition abroad. The familiarity
of educated Englishmen with the French language, and
even with French literature as represented by the novel
and the drama, has not promoted to much purpose the
culture of French poetry. And while the appreciative
criticism of certain journals is ready to bear witness that
there are English writers who possess a consummate
knowledge of French verse, its beauties have hitherto been
more or less neglected. It is true that of late years a
change has come over the indifferent feeling with which
this notable branch of literature was so long regarded in
England. Evidences of a growing interest in French
poets and poetry have been afforded by occasional translations from Musset or Gautier and occasional essays
on Baudelaire or Verlaine. The anthology edited by
George Saintsbury has helped to give a general notion of
the character and scope of French verse to fluent readers
of the language. If such unambitious specimens as Dean
Carrington's *Translations from the Poems of Victor Hugo*
may have failed to perform a similar service for the un-
initiated, it cannot be said that the characteristics of
French lyrical form and melody have been neglected in
the excellent fugitive translations of Austin Dobson,
Arthur O'Shaughnessy, Andrew Lang, Cosmo Monk-
house and other English writers. The purpose of the
experimental translations which are published in this
volume is simply to convey to those readers who are not
in touch with the original language some perception of

the peculiar qualities of French poetry, in so far as these may have been reflected in a diversely constituted tongue.

* * * * * *

'Speaking generally, it is not in respect of form, but 'in respect of matter, that our poets are inferior to the 'English poets'* says Gabriel Sarrazin in his admirable series of studies entitled *la Renaissance de la Poésie anglaise*: *1798-1889*. In this distinction between spiritual substance and artistic shape the French writer has seized at least one characteristic which gives English poetry the supreme place in modern literature. Other French critics have observed it, for example, Taine, who confesses in his *Notes sur l'Angleterre*:—'To my mind there is no poetry 'equal to English poetry, and none which speaks so 'strongly and so clearly to the soul'. Théophile Gautier was likewise able to appreciate, if not to emulate, those inherent qualities which give to English verse its enviable supremacy, for he has somewhere vaguely defined them as 'the Scottish element' in song.

It would, of course, be false to assume that the higher faculties of imagination and moral force have exercised no influence on French poetry. Yet it is certain that the peculiar pathos of the *Elegy written in a Country Churchyard*, the wild fantastic charm of *The Ancient Mariner*, and the subtle emotion that breathes through *The Solitary Reaper* or the *Ode to a Nightingale* have found no such perfect expression in the French language, rich as it is in poetical ideas and images, and possessed of such artistic resources. And if, in a general sense, refraining from futile individual comparisons, we take Keats for André Chénier; Wordsworth, Shelley, Coleridge and Landor for

---

* 'Ce n'est point en général par la forme, mais par le fond, que nos poètes 'sont inférieurs aux poètes anglais.'

Lamartine, Barbier, Sainte-Beuve and Gérard de Nerval
(forgetting Victor Hugo); Byron for Alfred de Musset;
and Browning, Rossetti, Tennyson, Swinburne, Matthew
Arnold, William Morris and George Meredith for Théophile Gautier, Théodore de Banville, Leconte de Lisle,
Charles Baudelaire and the whole school of contemporary
French singers, such a parallel is on the whole unfavour-
able to France, especially when those things which seem
to be the essence and soul of poetry are divested of their
outward limbs and flourishes. But, in making this
comparison, it must be remembered that although the
combination of moral force with ideal vision which is
conspicuous in Wordsworth, Browning and Tennyson is
not so manifest in Keats, Shelley and Swinburne, these
poets have nevertheless achieved great things and taken
a place with all but the highest names in English song.
Perhaps it is unfortunate for French verse that so much of
it has been inspired by Parisian experience, and that it
often reflects the artificial emotions of a highly-corrupted
civilisation, instead of seeking fresh colour and life from
the healthy influences of natural beauty and spiritual
solitude. For this is the secret of the power which lies in
the best English poetry. Its spell has been woven from
the deepest and widest experiences of human life. Those
elements of reflection and force, kindled by imagination and
feeling, with which it is so largely suffused are drawn from
the remote and complex characteristics of a race in which
the robust Saxon, the calculating Norman, the audacious
Dane and the dreamy Celt have for ages blended their
activities, their thoughts and their ideals.

      *   *   *   *   *   *

The poetry of any people necessarily derives its
external characteristics from the peculiar attributes of the
national tongue, for the mould in which the poet's thought

is cast must be determined by the nature of the rhyme and the limitations of the rhythm which are indigenous to his own language. Let the emotion be ever so fervid and the imagination ever so lofty, their rough-cast creations will have to be chiselled, when they cool down, in the material which the craftsman's native speech has placed at his service. Hence the 'mechanic exercise' to which Tennyson alludes in one of the most spontaneous and at the same time one of the most highly elaborated of his works. The critic of poetry, in his pursuit of 'conceptions' and 'atmospheres' and 'periods of evolution', is perhaps prone to overlook the importance of this purely artistic element in verse. And yet the accidents of rhyme, the facilities of alliteration and the felicities of assonance are inseparable aids to song. They have often given birth to a beautiful thought, suggested a brilliant image and contributed to the force of an antithesis. They help the poet to express himself in a more melodious and captivating fashion. French poets have naturally displayed a no less ingenious art than their English brethren in availing themselves of the ready-made ideas involved in rhyme and in diversifying these ideas a thousand-fold. But there is one almost vital difference in their method, arising chiefly from those limitations which the more precise character of the French language has imposed on poetical expression. An example taken from two writers of English verse will serve as a simple illustration. Longfellow, who, with all his learning and lyrical capability, often failed to achieve that perfect harmony between word and idea which is the glory of imaginative poetry, has the following couplet in *Flowers* :—

'Others, their blue eyes with tears o'erflowing,
'Stand, like Ruth, amid the golden corn'.

INTRODUCTION

Keats, the greatest master of his art since Shakespeare and Milton, sings in his *Ode to a Nightingale* of

' . . . the sad heart of Ruth, when, sick for home,
' She stood in tears amid the *alien* corn '.

The conception in each case is highly poetical and the illustration is almost the same, but how the poetry seems to evaporate when an ordinary descriptive adjective is substituted for the spiritual one in which Keats, with his unerring instinct, has summed up the true pathos of Ruth's loneliness !

It is precisely in the lack of this power to transfigure common words by the light of imagination that French poets have often failed to reach the height to which English poetry has so easily attained, owing to the vague and fluctuant largeness of our English speech. Hence, also, the abuse of such adjectives as *sombre, sacré, divin* and *suprême* by French poets to whom Milton's 'blind mouths' or Shakespeare's daring metaphor ' to take arms against a sea ' of troubles ' would seem monstrous, because of the exactness into which the logical French mind has fashioned the national idiom.

*   *   *   *   *   *

There are some essential characteristics of the French language which contribute to give to French poetry an artificial form. Its derivation and structure, which are scholastic rather than vernacular,* have endowed it with a

---

* Since so much is made of the Celtic elements in the French nation (and properly so as regards its ethnological origin) it is significant that modern French has about 2000 Latin and 1000 Greek radicals and only 700 from the Germanic and Celtic languages ; indeed the purely Celtic contribution is represented by less than 100 roots, and many of the words derived from these are of purely local application. (See Henri Stappers : *Dictionnaire synoptique d'étymologie française :* Bruxelles : 1885.)

limited capacity for the expression of homely sentiment, such as is congenial to the rich root-soil of German speech. For this reason the French chanson and lyric have so often a cold and conventional air, when compared with the *lied*. In like manner, the deliberateness of French poetical diction, contrasting as it does with the quick incisiveness of the colloquial language,* tends to deprive it of that force and fervour which the fine frenzy of the singer would otherwise infuse into it.

To these natural limitations of the French language must be added the academical restrictions to rhyme, the lack of rhythmical accents, and the use of the symmetrical cæsura which custom has imposed on poetical speech. Heine likened the French metrical system to 'a strait-'waistcoat' and Zola describes it as 'a steel corselet'. Such impediments to rhythmical movement and emotional expression have forced French poets to seek relief from monotony in richly-coloured imagery, in variety of rhyme and in devices of melody ; often to such a degree that the reader is tempted to exclaim, like Gertrude, 'More 'matter, with less art!' 'French poetry', says Gabriel Sarrazin, 'has been striving for a century to reach by 'powerful effects of music and colour that which the 'Anglo-Saxon instinct has unconsciously achieved'. (*Poètes modernes de l'Angleterre.*) Moreover, their inheritance of artistic traditions and their culture of the sensuous arts † has exaggerated in many of the best French poets a natural devotion to form. Hence the cunning conveyance of subtleties embellished by fancy

* 'La lenteur de notre chant, qui fait un étrange contraste avec la vivacité de notre nation.' (Voltaire : *Supplément au Siècle de Louis XIV.*)

† Victor Hugo, Barbier, Gautier, Gérard de Nerval, Baudelaire, Villiers, Dierx, Mendès and many other French poets have either been draughtsmen, painters and musicians themselves or accomplished connoisseurs and critics of the fine arts.

xxii

and sentiment; and hence a striving after unfamiliar rhymes and images which has usurped in many of them the place of strong emotion seeking utterance in song. Often the French poet seems to choose a landscape scene or a phase of human experience for the express purpose of painting a picture, instead of weaving external nature into the mood and emotion of the moment, as in *The Excursion* or *In Memoriam*. But in their own sphere of art the French poets are supreme. They may claim a place by themselves as masters of purely intellectual expression. In no other literature have there been such expert artificers in verse as Gautier, Baudelaire, Mendès, Mallarmé and Verlaine, men whose verbal work at its best is unrivalled in visible beauty. By diligently cultivating and developing their poetical language on its own lines, such artists have carried to perfection in verse all those qualities which distinguish French art in general from English or German or Italian art, and which have given to French music, French sculpture and French painting a peculiar grace and individuality. Delicacy of outline, beauty of form, freshness and brilliancy of colour; everything that betokens dexterity of touch and absolute lucidity of vision; declamatory force, harmonious modulation and dramatic movement—all are there! And if in French verse there is more of the superficial play of fancy than the transfiguring glow of imagination; a sensuous worship of palpable loveliness rather than a revelation of the inner pathos of natural things; let it not be supposed that French poetry is by any means devoid of the higher attributes of impassioned speech. The fiery particle has never been extinguished in a poet because he had to contend with the difficulties of an extremely complex metrical system. Who will venture to assert that the observance of the dramatic unities in Greek tragedy fettered the passion of Euripides, the pathos of Sophocles and the sublimity of Æschylus? Not one of these essential qualities of pure poetry is wholly lacking in the French verse of the nineteenth century, and, if in certain schools the artistic attributes are paramount, many of the higher imaginative and emotional elements are to be found abundantly in Lamartine and Musset, while there is ample measure of every one of them in Victor Hugo.

* * * * * *

The melody of the French language has been loudly denied by English writers and especially by those whose knowledge of French verse was limited to the alexandrines of Corneille, Racine and Voltaire. The nasal 'n' is naturally the head and front of offence. It is difficult for a foreigner to judge impartially of these things, for he almost inevitably ignores similar cacophonies with which custom has made him familiar in his native speech. The English hissing plural and many of our harsh consonantal combinations (rnt : rbd : sht) must seem unmusical to an Italian, particularly when they occur as verse terminals. Take for example a stanza from *In Memoriam*:—

> 'I held it truth, with him who si*ngs*
> 'To one clear harp in dive*rs t*ones,
> 'That men may rise on steppi*ng-st*ones
> 'Of their dead selves to higher thi*ngs*'.

Not only has the poet ended all his rhymes with the sibilant, but he has placed them all on the same consonant, and some of them in uneuphonious combinations. And yet Tennyson's supremacy among the modern masters of verbal harmony is indisputable. It would be worse than hypercritical to insist on the point. The Germans have their ʀſſt and ᴕſt and the Russians their Щ (shtch) and ЧНИК (tchneek), but the employment of these harsh sounds in poetical language does not rob it of harmony and melody. The modern masters of French versification have handled their nasal consonant with wonderful discretion, and, however discordant it may be on the lips of a *café-chantant* singer, its pronunciation in poetry by a true artist need not offend the most sensitive ear. Perfect euphony is not the highest charm of a language, for almost in proportion as speech becomes merely mellifluous it loses in virility and vigour, owing to the absence of concussive sounds. There is as much real melody in Baudelaire's or Verlaine's French and in Tennyson's or Swinburne's English as in the finest Italian. Let not the persuasive eloquence of silver-tongued De Quincey nor the loud-mouthed declamation of Walter Savage Landor prejudice any one against the melody of French verse. Their examples of dissonance are generally chosen from the worst verses of eighteenth-century writers, who had not the cultured sense of verbal beauty which is now common among French writers, whether of verse or prose. The later French poets have discovered marvellous harmonies in their native tongue, as the following examples will shew :—

' Car je ne puis trouver parmi ces pâles roses
' Une fleur qui ressemble à mon rouge idéal '—
(*Charles Baudelaire.*)

' Plus vides, plus profonds, que vous-mêmes ô Cieux !'—
(*Charles Baudelaire.*)

' Et ce vague frisson de rose d'Orient
' Où la lumière passe et joue en souriant '—
(*Théodore de Banville.*)

And this magnificent quatrain which, notwithstanding the

consecutive nasal sounds in the second line, is one of the most majestic in the whole range of French verse :—

'Et toi, divine Mort, où tout rentre et s'efface,
'Accueille tes enfants dans ton sein étoilé,
'Affranchis-nous du temps, du nombre et de l'espace,
'Et rends-nous le repos que la vie a troublé!'

(*Leconte de Lisle.*)

No nobler and deeper music has ever been moulded by the lips of man.

* * * * * *

Those who wish to study the structure of French verse and the rules which govern its rhyme and measure will find an exhaustive historical analysis in Adolf Tobler's *Vom französischen Versbau alter und neuer Zeit* (Berlin : 1880). This author is more thoroughly scientific than any French writer on the subject, and his work is admittedly superior in respect of lingual and archaic learning to those of Louis Quicherat * and Becq de Fouquières.† An excellent if in no sense profound discourse on French versification is Théodore de Banville's *Petit Traité de Poésie française.* Two other poets—Sully Prudhomme in *Réflexions sur l'Art des Vers* and Stéphane Mallarmé in *Relativement au Vers*—have vouchsafed on the same subject some purely philosophical observations, but these do not cope with the problems of metrical construction, although they give evidence of the predilection for form which is so characteristic of French versifiers.

Any attempt to apply a theory of accent or quantity to the metre of French verse would be lost labour. Théodore de Banville's dictum is at once simple and conclusive :—
'French verse has no rhythm, like that of other languages,

* *Traité de Versification.* (Paris : 1850.)
† *Traité général de Versification française.* (Paris : 1879.)

' formed by a certain interlacement of long and short
' syllables. It is simply the grouping of a certain regular
' number of syllables, divided in certain kinds of verse by
' a pause or rest which is called the cæsura, and always
' terminated by a sound which cannot exist at the end of
' one line without being repeated at the end of another, or
' of several other lines, and the return of which is called
' Rhyme'. If this definition be accepted (and there is
no doubt of its accuracy) it follows that French verse has
not a woven harmony of accents, with a regular beat and
rhythm—*tempora certa modosque*—but is rather an even
flow of vocal utterance, saved from endless monotony by
the hiatus, and endowed with melody by the devices of
assonance, alliteration, elision and rhyme. The following
example of nonosyllabic verse from the *Art poétique* of Paul
Verlaine will serve as an illustration to Banville's thesis :—

'Car nous voulons | la Nuance encor,
'Pas la Couleur, | rien que la nuance!
'Oh! la nuan- | ce seul.. e fiance
'Le rêve au rêve | et la flûte au cor!'

On no other metrical system can these lines be scanned.

The almost exaggerated importance attached by French
poets in general and by Théodore de Banville in particular to the function of rhyme may be measured by
his bold assertion that 'the imagination of Rhyme is,
' above all, the faculty which constitutes the poet'; and
further that 'the only word which you hear in a verse is
' the word which is in the rhyme, and this word is the
' only one which operates in producing the effect aimed
' at by the poet'. The proper significance of Banville's
paradox is only observed when he goes on to. explain
that it is necessary to think in verse because a poet

cannot have the right rhyme until he has the vision in his brain which gives birth to the rhyme. It follows from the French metrical method, with its compulsory hemistich in lines of nine or more syllables, that, unless the language is handled with consummate art, there is a tendency to tameness and uniformity in the movement of the verse, a disadvantage of which certain critics, and among them Jules Janin, have been expressly conscious. But the great masters of French verse have contrived by various devices to give to it a wonderful richness and diversity. If in a line of equal syllables we miss the anapæstic trip of Shelley or Swinburne, we have at all events a release from monotony in the alternation of masculine and feminine rhymes, in the harmony of sonorous consonants and assimilated vowels, and in the verbal resources which distinguish the diction of poetry from that of prose in every language. Much of Victor Hugo's verse is so flexible and so forcible that it is almost impossible to .read it without such emphasis as almost endows it with a rhythmical accent. He revolutionised the alexandrine by his masterly art in phrasing so as to shift the cæsura from syllable to syllable according to the demands of his imperious poetical instinct. In vigour and grandeur, in resonance and splendour, he is immeasurably superior to every other French poet. None, save now and then Baudelaire, has such sonorous lines as

'Fleur de bronze éclatée en pétales de flamme '—

(*L'Année terrible.*)

'Toi, derrière Lagide, ô reine au cou de cygne '—

(*Les Châtiments.*)

'Tourbillonnaient dans l'ombre au vent de leurs épées '—

(*La Légende des Siècles.*)

xxviii

lines in which the supreme resources of French poetical diction have been demonstrated. The elasticity of his vowel elision is admirably illustrated by the following couplet, in which the rough force of the first line contrasts with the exquisite tenderness of the second :—

> ' Je te proclame, toi que ronge le vautour,
> ' Ma patrie et ma gloire et mon unique amour ! '
> (*L'Année terrible.*)

Some of the rigid rules of French versification are obviously intelligible. Thus a singular (such as *lieu*) must not be rhymed with a plural (such as *cieux*), although there is no difference in the terminal pronunciation. Nor should two similar sounds, one ending with a consonant and the other ending with a vowel, to wit, a masculine and a feminine word like *noir* and *gloire*, be rhymed. Both these prohibitions have been boldly contravened by one or two poets of the advanced school, notably by the late Jules Laforgue and by Jean Moréas, but a definitive adoption of such heresies would discredit the system on which the whole volume of French verse from Villon to Verlaine is composed. The alternation of masculine and feminine rhymes, which custom had rendered almost obligatory in French verse, has been disregarded by one or two living poets who are by no means revolutionary in their rhythmical methods, especially by Paul Verlaine in the Sapphic celebrations of *Parallèlement* and by Jean Richepin in his *Chanson du Sang*. The former poet has aimed at the expression of a voluptuous languor in the sole employment of feminine rhymes, and the latter at a virile and barbaric robustness in his exclusive use of masculine rhymes. In both cases the success of the abnormal experiment is vindicated by its specific purpose.

The so-called 'mute e' seems to have derived its value in French verse from the Italian and Provençal models of the early French poets. English poetry had a narrow escape from the same influence, for Chaucer invariably gave the feminine termination its full rhythmical effect, both in the singular and in the plural, and if it be disregarded the melody and rhythm of his verse is entirely spoiled. The precise value of the feminine 'e' in the declamation of French verse is a controversial point, and, as the poetical language owes much of its plasticity and most of its melody to the proper employment of this vowel, the vocal significance thereof is worthy of some attention. There is, indeed, little or no difference of opinion as to its syllabic value in versification, but the currency which should be given to it in the recitation of verse has been a fertile subject of discussion among authors, critics, actors and musicians. When the vowel occurs at the end of a line its utterance seems by common consent to have become so attenuated as to be almost inaudible. Théodore de Banville deliberately avers that the final 'e' of the feminine line is not pronounced, and does not count in the enumeration of the syllables of which a verse is composed. Sully Prudhomme says that ' in words which are terminated by the vowel *e* (*e mute*) ' the latter has gradually grown weaker to such a degree ' that it is scarcely pronounced at all . . . and is no longer ' reckoned a sound at the conclusion of a line'. Against such authorities there is nothing to be urged, but it is evident that the terminal 'e' had a distinct declamatory value when the French language was in process of formation, and when a fuller and larger fashion of pronunciation prevailed. This value has always been recognised by musical composers, so that in a song of Victor Hugo's set to music by Gounod the terminal 'e' at once resumes its full syllabic significance.* But even here the instinct of the consummate artist is exhibited in his treatment of the vowel. Songs like the *Marseillaise* and *Une dame noble et sage* (in Meyerbeer's opera of *les Huguenots*) offer repeated examples of a coarse and clumsy manipulation of the final 'e'. On the other hand, in the *Nuits d'été* of Berlioz, in such an air as *Plus grand dans son obscurité* (Gounod's *Reine de Saba*) and in any melody composed by Massenet or Saint-Saëns the discreet and delicate treatment of this terminal vowel gives a charm to the music which is peculiar to the French lyrical language. In a witty letter written by the last-named composer to Francisque Sarcey on this subject, he declares that 'the ' prolonged *e mute*, that is to say *eu, eu, eu*, . . . is due to ' our singers, who love to dwell on all *finales*, whether ' masculine or feminine '.

The function of the feminine 'e' in the body of the verse is a much more important problem. Some German *savants* have enunciated a heterodox theory to the effect that this 'e mute' has no rhythmical value in poetry, that it plays only a trivial part in dramatic diction, and that it tends to disappear altogether from French verse. A fierce controversy recently arose in Paris owing to the adoption of their opinion by Jean Psichari, a Franco-Greek contributor to the *Revue bleue*, who boldly declared that 'the *e mute* is not pronounced in French verse, un- ' less in the single case where its disappearance would ' bring about the encounter of three consonants '. The practical acceptance of such a theory would, of course, eliminate from French verse every element of melody and rhythm, and necessitate the entire reconstruction of its

* 'This *e*, which is not pronounced in ordinary declamation, *is* pronounced ' in noted declamation, and that in a uniform manner.' (Voltaire : *Supplément au Siècle de Louis XIV.*)

metrical system. No better refutation of this fallacy can be adduced than the invariable recognition which the feminine 'e' has obtained in the verse of every notable poet of purely French nationality. Omitting this vowel in the declamation of their lines, the cadence would be destroyed, the harmony emasculated and the measure falsified. French verse, as we know it, would become a chaotic assemblage of harsh sounds, and the vaunted alexandrine would be converted into irregularly alternated lines of eight, nine, ten, eleven and twelve syllables. 'Foreign critics have too readily believed'—says an actor and teacher who speaks with some authority—'that our ' verse, devoid of the quantities which form the basis of ' other prosodies, lives only by its rhyme. Failing to find ' in it the cadences due to long and short syllables, they ' have accused it of dragging itself along in the uniformity ' of restricted rhythms, of stretching itself out to a fatal ' monotony by the repetition of an unvarying number of ' equal syllables, and, in fine, of achieving only an artificial ' existence and a conventional harmony in the puerile ' play of rhymes. They have been unable to feel that '. . . these long and short syllables which they deny to ' us are often created delicately and deliciously by this ' so much misunderstood *e mute*'. (L. Brémont: *le Théâtre et la Poésie*: 1894.)

Any one who is familiar with French verse, and who cannot enunciate the 'mute e' with that 'delicate and ' delicious' ease which is the privilege of tongues to the manner born, will prefer to give it a fuller rather than a fainter emphasis if he wishes to realise its value in the euphony of French verse. The precise significance of the vowel is determined more by instinct, taste and sense of melody than by any recognised standard. Some French actors carelessly slur it over and others ignore it in a most

reprehensible fashion. 'In poetry'—says Francisque
Sarcey—'its employment admits of a marvellous variety ;
'for it may be simply recalled to the ear by an almost
'insensible suspension of the utterance, or indicated by a
'breath, or more heavily accentuated, or even sounded
'outright'. And it must be remembered, in reading
Racine and Lamartine or Corneille and Victor Hugo,
that the melody of their verse can only be appreciated by
those who have mastered the musical effect of the feminine
'e' and learned to enjoy the cadence, the suppleness and
the harmony which this peculiar vowel gives to the un-
dulating alexandrine.

It may be noted in passing that one or two contemporary poets have so far broken with tradition as to
try experiments with the occasional suppression of the
'mute e' as a syllabic factor in verse. This practice
must, however, be regarded as a bold imitation of the
vernacular elision which is customary in popular songs,
and particularly in Parisian doggerel, for no French poet
of importance has attempted to dispense altogether with
the rhythmical employment of the vowel, nor would it be
possible to do so unless strongly-marked accents or some
other metrical device were substituted.

* * * * * *

No individual value can be given to the feminine 'e' in
an English translation of French verse. But as it often
confers a greater number of syllables on the French
poetical line than the prose pronunciation of the same
words would warrant, it may be accepted as a general
rule that the double alexandrine is adequately represented
in English by the decimal or so-called heroic couplet, and
this equivalence has been assumed in the following translations. It would have been rash to attempt an English
twelve-syllable verse in the face of *Fifine at the Fair*,

since a master in the art of moulding difficult measures has often failed to give the desired flexibility to that long and heavy line with its monotonous cæsura.

Since the metrical regularity of French verse is redeemed by the elision of vowels and the employment of the feminine terminal, it becomes necessary, in an English translation, to relieve the comparative monotony of the trochaic and iambic measures with dactylic and anapæstic rhythms, or by some variety of rhyme. Having regard to the fact that simple metres in English are more congenial to the French rhythmical method, those have been generally employed in the translations which follow, but diversity has been sought in the occasional use of mixed masculine and feminine rhymes, as giving at least an approximate idea of the difference which once appealed to the ear and still appeals to the eye in the alternating rhymes of French verse. The difficulty might have been met by an alternate employment of long-vowel and short-vowel monosyllabic rhymes, but this device would hardly have been acceptable. The mechanical labour of translation has been considerably increased by the adoption of trochaic rhymes. It may be observed that Rossetti employed this method of rhyme in his beautiful version of Villon's *Ballade des Dames des temps jadis*, and the practice will probably commend itself to those who have an intimate acquaintance with French versification. In doing this, some rhymes have been used which would not pass muster in the original, for in French verse 'there are 'no licences', as Théodore de Banville says in his decided fashion. No apology, however, should be necessary for the juxtaposition in rhyme of 'blossom' and 'bosom' or 'meadow' and 'shadow,' which are sanctioned by the genial freedom of English verse and the custom of the masters. Had such vocables as 'blossom', 'meadow', 'murmur' and 'splendour' had a hundred metrical sisters, instead of existing in single blessedness, there would have been no excuse for imperfect rhymes. But surely the limits allowed by Keats and Shelley and Swinburne may be regarded as permissible to any writer of verse who refuses to follow Elizabeth Barrett Browning in her wanton freedom with dissyllabic rhymes or to repeat the present participle *ad nauseam* after the fashion of Felicia Dorothea Hemans.

The variety of rhymes at the disposal of French poets renders it difficult to translate into English with any approach to accuracy some of their highly artificial and elaborate forms of verse, such as the Ballade and the Rondel; indeed, if feminine rhymes are considered essential, the task of giving an English version of French poems in reverberant verse is an impossible one. Many of these poems seem to have been written chiefly as exercises in rhyme or to display the composer's craftsmanship and resource. It is an indisputable fact that the French language has a greater abundance of rhymes than any of the European languages which are cognate to it. The number of rhymes is increased by the rule which permits words having the same sound and spelling to be used as rhymes, and, indeed, regards the rhymes as richer in proportion to their identity. Rich rhyme is composed of such consonances as *rose : morose ; dix : jadis ; avide : livide ;* and poor rhyme of such consonances as *brume : plume ; cœurs : douleurs ; fière : poussière ;* whilst a leonine rhyme is one in which the consonance is carried through two or more syllables, such as *écumante : fumante ; saillir : jaillir ; violet : triolet.* There are also numerous varieties of recurrent and mimicking rhyme which properly belong to the museum of poetical curiosities.

In English poetry there are only a few examples of the French form of 'rich rhyme', which is not congenial to our prosody. The poet, in such cases, appears to have permitted a solecism rather than disturb the mould into which he had already cast his thought, as in Tennyson's *Literary Squabbles* :—

'And strive to make an inch of room
'For their sweet selves, and cannot *hear*
'The sullen Lethe rolling doom
'On them and theirs and all things *here*'.

Some illustrations of French rhyme may also be found in Swinburne, who has thoroughly and lovingly studied the French poets.

The rule laid down by Robert Browning in his superb preface to *The Agamemnon of Æschylus*, that a translation should be 'literal at every cost save that of 'absolute violence to our language', is too sound to be disputed. This rule, however, can be observed in its strictest sense only in a prose or a blank-verse rendering ;* some latitude must be allowed to a transcription in rhyme. Now rhyme plays such an important part in French verse that translation into English prose or even into unrhymed verse would be eminently inappropriate. Absolute fidelity alike to word and thought is the ideal, but it is evident that in interchanging the rhymes of two

* The glaring unfitness of blank-verse for the transcription of rhyme is witnessed in the English translations of the *Divina Commedia*. The fine Miltonic verse of Cary gives neither the rhyme and the rhythm nor the cadence and the accent of the *terza rima*, and Longfellow's unrhymed triplets approach so closely to prose that they seldom suggest either the supple movement or the subtle harmony of the original. In brilliant contrast to these is Rossetti's version of Villon's ballade before mentioned. In form and matter it is as perfect a transcription of the charming original as handicraft and artistic cunning could achieve ; and a single glance at the prosaic versions signed by Walter Thornbury and John Payne is sufficient to demonstrate its absolute supremacy as a poetical translation. But only a poet can transcribe with such success, and poets naturally prefer indigenous cultivation to the transplanting of exotics.

languages which are so diverse in structure and syntax the sound must now and then be sacrificed to sense and the sense occasionally subordinated to sound. And although the substance, the shape and the harmony ought to be all preserved as far as is attainable, the verbal effect rather than the literal signification has sometimes to be sought. Especially is this the case with translations from the French, a language in which the *cheville*, or interpolated turn to comply with the demands of rhyme, is a recognised poetical device. But the true principles of translation, though easy to enunciate, are hard to carry into execution. In the following experiments an attempt has been made to convey the sense of the original, whilst imitating the harmony, the cadence and the characteristics thereof, with some attention to the alternations of masculine and feminine rhyme which are inseparably associated with French verse. They will give at best but a faint reflection of those rich effects of colour and melody which have been achieved by the French singers of this spacious century, and must therefore be regarded rather as an unworthy tribute to the poetical literature on which Catulle Mendès bestows so magnificent an encomium :—

'Our admirable French verse, glimpsed by Ronsard, desired
'by Corneille and dreamed by Chénier; that verse which
'is perhaps so little understood by alien ears and has been
'inconsiderately decried, but which, diverse and supple,
'endowed with harmonious numbers, and as well fitted to
'be filled with things as the metrical verse of Homer and
'Lucan, bears like a flapping banner on the summit its
'resounding rhyme, multiform and inexhaustible, the effect
'of which, peculiar to our language, is lacking in all poesy
'save our own'.

(La Légende du Parnasse contemporain.)

*   *   *   *   *   *

Thy name, imperial poet, I invoke !
Hugo, whose genius first on fiery wings
Plunged into measureless space sublime and broke
　The speechless bounds.　With trumpet thunderings,
　Tempest and pale eclipse of mortal things
Thy clamorous lips the empyreal echoes woke ;
　Anon in cloudless blue thy spirit sings,
Lulls the world's cry, lightens the human yoke,
　And with sweet pity thrills love's tremulous strings.

And thine, O hapless Chénier ! with the fair
　White blossom blighted when the chill frost fell ;
Lamartine, Musset, whose melodious air
　Played whispering prelude to the wilder swell
　Of Hugo's clan.　Gautier, thy puissant spell !
Gérard and Mürger, souls of beauty rare.
　Flamboyant Barbier, fugitive Borel,
Pale Glatigny and sombre Baudelaire
　Whose song-fire glows with sullen flames of Hell !

Yours, too, sweet acolytes in the courts of song,
　Prudhomme and Coppée that with hymns adore
In faultless rhyme no gods of shame and wrong :
　Subtile Verlaine, quaint Mallarmé whose lore,
　Sphinx-like, with symbols dim is sculptured o'er,
And yours, last of the proud Hugonian throng,
　Leconte and Banville, bards that evermore
With pæans loud triumphantly prolong
　The timbrel-clash and clarion-calls of yore !

A CENTURY OF FRENCH VERSE

André Chénier.

Born in Constantinople, 1762 . . . Died in Paris, 1794.

It was well said of the French Revolution that, like Saturn, she devoured her own children. The times were not propitious to idealists and singers, and the only poet of uncommon promise produced during that stormy period was sent to the guillotine at the age of thirty-two and 'died without emptying his quiver'.*

Louis Chénier, the poet's father, was an *attaché* of the French Embassy to the Sublime Porte, and not Consul-General of France at Constantinople, as he is often erroneously designated. He married a Greek girl of great beauty, high character and exceptional intelligence. Her name was Elisabeth Santi-Lomaca, and she belonged to Cyprus, the island of Aphrodite. There is a tradition that she was descended from the illustrious crusading family of Lusignan. She died at Paris in 1844. Her open letters on Greek dances, Greek burials and Greek tombs were collected and published by Robert de Bonnières in 1879.

André Chénier was brought to Paris in 1765, when his father returned home with a wife and four children, as well as a dilapidated fortune. Louis Chénier soon afterwards left his family for fifteen years, on receiving the appointment of Consul-General in Morocco, and when he came back to France he obtained for André a nomination as gentleman-cadet in the Angoûmois regiment of infantry.

* 'Mourir sans vider mon carquois !' (*Ïambe III.* André Chénier.)

A   I

ANDRÉ CHÉNIER

A few years later André became *attaché* to the French Embassy in London, and he complained bitterly of isolation and weariness during his sojourn in England. Like Camille Desmoulins, and along with his own brother Marie-Joseph, André Chénier began early to dabble in literature. He had been nourished on Greek poetry, and is credited with a translation of Sappho's fragments and Anacreon's odes, executed at the age of fourteen. Until the popular movement became pronounced, all the Chénier family were 'aristocrats'. André signed himself Chénier de Saint-André; Marie-Joseph posed as the Chevalier de Chénier. Their discontent with the slow progress of their fortunes under the monarchy led them to throw in their lot with the leaders of the democratic agitation. Marie-Joseph became an advanced demagogue. André published in 1791 an *Avis aux Français*, in which he counselled moderation and respect for the laws, in opposition to the furious spirits of the revolution. Marie-Joseph voted for the death of Louis XVI. André not only disapproved this act of injustice, but expressed his opinion so openly that he became a 'suspect' to the extreme party. He was arrested during the Terror, and guillotined at the *barrière de Vincennes* on 7 *thermidor*, only two days before the fall of Robespierre. Save the divine and heroic Charlotte Corday, no more interesting figure than that of the young poet was eclipsed with all the beauty and bravery which perished in that pitiless Revolution.

It is an almost accepted legend that André Chénier was the protagonist of French poetry in the nineteenth century. 'All the poets of the nineteenth century, save Lamartine' . . . , says Arsène Houssaye, 'set out in the ' golden argosy of André Chénier, to sail across the Ionian ' sea, and listen to the sirens of Homer and Sappho'. His verse was 'a fresh breath from Greece', says Théophile

Gautier, with less exaggeration. Sainte-Beuve, in his *Pensées de Joseph Delorme*, seems to have been largely responsible for the promulgation of this legend. Baudelaire believed that André Chénier had no influence whatever on the poetical development of the nineteenth century ; and indeed it was Lamartine who gave the first fresh impulse to the lyrical movement of his age. Chénier's poetry was entirely neglected by his own contemporaries, and it was only in 1819 that a very imperfect collection of his verses, with an inaccurate memoir by Henri de Latouche, was given to the world. The Revolutionary and Napoleonic epochs had not been favourable to lyric art, but there can be no doubt that when Chénier's poems were published they did contribute a little to the efflorescence of 1830, which was chiefly the work of Chateaubriand, Lamartine, Musset, Alfred de Vigny, Sainte-Beuve and Victor Hugo.

Chénier's poetical style and metrical treatment do not differ fundamentally from those of the French versifiers of the eighteenth century, to which era he belonged by birth and tradition. But he gave a fresher and freer play and a fuller harmony and rhythm to the classical mythology which underlies all the writings of that period. He restored suppleness to the stiff old alexandrine, and his ideas and images had a much more vivid individuality than those of his predecessors. He had vigour and grace, along with which he achieved at times the true lyrical swing and gait. On this ground, if on no other, he claims a place among the poets of the present century, to whom he is akin also in the dignity and forthright earnestness of his utterance. His political poems have an accent of sincerity which makes them models of their kind. Perhaps he felt, when face to face with death, that he had not done all he might have done with better opportunities and a more encouraging public. But it does not appear that he would have become the leader of a new movement in letters, if his measure may be taken from the plan of *Hermès*, which was discovered among his posthumous papers. Specimens of this work were first published by Sainte-Beuve, along with other reliques of Chénier's poetry. *Hermès* was to have been a descriptive and philosophical poem in three books, containing imitations of Vergil's *Georgics*, and of Lucretius, Lucilius, Ovid and other Latin writers, with whom Chénier had a large acquaintance. The formation of the earth, the creation of animals and man, the development of the human mind, the growth of religions, the organisation of society and the evolution of customs, morals, polity and science were comprised in the scheme of *Hermès*. From the fragments which have come down to posterity, this poem would seem to have been admirably fitted to close the work of Lebrun and Delille in the eighteenth century, instead of preluding the melodious bursts of 1830. But the fame of Chénier must naturally rest on what he did, rather than what he might have done. His virile, sonorous and often beautiful verse, his tragic career, and the premature extinction of his ambitious genius, will give him an ever-lasting place in French literature, and leave not unfulfilled, in a wider sense than he conceived it, the fate fore-shadowed in the last lines which he wrote whilst awaiting his turn in the prison of Saint-Lazare:—

' Le messager de mort . . . .
' Remplira de mon nom ces longs corridors sombres ! '

(Iambe IV: unfinished.)

Bacchus.

Come Bacchus, come Thyoneus ever young,
As Dionysus or as Leneus sung!
O come, as when in Naxos lone and wild
Thy voice did soothe the fears of Minos' child!
The towered elephant, slain in glorious war,
Had fashioned with his spoils thine ivory car;
Vine-leaves and tendrils linked in flowing chains
The broad-flanked tiger, furrowed with dark stains,
And dusky pard, fierce panther and starred lynx
That led thee with thy courtiers to these brinks.
On wheels and axles gold shone everywhere;
The Mænads ran with loose and streaming hair,
And Io Bacche! Evohe Bacche! sung,
Leneus, Evan, Thyoneus ever young,
And all thy splendid names in Greece renowned,
Till rock and vale echoed the jovial sound.
Lo, now with wreathëd horns and flutes they come,
Crotals and clamorous cymbals and hoarse drum
Waved on thy noisy path with song and dance!
Satyr and Faun and sylvan gods advance
Trooping at random round Silenus hoar,
Who, cup in hand, from the far Indian shore,
Drunken and drivelling as of old, will pass
With slow pace tottering on his lazy ass.

Bacchus.
(*Idylles: IX.*)

The Young Captive.

The green ear ripens while the sickle stays,
The ungathered grape, clustering in summer days,
    Drinks the dawn's dewy boon ;
Like theirs my beauty is, my youth like theirs,
And though the present hour has griefs and cares
    I would not die so soon.

Let tearless Stoics seek the arms of Death !
I weep and hope ; before the black wind's breath
    I bend, then raise my head.
Among my bitter days some sweet I find !
What honey leaves no satiate taste behind ?
    What seas no tempest dread ?

Life's fresh illusion dwells within my breast.
My limbs in vain these prison-walls invest ;
    Hope ever gives me wings.
As when, escaped the cruel fowler's snare,
More light, more joyful in the fields of air
    Philomel soars and sings.*

Why should I wish to die ? From peaceful sleep
Peaceful I wake ; not with remorse I weep,
    Nor crimes my rest destroy.
My welcome to the dawn in all things smiles ;
On sombre brows my look almost beguiles
    A reawakening joy.

* The young captive says *Philomèle*, but perhaps she is thinking of the lark.

6

ANDRÉ CHÉNIER

I seem so far from the bright journey's end!
These elms that fringe the path on which I wend
    Stretch forth in endless rows.
Fresh at the feast of life, like a new guest,
One moment only my fond lips have pressed
    The cup that overflows.

'Tis spring; the harvest is not yet begun;
From season to new season, like the sun,
    I would fulfil my year.
Flower of life's garden, shining on the bright
Spray, scarce have I beheld the morning light,
    And noon is not yet near.

Death, come not nigh me now . . . depart, depart!
Console the sons of fear and shame whose heart
    Sinks in despair's pale swoon:
To me green Pales with her flock belongs,
The Loves give kisses, and the Muses songs;
    I would not die so soon.

*   *   *   *   *   *

La jeune Captive.
(Ode XI.)

7

Alphonse de Lamartine.

Born in Mâcon, 1790 . . . Died in Paris, 1869.

Alphonse-Marie-Louis de Lamartine * is the master of French reflective verse, and his influence on modern poetry has been real and lasting. His early youth was passed in the country-house of Saint-Point, under the wing of a fond mother and with refined sisters ; his education was superintended by a romantic priest and completed at the Jesuit seminary of Belley. His youthful faculties were fed on the Bible, on Bernardin de Saint-Pierre, on Rousseau and on Chateaubriand, with some of the older English and Italian poets, and he began early to express his emotions in verse. After a visit to Italy he entered the military household of Louis XVIII in 1814, and soon became a familiar figure in the best royalist *salons* in Paris. His health had always been somewhat fragile, and his sentimental melancholy led him into many strange experiences of the tender passion in his youth.

The publication of the first volume of *Méditations* in 1820 caused an unwonted commotion in literary circles. It was the most brilliant success, said Sainte-Beuve, since Chateaubriand's *Génie du Christianisme.* Lamartine leaped into fame with one bound, and yet, if the circumstances be considered, it is easy to understand the sudden

* The repeated assertion that Lamartine's real name was Prat is inaccurate. The family name was Lamartine, but the poet's father, a younger son, bore the courtesy-title of Chevalier de Prat. The family was an old but obscure territorial one.

8

celebrity of his early poems. These glimpses of pure affection, nursed in devotion and faith, and this return to the love of nature refreshed an age which was suffering from weariness after the bloody terrors of the Revolution and the brutal splendours of the Empire. Not only did Lamartine's verses reveal a fine vein of contemplation, which expressed simple thoughts and emotions in a simple way, without recourse to classical allusions and conventional imagery ; they came at a time when there were few singers in France and certainly no great one. Casimir Delavigne had been the Triton among such minnows as Millevoye and Chênedollé and Désaugiers. Victor Hugo, Alfred de Vigny, Alfred de Musset and Auguste Barbier had not yet begun to publish their poems ; all these men of the future were then under twenty years of age. Louis XVIII gave his patronage to Lamartine and granted him a pension. ' A poet is born to us this night ', exclaimed Talleyrand, after reading through the *Méditations* in a single sitting. So generally was this judgment approved that Lamartine was encouraged in 1823 to issue a new volume of *Méditations*, for which he received 14,000 francs. He seemed to be on the high road to fortune. He had been appointed secretary to the French Embassy at Naples, and was married to a young Englishwoman who brought him a considerable dowry, or at least an assured income. The French Academy elected him in 1830, the year of his *Harmonies poétiques et religieuses.*

Lamartine's royalist opinions had been undergoing a change as he grew older, and he thereupon renounced the diplomatic career, chartered a vessel, and made a voyage to the East with his wife and daughter, travelling like a *grand seigneur.* In 1835 he published a volume recording his impressions of Eastern travel ; in 1836 came *Jocelyn*, in 1838 *la Chute d'un Ange*, in 1839 the *Recueille-*

ments poétiques, and in 1847 the *Histoire des Girondins*. But his fame had already been overshadowed by that of Victor Hugo and the brilliant men of 1830-1840, and he himself had lost the touch which made his earlier poems so fascinating. Moreover, he could not be compared as an artist with the writers of that period. His facility of improvisation was fatal to the severe discipline which forms a poet of the highest order. He had always been a loose and careless writer, and so disliked the labour of revision that when Hachettes were about to publish a new edition of *Jocelyn* he could not make up his mind to correct the faulty verses, and finally proposed that a literary hack should finish them. And yet this was the poem in which Béranger, so debonair in his judgments, found flaws, negligences and *longueurs* which, even to his indulgent eyes, were only redeemed by its numberless beauties.

Lamartine's active intervention in politics, his participation in the overthrow of Louis-Philippe in 1848, and his courageous and successful resistance, as a member of the Provisional Government, to an armed multitude in the streets of Paris, are familiar to readers of French history. He was almost the absolute master of France for three months. His decline was rapid and irretrievable. A year later he could not find a department in France willing to elect him as its parliamentary representative. He soon retired into private life, disappointed and impoverished. His resources had been badly administered in the day of his prosperity. Princely expenditure and unhappy speculations, travelling, elections, charities, and a hundred other things, had exhausted his fortune. In 1860 he had to leave Milly, the family domain in the Mâconnais, after selling his furniture and heirlooms. Thenceforth he lived in an obscure lodging in Paris with his devoted wife, while Victor Hugo, exiled, was writing *les Misérables* in his island solitude. Lamartine's efforts to free himself from debt, says Ernest Legouvé, a friend of his later days, were superhuman. The author whose *History of the Girondins* had been sold to a publisher for 250,000 francs before he had written a single line, now slaved for journals and magazines, furnishing political and historical criticism, confidences, memoirs and occasional verse for the wherewithal to face dishonoured bills, accumulated interest, and the demands of urgent creditors. This proud man had to sacrifice his pride, his ambition, his health and his happiness in the desperate struggle. The French Chambers voted him a substantial allowance in 1867, but this welcome relief came too late. And so Lamartine, who might easily have had all that should accompany old age, died in poverty and loneliness, a shadow of his former self, in the midst of new political and literary movements to which he was a stranger. More than once he had failed to take at the flood that tide in the affairs of men which leads on to fortune.

Lamartine's character was in many respects a great one. He was tolerant in his opinions, liberal in his ideas and just in his actions. When the events of 1848 placed power in his hands he not only governed with moderation and dignity but he showed himself absolutely disinterested. He had the gift of seizing quickly the superficial significance of things, yet he lacked perseverance, and rarely followed up his first enthusiasm with energy and goodwill. Had he disciplined his literary faculties and turned aside from political popularity he might have been one of the first poets of the century. As it is, he has exercised a larger influence on French poetry than either André Chénier or Alfred de Musset, and no lover of verse can be insensible to the melodious charm, the contemplative beauty and the tender melancholy of his Muse, so free from every disposition to revolt and violence. His ideals of the poetic vocation differed widely from those of his chief contemporaries in France, and were rather akin to Wordsworth's. 'You ask me', he says in the beautiful preface to his *Recueillements poétiques*, 'how, in the midst ' of my agricultural labours, my philosophical studies, my ' travels, and the political movement which carries me ' occasionally into its tumultuous and impassioned sphere, ' I can keep some freedom of mind and some hours of ' audience for that poesy of the soul which speaks only in ' a low voice, in silence and in solitude. It is as if you ' should ask the soldier or the sailor if he has a moment to ' think on those he loves, and to pray to God, in the noise ' of the camp or amidst the agitations of the sea'.

Although the fitful reaction from time to time in favour of Lamartine has not restored his popularity, there is little doubt that he will occupy in French literature that place which the rapidity of historical evolution and the bewildering changes in literary taste have so long denied to him. 'Lamartine', says Théodore de Banville, 'was to ' Victor Hugo what the dawn is to the sun'. With his generosity, his humanity, his noble ideals, and his pure poetical talent, so simple and so emotional, the fame of Lamartine has deserved a better fate. 'There is', wrote Jules Claretie in 1881, 'and I say it to the shame of the ' new generations, a want of taste, and also a want of feel- ' ing, in the discredit into which Lamartine has fallen. ' In him the poet was a great poet and the man a good ' citizen'. Since this was written other powerful voices— those of Jules Lemaître and Gaston Deschamps not the least—have pleaded for the rehabilitation of Lamartine, and it will be passing strange if they have always to plead in vain.

The Lake.

Thus ever driven, as one that aimless steers,
  And borne towards night eternal drifts away,
Shall we not once, on the swift tide of years,
    Cast anchor for a day?

O lake! one fleeting year hath scarcely flown;
  Yet, by the cherished waves she loved to greet,
See, where she watched thee, seated on this stone,
    Alone I take my seat!

Thus wert thou moaning on those rocks profound;
  Thus broke thy billows on their riven flanks:
Thus at her worshipped feet the wild wind crowned
    With foam thy wave-kissed banks.

One night—hast thou forgotten?—we did float
  In silence; hushed were sky and stream and cave;
Only the sound of oars in cadence smote
    On thy harmonious wave;

When, suddenly, strange speech, as from above,
  Woke the charmed echoes of thy listening shore;
The waves grew still, and, from the lips I love,
    These words the breezes bore:—

'O Time, suspend thy wing! And you, blest hours,
  'Suspend your rapid flight!
'Leave us awhile to taste the bliss that dowers
    'Our days with brief delight!

'Too many wretches groan in yon sad world:
    'O speed for them the suns;
'Let their slow sorrows on your wings be whirled;
    'Forget the happier ones.

'Yet vainly I implore a brief delay;
    'Time flies, swift as a dream;
'I pray for night to linger, and the day
    'Even now begins to gleam.

'Haste, then, to love! Seize happiness before
    'The fleeting moments fly!
'Man has no haven here, and Time no shore:
    'Life flows, and we glide by!'

O envious Time, must the hour when raptures spring,
    When love pours out long draughts of happiness,
Sweep far beyond us, borne on swifter wing
    Than days of sore distress?

What! wilt thou leave us not at least a trace?
    What! wholly flown? what! lost for evermore?
The bliss that Time bestowed shall Time efface,
    Nor once its boon restore?

Space and oblivion, sombre gulfs of time,
    Where are the days ye swallow and destroy?
Speak! shall ye not bring back those hours sublime
    Ye ravished from our joy?

O lake! O voiceless caves! Woods dark and deep!
    You that Time spares, or freshens in his flight;
Keep thou at least, belovëd Nature, keep
    Remembrance of that night!

Let it be in thy storms and in thy rest,
    O lake, and in the shores thy ripple laves,

And in those gloomy pines, and rocks whose crest
  Frowns on thy laughing waves !

Let it be in the breeze that shivers past,
  And in the murmur of thy tribute stream,
And in the whiteness of thy surface, glassed
  From the Star's silvery beam !

And may the wind that wails, the reed that sighs,
  The light-winged fragrance of thy breath divine,
And all that soothes the soul and charms the eyes
  Whisper : Their love was mine !

        Le Lac.
        (*Premières Méditations poétiques.*)

The Valley.

My heart, in which even hope has ceased to live,
  Shall weary fate no more with idle breath ;
Give me, O valley of my childhood, give
  Me shelter for a day to wait on death !

Here the strait pathway leaves the open glade :
  Along its devious slopes hang the dense boughs
That, bending over me their mingled shade,
  With blissful calm and silence crown my brows.

Two rivulets there through verdant arches gleam,
  Thence down the valley wind with serpent course ;
A moment blend their murmur and their stream,
  And, lost in one, forget their nameless source.

Like theirs the current of my youth did roll
  Beyond recall, noiseless and nameless passed :
Their wave is clear, but in my troubled soul
  The morning beam no bright reflection cast.

The freshness of these beds, with shadow crowned,
   Chains me all day on banks the streamlet laves ;
Like a child soothed by song's monotonous sound,
   My soul grows drowsy with the murmuring waves.

Ah ! here, girdled by ramparts ever green
   Whose narrow bound my vision satisfies
I love to linger, and alone, unseen,
   Hear the stream only, only see the skies.

Too much my soul has lived and loved and striven ;
   Living I come to seek Lethean calm ;
May blest oblivion by these shades be given,
   For save oblivion naught can bring me balm.

My soul finds silence here, my heart repose ;
   The turmoil of the world comes muffled here,
Even as a distant sound that feebler grows,
   Borne on the wind to the uncertain ear.

Hence over life a cloudy veil is thrown,
   The past through shadow casts a fading gleam ;
Love alone dwells, as some vast shape alone
   Survives the awakening from a vanished dream.

Linger, my soul, in this last resting-place,
   Even as a traveller, in the dwindling light,
Before the gates of refuge rests a space,
   And breathes refreshed the balmy air of night.

Let us, like him, shake from our feet the dust ;
   The path of life once trod our journeyings cease :
Let us, like him, o'erwearied, breathe in trust
   This calm, precursor of the eternal peace.

Thy days, sombre and brief like autumn days,
   Decline, as on those slopes the night-shades gloom ;

When love forsakes thee, and thy friend betrays,
Alone thou treadst the pathway to the tomb.

But Nature's welcome here thy love shall claim ;
Plunge in her breast, that ever open lies ;
All else may change, but Nature is the same,
And all thy days behold the same sun rise.

Her breast with light and shadow still is stored.
Turn from false loves and dreams that fade erelong ;
Adore the voice Pythagoras adored,
Give ear, like him, to the celestial song.

Fly with the north wind on her aëry car ;
Follow the noonday glow, the twilight pale :
Beneath the beam of eve's mysterious star
Steal through the woods when shadow swathes the vale.

In Nature seek the soul ; blind though thou art,
God gave thee light to know him and rejoice ;
A voice speaks in his silence to the heart.
Who has not heard the echo of that voice?

> *Le Vallon.*
> (*Premières Méditations poétiques.*)

The West.

Then the sea dwindled, as a boiling urn
Wanes when the furnace burns less fiercely red,
And waves, blown foaming on the sandy bourne,
Fell back, as if to sleep, in her vast bed.

And lo ! the sun, sinking from cloud to cloud,
Poised on the blood-red wave his rayless star,
Then plunged, half-swathed, as in its fiery shroud
A burning vessel sinks on seas afar.

And half the world was darkened, and the breeze
Breathless and voiceless shrank within the veil ;
And shadows gathered round, and skies and seas
Beneath their dusky wing grew sudden pale.

And in my soul, that likewise waned and dreamed,
All sounds, all splendours dwindled with the day,
And, as in Nature, something in me seemed
By turns to grieve and bless, to weep and pray.

And towards the West alone, with splendour rent,
The wavering flame blazed as a golden pyre,
And, wrapt in purple clouds, was like a tent
That veils, but quenches not, a burning fire.

And clouds and winds and waves with hurrying
wings
Rushed towards that flaming vault in rapid flight,
As though wide Nature and all living things
Were doomed to death if they should lose the light.

The dust of twilight floated from the ground,
Upwards the white foam from the black waves flew,
And in mine eyes, that wandered sadly round
To watch their flight, tears gathered like the dew.

Then the light vanished, and my soul oppressed
Grew void, swathed like the sky with cloudy bands ;
And one sole thought rose in my troubled breast,
Sole as the pyramid on desert sands. . . . . . .

O light ! where goest thou ? Orb forlorn of flame,
And clouds and winds and waves, and thou my
soul,
Foam, dust and darkness, if we know, proclaim
What course is yours, and where your final goal !

In thee, vast All, whose star is the pale light
Where night and day, and soul and substance blend !
Life's universal tide in flux and flight ;
Wide sea of Being in whom all things end ! . . .

L'Occident.
(*Harmonies poétiques et religieuses.*)

Epistle to Adolphe Dumas.

18 September, 1838.

Musa pedestris.

*   *   *   *   *   *

Still the true poet's soul soars high and higher !
So, friend, for thee the sum of my desire
Is freedom, and oblivion of the world,
And prose and verse into the black gulf hurled ;
But in thy heart of hearts a plenteous spring,
Where inspiration daily dips her wing,
And whose sweet murmur, while it soothes the mind
Flows in that silent verse no hand hath signed ;
A soul that still with quenchless rapture glows,
Whence admiration brims and overflows ;
Those sacred transports in the work of God
That make a temple spring on every sod ;
That commune of the soul's mysterious deeps
Held with the wave that sings, the wind that weeps,
And bird, and bush, and starry firmament,
And all that thrills, with thought and feeling blent :
A sunny nook o' the trellised wall where comes
The bee, afloat in the bright beam, and hums ;
Beneath green sunshade of the noonday pines,
A meadow on whose slope the warm sky shines,

While through the haze, far as thine eye can reach,
The blue sea flings its white foam on the beach,
And the white sail, remote on billowy seas,
Bends like a wave-borne tree beneath the breeze,
And whence the thunderous sound of floods distraught,
Breaking amain upon thine aëry thought,
Reveals in dreams that mirror vast and clear,
Reflex of the infinite, that brings God near! . . .
A heaven that sheds its beams above thy soul;
Thy heart in tune with life's harmonious whole!
A peaceful conscience slumbering in thy breast,
As in its bed the untroubled pool doth rest;
On the hill slope, outstretching many a mile,
Thy realm; a roof of thatch, or slate, or tile,
Whose shadow is thy world, whose threshold saves
Its lord a hundred years from the cold grave's;
There, slumbers light, that waken with the lark,
The cheerful furrow, ploughed from dawn to dark;
A frugal board, where, between leaf and flower,
Smile fruits to which thy graft gave double dower;
On walnut, shining with thy woven flax,
A wine whose fragrance of thy vineyard smacks;
A summer shade; a winter hearth aglow,
Where oft thy hand the olive-stone shall throw;
Candles of bees-wax perfumed in thy hives,
Whose flame on many a well-read book revives
Consoling lamps that, for our souls' relief,
The storms of time have left on the bare reef,
And, though our fickle winds fan not their flame,
High in the spirit-sphere shine still the same! . . .
Then, lest the dregs of age no sweetness leave,
A mother's, sister's love to cheer life's eve,
A friend of old, whose solitude lies near,
True as the needle and to custom dear,

Who comes each night, with his familiar smile,
The hearth with friendly converse to beguile.

With these, dear friend, let the keen critic's claw
Mark on our tuneful page each fatal flaw,
Let Paris hiss us, while our suns entice;
I long for fame . . . to sell it at this price!

Épître à M. Adolphe Dumas.
(Recueillements poétiques.)

To a Young Girl who begged a lock of my hair.

My hair! that Time turns white, and withering mocks!
My hair! that falls before the winter's frown!
Why should your fingers pleach these fading locks?
Green boughs are best if you would weave a crown.

Think you the brows of manhood, fair young girl,
That forty seasons load with joys and fears,
Wear the blond ringlets in their silken curl
Wherewith Hope plays, as with your seventeen years?

Think you the lyre, attuned to the soul's rhyme,
Sings from our heart of hearts in the full throat,
With never a string that snaps from time to time,
And leaves beneath the touch a silent note?

Poor simple child! What would the swallow sing,
When winter winds beat round her ruined tower,
If thou shouldst crave those feathers from her wing
The ruthless vulture strips and tempests shower?

À une jeune fille qui me demandait de mes cheveux.
(Recueillements poétiques.)

Victor Hugo.

Born in Besançon, 1802 . . . Died in Paris, 1885.

. . . . he above the rest
In shape and gesture proudly eminent.

It is needless to recapitulate the chief incidents of a life which has filled so large and luminous a space in the literature of the nineteenth century as that of Victor Hugo.* No poet ever lived so much in the full light of day. Every reader is more or less familiar with the legend of his glory as the chief of the Romantic Movement of 1830; his wonderful fertility from 1830 to 1840 in poetry, drama and romance; his exile of nearly twenty years after the Napoleonic *coup d'état* in 1852, and the sublime visions which he gave to the world from his island refuge; his return to Paris after the fall of the second Empire; his popular triumph in 1881, when Paris was covered with flags and flowers, whilst a procession of two hundred thousand persons passed before his dwelling; and, four

---

* His father was General Joseph-Léopold-Sigisbert Hugo, afterwards Count de Cifuentes and de Siguenza, in the Spanish peerage of King Joseph Bonaparte. The Hugo family was of very humble origin. Victor Hugo's grandfather was a carpenter, and three of his aunts supported themselves by dressmaking. In spite of his democratic professions the poet took no end of pains to graft his ancestry upon that of the Franco-German seigneurial family of Hugo von Spitzemberg, and even assumed their armorial bearings, but there is not a particle of evidence to substantiate this pedigree. The authentic genealogy of Victor Hugo is established beyond a doubt by the documents cited in Edmond Biré's *Victor Hugo avant 1830* (Perrin: Paris) of which a new edition was published in 1894.

years later, his public funeral, which called forth a demonstration of sorrow and enthusiasm such as had never accompanied the remains of a mortal man to their last resting-place.

A study of the vast work of Victor Hugo would also be futile unless a whole volume could be devoted to the purpose. The mere enumeration of a list of literary achievements which includes *Hernani*, *Marion de Lorme*, *le Roi s'amuse*, *Ruy Blas*, and *les Burgraves* in tragedy, *Notre-Dame de Paris*, *les Misérables*, *les Travailleurs de la Mer*, *l'Homme qui rit*, and *Quatrevingt-treize* in romance, and that marvellous series of lyrical creations in which well-nigh every note of human emotion is sounded and every phase of human contemplation represented, would be enough to recall to those who are in touch with French literature the incomparable power and versatility of Victor Hugo's genius. Those who are not at home in French literature may refer to Algernon Charles Swinburne's *Study of Victor Hugo* (London: Chatto and Windus: 1886) in which the only blemish is perhaps a too enraptured strain of exuberant eulogy.

The glory of Victor Hugo has not lacked disparagement, and an impartial admiration will hardly be blind to the faults which are inseparable from such a phenomenon of genius. When the flux of images and metaphors at the poet's command pours in almost ludicrous disproportion to the magnitude of the thought; when grotesque antithesis and superfluous analogy are piled up to disguise the occasional lack of intense passion or sustained imagination; when an apparently egregious conceit finds expression in familiar colloquy with the majestic forces of Nature until it verges on the burlesque;—what can the judicious do but grieve? And yet all the trivialities, and all the platitudes, and all the tumid disfigurements

that may be discovered in a critical analysis of Victor
Hugo's work, are small in comparison with the grandeur
and vastness of the whole. The historical anachronisms
and verbal blunders of which so much has been made may
be individually absurd, but they count for little in the
splendid sum, and such inaccuracies are not to be found
in anything of Hugo's which is the record of direct personal observation. The beauty of a wide landscape is
none the less refreshing to the senses and inspiring to
the soul because the beholder knows that if he dissects
the material of which it is composed he may discover
many things on which he would fain close his eyes and
stop his nostrils. Milton leads us sometimes into the
arid wilderness where insipid personages discourse, not
always with the tongues of angels ; nor are Dante's dry
dissertations invariably radiant with the triple influence
of the stars ; even Shakespeare has occasional lapses
into persiflage not unworthy of a farce at the fair. And
Victor Hugo, sublime as these in his supreme moments,
must be judged by the general sweep and power of his
genius, regardless of spots that appear and disappear in
the solar radiance.

It was inevitable, also, that the acts and opinions of a
man whose evolution led him from Roman Catholicism to
absolute independence of creed, from the worship of
imperialism and faith in royalty to the glorification of
the ideal republic, and from literary tradition to the individual expression of his own genius, should have aroused
animosity in many religious, conservative and conventional
minds. This poet who at nineteen adored Delille and
at twenty-one revealed himself as the creator of a new
form of French lyrical art ; this leader of a revolutionary
movement in letters and politics who became a member
of the Academy and accepted a seat in the Senate ; this

peer of the realm who preached humility to the poor and patience to the oppressed ; this evangelist of equality who loved the literary throne and breathed with delight the incense of popular praise ; this courtier of fame who never wrote a line of congratulation or condolence * without the pomp and circumstance of an epistle addressed to posterity ; this author who accumulated a vast fortune from his literary labours † and was carried to the grave (by his own desire) in a pauper's coffin : offered himself readily enough to the sarcasm of detractors in an age of publicity when every contradiction and foible could not fail to be bitterly discussed.

The glory which illumined Victor Hugo's later days was not gained without dust and heat, nor, it must be confessed, without some judicious sounding of trumpets and beating of drums. For many years he was the pet aversion of the professors and officials of literature. Each one of his titles to fame was fiercely contested, and those writers who championed his cause, as for example Théodore de Banville and Auguste Vacquerie, were dismissed from the service of the journals to which they contributed. It is difficult in these days to understand the furies which were let loose on that innovator who dared to introduce such an ignoble word as '*cheval*' into serious verse and smuggle a low epithet like '*gamin*' into respectable prose.

Victor Hugo had a singularly robust physical frame, with uncommonly keen eyesight, and a memory so clear and so precise as to be almost phenomenal. The exceed-

* See his letter of 16 March, 1869, addressed to Lamartine's widow, and ending with the phrase : 'Henceforth he beams with a double radiance : in ' our literature, where he is a soul, and in the great unknown life, where he is ' a star '.

† The rights of publication in *les Misérables* were sold to Lacroix and Verboeckhoven for half-a-million francs.

ing vividness with which he could depict and present natural objects was due to his naturally quick and carefully cultivated faculty of observation. While he walked he dreamed and created; hence the appropriateness of Baudelaire's characterisation of him as '*Méditation qui 'marche*'. Indeed one of the secrets of Victor Hugo's inexhaustible energy and lifelong capacity for indefatigable labour—equal to that of Balzac or Littré—was his healthy love of exercise. Although he was fond of social pleasures he eschewed those voluptuous indulgences which have been the moral and material ruin of so many French poets. He kept his vigour fresh and unimpaired long after the time when the average man is worn out: in old age his eye was not dim nor his natural force abated. And there was always in his nature that real simplicity which finds its sustenance in the love of flowers and children and in the sweetness of household affections. These feelings, expressed in his poetry, have left a trail of exquisite tenderness even on the fierce invective of *les Châtiments* and over the blood and desolation of *l'Année terrible*.

Looked at in large, the character of Victor Hugo, like that of every truly great man, was good and noble. His voice, no less than Voltaire's, was continually lifted up against cruelty, ignorance and oppression. He pleaded for clemency; and although his personal likes and dislikes were equally pronounced, and sometimes indulged to excess,* he was a faithful believer in tolerance and liberty. His charities were as ample as they were unostentatious. To political refugees and literary aspirants he was often a prudent counsellor and always a generous friend. It is a

* A notable instance is the savage animosity of his poem on the death of Marshal Saint-Arnaud, published by Paul Meurice and Auguste Vacquerie in the last volume of *Toute la Lyre* (*Poésies inédites*).

notable fact that all the younger men of letters who enjoyed the intimacy of Victor Hugo retained through every change, and to the last, their affection and admiration for the master. For many years he reserved in his Parisian residence a chamber which poor authors, fed at his table and cheered by his discourse, could occupy for a few months at a time, and so work in freedom on some cherished volume. Gérard de Nerval, Édouard Ourliac and Albert Glatigny were among the temporary recipients of this bounty.

It is not literally true, as some admirer has asserted, that in the nineteenth century all French poetry worthy of the name is derived from Victor Hugo. Lamartine and Musset must claim a share in the impulse given to lyric art. But the supremacy of Victor Hugo has been recognised by every poet of importance since 1830, and, like Voltaire in the eighteenth century, Victor Hugo is by general consent the great representative genius of France in the nineteenth century. No writer has excelled him in weaving the elements either of human passion or of natural force into a vast 'tragic landscape'. His colossal architecture has a beauty of outline and a majestic unity of structure which justifies the epithet of ' *Magister de lapidi-* '*bus vivis*'. His verse, which has been the envy and admiration of three generations of French singers, is distinguished by its extraordinary vigour and vehemence ; the rhythmical sweep is superb and the inwoven melody inimitable ; the fertility and felicity of illustration are boundless. Even a superficial comparison of his work with that of the older French poets must manifest his immense superiority, both as singer and artist. Their cold declamation is charged with passion ; the note of tenderness is truer and deeper ; the harmony is rich and sonorous ; the imagery glowing and original ; the dramatic intensity at times almost overpowering. His finer verse is most delicate and fanciful, and in the manipulation of narrow rhythms and difficult rhymes he displays the absolute ease of a master.*

No poet was ever more profoundly and diversely human than Victor Hugo, and none, with the single exception of Shakespeare, has so divinely interpreted

. . . . 'the prophetic soul
'Of the wide world, dreaming on things to come'.

---

* The short rhythms which Victor Hugo handled with such consummate art cannot be adequately translated into English. Some wonderful achievements in similar compass have been performed by Shelley and Swinburne and Beddoes, but in translating it is impossible to turn the necessary rhymes round in so limited a space without excessive violence to the thought. Victor Hugo's ample alexandrines also lose much of their effect in the English rhymed heroic verse, because the latter runs naturally into couplets, whereas the long French line resolves itself into two hemistiches, and thus lends itself to the completion of a comparison or antithesis in the space of a single line. The decasyllabic verse is too abrupt when treated in this fashion, and if the two alexandrines are fused into one heroic couplet there is often a mixture of metaphors and a redundancy of images which becomes confusing. It must not be imagined that the ensuing translations are intended otherwise than as mere specimens of Victor Hugo's verse. They will give but a glimmering of the splendour and scope of his genius as a lyrical and declamatory poet. A copious selection from each of his twenty volumes of verse would be needed to represent the manifold and multiform incarnations of his poetical spirit. The only living Englishman capable of doing justice to the rush and splendour of the rhythm and the beauty and variety of the rhyme is Algernon Charles Swinburne.

Her Name.

Nomen aut Numen.

A lily's fragrance rare, an aureole's pale splendour,
    The whisper of the waning day ;
Love's passionate pure kiss of virginal surrender ;
The hour that breathes farewell, mysterious and tender ;
    The grief by comfort charmed away ;

The sevenfold scarf by storm emblazed and braiden,
    A trophy to the victor sun ;
The sudden cadence of a voice with memories laden ;
The soft and simple vow won from a shamefast maiden ;
    The dream of a new life begun ;

The murmur that with orient Dawn, rising to greet her,
    From lips of fabled Memnon came ;
The undulant hum remote of some melodious metre :—
All the soul dreams most sweet, if aught than these be
    sweeter,
    O Lyre, is less sweet than her name !

Even as a muttered prayer pronounce it, breathing
    lowly,
    But let it sound through all our songs !
Be in the darkened shrine the one light dim and holy !
Be as the word divine the same voice, chaunting slowly
    From the deep altar-place prolongs !

O world! ere yet my Muse, upborne in ample azure,
 Her wings for wandering flight unfolds,
And with those clamorous names, profaned of pride or
 pleasure,
Dares blend that chaster one that, like a sacred treasure,
 Love hidden in my heart still holds,

Needs must my song, while yet of silence unforsaken,
 Be like those hymns we kneel to hear,
And with its solemn strains the tremulous air awaken,
As though, with viewless plumes and unseen censers
 shaken,
 A flight of angels hovered near!

Son Nom.
(*Odes et Ballades.*)

1823.

To a Woman.

Child! if I were a king, my throne I would surrender,
 My sceptre, and my car, and kneeling vavassours,
My golden crown, and porphyry baths, and consorts
 tender,
And fleets that fill the seas, and regal pomp and splendour,
 All for one look of yours!

If I were God, the earth and luminous deeps that span it,
 Angels and demons bowed beneath my word divine,
Chaos profound, with flanks of flaming gold and granite,
Eternity, and space, and sky and sun and planet,
 All for one kiss of thine!

À une Femme.
(*Les Feuilles d'automne.*)

8 *May*, 1829.

New Song to an Old Air.*

If there be a fair demesne,
Fresher than the rose is,
Where each season's shower and sheen
Some new bloom uncloses;
Where one gathers, hour by hour,
Jasmine, lily, honey-flower,
Would that such might be the bower
Where thy foot reposes!

If there be a loving breast,
Honour so disposes,
That of all her gifts the best
Love therein encloses;
If this noble bosom yield
High desires to love revealed,
Would that such might be the shield
Where thy head reposes!

If there be a dream of love,
Odorous with roses,
Whence each day that dawns above
Some sweet thing discloses;
Dream that God himself hath blessed,
Wherein soul with soul may rest,
Would that such might be the nest
Where thy heart reposes!

Nouvelle Chanson sur un vieil Air.
(*Les Chants du Crépuscule. XXII.*)

18 *February*, 1834.

* See Note on page 50.

In a Church.

* * * * * *

O woman! why these tears that dim your sight,
   These brows with sorrow drawn?
You, whose pure heart is sombre as the night,
   And tender as the dawn?

What though the unequal lot, to some made sweet,
   To some deals bitter dole;
Though life gives way and sinks beneath your feet,
   Should that dismay the soul?

The soul, that seeks ere long a purer realm,
   Where beyond storm is peace,
Where, beyond griefs that surge and overwhelm,
   This world's low murmurings cease!

Be like the bird that, on the branch at rest
   For a brief moment, sings;
For though the frail bough bends beneath her breast
   She knows that she has wings!

         Dans l'Église de . . .
           (*Les Chants du Crépuscule.*)
25 *October,* 1834.

This Age is great and strong.

This age is great and strong. Her chains are riven.
   Thought on the march of man her mission sends;
Toil's clamour mounts on human speech to heaven,
   And with the sound divine of Nature blends.

In cities and in solitary stations
   Man loves the milk wherewith we nourish him;

And, in the shapeless block of sombre nations,
  Thought moulds in dreams new peoples grand and dim.

New days draw nigh. Hushed is the riot's clangour.
  The Grève is cleansed, the old scaffold crumbling lies.
Volcano torrents, like the people's anger,
  First devastate and after fertilise.

Now mighty poets, touched by God's own finger,
  Shed from inspirëd brows their radiant beams.
Art has fresh valleys, where our souls may linger,
  And drink deep draughts of song from sacred streams.

Stone upon stone, remembering antique manners,
  In times that shake with every storm-wind wild,
The thinker rears these columns, crowned with banners—
  Respect for grey old age, love for the child.

Beneath our roof-tree Duty and Right his father
  Dwell once again, august and honoured guests,
The outcasts that around our thresholds gather
  Come with less flaming eyes, less hateful breasts.

No longer Truth closes her austere portals.
  Deciphered is each word, each scroll unfurled.
Learning the book of life, enfranchised mortals
  Find a new sense and secret in the world.

O poets! Iron and steam, with fiery forces,
  Lift from the earth, while yet your dreams float round,
Time's ancient load, that clogged the chariot's courses,
  Crushing with heavy wheels the hard rough ground.

Man by his puissant will subdues blind matter,
  Thinks, seeks, creates! With living breath fulfilled,
The seeds that Nature's hands store up and scatter
  Thrill as the forest leaves by winds are thrilled.

Yea, all things move and grow. The fleet hours flying
  Leave each their track. The age has risen up great.
And now between its luminous banks, far-lying,
  Man like a broadened river sees his fate.

But in this boasted march from wrong and error,
  Mid the vast splendour of an age that glows,
One thing, O Jesus, fills my soul with terror:
  The echo of thy voice still feebler grows!

                              Ce Siècle est grand et fort.
  15 *April*, 1837.   (*Les Voix intérieures.*)

Mixed Commissions.

They sit in the shadow while 'Justice prevails!'
They people with heroes their dungeons and gaols,
    And the hulks, a detestable cloister
That floats like the blackness of night on the tides
While the sun on the sea gilds its glittering sides
    Like scales on the shell of an oyster.

For harbouring an outlaw beneath his poor roof
An old man is crushed by the law's iron hoof,
    His cries with their curses they stifle:
To the galleys for branding these rogues of our Vote,
These thieves that seized Popular Rights by the throat,
    His pockets the better to rifle!

They sentence the son that defended his sire,
The wife that took bread to her husband through fire,
    The friendship by Freedom begotten;
Honour?... they banish: and Truth?... they exile:
From judges like these issues Justice as vile
    As a graveworm from flesh that is rotten.

                              Les Commissions mixtes.
  BRUSSELS: *July*, 1852.   (*Les Châtiments.*)

Jericho.

Sound! trumpets of the soul, for ever sound!

When Joshua, vexed at heart, went marching round
The walls, with high head, dreaming ; when the clang
Louder and louder of shrill trumpets rang,
At the first blast the king laughed in his sleeve ;
The next he laughed to scorn :—' Dost thou believe
' With wind my city-walls to overthrow ? '—
The third time, as the ark, solemn and slow,
With clarions went before the marching ranks,
A troop of children mimicked in their pranks
The trumpet-blare, and spat upon the ark.
At the fourth blast, by Levi's sons blown stark,
Dusk women, seated at the distaff, spun
Between the crennelled towers, moss-grown and dun,
And flinging stones on the pale Hebrews, jeered.
The fifth time, on those gloomy walls appeared,
With cries, the halt and maimed and blind in crowds,
And mocked the clarion blown beneath the clouds.
The sixth, beneath that rampire's granite crest,
So high that there the eagle builds his nest,
So hard that there the lightning bursts in vain,
The king, with full-gorged laughter, came again
Crying : ' These Hebrews make rare minstrelsy ! '—
Round their gay king the elders laughed with glee,
Though wont to ponder grave in judgment-halls.

But with the seventh blast crumbled the proud walls!

(Les Châtiments.)

JERSEY : 19 *March*, 1853.

35

Stella.

One night I slumbered on the salt sea shore.
A fresh wind woke me, and I dreamed no more,
But watched with rapturous eyes the morning-star
Supreme, that rose in skies profound and far,
Swathed in white splendour, wonderful and soft.
The north wind, flying, whirled the storm aloft.
The bright star smote the clouds in vapours wreathed,
It was a light that thought, and lived, and breathed ;
It calmed the rock whereon the waves unfurl ;
And shone even as the soul shines through a pearl.
Though night was there, in vain the shadow gloomed
I' the welkin, by a heavenly smile illumed.
The top of the slant mast caught silvery light ;
Black was the vessel, but the sail was white :
The seamews, poised upon the ragged scar,
With brooding looks gazed gravely on the star,
Seen like some heavenly fowl with plumes of flame.
The sea, whose swell is like the people, came
And with hoarse murmurings low looked on the light
Trembling, lest backward it should turn in flight.
All space with love ineffable was filled.
The green grass at my feet shivered and thrilled ;
Birds in their nests held converse ; the new birth
Of flowers sang sweetly : We are stars of earth !
And, as the darkness her long veils unwove,
I heard a voice fall from the star, that clove
The heavens and said :
      ' I am the star of doom,
' She that seemed dead and rises from the tomb.
' On Sinaï, on the Spartan rock I shone ;
' A golden pebble winged with fire and thrown,

' As from God's sling, at the black brows of night.
' From ruined worlds I rise reborn and bright,
' O Nations, as the burning sun of song!
' The fire on Moses' brow and Dante's tongue
' Was mine. With love of me the ocean sighs.
' I come. . . . . .
     Faith, Virtue, Courage, rise!
' Mount to the towers, ye souls that watch below!
' Blind eyelids open, darkened eyeballs glow;
' Earth, thrill thy furrows; speech, inspire the dumb;
' Up, ye that slumber, for behold I come,
' Vaunt-courier of their march that sunders night,
' The giant Liberty, the angel Light!'

      Stella.
      (*Les Châtiments.*)
JERSEY: 31 *August*, 1853.

Dusk.

The pool glimmers white, like a mystical shroud;
 In the depths of the woodland are glimpses of glades;
The boles are a shadow, the branches a cloud;
 Is it Venus that shimmers through leafy arcades?

Is it Venus that silvers the slopes with her light?
 And you, are you lovers that pass in the gloom?
With a sheen of soft lawn the dusk pathways are white;
 The meadow awakens and calls to the tomb.

What song from the grass and what voice from the grave?
 Night comes: they are cold that sleep under the yews.
Let lip cling to lip! Seek love, hearts that crave!
 Let the living be glad while we slumber and muse.

God smiles on the lovers. Live, envied and blest,
O couples that pass on your leaf-covered way!
The love we bore with us to earth's chilly breast,
From the land of the living, is left us to pray.

The thatch looming black hides a hearth that is bright;
The tread of the reaper is heard in the field;
A star from the blue, like a blossom of light,
Bursts forth in the freshness of splendour revealed.

'Tis the month of ripe berries, the month of sweet things.
Night's angel floats dreaming on winds overhead,
And blends, borne aloft on his shadowy wings,
The kiss of the living, the prayer of the dead.

Crépuscule.
(Les Contemplations.)
CHELLES : *August*, 18 . .

A Hymn of the Earth.

Her throne is the meadow, the field and the plain,
She is dear to the sowers and reapers of grain,
To the shepherds that sleep on the heather;
She warms her chill breast in the fires of the suns
And laughs, when with stars in their circle she runs,
As with sisters rejoicing together.

She loves the bright beam that caresses the wheat,
And the cleansing of winds in her æther is sweet,
And the lyre of the tempest that thunders;
And the lightning whose brow, when it shines and takes
flight
In a flash that appals and appeases the night,
Is a smile from the welkin it sunders.

VICTOR HUGO

Glory to Earth! To the dawn of God's gaze!
To the swarming of eyes in the woodland ablaze,
    To nests by the sunrise made splendid!
Hail to the whitening of moon-smitten heights!
Hail to the azure that squanders her lights
    From treasuries never expended!

Earth loves the blue heaven that shines equal on all,
Whose radiance sheds calm on the throne and the thrall,
    Who blends with our wrongs and remorses,
With our sorrows, that burst into laughter too bold,
With our sins, with our fevers of glory and gold,
    The song of the stars in their courses.

Earth is calm when the sea groans beneath her and
    grieves.
Earth is beautiful; see how she hides under leaves
    The maidenly shame of her blushes!
Spring comes, like a lover, to kiss her in May;
She sends up the smoke of the village to stay
    The wrath of the thunder that rushes.

Smite not, O thunder! the humble lie here:
Earth is bountiful; yet is she grave and severe;
    And pure as her roses in blossom:
Man pleases her best when he labours and thinks;
And her Love is the well-spring that all the world drinks,
    And Truth is the milk of her bosom.

Earth hoards up her gold, but her harvest she wears;
In the flank of dead seasons that sleep in her lairs,
    The germs of new seasons assemble;
She has birds in the azure that whisper of love,
Springs that gush in the vales, and on mountains above
    Vast forests of pine-trees that tremble.

39

Wide weaver of harmonies under the skies,
She bids the salute of the slender reed rise
    With joy to the height of the cedar ;
For her law is the lowly that loves the sublime,
And she bases the right of the cedar to climb
    On the will of the grasses that feed her.

She levels mankind in the grave ; at the end
Alexander's and Cæsar's proud ashes descend
    With the dust of the cowherd to crumble ;
The soul she sends heavenward, the carcase she keeps,
And disdains, in the doom of oblivious deeps,
    To distinguish the high from the humble.

Each debt she discharges ; the branch to the root,
The night to the day, and the flower to the fruit ;
    She nourishes all she engenders ;
The plant that has faith when the man is in doubt ;
O blasphemy, shame against Nature to flout
    With his shadow the soul of her splendours !

Her breast was the cradle, her breast is the tomb,
Of Adam and Japheth ; she wrought out the doom
    Of the cities of Isis and Horus ;
Where Sparta lies mourning, where Memphis lies
    crushed,
Wheresoever the voice of man spake and is hushed,
    The grasshopper's song is sonorous.

For why ? That her joy may give comfort to graves.
For why ? That the ravin and wreck of Time's waves
    May be guerdoned with glorification,
The voice that says No with the voice that says Aye,
And the passing of peoples that vanish and die
    With the mystical chaunt of creation.

VICTOR HUGO

Earth's friends are the reapers; at twilight her face
On the broad black horizon would gladly give chase
    To the swarm of the hungering ravens;
At the hour when the oxen in weariness low,
When homeward with joy the brown husbandmen go,
    Like ships that return to their havens.

She gives birth without end to the flowers of the sod;
The flowers never raise their reproaches to God;
    From lilies, still chaste in their splendour,
From myrtles that thrill to the wind not a cry,
Not a murmur from vineyards ascends to the sky,
    On their innocence smiling and tender.

Earth spreads a dark scroll beneath the dense boughs;
She does what she can, and with peace she endows
    The rocks and the shrubs and the rivers,
To enlighten us, children of Hermes and Shem,
Whose pages the porings of Reason condemn
    To a lamp-light that flickers and shivers.

The end of her being is birth and not death;
Not jaws to devour, but a life-giving breath;
    When with havoc of battle is riven
Man's furrow and blood-bathed the track that war
    cleaves,
Earth turns her wild look, that is angry and grieves,
    From the ploughshare by wickedness driven.

Blasted, she asks him : Why kill the green plain?
What fruit will the wilderness give, and whose gain
    Shall be garnered from ruin and ravage?
No boon to her bounty the evil one yields,
And she weeps on the virginal beauty of fields
    Deflowered by the lust of the savage.

Alma Ceres was Earth, and Earth's goddess of old,
She beamed with blue eyes over meadow and wold,
And still the world rings with her pæan ;
' Sons, I am Demeter, divine of divine,
' Ye shall build me a temple of splendour to shine
' On the slopes of the Callichorean '.

La Terre : Hymne.
(*La Légende des Siècles. I.*)

Frondage.

Orpheus heard, as star rose after
    Star and touched the woods with light,
The obscure and ominous laughter
    Of the worshippers of night.

Phtah, the Theban priestess holy,
    Gazing from her dusky shrine,
Saw the ebon shadows slowly
    Dance along the starred sky-line.

Æschylus, after sunset, lingered
    In the dun Sicilian shades,
Charmed by flutes that deftly fingered
    Flung sweet echoes through the glades.

Pliny, couched among the myrtles,
    Deemed the nymphs of Melita fair,
When the wind neath whirling kirtles
    Kissed their rosy limbs blown bare.

Plautus wandered through the glowing
    Orchards, sometimes turning o'er
Tasted fruits i' the herbage, showing
    Where some god had gone before.

In Versailles, with beauty haunted,
  Comes the faun, where fountains flow,
Proffering to Molière the enchanted
  Rhymes that so amazed Boileau.

Dante, when his glass grew dimmer,
  Blurred with dark-souled images,
Watched athwart the twilight-glimmer
  Women glide between the trees.

Chénier, peering through the slender
  Willow-boughs, bewildered hung
On those flying breasts whose splendour
  Vergil, like a lover, sung.

Shakespeare, ambushed in the shadows
  Of the drowsy-branchëd oak,
Caught faint trippings from the meadows
  When the light-foot fairies woke.

Thus, O foliage, are my fancies
  Lured within the bosky bourne!
Pan dwells there, and there in dances
  Still the dizzy Satyrs turn.

> *Floréal: II.*
> (*Les Chansons des Rues et des Bois.*)

Reality.

Nature is everywhere the same,
  At Timbuctoo as on the Tagus;
Chlamys is petticoat, save in name:
  And Douglas Home is Simon Magus.

Lavallière in her coach, aquest
  Of Louis or Mars to quench her passion,
Was just as fiercely love-possessed
  As in her shell the bright Thalassian.

O sons, O brothers in poesy,
  If the thing is, let the word be spoken!
Nothing is low when the soul soars high ;
  Be pure in spirit and pass the token!

You hear in Pæstum's rose-demesne
  The hiccuping of old Silenus!
Is Bottom amiss on Shakespeare's scene
  When Horace stales the son of Venus?

Truth laughs at limits, the veil she scorns,
  And, thanks to beast-god Pan, earth's Real
Sprouts unashamed, and shows his horns
  On the blue brows of the Ideal!

Réalité: Les Complications de l'Idéal.
(*Les Chansons des Rues et des Bois.*)

The Streets and the Woods.

Beware, my friend, of pretty girls ;
  Shun the bower of the fallen goddess:
Fear the charm of the skirt that whirls,
  The shapely bust and the well-laced bodice.

Look to your wings, bird, when you fly!
  Look to your threads, O doll that dances!
Turn from the light of Calypso's eye,
  And flee from the fire of Jenny's glances!

When they grow tender, then be sure
    That slavery lurks within their rapture ;
Love's A B C is Art to allure,
    Beauty that blinds and a Charm to capture !

The sun-light gilds a prison-cell ;
    A fragrant rose the gaol refreshes :
And just like these, you see, is the spell
    Of a girl that lures you into her meshes.

Once caught, your soul is a sombre lyre,
    And in your thought are storms that thunder !
And weeping follows dead desire
    Ere you have time to smile and wonder !

Come to the fields ! Spring's gladsome voice
    Thrills the vast oaks and wakes the mountains,
The meadows smile, the woods rejoice,
    Sing O the charm of crystal fountains !

      Pour d'autres : IX.
      (*Les Chansons des Rues et des Bois.*)

To the Imperious Beauty.

L'amour, panique
    De la raison,
Se communique
    Par le frisson.

Laissez-moi dire,
    N'accordez rien.
Si je soupire,
    Chantez, c'est bien.

Love, like a panic
    Seizing the will,
Leaps to tyrannic
    Sway with a thrill.

Let me beseech you,
    Turn and refuse ;
When my sighs reach you,
    Sing, if you choose.

Si je demeure,	If I come kneeling,
Triste, à vos pieds,	Near you to dwell,
Et si je pleure,	See my tears stealing,
C'est bien, riez.	Laugh, it is well.
Un homme semble	Man may dissemble
Souvent trompeur.	So to ensnare :
Mais si je tremble,	But if I tremble,
Belle, ayez peur.	Beauty, beware !

À la belle impérieuse : L'éternel petit roman.
(*Chansons des Rues et des Bois.*)

Forerunners.

On Being and the Thing that is
  Man in all ages broods forlorn,
And ever asks of the abyss
  'O Nature! Wherefore was I born?'
Believers now, atheists betimes,
We, to the height Prometheus climbs,
  The Euclids and the Keplers send ;
Our doubts like clouds funereal rise,
And, filled with darkness, seek the skies,
  Whence, filled with lightnings, they descend.

O brows whereon the Ideal beams !
  From the gulf's edge, in depths of space,
What faces peer with luminous gleams !
  What looks are on each mystic face !
See where the starry eyeballs glow
Of Milton and Galileo !
  Dim-visaged Dantes, sombre-hued,
Your heels are worthy of the stars !

VICTOR HUGO

Your spirits, on their fiery cars,
  Are coursers of Infinitude!

Rise and descend, for all is there;
  Be bold to seek and seize, for still
Jason proclaims himself 'To dare!'
  And Gama's blazon is 'I will!'
And when the searcher, shrinking yet,
With eyes on dawn and darkness set,
  Backward before the mystery springs,
Trembling to read the hieroglyph;
Lo! Will, a rearing hippogriff,
  Above the sunrise spreads his wings!

This terrible steed was his to urge
  When human Genius durst aspire
To pass beyond the inviolate verge,
  Armed only with his torch and lyre.
Then on his springing soul from far,
Reason the sun and Love the star
  Rose radiant in the yawning blue,
Where darkness spins her sombre snares;
And these two planets were God's phares
  Shining to guide the giant through.

The hearts wherein God kindles fire,
  Though all around them fleet like fume,
Keep sacred still their wild desire
  To explore the gulf and pierce the gloom;
Deep in the gulf all knowledge lies.
They look, they plunge, they agonise:
  Life lags too long in aimless ease.
Madness is sire to the sublime;
And down the same abyss in time
  Columbus seeks Empedocles!

O seas to sound! O skies to scale!
 Each dauntless seeker of the True
Unfurls to the infinite his sail,
 Fulton the green, Herschell the blue.
Magellan launches, Fourier flies ;
The frivolous crowd, with scornful eyes,
 Too ignorant their dreams to sound,
Watches them vanish from the coast
And cries 'Behold! a soul is lost':—
 Nay, scoffing crowd, a world is found!

Les Précurseurs.
(L'Année terrible.)

Change of Horizon.

The bard of the old days was Homer; war
Was law; age grew beneath a vulgar star.
The living flew, with strenuous blood and breath,
To meet the sinister embrace of death.
A glorious shroud for liberated Rome,
For Sparta and her laws some holy tomb,
Were the best gifts the Gods could give to man :
The haggard youth rushed frantic in the van ;
He that leaped first into the open grave,
And ran his proud career, was counted brave.
Seek death with glory, O sublime behest!
Achilles' wrath the sage Ulysses guessed ;
A strumpet tore her robe from top to toe,
And all exclaimed: 'Behold our lord lies low!'
And the fierce virgin of the Scyrian isle
Masked heroes with august and fatal wile.
Man was the faithful bridegroom of the sword.
Above the Muse hovered a vulture horde ;

Savage, she lured her ghouls to the grim field ;
Vast singer, she, of clashing spear and shield ;
Ogress of Evil, tigress tearing Peace,
Black cloud that lowered on the blue hills of Greece ;
Her clamours shook the heavens with desperate cry ;
She bade the victor ' Kill !', the vanquished ' Die !'—
She gashed the flanks of monstrous steeds and rose,
With wind-blown tresses, glaring on the throes
Of demigods in Titan's clenched embrace :
With fires of hell she lit the hero's face,
From Ajax' sheath showered lightnings and with thongs
Trailed Hector's corse before the Trojan throngs.
When warriors blenched, stung by the whizzing steel,
And with red-streaming flanks did faint and reel,
When skulls, yawning like sombre urns, were cloven,
When lances pierced her veil of darkness woven,
When snakes along her white arm writhed and curled,
When through the Olympian realm loud war was
      whirled,
Dreadful and calm she sang, and her wild lips
Foamed blood in the fierce clarion ; dim eclipse
Of towers and tents and helms and wounded hosts,
Black swarms of dead, heaped on the grisly coasts,
Whirlwinds of banners, chariots overthrown,
And swords and shields on the epic blast were blown !

But now the Muse is Peace ; she binds no greaves
On her white limbs ; her head is crowned with sheaves :
To Death the bard says : ' Die, war, shadow, strife'!'—
And gently leads the march of man towards life :
Her songs, like tears, fall softly in slow showers
On children, and on women, and on flowers ;
Stars burst in splendour on her wingéd brows ;
Her music makes green buds break from the boughs ;

D   49

Her dreams are woven of dawn ; with lips of love
She sings and laughs, clear as the heavens above.

Vainly, with clenched fists, in thy sullen wrath
Thou threatenest still, black past : *there* leads thy path !
Thy day is done.   Henceforth the living know,
If they but will, thy hideous towers of woe
Shall crumble, that the light at last shines through ;
That what they shall be springs from what they do :
That men must succour men, that man's fate feeds
On his own treacherous dreams and coward deeds.
I, exiled, travail towards the sacred time
When from man's fears shall issue hopes sublime
To pluck, watching dawn out of darkness rise,
Hell from his heart, with heaven before his eyes.

Changement d'Horizon.
(*La Légende des Siècles. IV : XLV.*)

Note on
New Song to an Old Air.

The 'old air' to which this song was written is *La bonne aventure*, well known to generations of English children as ' In my cottage by a wood' or ' Holy Bible, book divine'.   The rhythm of the English version has been vulgarised by the substitution of two distinct syllables for the graceful feminine cadence of the French original. *La bonne aventure* is simply a nursery song, but the genius of two great poets has matched the melody with words which are worthy of its exquisite beauty.   Molière touched it with tenderness in *le Misanthrope*, for there Alceste sings :—

Si le roy m'avoit donné
Paris, sa grand'ville,
Et qu'il me fallût quitter
L'amour de ma mie,

VICTOR HUGO

Je dirois au roy Henry :
Reprenez vostre Paris,
J'aime mieux ma mie, au gué,
J'aime mieux ma mie.

And Victor Hugo gave a grander note to it in *les Misérables*, when
Combeferre sang in the staircase :—

Si César m'avait donné
La gloire et la guerre,
Et qu'il me fallût quitter
L'amour de ma mère,
Je dirais au grand César :
Reprends ton sceptre et ton char,
J'aime mieux ma mère, ô gué !
J'aime mieux ma mère.

Béranger and other chansonniers have also paid their tribute to this
charming melody, more beautiful in its simplicity than all the
cavatinas and arias of Mozart and Rossini. But it would be vain to
seek in French verse, from Malherbe to Musset, for anything so light
and delicate as Victor Hugo's setting. It will be observed that Dean
Carrington's version of this *New Song to an Old Tune*, which is given
below, does not reproduce the feminine rhyme and is in some other
respects unfaithful to the lyrical symmetry of the original :—

If some fragrant lawn be found,
By dews of heaven blest,
Where are seen, the whole year round,
Flowers in beauty dressed ;
Where rose, pink, and lilies rare,
All in rich profusion are—
I would make a pathway there
For your foot to rest.

If there be that well can love,
Some devoted breast,
Which all virtue doth approve,
All things base detest ;
If that bosom always beat
To perform heroic feat—
There I find a pillow meet
For thy brow to rest.

VICTOR HUGO

If a dream of love there be,
  By all sweets possest,
Where each fleeting hour we see
  Whatsoe'er is best—
Dream, God-hallowed, bright and kind,
Where the soul to soul is joined—
There a shelter would I find
  For your heart to rest.

(*Translations from the Poems of Victor Hugo.*)

52

Joseph Delorme.

Born in Boulogne-sur-Mer, 1804 . . . Died in Paris, 1869.

Charles-Augustin Sainte-Beuve began his literary life as a disciple of the Romantic school and assisted in the Renaissance of French poetry in 1830. If not so fervent in his later days as in the flush of youth, he always judged the movement and the men with critical impartiality; and praise from him was praise indeed.

Sainte-Beuve's father died before the boy was born. The child's education was supervised by his mother, a woman of good-sense and strong character. He completed his course at the *collège Charlemagne* in Paris and reluctantly sacrificed his taste for letters to the study of anatomy and surgery. At twenty-two years of age he left the hospital to which he was attached and published some literary criticisms in the *Globe*. In 1828 he issued his *Tableau historique et critique de la poésie française et du théâtre français au seizième siècle*, the first important essay in modern historical and philosophical analysis applied to letters.

Sainte-Beuve's admiration for Victor Hugo gave birth to the imaginary young poet whose productions (*Vie, Poésies et Pensées de Joseph Delorme*) appeared in 1829. The volume was generously appreciated. It was followed in 1830 by *les Consolations* and in 1837 by *Pensées d'août*. In all these poems there is evidence of a healthy and well-nourished mind, refreshed in the contemplation of nature and expressing itself in noble and harmonious

numbers. The influence of English literature was acknowledged in translations and imitations of Byron, Wordsworth, Charles Lamb, Coleridge, Bowles and Kirke White;
indeed the French poetry of the period immediately preceding 1830 is more nearly akin to English poetry in
simplicity and pathos than that of any other period.

Joseph Delorme died on the threshold of manhood, and
in answer to the remonstrances of a friend all that Sainte-
Beuve could say was that he had no longer any love in
his heart or any song in his voice.* The disappearance
of Joseph Delorme was a great loss to French poetry, for
he combined something of Wordsworth's spiritual insight
with the simple emotion of Lamartine, and brought a
calm and meditative note into the transports of Victor
Hugo and the complaints of Alfred de Musset. He was
a poet of observation and sentiment rather than passion,
and altogether lacked the lyrical buoyancy.

It is unnecessary to say much of Sainte-Beuve's critical
works, which are a permanent portrait-gallery of French
literature in his own and all preceding epochs. His vision
was wide in its sweep and keen in its scrutiny. When
he took up the study of a man of letters he contrived not
only to reconstitute the atmosphere of his time, but to
ascertain 'the central point of his work and the dominant
'feature of his character'. Sainte-Beuve's sympathies were
many-sided, and he never affected that deliberate attitude
of contradiction and superiority which vitiates so much
contemporary criticism ; nor did he disdain to study small
men. His kindly and appreciative notices of such minor
poets as Hégésippe Moreau and Louis Bertrand are an

---

* 'Mon cœur n'a plus rien de l'amour,
'Ma voix n'a rien de ce qui chante'.

Réponse à M. Édouard Turquety.
(Poésies complètes de Sainte-Beuve.)

everlasting memorial of the greatness of his intellect and a perpetual lesson to the literary Pharisee.

Sainte-Beuve was a conscientious and unwearied worker, with an immense range of general knowledge and a most precise memory. He assimilated everything—the beauty of a landscape, the soul of a book, the character of a visitor, the structure of an epoch—with the same unerring faculty. His prose, if not of the highest distinction, is never trivial: it is clear, sober, convincing, carefully fashioned, instinct with thought and finely analytical. A certain English austerity in relation to literary morals is visible in his critical judgments. His mother had English blood in her veins, and to her, more than to his father, Sainte-Beuve attributed the healthy robustness of his nature. That intelligent sympathy with which he divined the English character is admirably manifested in his articles on William Cowper in the *Causeries du lundi*.

It is scarcely an exaggeration to say that Sainte-Beuve's life was wholly dedicated to letters. He was a senator, but not a politician, in his later days; and a member of the French Academy. After having passed through several phases of philosophical belief, he died unfurnished with the sacraments, and, by his own wish, was buried without religious ceremony.

This excellent poet, philosopher and critic was an earnest seeker of the truth and a robust and independent thinker.

To Rhyme.

Rhyme, to whom the sounds of song
      Sole belong,
Rhyme, in whose harmonious numbers
Verse, that rings with accents true
      Thrilling through,
Wakes the soul from voiceless slumbers ;

Rhyme, now echoing as when flute
      Sighs to lute,
Now with burst of trumpet splendour ;
Last farewell, in whispered word
      Faintly heard,
Wafted back with cadence tender ;

Rhyme, whose measured sweep and chime,
      Keeping time,
Oar-like cleaves the foaming surges ;
Golden bridle, spur of steel,
      When the heel
Onward the swift courser urges ;

Buckle that on naked breast,
      Closely pressed,
Clasps the girdle of Love's charmer ;
Baldrick by the warrior bound
      Firmly round,
Girding on his linkëd armour ;

JOSEPH DELORME

Narrow nipple whence the spring
        Issuing
Shoots to heaven a crystal tower,
Thence, with roseate tissue spun
        By the sun,
Bursts in rainbow-coloured shower ;

Adamant ring whose diamond shine
        Near the shrine
Sparkles as the air grows denser,
Where the paling lamp-lights swim
        Wreathed in dim
Vapours from the smoking censer ;

Key that keeps from mortal eyes
        Mysteries
In the sacred ark enshrouded,
While on Truth's embalmëd vase
        Angels gaze,
Veiled in wings with glory clouded ;

Rather sylph whose lissome feet
        Skim the fleet
Winds and spurn the earth beneath her,
When she guides the poet's car,
        Like a star
Trailing light through fields of æther ;

Rhyme ! O whatsoe'er thou be,
        On the knee
Bending, I confess my treason ;
Humble hence my rebel pride
        Shall abide
Loyal to thy laws of reason.

Fly not when I court the Muse,
      Nor refuse
Help to him whose song adores thee ;
Turn, O turn thy kind regard
      On the bard,
On the bard when he implores thee !

If a verse deflowered and bare,
      In chill air,
Lies beneath thy stern look blighted,
Let no solitary tone
      Sigh and moan,
Like a lonely voice benighted.

Erst, when on my trembling lyre
      Young desire
Dallied with unskilful finger,
In her flight a soft white dove,
      Poised above,
Near the lute seemed fain to linger ;

But ere yet my chords could ring,
      Vibrating,
Plaintively the bird did hover,
Sad as one whose lonely fate
      Mourns her mate,
Mourns her mate the exiled lover.

Ah ! sweet songsters, two by two,
      Lovers true,
Henceforth shall ye wed twin-voices,
Let your kisses, let your wings,
      Thrill the strings,
When my tremulous lyre rejoices ;

Else, with golden thread for rein,
　　　Let your wain
On the light clouds, wreathed in roses,
Draw me, cherished steeds of love,
　　　To the grove
Where the Cyprian queen reposes!

À la Rime.
(*Poésies.*)

To Victor Hugo.

Great is your genius, Friend, your thoughts upborne
　As on Elijah's living car ascend ;
　Before your breath we are like reeds that bend ;
Beneath the fiery blast men's souls lie shorn.

And yet how fearful lest you wound us, Friend!
Noble and tender, in your heart you scorn
The thoughtless word that pierces like a thorn,
　And still with kind embrace your arms extend.

As the iron warrior, he that laughs at fears,
Lifts from the field a nursling bathed in tears,
　And bears him safely through the armèd band,

Gauntletted, soothing him with fond caress :
No nurse could shew more skill in tenderness,
　Nor could the mother have a softer hand.

À V. H . . .
(*Les Consolations.*)

To the Muse.

Florem . . . bene olentis anethi.

Poor Muse, driven homeward, crushed, abused, betrayed ;
   Innocent child that erst in pilgrim guise
   Fared forth for me, with songs to charm deaf skies,
Thy drooping brow shall on this breast be laid.

They heard thee not, O dear deluded maid,
   Now more than ever dear ; yet cease these cries !
   Sweeter thy fragrance is when storm-winds rise ;
The bee still loves thy blossoms disarrayed.

A heavenly smile on earth strewed heliotrope,
   Lily and hyacinth, windflower and the rest
That Homer rained on the Idalian slope.

   Even fields and hedges shine in beauty drest,
   And the bold may-bloom laughs, but I love best
The soft blue eye that humble violets ope.

À la Muse.
(*Notes et Sonnets.*)

Lausanne.

Be it at nightfall when beneath a cloud,
    Stretched wide from dusk to dark, the skies lie furled,
    While beyond Chillon, higher and higher curled,
Summit on summit sleeps in dense blue shroud.

When all those towering giants, in close crowd,
    Loom like the barriers of a far-off world,
    Gainst which in vain eternal storms are hurled,
Or antique Thule's battlements steel-browed!

Enchantment vast and vague! Scarce the wave throbs,
    Nor in the clouds nor on my brows one breath ;
    What foil divine to dreams of change and death!

O Byron, O Beethoven, hush your sobs !
    —Sole in the silence, while my thought takes wing,
    From coverts nigh the shrill cicalas sing.

                                    Lausanne : II.
                                    (*Notes et Sonnets.*)

Auguste Barbier.

Born in Paris, 1805 . . . Died in Paris, 1882.

. . . . from the book of honour razèd quite,
And all the rest forgot for which he toiled.

Henri-Auguste Barbier was bred for the law by the
decree of his parents, and betook himself to letters of
his own free will. He is one of the forgotten glories of
the French Romantic Movement. A true republican, like
Shelley and Landor, he threw a trumpet-note into the
melley of 1830. Balzac adored him, and Berlioz, who had
a keen sense of poetical beauty, went to 'the terrible poet
of the *Ïambes*', as the nearest to Victor Hugo, for the
libretto of *Benvenuto Cellini.*

These *Ïambes*, collected in 1832 from the gazettes for
which they had been written, are a satire on the worship
of glory and the lust of political power, composed in the
couplet form first employed by André Chénier in his latest
poems. The same measure had been used in stanza form
by other poets of the eighteenth century, but Auguste
Barbier gave this verse a freedom, a vigour and a resonance which no previous poet had ever attained in it. The
alternate twelve-and-eight-syllable lines, with crossed
rhymes, give no idea of the classical iambic, but were
intended to recall it by their ' free and rapid gait '.

Barbier's verse is bold and brilliant, and has much pomp
and amplitude of movement. He is usually robust and
seldom delicate. The author of the *Ïambes* had not that

passion for finely-chiselled handiwork which has distinguished so many French poets of this century. But he
had a wonderful way of throwing off a large line when he
loved his subject. To him Italy was the

'Divine Juliette, au cercueil étendue';

and he celebrated Ireland as

'La verdoyante Érin et ses belles collines'.

The poet had visited Italy in the company of Auguste
Brizeux, the Breton bard, and in *Il Pianto* (1832) he sung
her departed glories and later degradation in some superb
sonnets and stanzas. In *Lazare* (1833) he recorded his
impressions of a visit to England, satirising in powerful
verse the mingled splendour and misery which he witnessed in her capital, and the doom of her labourers
bound beneath the tyranny of wealth.

Barbier's poetical triumph was brief, his fall sudden
and decisive. He withdrew into lasting obscurity, and
although he issued volumes of verse from time to time—
such as *Chants civils et religieux* (1841) *Rimes héroïques*
(1843) *Silves et Rimes légères* (1864) . . . these not wanting
in freshness and grace . . . and *Satires et Chants* (1865)—
he seemed gradually to lose vigour as he left behind him
the enthusiasm and fervour of 1830. He was a man of
high culture and learning. Among his miscellaneous
works were a metrical translation of Shakespeare's *Julius
Cæsar* in 1848; some *Études dramatiques; Chez les Poètes*,
a collection of translations and imitations of ancient and
modern verse; and *Contes du Soir* and *Trois Passions*,
prose tales.

The later days of Auguste Barbier were passed in solitude and penury. A shabby little old man, who shrank
in conscious self-effacement and to whose presence the

unwelcome visitor could obtain access only after much knocking and unlocking of doors, was all that remained of the once 'terrible poet of the *Ïambes*'. His time was spent in conjuring up ghosts of his old poems and in drawing sketches to illustrate histories of travel and adventure which he compiled to earn his poor livelihood. Once or twice only he emerged from his obscurity—the last occasion was in 1870, when he delivered his reception speech at the Academy and amazed everybody by the artificial feebleness of his antiquated diction. The author of the brilliant *Ïambes*, so celebrated at twenty-seven years of age, died almost unnoticed at seventy-seven; all his triumphs forgotten and all his glory extinct . . . *nominis umbra.*

Popularity.

*   *   *   *   *   *

The People's Love ! She is the shameless goddess
  With world-embracing arms,
The antique nymph that flaunts, with open bodice,
  To all her naked charms !
She is the Sea ! the Sea ! now calm and smiling
  When dawn first breaks above,
Like a young queen that sings, man's soul beguiling,
  Blonde siren, full of love.
The sea, kissing the sand, a perfumed blossom
  Borne on bewitching waves,
And cradling in her undulant wanton bosom
  Her race of dusky slaves ;
The sea, anon, that frenzied and defiant
  From her calm couch doth rise,
Towers with enormous head and, like a giant,
  Threatens the sombre skies ;
Thence to and fro, dishevelled, riven asunder,
  Bounds in her headlong flight
Through the vext surges, fierce beneath the thunder
  As thousand bulls in fight ;
Then, with flanks whitened as in foaming madness,
  Warped lips and wandering eyes,
Rolls on the shore, deep moaning with the sadness
  Of one that writhes and dies ;

And, like the Mænad, worn at last with anger,
    Crawls wearied to her bed,
Still tossing on the beach, in powerless languor,
    Torn limb and bleeding head!

La Popularité : V.
(Les Ïambes.)

Michael-Angelo.

How wan thy brow, how sad thy looks and wild,
    O Michael-Angelo, proud marble-bender!
    No soft tear ever made those eyelids tender;
Nor once thy lips, like Dante's, may have smiled.

The Muse with milk too strong suckled her child;
    Art alone claimed thy love and life's surrender:
    Through sixty years, aureoled with threefold splendour,
No heart with tenderness thy heart beguiled.

    Poor Buonarotti! thine was one sole gladness,
    To carve in stone sublimity and sadness;
Puissant as God and girt like him with fears:

    So, when the dwindling sunset of thy glory
    Left thee a wearied lion grim and hoary,
Death lingering took thee, full of fame and years.

Michel-Ange.
(Il Pianto.)

66

Allegri.

Though in my heart Christ's antique faith may perish,
  Art, towering like a marble tomb, shall shine,
  As when, from heaven's high vault, suns in decline
Its gloom with glimpses of lone light reflourish.

So thou, austere Allegri, wont to nourish
  The seed of sacred song in days divine,
  Leadst me where faith and love, in hallowed shrine,
The dead limbs of the World's Redeemer cherish.

Then my vain soul, wherein no reverence dwells,
My soul, borne on the song thy rapture swells,
  Soars to the blest abode of bright archangels ;

Whence, swathed in mystery from heaven's depths that glow,
I hear the holy ones, in robes of snow,
  Chaunt on their golden lutes divine evangels.

Allegri.
(*Il Pianto.*)

Shakespeare.

Alas! shall the pure brows that glory kindled
  Be blasted by the winter's icy breath,
And must the gods of genius, sadly dwindled,
  Go, like the other gods, to dusty death ?

67

To these dull days great Shakespeare's tragic wonders
  Unfurl the enchantment of their scenes in vain ;
Men have no ears for the proud Briton's thunders :
  Voiceless and lonely lies his echoing fane.

Albion no longer loves his sacred symbols ;
  Outwearied with their truth the wandering throng
Harks back to barbarism, while tinkling cymbals
  Speak louder to the heart than loftiest song.

And yet what Titan, heavenly splendours bearing,
  Lightened like him the pools of human slime ?
Plunged in the salt sea's breast, more greatly daring,
  And deeper dived into the gulfs of Time ?

What wizard woke like him the sombre passions,
  Enormous reptiles swarming in man's heart ;
Dragons obscure that in a thousand fashions
  Curl writhing in their nest ?   What hand with art

Like his could in their dark recesses take them
  And, with discovered face in the pure light,
Like Hercules before the dazed world shake them,
  Shrieking in chorus their funereal fright ?

Must we behold base Matter boldly planted
  With brutal feet firm on her heavy car ;
Must England choose false lights for ever flaunted
  Before the beams of that imperial star ?

On this dull earth shall Beauty cease to hover,
  Lost utterly in the wide realm of Night ?
Nay !   Night with sombre clouds the sky may cover,
  She shall not quench the lamps of heavenly light !

AUGUSTE BARBIER

O thou, of Nature's womb the rarest blossom!
Nursling robust, child borne in her strong arms;
Thou that didst cling and, suckled at her bosom,
    With puissant lips drain Truth from all her charms;

All that thy fancy touched with aëry pinion,
    All things to which thy glance gave birth below,
All the fresh shapes that filled thy vast dominion,
    Woundless of death eternally shall glow!

Shakespeare! In vain beneath these vaults supernal
    Inconstant mortals in vile cohorts pass;
In vain the abyss of Time sees sempiternal
    System on system piled in ruinous mass:

Thy genius, like the sun that rises slowly
    And moveless shines at noon's empyreal height,
Still calmly pours its light supreme and holy
    Above the wild waves in tumultuous flight!

Shakespeare.
(Lazare.)

Gérard de Nerval.

Born in Paris, 1808 . . . Died in Paris, 1855.

The lunatic, the lover and the poet
Are of imagination all compact.

Gérard La Brunie or Labrunie (by anagram changed to
Nerval) was the son of a Picardese surgeon-major in the
army of Napoleon. He lost his mother in early childhood ; she died of fever at Glogau during the disastrous
Russian campaign. The boy had a curious education
under his father's care. The elements of Latin and
Greek, Italian and German, and Arabic and Persian, with
a course of Oriental calligraphy, were included in his
curriculum. He was afterwards sent to the *collège Charlemagne*, and, while yet a schoolboy, his *Élégies nationales*,
composed under the influence of Casimir Delavigne's once
famous *Messéniennes*, attracted the attention of literary
observers. Before he was twenty years old he had translated *Faust,** an achievement which drew from Goethe
the· precious compliment that he had never understood
his own poetry better than in reading this French transcription. ' Here everything lives and moves anew with
' freshness and vivacity', said Goethe to Eckermann ; ' and
' this young man ', he added, 'will become one of the
' purest writers of France '. Goethe's eulogium 'was well
deserved, for although the Frenchman's knowledge of

---

* Issued in 1828 : second edition 1835 : republished, with the second *Faust*
and translations from several German poets, in 1840.

German must have been imperfect he had the indispensable
poetic insight and sympathy, to which he joined the rare
art of preserving the depth and fervour of the original
whilst endowing it with the natural lucidity of his own
language. This is abundantly demonstrated by his experiments in translating from Schiller, Klopstock, Bürger,
Körner, Uhland, Hoffmann, Richter and Heine.

Gérard de Nerval's native dreaminess led him into
many other unfamiliar and fascinating paths of human
idealism. If he had not the marvellous instinct of
Oriental things which is attributed to Méry (who collaborated with him in several dramas) he was nevertheless
conversant with the secular myths and religions of
humanity, and 'even invented some himself' if Gautier is
to be believed. He had absorbed the mystical elements
of Bouddhism and Catholicism, and the spiritual essence
of the legends of Greece and Israel, as well as the influences of the modern visionaries down to Swedenborg.
'But you have no religion' said some sceptical friend.
'No religion?'—answered Gérard—'Why, I have seventeen
'. . . at least!'

This rare genius was a man of most sweet and gentle
nature ; he was unassuming even to humility, and yet of a
proud and sensitive disposition. His clear complexion,
golden hair, grey eyes and finely-moulded features gave
him in the freshness of youth that appearance of physical
frailty allied to intellectual beauty which was the charm
of Shelley. But as Gérard, short in stature and near-
sighted, grew prematurely bald, he lost in early manhood
the attractiveness of his youth.

His characteristic condition of mind was a mixture of
extreme simplicity and subtle mysticism. He firmly
believed in the efficacy of talismans and exorcisms, drew
horoscopes with touching faith, and had withal a cunning

gift of observation, which is evinced in his writings by excessive delicacy and vividness of description.

The first years of Gérard's literary life were spent in that miserable lodging in the *impasse du Doyenné* which he shared with nine other Bohemians, among whom were Théophile Gautier, Arsène Houssaye, Édouard Ourliac, Roger de Beauvoir and Alphonse Esquiros. Their lot was occasionally enlivened by the visit of girls from the Opera, presided over by the *Cydalise* whose charms Gérard has so tenderly sung. Gérard's habits of life were abnormal. He rarely slept in his bed-chamber, but wandered about the streets of Paris night after night, and dozed anywhere during the day. He was familiar with every nook and corner of the city, and a friend of his nocturnal wanderings tells how he took a childish pride in knowing where to find the best brandy or *blanquette* or tea-punch; where a delicious cup of chocolate could be had at two o'clock in the morning; and where the only good beer in Paris was served by two red-haired damsels, on whom Gérard would gaze with 'calm and ecstatic admiration'. From time to time he had an access of insanity, and was taken to an asylum at Passy. More than once he passed a few months in this friendly retreat.

Gérard's literary work was intermittent, and yet he had the essential virtue of an artist, for, although he never developed and completed any long poem or romance, he turned and re-turned his thoughts until he had given them their fullest expression. His wavering reason could not face severe and solid work. He had planned a great drama on the Queen of Sheba, that sphinx-like Balkis or Belkiss whose fascinations seem to have fixed themselves on the imagination of so many French men of letters during the Romantic era, and to whose inspiration we owe the most pathetic and most entrancing of all short stories, Charles Nodier's *Fée aux Miettes*. This enchantress haunted Gérard like a passion. He plunged deeply into Oriental lore to saturate himself with the warmth and colour of the legend, and for a time could speak and think of nothing else. His mysticism led him into another passion, no less æthereal and equally innocent. He fell in love with Jenny Colon, a famous vaudeville actress and singer of the day. A legacy of some two thousand pounds which fell to him about the same period enabled him to launch into a brief career of luxury and dandyism, and gave him the means to express his harmless affection. He addressed bouquets and love-letters to his blonde deity, and founded a journal in which to celebrate her theatrical talent, but it is not known that he ever addressed a word to her in proper person. Then he frittered away the remains of his small fortune on sham curiosities and spurious antiquities. He furnished his apartment with rococo carvings and Gothic chairs and ecclesiastical ornaments, to fit the shrine for his divinity. The climax of this mediæval lunacy was his acquisition of a treasure—a 'monumental bed' of the period of Diane de Poitiers, which he caused to be restored and embellished for the nuptial chamber, and which in some way his imagination associated with the inevitable Queen of Sheba. His friends became alarmed by his extravagance, his outbursts of bizarre enthusiasm, his disordered speech. He was discovered one day trailing a lobster about the *Palais-Royal*. He had attached a blue ribbon to it, and reasoned eloquently with his friends that a tame lobster was not a more ridiculous animal to lead about than a dog or a cat. 'Lobsters neither bark 'nor bite', said he, 'and besides, *they know the secrets of the* ' *sea*!'

In 1845 this strange enthusiast visited Turkey, Egypt

and the Holy Land. His records of travel denote the
rare faculty of observation and sympathy which was inherent to him, but he was in a state of hallucination all
the time and idealised everything. At Cairo and Constantinople he slept in the common khans and lived by the
way, lounging in the bazars and following no regular plan
of perambulation. In the bazar at Cairo he bought a
dark-skinned damsel—Abyssinian say some, Cinghalese
according to others—and married her; but he deserted
her when he turned his face homewards. After his return
to Paris he had a long spell of mental tranquillity (1846
to 1850) and did more active and healthy work than at
any period during his life. To this lucid interval belong
Aurélia, ou le Rêve et la Vie, one of his strangest and
most characteristic creations ; his *Scènes de la Vie orientale*,
contributed to the *Revue des Deux Mondes* and afterwards published as the *Voyage en Orient*; and a number
of miscellaneous articles which have never been collected
from the magazines and journals in which they appeared.
His productions for the theatre were also of some importance. He furnished the libretto for Armand Lim-
nander's opera of *les Monténégrins*, which had a brief
popularity. In conjunction with Méry, he produced at the
Odéon an adaptation of one of the oldest Hindu dramas,
The Terracotta Chariot, followed by *l'Imagier de Harlem*,
a fantastic piece written in mixed verse and prose.
These, and several other plays to which he contributed,
had either a transient success or failed altogether.

All the prose work of Gérard which has been preserved
is of exceeding beauty, and everywhere impregnated with
the vague and vaporous poetical charm which was peculiar
to his subtle genius. His claim to rank among the
masters of French prose is beyond dispute.

To his later period belong also the best of the *Chimères*,

a series of sonnets which vie with the finest examples of *rime riche* in the French language. In these poems the spiritual essence of diverse mythologies is fused with a felicity which shews how thoroughly this dreamer of dreams had deciphered the symbols of human worship. Though often obscure in their intense mysticism, the woven melody and luminous depth of some of his lines are matchless. Like Cowper in *The Castaway* and Gilbert in the *Ode imitée de plusieurs Psaumes,* he found in the shadow of imminent madness and death an efflorescence of pathos which is not visible in his earlier poems. Much of Gérard's poetry, however, instead of being crystallised into verse, was diffused throughout his prose writings, as in *les Illuminés* and *les Filles du Feu.*

Gérard had a terrible relapse of lunacy about the end of 1854, and vainly sought relief in a visit to the countries beyond the Rhine. His dreaminess had degenerated into melancholy, his melancholy into madness, and his madness became a settled despair. For two or three years his existence had been a hopeless struggle with the blackest destitution, and in the misery of his unfulfilled hopes and failing intellectual powers he had recourse to stimulants. One chill grey dawn in January witnessed the last scene of this dreadful tragedy. Gérard's body was found by a rag-gatherer hanging in the gutter near the foot of a narrow staircase which led up from the squalid little *rue de la Vieille-Lanterne,* one of the filthiest courts of old Paris. The stones were sprinkled with snow, and on the steps a tame raven was hopping about. From the grating of a vent-hole above the staircase Gérard had hanged himself with one of his antiquarian treasures, a cook's apron-cord which he had bought for the girdle of Madame de Maintenon, and which his delusion converted into the Queen of Sheba's garter.

75

GÉRARD DE NERVAL

Gérard de Nerval was the most beautiful of all the lost souls of the French Romance. With spiritual intelligence at once lucid and visionary, he had a frail hold on the material conditions of life. His kingdom was not of this world, for he floated in a loftier atmosphere, which was composed of the dreams and ideals of the human soul in all ages. 'The best part of man', he said, 'is that which 'thrills and vibrates in him'. No one who is responsive to the sorrows of genius can refuse an emotion and a tear to the fate of this creature so exquisitely gifted, a victim to that sense of the supernatural which to finer spirits is at once the charm, the mystery and the scourge of existence.

April.

Once more the sun, the dusty ways,
A heaven of blue transparent haze,
    And luminous walls and twilights long ;
Not yet grown green the gaunt trees wear
A rosy blush that hides the bare
    Black boughs, forlorn of leaf and song.

The season irks and overpowers.
For only after daylong showers
    Shall Spring, as from a radiant dream,
Rise garmented in green and rose,
Like a fresh nymph, with cheek that glows,
    New-blown and smiling from the stream.

Avril.
(*Odelettes rythmiques et lyriques.*)

Neither Good Morning nor Good Night.

Νὴ Καλημέρα νὴ "Ωρα καλή.

Morn is no more, nor yet the twilight trembles,
    Though from our eyes love's paling splendours flee.

Νὴ Καλημέρα νὴ "Ωρα καλή.

But rosy dusk the rosy dawn resembles,
    And, with Night's shadow, shall oblivion be !

Ni bonjour ni bonsoir.
(*Odelettes rythmiques et lyriques.*)

77

Lost Lovers.

O death! where are our lovers?
   They slumber in the tomb.
Their happier dream discovers
   A dawn beyond this gloom.

Their converse is with angels,
   In heaven's blue depths serene
They sing the sweet evangels
   Of Mary, Virgin Queen!

O pure and sinless maiden!
   White spouse whose bloom was brief!
Forsaken soul, love-laden,
   That withered, worn with grief!

The light of heavenly morrows
   Smiled in your radiant eyes:
Quenched lamps of this world's sorrows
   Relumed in lovelier skies!

*Les Cydalises.**
(*Poésies diverses.*)

---

* 'The ode entitled *les Cydalises* came to me, in spite of myself, in the form
of a song. I found at once the verse and the melody—and the latter, which
I have had noted down, has been recognised as very suitable to the words.
Ni bonjour ni bonsoir is composed on a Greek air. I am persuaded that
every poet could easily furnish the music for his own verses if he had some
knowledge of notation.'   (*La Bohème galante—Musique.*)

Anteros.

Why do I bear a breast so swollen with ire,
  And on lithe neck a head indomitable?
  Against the conquering god, as ancients fable,
I turned his darts . . . Antæus was my sire!

Yea, I am he the Avenging Ones inspire;
  They branded on my brows their angry label,
  And on the pale blood-sprinkled lips of Abel
Burns the red rage of Cain's relentless fire!

Jehovah, vanquished by his foes that fell,
Cursing their tyrant from the depths of hell,
  Was Baäl my grandsire and my father Dagon...

Though thrice they plunged me in Cocytus wave,
The Amalekite, my dam, I shield and save,
  Sowing again the teeth of the old dragon.

Antéros.
(*Les Chimères.*)

Delphica.

Ultima Cumaei venit jam carminis aetas. . . .

O Daphne! knowest thou that old-world chorus,
   Beneath green olive or pale laurel sung,
   Or myrtle, or where trembling willows hung,
That song of love . . . with echoes still sonorous?

Knowest thou this lofty temple towering o'er us,
   These cloven citrons bitter to thy tongue,
   That cave, wherein the old dragon's seed once flung
Lies slain, now sleeping cold and void before us?

The Gods shall come again to stanch thy tears!
Time shall roll back the tide of ancient years:
   Earth thrills even now with breath of things immortal.

Though yet the Sibyl of the Latin shrine
Slumbers beneath the arch of Constantine,
   And not a tremor stirs the rigid portal!

Delfica.
(*Les Chimères.*)

Tivoli: 1843.

Artemis.*

The thirteenth comes again ! . . . She is, moreover,
  The first and sole—or one sole moment seen :
  O thou ! the first or last, art thou the queen ?
Art thou the king, thou sole or the last lover ? . . .

Love thou whose love thy birth and bier did cover ;
  She whom I loved loves me no less, I ween :
  Death—or one dead—O ecstasy ! O teen !
On the dusk rose she holds dense shadows hover.

Pale Saint-Gudule, whose hands are full of flame,
  Whose breast the purple-hearted rose doth cherish ;
Hast thou too found thy cross in wasted skies ? . . .

White roses fall ! Ye flout our Gods with shame :
  White phantoms fall from burning heavens and perish ;
The saint of Hell is holier in these eyes !

Artémis.
  (*Les Chimères.*)

---

* The meaning of this somewhat obscure sonnet may be elucidated by a
reference to Dante Gabriel Rossetti's sonnet on *Vain Virtues* and Charles
Baudelaire's sonnet on *Femmes damnées.* The 'dusk rose' in the original is
rose-trémière or hollyhock. Gérard calls Saint-Gudule 'a Neapolitan saint',
but Saint-Gudula or Goule, the patron saint of Brussels, was of Flemish
origin. She 'consecrated her virginity to God', and is commonly represented
in pictures with a lamp in her hand, because she was accustomed to leave her
father's castle in the early morning, accompanied only by her maid bearing a
lantern, to say prayers in a church two miles off. (See Alban Buckley's
Lives of the Fathers, Martyrs and other Principal Saints. James Duffy :
Dublin : 1866.)

Petrus Borel.*

Born in Lyons, 1809 . . . Died in Algeria, 1859.

Petrus Borel—the Lycanthrope and Basileophagus (as he loved to call himself)—represents the most extravagant phase of the French Romance of 1830 to 1840. When Victor Hugo was boldly preparing to follow up the triumph of *Hernani* with *Marion de Lorme* and *le Roi s'amuse*, to endow dead ages with life in *Notre-Dame de Paris* and to give his lyrical wings a wider sweep in *les Feuilles d'automne*; when Honoré de Balzac was working sixteen hours a day in his solitary chamber in *rue de Tournon* and shaping in his dreams the phantasmagoria of the *Comédie humaine*; when Hector Berlioz was refashioning his *Symphonie fantastique* in Rome and foreshadowing in his overtures to *Rob Roy* and *King Lear* the wonders of a new world of orchestration ; when Eugène Delacroix was looked upon as a madman in art, while Paul Delaroche was gazing within the friendly gates of the Institute ;—Petrus Borel was engaged in a melodramatic attempt to give Bohemianism a local habitation and a name on the heights of Montmartre.

In 1831 the tribesmen of 'The Tartars' Camp' pitched their tents beneath the blue sky on an open space in *rue*

---

* Often and perhaps correctly written Pétrus Borel. His full name was Joseph-Pétrus Borel d'Hauterive, and he belonged to a noble family of Dauphiny, which was reduced to poverty and driven into exile by its resistance to the Republican army during the Revolution.

Rochechouart. Their laws were summed up on a placard in the precincts :—

> *Clothing is prohibited..*

They had no political opinions, other than a ferocious Republicanism ; no social ideals and no defined aims in literature or life. The only sentiments that bound the Tartars together were the vanity of solecism and a blind frenzy against the *bourgeoisie* with its pernicious influence on art and letters. The members of the camp cursed society and lived ; they flourished daggers, danced and gesticulated wildly, sneered at convention, and paraded a pessimistic discontent with everybody and everything in the worst of possible worlds. Expelled by their landlord for riotous conduct, they transferred their camp to a building in *rue d'Enfer*, and celebrated the occasion by a colossal feast. There are sinister legends of drinking cream from a skull, and of a masked ball in which the domino was the sole apparel. It is certain that when the Tartars sallied into the streets, clothed but scarcely in their right mind, they fell foul of the police and were now and again locked up for disorderly conduct.

The misfortune of the Romantic Movement was that most of the men thrown into its whirlpool belonged to that morbid, nervous and demoralised generation which was produced in France during and immediately after the Revolutionary period. They were the children of frenzy and enthusiasm begotten by the Revolt of the People, by the sanguinary excesses of the Terror, by the transports of Republican conquest and by the glories and despairs of Napoleon's campaigns. The horrors of battle and murder and sudden death brooded over their birth ; their genius was the diseased efflorescence of that terrible epoch.

83

Many of them lived a feverish existence on the border-
land of insanity, and their moral and intellectual disarray
too often ended in violence and suicide. Charles Dovalle,
author of *le Sylphe* (1830), was killed in a duel at twenty-
two years of age. Louis Bertrand (1807-1841), whose
exquisite prose poems were published under the sinister
name of Gaspard de la Nuit, lived in abject misery, died
in a charity hospital, and after dissection was flung naked
into a coffin and buried without consecration or ceremony.
Charles Lassailly, the phenomenally lean author of a
haggard romance entitled *les Roueries de Trialph, notre
contemporain avant son suicide*, perished in a madhouse at
the age of thirty-one, a victim to Balzac and black coffee.*
Édouard Ourliac, another of Balzac's hapless secretaries,
after a youth of lively gaiety and a discouraging struggle of
six years against ill-health and exhausted energies, ended
his miserable existence in the hospital of the *frères de
Saint-Jean de Dieu*, at the age of thirty-five. Louis-Charles
Barbara (1822-1866) threw himself out of the window of
an asylum, after losing wife and child and reason in a
plague. Gustave Drouineau, prolific writer of romances
and plays, who saluted the Revolution of 1830 with his
Soleil de la Liberté, was consigned to a madhouse at
thirty-five, and lingered there for forty-three years. And
these were but a few of the obscure and ill-starred victims
of the time—the very names of many others have long
since gone down to dust and damned oblivion.

Petrus Borel was in many respects a remarkable man.

---

* Balzac had several young men of exceptional talent as secretaries.
Théophile Gautier and Jules Sandeau are said to have served him in this
capacity in their early days. Balzac's laborious system of revision necessi-
tated literary assistance in his novels and plays, and his service was a form
of slavery, recompensed by poor pay, disturbed slumbers, copious libations
of black coffee, and a novel system of cheap feeding, in which spinach and
a *purée* of onions played the principal part.

There was a kind of method in his madness, and had he not deliberately chosen the wrong way there is no telling what he might have accomplished. At one time he so impressed his fellows and followers that with one accord they acclaimed him the chief of the Romantic Movement. Even Théophile Gautier acknowledged his genius and confidently expected that whenever he chose to assert himself Victor Hugo would have to hide his diminished head. But the poor lycanthrope was not destined to eclipse the supremacy of the real leader of the literary revolution.

Petrus Borel had a commanding presence and uncommon physical attractions. Of medium stature, his fine features and long flowing beard gave him the appearance of an Arab sheik or Hebrew patriarch. In his earlier association with the Romantics he displayed a Castilian dignity of manner, and even shewed a disposition to hold aloof from his wilder comrades. His education had been entirely neglected. He left school at fifteen years of age to serve his apprenticeship to an architect, and afterwards took lessons in painting from Eugène Devéria. So absolute was his destitution that he often lived in the cellars of houses in course of construction, and fared on potatoes cooked under ashes, with cold water for his drink. When he established 'The Tartars' Camp' many of those who rallied round him were young men of considerable talent. Gérard de Nerval; Théophile Dondey de Santeny (known as Philothée O'Neddy) author of *Feu et Flamme*; Joseph Bouchardy, the prolific playwright; Jules Vabre, the architect, notorious for his mad admiration of Shakespeare; Jean (otherwise Jehan) Duseigneur, the sculptor; Auguste Maquet (Augustus Mac-Keat) who collaborated with the elder Dumas in *les Trois Mousquetaires* and was destined to outlive all his literary comrades save Alphonse Brot; Louis Boulanger, the designer; Célestin

Nanteuil, a neglected artist of distinct ability; Achille
Devéria, engraver, a brother of the better-known painter ;
and Louis (alias Ludovic, Aloysius or Aloïsius) Bertrand :
—these were a few among the many who gathered round
Borel, and listened to the impassioned expression of his
revolutionary opinions on art, or gravitated towards the
cénacle of *les Jeunes-France*, over which Théophile Gautier
and Gérard de Nerval held undivided sway. All were
steeped in poverty to the lips, and many a time they
turned from their dreams of fame to wish that ‘the moon
‘ were a silver crown and the sun a golden pound’.* Petrus
Borel was the bright particular star of that sombre sky.

Bohemia was not the blind-alley to Borel which it was
to so many of his associates. He tried hard, but without
success, to make a name in literature and a living by journalism. In 1846 he obtained, by the influence of Théophile
Gautier, the appointment of Inspector of Colonisation at
Mostaganem in Algeria—for which his experience in ‘The
Tartars’ Camp’ was perhaps his chief qualification—but
he was cashiered in 1848. Thanks to the intervention of
Marshal Bugeaud, he soon received a similar appointment
at Constantine, where he married. Again he was deprived
of his position, this time because he had frankly denounced
some malversations, although the ostensible cause of dis-
missal was his practice of writing the official reports in
rhyme. After a hopeless effort to live by agricultural labour
on his allotment of land, he died of cerebral congestion
from sunstroke, a disappointed and disappointing man.
It was his own fate which he had foreshadowed in his
finest piece of verse, the prologue to *Madame Putiphar* :—

‘ Quand finira la lutte, et qui m'aura pour proie—
‘ Dieu le sait !—du Désert, du Monde, ou du Néant ? ’

* ‘ La lune écu d'argent, le soleil louis d'or.’—Alphonse Esquiros.

The mediocrity of Borel's poetry has cast a shade over his reputation. He had no great lyrical gift, he lacked imagination, he was incoherent in expression and penurious of ideas; and yet one or two of his pieces prove that he could have done better things. His *Rhapsodies* (Levavasseur: Paris: 1832—second edition, Bouquet: Paris: 1833—reprinted as *Rapsodies* at Brussels in 1868) are not rhapsodical in any sense which implies dithyrambic inspiration, although there are a few fine verses in the volume. But those who say, with Catulle Mendès, that the man was 'destitute of talent' are strangely deceived, for he was a prose-writer of singular genius.

Madame Putiphar (Ollivier: Paris: 1839) deserves to be ranked with the most real and living historical romances now extant. Why it has fallen upon neglect is one of the wonders of literary injustice. There is no more poignant and pathetic story in human fiction than the adventures of those two young Irish lovers, cruelly separated and persecuted because the husband shewed himself insensible to the seductions of Madame de Pompadour. The plot, taken from a chapter in the miscellanies of Camille Desmoulins, is worked out with a master-hand. *Madame Putiphar* is not a tale of 'lewdness 'swathed in sentiment', as the title might intimate, but a secular reconstruction of heroic proportions, handled with powerful reserve, full of vivid description and alive with incident and character. The court of Pharaoh (Louis XV) serves as a background to the picture of Patrick and Déborah, faithful to one another through the scandals and intrigues of the time; the husband buried alive in an unknown dungeon, the wife left a prey to libertine assaults. Then comes the tragic death of their son, whose life had been devoted to revenge for the fate of his father; followed by the ghastly meeting of man and wife—he mad from suffering, and she dying in agony at the sight of him, after long years of hope and anxiety—when at last he is liberated from his prison. Altogether, in spite of occasional extravagances and affectations, one of the great dramatic creations of the nineteenth century. The closing chapter on the capture of the Bastille is a triumph of vigorous description, worthy of Carlyle, and the fitting crown to a work of genius.

Madame Putiphar was written in Champagne, during a period of sane resolution and laborious energy, but in the midst of such black misery that Borel had from time to time 'to issue forth from his den and glean his nourish-'ment in the country-side'. He was paid 200 francs for this masterpiece of true romantic art. Like Milton and Landor, he had his own ideas about orthography, and *Madame Putiphar* was written thereafter. A fine reprint of the work was published in 1877 by Léon Willem of Paris, with a preface by Jules Claretie, but the two original volumes are scarce, and were so little known that when the editor visited the National Library in Paris to consult them he found that they had been lying there for more than a quarter of a century, unopened and uncut.

Among the miscellaneous literary works of Petrus Borel are *Champavert: Contes immoraux* (1833); a translation of *Robinson Crusoe* (1836) with a life of Daniel Defoe by Philarète Chasles and illustrations by Nanteuil, Devéria, Boulanger and Napoléon Thomas; and a grand romantic drama, entitled *le comte Alarcos*, which has never been published. In most of his writings there is evidence of a powerful satirical talent and of the capacity to create living character. He had all the gifts of a successful man of letters, save one. . . .

'Unstable as water, thou shalt not excel'.

To Iseult . . . a medallion.

L'amour chaste agrandit les âmes.

Enchanting bronze that gives the soul love's fever,
  Green emerald, whose radiant beauties shine;
  Iseult, angel with saddened looks divine,
Oh! could such bliss be given to me for ever,
      Only to press my lips on thine!

Chaste ecstasy, my soul's one aspiration,
  For never durst these fingers with desire
  Touch one so pure, nor thrill her with love's fire;
I gaze on her with such hushed exultation
      As pilgrims glimpse the holy spire.

So much her beauty on my soul holds power,
  So in my heart her flame doth purely burn,
  So seems her mouth to me a holy urn;
So do I worship, as a drooping flower
      Towards the golden dawn doth turn.

No blossom e'er disclosed so sweet a chalice!—
  Furl up thy soul, no longer filled with fears;
  Passionless as the grave thy face appears:
Calm is thy look, that chases shame and malice,
      Calm as the everlasting years.

Abide, while exile lasts, thou heavenly angel!
  Sombre, but pure as snow, with us abide!
  Even in the crowd the friend leaves not thy side;
He loves, reveal to him thy dreamed evangel,
      And he thy wandering feet shall guide!

No more, with thee, is solitude propitious ;
   Figure divine, thy visage sweet and young
   Is like to one beloved, whose nectared tongue
Is in my heart a serenade delicious,
      By soft and fragrant breezes sung

  .   .   .   . *

         Au Médaillon d'Iseult.
            (*Les Rhapsodies.*)

Odelet.

Would that I had lived i' the Middle Ages
   Days that bards and troubadours desire.
Then the singer served with love for wages,
Sung as linnets sing in golden cages,
   Slave of love and of the lyre !

Song and sword to him were wine and wassail ;
   All his wealth beneath his cloak he wore ;
Song that welcomed him in bower and castle,
Sword that was his lady's loyal vassal,
   Brandished at her word he bore.

         Odelette.
            (*Les Rhapsodies.*)

The Old Breton Minstrel.

Come, children, come, the maple-branches tremble,
   Dance, Bretons, to the sound of the binew ;
To hear my plaintive song with smiles assemble ;
   Once, in life's spring, I danced and sang like you.

* The last verse, omitted in this translation, is in praise of Jehan Duseigneur, the sculptor of *Iseult.*

Cold death to-morrow may benumb my fingers,
  For now, grown frail, I totter towards the grave. . . .
Come then and learn, while yet your minstrel lingers, ✮
  The old refrains that to your youth I gave.

Remember! every son of hers remembers
  How Breton soil was once 'the field of rest';
How Gaul sent forth, as fire from smouldering embers,
  A thousand heroes from her magic breast.
Freedom, whose stripling tree these shores once
    nourished,
  Over your youth her branches doth expand;
Let bold Duguesclin's heritage be cherished,
  Virgin of tyrants is our native land!

Dolmen and menhir, ruins of your glory,
  Scattered along those granite ridges lie.
Within these forests bard and druid hoary
  Revealed to your proud sires their destiny!
Wild days! when fiercely against Cæsar's ravage
  The Roman saw her warriors issue forth;
Wild speech! with these same Celtic accents savage
  His clansmen cheered the Chieftain of the North!

But now the light flies. Darker on the frondage
  The night-shades fall, the mist clings round your
    eaves;
Soon the black wizards, waking from day's bondage,
  Shall wind the unholy spell that darkness weaves.
Fly! fly! for I discern on the far mountains
  The elves that dance round the wild peulvan-ring;
The kelpies shout and plunge in the cold fountains:
  Fly, Breton folk, ere midnight spreads her wing!

       Le vieux Ménétrier breton: Villanelles.
                (*Les Rhapsodies.*)

Alfred de Musset.

Born in Paris, 1810 . . . Died in Paris, 1857.

The ease and sprightliness of Musset's lyrical talent, the versatility of his character and the personal emotion which breathes through his verse have contributed to give him a large place in French poetical literature, but perhaps scarcely so large a place as he deserves. Lamartine hardly deigned to notice him. Victor Hugo affected to treat him as one of those ephemeral artists who owe their notoriety to the caprices of fashion, and yet Heine held in 1840 that Musset was as far above Victor Hugo in poetry as was George Sand in prose. Jules Janin classed him with living poets of the third rank, and Sainte-Beuve valued him likewise; although after Musset's death the author of the *Causeries du lundi* assigned to him a much higher literary rank that he was willing to allow him when alive. Like Byron and Mendelssohn, Alfred de Musset seems to possess an individual fascination which is proof against the vicissitudes of taste and the glamour of great names; and many admirers of French poetry will be disposed to agree with Théophile Gautier and Maxime Du Camp in placing him among the three masters of his art in the nineteenth century.

Louis-Charles-Alfred de Musset was descended from an old but decayed aristocratic family of Vendôme. His father, Victor de Musset (sometimes designated Musset de Pathay), held a lucrative appointment in the offices of the Ministry of War and was known in letters as an editor of the works of Jean-Jacques Rousseau. Had Alfred de Musset been born, like Henry Mürger, in the slums of Paris, he would certainly have found his way to the *quartier latin,* for he was a Bohemian by nature. As it was, he blossomed in early youth into a dandy. He was dressed by the fashionable tailor. He gambled at the clubs, he rode in the *Bois,* he ran deeply into debt; his nights were passed with boon companions or at the shrine of *damnosa Venus.* He was the spoiled darling of frivolous women in the choice *salons* of Paris.

Musset's first prose work, the *Contes d'Espagne et d'Italie,* was published in the year of glory 1830. He was already known in literary and aristocratic circles as the author of some promising poems. The encouragement of the brothers Deschamps, and later of Sainte-Beuve and Victor Hugo, with the practical assistance of François Buloz, the celebrated editor, helped him on his way. Chateaubriand and Byron had more influence than any of the Parisian poets of his own time upon Musset. He followed neither Lamartine nor Victor Hugo ; indeed, he prided himself on his individuality* and rallied Émile Deschamps and others on their servile adulation of the leader of the Romantic Movement.

For many years the fame of Musset was almost confined to the fashionable assemblies of Paris, at a time when it was customary for poets to read their own verses to idolising circles. But he was also the poet of youth ; and his exquisite sensibility, his tender scepticism and his fascinating melancholy were made to charm the heart of the age. In ten years he sent forth ten volumes of poems and plays, among the latter those captivating *Comedies* and *Proverbs,* so full of sparkling wit, which are

---

* ' Mon verre n'est pas grand, mais je bois dans mon verre.'

(*La Coupe et les Lèvres.*)

in their kind the best things ever written. It was only in 1847, when he was already exhausted and disheartened, that his fame began to extend. The tardy performance of *Un Caprice* at the *Comédie-Française* disclosed a brilliant and accomplished playwright, and one whose works have never since been entirely banished from the national stage.

The popularity of the poet did not gain much by his theatrical success; indeed it had been steadily declining, and the vapid prose and feeble verse which he doled out during the last fifteen years of his life shewed that the spring of his genius was already drained dry. His capricious disposition, rapidly passing from one extreme to another, rebelled against patient labour; his excesses of passion and the reckless dissipation of his energies hurried him on to untimely old age. Since the death of his father had thrown him too early on his own resources his life had been an incessant struggle with ways and means. He never learned to work for a livelihood, and the small revenue which he derived from his writings and from a government appointment as librarian was miserably disproportionate to his extravagant scale of living. A long period of physical prostration and intellectual melancholy ended in premature death from disease of the heart, an affection from which he had suffered for many years.

Heine's maundering sentiment on the *liaison* of Alfred de Musset and George Sand has cast over this episode of the poet's life a halo which fades away in the fierce light of friendly indiscretion and hostile criticism. Much may be forgiven to the first love of two beautiful young souls, however little their union owes to the blessing of the church and the sanction of the community, but it would be difficult to find anything idyllic in this amour of the experienced woman of thirty years with the precocious libertine of twenty-three. It is only too certain that all the morbid violence of Musset's emotional character was aggravated by that visit to Italy in the winter of 1833-34 from which he returned to his mother's house with 'a ' diseased body, a dejected soul, and a bleeding heart'. His *Confession d'un Enfant du Siècle* (1836) is an incoherent record of the transports and disillusions of this suffering soul; and the painful self-analysis of the confession is not redeemed by its literary style, which can by no means claim to be a model in the language which boasts so many masterpieces of autobiographical prose. And no worse service was ever rendered to Musset's memory than the vainglorious and saddening notice of the poet's life published by his elder brother Paul, author of *Lui et Elle*.

Musset's legacy of literary work is a considerable one, for he was a feverishly rapid if at no time a steady worker. He had the gift of inspiration, and would throw off his verses beneath the chestnut-trees of the Tuileries gardens or in his bed-chamber after a noisy supper-party. His mobile and impressionable temperament is reflected in these verses, which have all the fervour of youth and the effervescence of precocious passion. Musset has left no immortal poem of singular beauty, like *The Ancient Mariner* or *Hyperion*; but if his verse lacks originality in structure and rhyme, and seldom reveals the devotion of an artist to perfection of form, there is often a freshness of conception, a spontaneous ease in expression, and withal a light fantastic grace which has its own peculiar charm. He had no firmly-defined ideals and little spiritual force. His verse, so full of sensibility, is often tinged with the melancholy of a spirit which was out of tune with the world and disappointed of aims which might easily have been fulfilled had his capacity for assiduous toil been equal to his inspiration. This careless singer has nevertheless left more fine lines than any French poet of his generation, and by pure genius has carved out verses far beyond the subtle and laboured art of Théophile Gautier. This tormented poet has thrilled strings which even the proud hand of Victor Hugo essayed in vain to sweep, and with a touch has drawn tears from deeps that to the dark soul of Baudelaire were as a hidden spring and as a fountain sealed. It is by this personal note of true emotion, in the midst of much that is frivolous and superficial, that his poetry lives, and with its blended grace and feeling justifies the felicitous phrase of Heine: 'The ' Muse of comedy has kissed him on the lips, and the ' Muse of tragedy on the heart'.

The Night in May.

THE MUSE.

Take thy lute, poet, kiss my lips and sing ;
The wild-rose feels her buds begin to swell.
The winds grow warm ; this night gives birth to Spring :
The wagtail, while the lingering dawn doth dwell,
Loves on the first green bush to rest her wing ;
Take thy lute, poet, kiss my lips and sing !

THE POET.

How black below the valley lies !
Methought I saw a veiled form rise
And hover on the woodland gray.
Along the mead she seemed to pass ;
Her light foot skimmed the flowering grass :
Like a strange vision, but alas !
Fainter it grows, and fades away.

THE MUSE.

Take thy lute, poet ; from her perfumed vest
Night shakes the zephyr on the sward and sighs.
The rose, a jealous virgin, shuts her breast
In which the pearly hornet swooning dies.
Dream thou of the beloved, while all things drowse !
To-night beneath the sombre linden-boughs
The beam of sunset leaves a sweet farewell.
To-night all things shall flower : immortal earth
Is filled with fragrance, love and murmuring mirth,
Like the blest couch where two young lovers dwell.

ALFRED DE MUSSET

THE POET.

Why leaps my heart with sudden throbs?
What in my bosom swells and sobs
With fears that on my senses brood?
Did not a hand strike on my door?
Why does my dwindling lamp-light pour
Its splendour in a sudden flood?
God! through my limbs what tremors run!
Who comes? Who knocks? Who calls me? None!
The hour-bell sounds; I am alone:
O poverty! O solitude!

THE MUSE.

Take thy lute, poet, for the wine of youth
Ferments even now as with a God's desire.
My troubled breast is torn with joy and ruth,
And parchëd winds have set my lips on fire.
See, wayward child, my beauty shines unveiled!
Has our first kiss no memory that charms,
As when, touched by my wing, with cheeks that paled
And tearful eyes, thou swoonëdst in these arms?
Then I consoled thee for a bitter grief!
Alas! so young, yet dying for love's sake.
Console me now, I die of hopes too brief;
I can but pray to live till morning break.

THE POET.

Is thine the voice that calls my name,
And art thou come, O my poor Muse?
O my flower! my immortal flame!
Sole being faithful even in shame,
Whose love of me my love renews!

Welcome again, my blonde delight,
Mistress and sister sweet thou art !
I feel thee near, through deepest night,
Bathed in thy golden garments bright
With beams that steal into my heart.

THE MUSE.

Take thy lute, poet.   I, the immortal love,
Have watched this night thy silence and thy tears,
And now, as when her nestlings call the dove,
Descend, to weep with thee, from highest spheres.
Thou sufferest, dear friend.   Though lonely grief
Consume thee, though despair thy soul destroy ;
Though love, such as earth wears, was all too brief,
A shadow of delight, a spectral joy :
Come, sing to God ; sing in thy thoughts again,
Sing thy lost pleasure, sing thy vanished pain ;
Soar, in a kiss, towards the unknown world.
Awake at will the echoes of thy lyre,
Tell us of glory and gladness and desire,
And let thy fancies float in dreams unfurled.
Discover realms that give our woes surcease ;
Fly hence, we are alone, the world is ours ;
Green Caledon, dusk Italy, fair Greece
My mother, with her honied crown of flowers,
Argos, red Pteleon of the hecatombs,
And Pelion's naked brow that glows and glooms ;
And Messa the divine, delight of doves,
And blue Eurotas, and, like silvery light
Glassed in the gulf whose wave the pale swan loves,
White Oloösone and Camyra white.
Tell me what songs shall lull our golden dream !
From what mysterious source our tears shall stream !

When this day's sunrise smote thy lids with dawn,
What seraph, bending pensive from above,
Shook lilac-blossoms from his robe of lawn
And, whispering low, breathed on thy couch his love?
Shall we sing songs of joy, or grief, or hope?
Drench in their blood the steel-embattled ranks?
Suspend the lover on his silken rope?
Fling on the winds the foam o' the courser's flanks?
Say from what hand unnumbered lamps above
Lighten by night and day in heavenly domes
The holy oil of life and deathless love?
Cry 'Tarquin, 'tis thine hour, the shadow comes!'?
Plunge and pluck up the pearl from deepest seas?
Watch the kid browse on bitter ebony-trees?
Lead Melancholy to the skiey shores?
Follow on scarpèd hills the hunter's horn?
The hind beseeches him, looks and implores;
Her heath-bed waits; her fawns are newly born:
He stoops, he slays her, and the quarry throws,
Still quivering, to his hounds that pant and reek.
Or shall we paint the virgin's crimsoned cheek
When, followed by her page, to mass she goes,
And, by the matron's side, with absent air,
Forgets on half-closed lips her pious prayer?
Trembling she hears, hard-echoing on the ground,
The spurs of a bold cavalier resound.
Shall we command the heroes of old France
To mount, full-armed, their many-crenelled towers,
And from oblivion wake the rude romance
Their glory taught to antique troubadours?
Swathe the soft elegy in white? Or woo
Wild war, and bid the man of Waterloo
Boast how his scythe mowed down the mortal bands,
Before the herald of eternal night

Swooped with swift wing on the green island-height,
And on that iron heart crossed his pale hands?
Shall our proud satire to the gibbet nail
The name o' the scribbler, seven-times-sold, that pale
And hungry issues forth from haunts obscure,
Shivering with envy and impotent despite,
To insult the brows of genius and to bite
The laurel sullied by his spume impure?
Take thy lute! Take thy lute! Give the song birth!
My pinion wafts me on the breath of Spring.
The light wind bears me hence; I quit the earth.
One tear from thee! God hears; 'tis time to sing.

THE POET.

Dear sister, dost thou crave but this,
From lips of love a willing kiss,
A tear that falls from tender eyes,
I give them gladly, that our love
May live in memory thereof
When thou returnest to the skies.
For now, neither of hope I sing
Nor glory, nor with joy rejoice,
Nor weep alas! with suffering;
On the lips Silence folds her wing
When in the heart she hears thy voice.

THE MUSE.

Dost thou then deem me as the autumn wind
That feeds herself with tears, even on the grave,
And grief, a drop of water from life's wave?
O poet! I kissed thee when thy soul had sinned.
The weed I fain would pluck from these choked sods
Is nourished in thy sloth; thy grief is God's!

What pain soever youth nursed in his core,
Let it find issue ; sacred is the sore
Black angels opened in thy heart's profound ;
With greatest sorrow greatest souls are crowned.
Yet stricken as thou art, O poet ! know
That not for silence lives thy voice below.
The noblest song with grief and anguish throbs,
And some I made immortal with pure sobs.
When the slow pelican, wearied of long flight,
Regains the shore and seeks his reedy home,
His hungered brood, lost in the haze of night,
Watching him from afar, swoop on the foam.
With beaks that on their hideous gorge agape
Already seize and share the prey, they shape
Their course to the parent bird, with joyful cries.
He, towards a high cliff slowly labouring,
Shelters the brood beneath his trailing wing
And, desperate, gazes sadly on the skies.
A stream of blood flows from his plumage torn ;
In vain he scoured the depths of the salt flood :
The sea was vacant and the shore forlorn,
And for sole nourishment he brings his blood.
Sombre and silent, stretched on the bare rock,
Succouring with father's flesh his little flock,
By love sublime sustained he soothes his wound
And, while the bleeding breast his offspring drinks,
Beneath the feast of death he reels and sinks,
As one with tenderness and horror swooned.
But sometimes, midst the sacred sacrifice,
Wearied in death so long to agonise,
He trembles lest they drain the living spring ;
Then, rising, opens on the wind his wing,
And flaps his bosom with funereal wail,
Sending through night such wild farewell abroad

That on the lonely beach the sea-mews quail,
And the belated traveller, turning pale,
Feels death in the air and gives his soul to God.
O poet! such is the great singer's fate:
He feeds awhile the joy of them that live ;
But the world's feasts on which his soul doth wait
Seem most like those the pelican's life-springs give.
When hopes beguiled at last thrill all his chords
With sadness and despair, with love and pain,
Such concert swells the hearts of men in vain.
His declamations are like flaming swords:
Though in the air they trace a dazzling ring
Still to their blade some drops of blood will cling.

THE POET.

O voice from the abysmal deeps,
Lay not on me this last command!
Man leaves no writing on the sand
When at its hour the north-wind sweeps.
There was a time when love, in sooth,
Rose ceaseless on my lips, and youth
Was ready, like a bird, to sing ;
But I have suffered, as through fire,
And should my silent griefs desire
To speak their anguish on my lyre
Their lightest breath would break the string.

La Nuit de mai.
(*Poésies nouvelles.*)

May, 1835.

Song.

When Hope, Love's wild capricious minion,
　　Brushes our elbow in her flight,
Then sweeps aloft, on aëry pinion,
　　And smiles and beckons from the height;

Whither flies man?　His dream he follows,
　　Light as the breeze the swallows skim;
And lighter-winged than wavering swallows
　　Is man when love allureth him.

Ah! frail and fugitive beguiler,
　　Thine is the song the sirens sung!
Why should old Fate, the ruthless spoiler,
　　House with a paramour so young?

Chanson.
(*Poésies nouvelles.*)

1840.

On One Dead.

She too was fair, if sombre Night,
　　Laid in the chapel cold and bare
To moveless slumber by the might
　　Of Michael-Angelo, is fair.

She too was kind, if kind they be
　　That passing drop from open palms
A gift God does not deign to see;
　　If, without pity, gold is alms.

She thought, if sweet and silvery tones
　　Of a voice softly murmuring naught
Like a brook babbling o'er the stones,
　　May seem the utterance of thought.

She prayed, if two bewitching eyes,
  Now turned to earth with pensive air,
Now raised with rapture to the skies,
  Deserves indeed the name of prayer.

She might have smiled, if the furled flower,
  That lies yet in the bud unblown,
Could open to the freshening shower,
  And breeze that woos it and is flown.

She might have wept, if once the hand
  On her cold bosom coldly pressed
Had felt the human clay expand,
  With dews of heaven embalmed and blessed.

She might have loved, had not her pride,
  Doomed like a useless lamp to dart
Its radiance by the coffin-side,
  Kept vigil in her barren heart.

She never lived and she is dead.
  Hers was life's semblance and life's look :
  From listless hands she dropped the book,
No line of which she ever read.

Sur une Morte.
(*Poésies nouvelles.*)

October, 1842.

Théophile Gautier.

Born in Tarbes (Hautes-Pyrénées) 1811 . . . Died in Paris, 1872.

Although Pierre-Jules-Théophile Gautier happened to be born in Gascony, he was of Provençal origin, but he had none of the restless garrulity and superficial vehemence which are characteristic of his race. He came to Paris when very young, and had made some progress in his studies as a painter before letters claimed his ambition. Gérard de Nerval and he were old school-fellows, and along with Arsène Houssaye, Camille Rogier, and one or two other Bohemians of the Romantic troop, these two poets founded their *cénacle* in a squalid lodging in *rue du Doyenné*, in the *quartier latin*. There Théophile Gautier passed his first youth, with ' its joyful miseries, its generous ' follies, its tender escapades and its charming faults, which ' are better than all the virtues of riper age '. There, too, with hard study of the early French poets and unwearied patience in imitating the Romantic masters, he wrote his *Comédie de la Mort* (published 1838) in the midst of poverty, wretchedness and obscurity, not unvisited betimes by the bright presence of that graceful *Cydalise* whose form and features the genius of Camille Rogier has immortalised.

The sane balance of Gautier's intellectual faculties saved him from the fate of Gérard and Bertrand ; his capacity for continuous work preserved him from the misfortunes of Borel and Baudelaire; and yet no poet of the Romantic period has written of these children of genius and disaster with so much sympathy and with such discernment as Théophile Gautier. Nor did any man of letters of his time remain so faithful to grand ideals of art and duty as he, long after the advent of Baudelaire and Flaubert had brought new aims and new forces into French literature.

The Romantic Movement, as represented by the dramas of Victor Hugo, found its foremost and one of its most vigorous champions in Théophile Gautier. He belongs to the legend of the Romance, with his grave sallow countenance and long black hair, as he witnessed the first performance of *Hernani*, wearing the famous crimson plush waistcoat which was regarded as the oriflamme of the fight for freedom of literary speech. But Gautier himself was not much given to sentimental extravagance. His literary style evinces a more scrupulous regard for measure and restraint than that of the most part of his militant contemporaries. Perhaps his cold control and his culture of the plastic arts saved him from the excess of zeal which inevitably accompanies a revolutionary movement in letters.

Gautier's life was one of ceaseless and indefatigable labour, broken only by excursions to Spain (1840) Algeria (1845) Italy and the Levant (1850-52) and Russia (1860). So little of adventure and incident relieved his existence that Baudelaire was justified in denoting it as 'an immense 'spirituality'. His own simple needs, and the family obligations which he fulfilled with heroic effort, doomed him to the slow martyrdom of journalism. His work for the newspaper press, that modern monster which, as Béranger laments, has 'devoured so many young talents', was remunerated by a pittance which would be scorned by a contributor of the same calibre to one of the great French or English journals of the present time. There is a world of satire in the placard which was posted in his room :—'Daily newspapers appear every day'. The energies thrown into this exacting and exhausting toil absorbed much of the thought and feeling which might have been devoted to the creation of great and durable works of art, such as the Greek dramas which he dreamed and never achieved, and a long-cherished translation of the Mahâbhârata into French verse. And yet he could have escaped from this drudgery but for his conscientious love of art and literary independence. He threw up his appointment on the *Presse*, and incurred the scorn of Émile de Girardin, rather than prostitute his pen by becoming the paid *attaché* of certain theatres, and so enriching himself by partial criticism. The sacrifice of this rare artist to the daily needs of existence is one of the most unfortunate examples of the difficulty of living on the wages of literature in days when any kind of meretricious talent may command a fortune if it falls in with the fashion or the fancy of the hour. Time brought no relief to Théophile Gautier. The Revolution of 1848, on which so many literary fortunes rose, was a disaster for him. It plunged him into even deeper poverty than he had known before, and his life thenceforth was one of constant anxiety, harassed to the day of his death by the demands of creditors and relations.

An unauthorised collection of Gautier's dramatic articles was published by Hetzel of Leipzig between 1858 and 1860, under the appropriate title of *Histoire de l'Art dramatique en France depuis vingt-cinq ans*. These criticisms cover an immense range of subjects, and show that in his ephemeral work the author's conscientious spirit, as well as his instinct of style, never failed him. Even when dealing with music, of which he had absolutely none in his soul, and which he once paradoxically described as 'the 'least disagreeable and most expensive of noises', his innate taste and cultivated judgment saved him from the expression of philistine opinions.

Notwithstanding his close application to work, and a certain proud reserve of disposition, this great artist was always accessible to his literary friends. His natural attitude was one of genial dignity and stately ease. He had the modesty of a genuine man of letters, without pose or pretension; and was indeed a living vindication of Heine's aphorism that 'Simplicity is always the *obbligato* ' accompaniment of genius'. He had the dislike of an idealist to society. His healthy and robust disposition shrank from morbid complaining; all ungainly objects, and all those things that pertain to the hideous paraphernalia of death, were hateful to him. It is characteristic in this respect that Gautier, with all his wit, had no great sense of humour, although he handled the grotesque and satirical elements in literature with considerable skill. He was inclined to despise laughter as a disfigurement of facial beauty and a disturbance to contemplative repose.

Théophile Gautier was an omnivorous reader. Like Victor Hugo and Balzac he had a large vocabulary and a wonderful faculty for the assimilation of rare words. He was the *virtuoso* of French prose. His knowledge of the arts gave him a command of uncommon technical terms; he held the key to architecture, archæology and heraldry; and he had an insight into the obscure sciences. His marvellous memory and systematic method made literary composition an easy task to him, and although his fastidious regard for style grew into a passion he wrote much that scarcely needed revision, so differing from Balzac, who spent in anticipation all the earnings of his pen and ruined himself in corrections and recast of copy. It may be that the verbal direction of Gautier's talent was to a certain degree determined by his comparative poverty of ideas, but his admirers are perhaps consoled by the recollection that in literature ideas are plentiful and artists few. He was not a member of the French Academy.

Théophile Gautier's work, when the conditions of his life are discounted, is of considerable volume and value. He never wrote a careless and rarely an uninteresting line. *Le Roman de la Momie* and *le Capitaine Fracasse* (planned between 1830 and 1840, but not published until 1863) are novels full of vivid description and romantic incident. In *la Morte amoureuse* and other short stories he displays that subtle and beautiful charm of style which has its masterpiece in *Mademoiselle de Maupin* (1835), one of the glories of French prose :

> '. . . the golden book of spirit and sense,
> 'The holy writ of beauty' . . . .

It was in this book, idolised by Swinburne and admired by such diverse men of letters as Balzac and Baudelaire, that Gautier's incomparable prose first assumed definite shape. Written in the full flood of the Romance, it came like a plea for the severest and purest beauty amid the violent excesses of that movement.

Gautier's records of travel (*Tra los Montes*: 1841—*Italia*: 1850) share with those of Gérard de Nerval the honour of having first impressed upon French prose that Oriental touch which is visible in the colouring of Eugène Delacroix and Prosper Marilhat; in the music of Félicien David and Camille Saint-Saëns; and, with a more accentuated note of exotic splendour in the verse of Baudelaire, Leconte de Lisle and Heredia. The keen observation of Gautier revealed to him the peculiar beauty and charm of each new country and people, and his consummate art enabled him to create that proper atmosphere which is everything in a book of travel.

THÉOPHILE GAUTIER

Théophile Gautier's early poems date from 1830. They denote a great inherent gift of versification and deal with a wide variety of themes. Some of them were inspired by the enthusiasm of Byron, whose fervent influence spread like an epidemic all over Europe, and found even in Russia a congenial response in the songs of that strangely original genius Pouschkin and in the gloomy imagination of Lermontoff. *Albertus: ou l'âme et le péché* (1833) was the chief outcome of this mania in Gautier, and, like Alfred de Musset in *Rolla*, the French follower out-Heroded Herod without ever reaching that sublime height to which Byron occasionally rose with a single sweep from the wastes of persiflage and the depths of cynicism. In 1845 Gautier published all the poems which he had composed during the romantic fever of 1830-1840, and thenceforth devoted himself to the cultivation of his individual style. In *Émaux et Camées* (1852-1856) he revealed himself as the supreme artificer of his time in verse. No single volume of French poetry contains so many flawless pieces,. excepting, perhaps, the *Fleurs du Mal*, and Baudelaire's are more uniform in tone and temperament. Alike in their perfection of form and in their verbal beauty the *Émaux et Camées* are unrivalled as works of art. They recall the most finished achievements of Tennyson and Rossetti in their absolute shapeliness. But, admirable as they are in artistic structure, there is no grandeur of conception or depth of passion in them. They are well named enamels and cameos, for they possess a luminous beauty of colour and a crisp delicacy of outline which belong to the lapidary's art, and are the work of a carver and jeweller of words rather than that of a spontaneous poet. There are no long lines pregnant with powerful thought, but within their limited range they are wonderfully rich and fanciful, and often attain in the octosyllabic line a firmness and dignity not to be found even in the favourite alexandrine of other French poets.

Théophile Gautier, worn out with life-long labour and partly paralysed, died not long after the horrors of the siege of Paris had been aggravated by the slaughters of the Commune. His death was commemorated by the publication of an album of verse (*Le Tombeau de Théophile Gautier*—Alphonse Lemerre: Paris: 1873) modelled on the fashion of the sixteenth century. This poetical tribute from no fewer than eighty men of letters was headed by the venerable name of Victor Hugo. Algernon Charles Swinburne sung the praises of Gautier in French, English, Latin and Greek; John Payne in French and English; and there were contributions by Swiss, Hungarian, Italian and Provençal poets in their accustomed speech. The fine medallion on Gautier's tomb, an etching of which serves as frontispiece to this memorial volume, gives an excellent presentment of his Olympian head and calm countenance, so expressive of serene reflection.

Unfaithfulness.

Here is the elm whose swinging shadow
    The well-known footpath keeps,
The eglantine that scents the meadow,
    The wood where silence sleeps ;
And here we loved to sit alone
At twilight on the bench of stone.

Here is the bower that breathes the fragrance
    Of clustering lilacs twined,
Wherein, when weary of love's vagrance,
    Together we reclined ;
Where, under coronals of flowers,
We watched the flight of sultry hours.

Here is the pool that breaks in bubbles
    When silvery fishes swim,
Where oft the frog leaps forth and troubles
    Its rippling surface dim ;
Here, as of old, beneath the wave,
Their feet the reeds and rushes lave.

Here, as of old, the spring-flowers sprinkle
    The turf of velvet green ;
And here the clambering periwinkle
    To kiss the sun doth lean,
Turning, half-filled with honey-dew,
Her chalice clear as heavenly blue.

Here, as of old, the fluttering swallows
    Skim by the donjon's gloom,
The swan a self-same circle follows
    And smooths her pure white plume :—
Soft sward below, blue sky above,
And nothing changed save you, my love !

Infidélité : Élégies.
(*Poésies* : 1830-1832.)

A Verse of Wordsworth.

No verse I know, save one, of Wordsworth's art,
    That rankled so in Byron's bitter leaven,
One verse that echoes ever in my heart
    Of 'spires whose silent finger points to heaven '.

It served as epigraph (how strange a place !)
    Heading a chapter from the loves impure
Of some frail girl ; the book a foul disgrace
    Drawn from the *Dead Ass* by a hand obscure.

This fresh and pious verse, among the loves
    Of a lewd volume lost, refreshed my sight
Like a wild blossom shed, or like a dove's
    White plume on the black puddle dropped in flight.

Now, when the Muse rebels, when to no sign
    Of Prospero's wand will Ariel's wing be given,
I fringe my margins with a quaint design
    Of spires whose silent finger points to heaven.

Un Vers de Wordsworth.
(*Fantaisies.*)

Secret Affinities.

A Pantheistic Madrigal.

Built in an antique temple high,
   Two blocks of marble, lit with beams
In the blue depths of Attic sky,
   For ages blended their white dreams.

Twin drops congealed in the same shell,
   Tears of the foam whence Venus sprung,
Two pearls, plunged in the deep sea-swell,
   Held converse in an unknown tongue.

What time the Moorish kings held sway
   In bright Alhambra, blown beneath
The ever-weeping fountain-spray
   Two roses mixed their fragrant breath.

In Venice, on the radiant dome,
   Two rose-tipped doves of snowy white
Ordained love's immemorial home,
   And nestled there a summer night.

Marble, and pearl, and rose, and dove,
   Decay and die.   Time melts the stone,
The pearl dissolves, the flower of love
   Falls withered, and the bird is flown.

Their dust, through changes manifold
   Dispersed, earth's deep alembic brings
To enrich the universal mould
   Whence Nature shapes all beauteous things.

By transmutation slow and strange,
  In diverse forms they recompose ;
White marbles into white limbs change,
  On rosy lips reblooms the rose.

Once more the dove with amorous coo
  The fresh young heart of love beguiles,
And pearls in clustered teeth renew
  Their whiteness wreathed in radiant smiles.

Thence hidden sympathies have birth
  In throbs imperious and sweet,
That teach the secret of the earth
  To souls when sister souls they greet.

Responsive to the spell that lies
  In perfume, colour, gleam or grace,
Atom to kindred atom flies,
  Like bee that seeks the flower's embrace.

Remembering thus their ancient dreams
  On temple or in sea beheld,
And flowery converse near the streams
  That from their crystal sources welled ;

And tremulous kiss and thrill of wing
  On domes grown golden in the sun,
The faithful atoms, vibrating,
  Desire and strive to blend in one.

Forgotten love from long eclipse
  Comes forth in vague new birth at last ;
The blossom breathes on vermeil lips
  Afresh the fragrance of the past.

The jewelled row that smiles enshrine
Recalls its splendour to the pearl;
Thrilled marble sees its beauty shine
In the white bosom of a girl.

A whisper to the dove reveals
Soft echoes of her former moan,
And love-dissolved resistance feels
The lover risen in one unknown.

Thou before whom I thrill and glow!
What wave, what shrine, what dome, what bower,
Knew us, in ages long ago,
As pearl or marble, dove or flower?

Affinités secrètes: madrigal panthéiste.
(Émaux et Camées.)

Ode in the manner of Anacreon.

Wouldst thou, O poet, have me love thee,
Bid not, with too much fervour, fly
My timid love that soars above thee,
Like a dove in shame's rosy sky.

The bird, in the hushed alley lighted,
Starts trembling at the faintest stir;
My passion, wingèd too, is frighted
And flies when one would follow her.

Mute as the Hermes carved in marble,
Beneath the elm stand still and see
The bird erelong, with joyous warble,
Descending fearless from the tree,

To breathe on temples flushed with brightness,
And fanned with fresh warm whisperings,
In one tumultuous whirl of whiteness
A palpitation of soft wings;

When the dove, nestling on thy shoulder,
Loses her shame in amorous bliss,
Pouts her rose-pointed beak, grown bolder,
And swoons bewildered with thy kiss.

Odelette anacréontique.
(*Émaux et Camées.*)

Apollonia.

I love thy name that like a chorus
Far-echoing from the sacred shrine
Hails thee, in harmonies sonorous,
Apollo's daughter and divine.

When with that name supreme and splendid
An ivory plectron thrills the strings,
Sweeter than love and glory blended,
Like bronze the resonant music rings.

Lo Greek! the elves, from forests lonely,
Plunge wailing in their lake forlorn;
Name by the Pythian priestess only
In Delphos fitly to be worn,

When, girding round her antique vesture,
Poised on the golden tripod high
She waits, with rapt prophetic gesture,
The god whose tarrying steps are nigh.

Apollonie.
(*Émaux et Camées.*)

118

The Nereids.

My chamber holds no canvas quainter
   And lovelier than this stretch of sea ;
Though rhyme and rhythm disown the painter—
   Theophilus Kniatowski.

Where the light foam's white fringes flash on
   The woven waters blue and gray,
Cluster three nymphs in sweet flower-fashion,
   Strange blossom of the bitter spray ;

Swung like drenched lilies on the surges
   With every silver whorl that swims,
And now sustains and now submerges
   The undulant dance of delicate limbs.

On tresses crowned with spoil o' the shingle,
   And reeds impleached with rushy plume,
Coyly these witching sirens mingle
   The bright sea's blazonry and bloom.

The shell, its lucent drops dispearling,
   Stars with a rare and precious chain
Each bosom, which the flood, unfurling,
   Sprinkles with purer pearls again.

And downwards, where the sinewy Tritons
   Those fine and shapely flanks uphold,
Their splendour, washed with azure, lightens
   Long trailing hair of dusky gold.

Below, with the blue billow blended,
   Their whiteness thrills the oozy sheen ;
And by a tail the torso ended
   Half woman and half fish is seen.

But what eye seeks that scaly swimmer,
  Whose folds the tremulous ripple laves,
Seeing those ivory busts that shimmer,
  Smoothed by the kisses of the waves?—

On the sky-line—quaint apparition
  That blends the fabulous and true—
A vessel veers athwart the vision,
  Startling these naiads of the blue :

Far off its flag tricoloured flashes ;
  Its funnels belch forth smoke and steam ;
Its wheel the sounding water lashes :—
  And the scared nymphs plunge in the stream.

Erewhile in fearless flock they followed
  The triremes of the gulf athrong,
While dolphins frisked, with arches hollowed,
  As erst to hear Arion's song.

But now the steamer's paddles speeding
  Soon would disperse them through the surge
With naked bodies bruised and bleeding,
  Like Venus under Vulcan's scourge.

  *   *   *   *   *   *

Farewell, fresh myth, to all thy fancies !—
  The packet, passing out of sight,
Leaves only on the dim expanses
  A shoal of porpoises in flight.

                    Les Néréides.
                    (*Émaux et Camées.*)

120

Carmen.

The gipsy's eye, bright as a jewel,
　Is circled by a bistre band ;
Her hair is black, her lips are cruel,
　The devil himself her skin has tanned.

A curse on her each woman whispers,
　But all the men are mad to see ;
The Archbishop of Toledo's vespers
　Are chaunted nightly at her knee ;

For on her neck of dusky amber
　Is twined a swarthy coil that swims
With long loose ripples in her chamber,
　And makes a mantle for her limbs :

And from the pallor of her bosom
　Her mouth with sovran laughter breaks ;
A crimson spice, a scarlet blossom,
　That from heart's-blood its purple takes.

So dowered, before this gipsy dwindles
　The proudest beauty, put to shame,
And from her eyes the warm light kindles
　In satiate souls their smouldering flame.

Her strange unloveliness possesses
　A salt trace of the bitter foam,
Whence, warm and panting for caresses,
　Venus in naked beauty clomb.

> *Carmen.*
> (*Émaux et Camées.*)

Art.

Art's noblest work from things
Rebellious to the trammel
    She wrings:
Rhyme, marble, gem, enamel.

No false constrainments use!
But so thy tread be stately,
    O Muse,
Bind on the buskin straitly!

A rhythm too easy spurn;
Sandals so wide of measure,
    In turn,
Each doffs or dons at pleasure!

Sculptor, since clay is vile,
Moulded with careless finger,
    The while
Thy spirit elsewhere doth linger,

Bend thou on marbles hard
And rare thy soul's endeavour;
    They guard
Their beauty pure for ever!

Seek Syracusan bronze
That, firmly graven thorough,
    Disowns
No proud and graceful furrow;

Or, with a delicate hand,
In veins of agate follow
    The grand
Grave profile of Apollo.

Limner, lest mildew shame
Thy tints too evanescent,
    Let flame
Fast fix them incandescent.

Make sirens blue that comb
Gold tresses trailing under
    The foam ;
Emblazon beasts of wonder :—

Jesus, with cross and globe,
The triple-haloed Virgin
    Whose robe
Bears lily-bloom and burgeon.

Time brings all things to dust :—
Art is Time's only rival.
    A bust
The city's sole survival.

The rigid disk some hind
Earthed in its urn funereal
    Doth find
Reveals a form imperial.

The gods themselves must pass :—
But sovran rhyme rings louder
    When brass
And iron are ground to powder.

Against the hard stone set
Thy hand ; hew, chisel, planish,
    Ere yet
The dream dissolve and vanish !

L'Art.
(*Émaux et Camées.*)

Leconte de Lisle.

Born in Saint-Paul (Réunion) 1818 . . . Died in Louveciennes, 1894.

The great Creole poet Charles-Marie-René Leconte, known as Leconte de Lisle, was the child of a Breton father and a Gascon mother. He had the Celtic clearness of vision and love of beauty, and the vigour and courage of the Pyrenean race. In his youth he travelled through the East Indies, and the vivid impressions of tropical colour and warmth which are visible in his poetry derive their value from the personal observation of nature in those regions.

Leconte de Lisle came to Paris in 1847, and as his first ambition was to become a power in politics he threw himself with ardour into the Revolutionary Movement of 1848. He was also an active disciple of the school of Fourier. His social passion soon cooled down, but he had brought some verses with him from the East, and he studied his art assiduously, giving lessons in languages and literature to provide for his daily subsistence. The appearance of his first volume established his relations with Alfred de Vigny, Victor de Laprade, Baudelaire and Banville, and gained for him a place among the foremost poets of the time.

No poet ever gave himself up to his art more thoroughly than Leconte de Lisle. He had no desire for wealth or luxury, and the small income which he earned by his literary labours, supplemented in later days by his emoluments as sub-librarian at the Luxembourg (Library of the Senate) enabled him to live his simple, austere and laborious life, and to provide for his small household—a wife without children. A grant of 300 francs a month, given to him by Napoleon III in 1870 and continued under the Republic, was a welcome auxiliary to his slender resources. In his later years Leconte de Lisle was the friend of Victor Hugo and the oracle of a select circle of men of letters, among them Mallarmé, Mendès and Dierx, who regarded him as their master. He served as a National Guard in the war of 1870 and succeeded to Victor Hugo's chair in the Academy in 1886.

Leconte de Lisle had a robust physical and intellectual character. His powerful forehead, clear cold eyes, ironical smile and exceedingly sarcastic speech were the external signs of a pronounced individuality. He always wore a single eye-glass and was seldom seen without a cigarette. His friends knew him as a lively controversial speaker, with great resources of eloquence and irony. He had strong prejudices and decided opinions. In religion as in politics he was a *révolté*. He published (anonymously) a democratic catechism and a popular history of Christianity. Frankly republican and atheist himself, he courageously avowed the disbelief in a divinity which so many men repudiate with their lips and practise in their lives. In later years he lost much of his vivacity and was somewhat embittered by disappointment—for his poetry was *caviare* to the general—and he also resented the failure of his laborious energy. His death definitively closed the Hugonian period in French poetry.

A scholar of exact and extensive learning, Leconte de Lisle has given to French literature a series of absolutely literal prose translations of Homer, Hesiod, Theocritus, Sophocles, Euripides, Æschylus, Horace and other classical authors. Like Robert Browning he introduced in his translations the proper spelling of Greek names, and incurred thereby much undeserved ridicule. His own experiment in classical tragedy, *les Érinnyes*, with music by Jules Massenet, was produced at the *Odéon* in 1872 and had as favourable a reception as could have been expected. But the poet was so conscious of his inability to achieve success in drama that he burned the manuscript of *Frédégonde*, a tragedy of which he had completed one act.

Leconte de Lisle's poetical renown is firmly established on the great trilogy: *Poèmes antiques* (1852), *Poèmes barbares* (1862) and *Poèmes tragiques* (1884). These have had a considerable influence on contemporary French and Italian poetry. His opinions on the poetical art are uncompromisingly and somewhat wildly expressed in the preface to the *Antique Poems* :—

'Since the days of Homer, Æschylus and Sophocles, who repre-
'sent poetry in its vitality, its plenitude and its harmonious
'unity, decadence and barbarism have invaded the human
'mind. In point of original art the Roman world is on
'a level with the Dacians and the Sarmatians; the entire
'Christian cycle is barbarous. Dante, Shakespeare and
'Milton have only the force and grandeur of their in-
'dividual genius; their speech and their conceptions are
'barbarous. . . . Modern poetry, a confused reflection of
'the fiery personality of Byron, the artificial and sensuous
'religiosity of Chateaubriand, the dreamy mysticism of
'Over-Rhine and the realism of the Lakists, is the poetry
'of disturbance and dissolution'.

With such exorbitant assurance did this great poet—
'a soul from which every modern idea is absolutely ban-
'ished', said Théophile Gautier—sweep away everything between Athens and himself. And in so far he is the father of the French decadence, which holds the opinion

that poetry should not be the expression of individual emotion and thought, but the pursuit of an ideal beauty and serenity in transfigured nature and spiritualised legend. A Romantic poet by his rich colouring, his splendid imagery and his choice of exotic subjects, Leconte de Lisle nevertheless belongs essentially to the Pagan group of nineteenth-century poets and is perhaps the greatest of them all. He renewed and widened the work of André Chénier, with a larger sense of beauty and a deeper range of sympathy, with a breadth and wealth of colouring which Chénier could never have attained, and sometimes with the bitter tinge of pessimism which belongs rather to the disillusioned end than to the ardent inception of a great movement in art.

Leconte de Lisle has been described as cold and un-lyrical. This is less than half true. His work is chiselled and polished as if to last. He had a rare eye for perfection of form, and in variety of theme and plenitude of treatment he is unapproachable. He scorned every concession to popularity, and followed his own way with decision and consistency. If there is not much personal passion in his work, there is an intellectual emotion which rises at times to the highest degree of intensity. Sometimes he has the lyrical sweep of Shelley and Swinburne, with the same disposition to heap up images and dazzle with colour. He gives the noblest expression to human revolt and desire, to ideal dreams, and to the pure and sometimes pathetic love of external nature. He is always truly French in the lucidity and directness of his speech. His tropical landscapes, his reconstructions of savage scenes, his studies of traditional epochs, are triumphs of learned imagination and splendid in their conception and clothing. No poet so richly endowed with the gifts of rhythm and declamation and melody has illustrated the latter half of the nineteenth century, save perhaps Giosuè Carducci or Algernon Charles Swinburne.

At the time of his death Leconte de Lisle had a new volume of poems in preparation. He also left unfinished *les États du Diable*, a vehement satire on the condition of Rome in the days of the Borgias. These reliques will probably be published by his widow, with the assistance of José-Maria de Heredia and the vicomte de Guerne, two intimate friends of the poet. Leconte de Lisle was most fastidious in weighing his own work, and destroyed everything which he judged unworthy of publication.

Pan.

Arcadian Pan, goat-hooved, with hornëd brows,
Whose shout stirs the pleased shepherds when they
  drowse,
Breathes through the fresh green reeds an amorous strain.
Soon as the dawn strows gold on slope and plain,
Vagrant he frisks amidst the dancing horde
Of Nymphs on the flowered moss and tender sward.
A lynx-skin clothes his limbs, his locks are crowned
With saffron and soft hyacinth wreathed round;
And with his resonant laugh the wild woods shake.
The Nymphs, half-naked, at his call awake,
Light-footed run and, near the limpid springs,
Troop round the god in swiftly whirling rings.
In vine-clad caves, in hollows cool and lush,
And where live rivulets through the woodland gush
Or clustering hollies weave a tangled bower,
Pan flies the ardours of the noonday hour;
He slumbers, and the boughs, with jealous screen,
Shelter his sleep from the sun's arrows keen,
But soon as the calm night, star-girdled, trails
O'er silent skies the long folds of her veils,
Pan, from familiar shades, enflamed with love,
Follows the flying virgin through the grove,
Swoops on her path, and, with transported play,
In the clear moonlight carries off his prey.

Pan.
(*Poèmes antiques.*)

I   129

The Spring.

A live stream sparkles in the bosky gloom,
  Hidden from the noonday glare ;
The green reeds bend above its banks and there
  Blue-bells and violets bloom.

No kids that batten on the bitter herb,
  On slopes of the near hill,
Nor shepherd's song, nor flute-note sweet and shrill,
  Its crystal source disturb.

Hard by, the dark oaks weave a peaceful screen
  Whose shade the wild-bee loves,
And nestled in dense leaves the murmuring doves
  Their ruffled plumage preen.

The lazy stags in mossy thickets browse
  And sniff the lingering dew ;
Beneath cool leaves, that let the sunlight through,
  The languorous Sylvans drowse.

White Naïs, near the sacred spring that drips,
  Closing her lids awhile,
Dreams as she slumbers, and a radiant smile
  Floats on her purple lips.

No eye, kindling with love's desire, has scanned
  Beneath those lucent veils
The Nymph whose snowy limbs and hair that trails
  Gleam on the silvery sand.

None gazed on the soft cheek, suffused with youth,
  The splendid bosom's swerve,
The ivory neck, the shoulder's delicate curve,
  White arms and innocent mouth.

But now the lecherous Faun, that haunts the grove,
　　Spies from his leafy trench
Those supple flanks, kissed by the oozy drench
　　As with a kiss of love ;

Then laughs, as when the Satyr's wanton imps
　　A wood-nymph's bower assail,
And waking with the sound the virgin pale
　　Flies like the lightning-glimpse.

Even as the Naiad, haunting the clear stream,
　　Slumbers in woods obscure,
Fly from the impious look and laugh impure
　　O Beauty, the soul's dream !

> *La Source.*
> 　　　　(*Poèmes antiques.*)

Pholoë.

Forget, O Pholoë, the lyre and the feasts divine,
The jovial gods and the nights too swift and the wine,
　　And desires in swarm on the lips that love uncloses ;
For Time, as he skims thee with wings that glide like a
　　dream,
Blends in those tresses, just touched by a silvery gleam,
　　　　The asphodel pale with thy roses.

> *Pholoë.　Études latines.*
> 　　　　(*Poèmes antiques.*)

Dies Iræ.

On life's rough road a day, an hour will come
　　When, bowed beneath its weight of woes and fears,
The soul of man halts wearied and with dumb
　　Desire looks back to immemorial years.

His life with fruitless expectation worn,
　　Deceived of God, who does not hear or see ;
He feels earth's childhood in his heart reborn,
　　He hears thy voice, O sacred memory !

The stars he loved of yore with glimpses pale
　　Silver the night's mysterious dusk abodes,
And shine on hallowed slope and antique vale
　　Where beneath black palms sleep his early Gods.

He sees earth free, and her green aureole
　　Float like fresh incense on the river's verge,
And, singing on their shores, blue seas that roll
　　To unknown deeps the immeasurable surge.

On mountain-tops, that nurse a generous race,
　　Rise murmuring floods, with whisper of green domes,
Hailing the vigorous growth in virgin grace
　　Of young Humanity in old-world Homes.

Blessëd were they ! For them the eternal globe
　　Held commune with the imperishable spheres ;
No soilure smirched man's still unblemished robe,
　　The new world's beauty blest his forceful years.

Then Love, that in the soul of man doth shine,
　　Through ages burned with undiminished ray ;
And simple faith and innocence divine
　　Watched in the tabernacle night and day.

Why then has pleasure's spring, once quaffed, run dry ?
　　Why these vain toils, these doubts that peer and
　　　grope ?
The winds have heaped dense clouds in the clear sky ;
　　One hour of storm has swept away man's hope.

LECONTE DE LISLE

O tent in the wilderness and on the hill,
  With pensive cedars shadowing dreams sublime,
And virgin Freedom shouting loud and shrill,
  And swelling transports of the human prime!

Vainly by anguish our desire is spurred:
  Henceforth whose eye the primal scroll shall read?
Since man has lost the sense of the world's word
  The spirit is dumb, the letter dead indeed.

No hand again towards mystic dusk shall draw
  The purple veil that hung before the shrine;
No ear on winds prophetic hear with awe
  This earth's first converse with the Voice Divine.

The flickering light of Heaven at last is flown;
  Impenetrable night the welkin loads:
Ormuzd lies dead beneath his starry throne;
  The East sleeps on the ashes of her Gods.

The spirit descends not on the chosen race
  To consecrate the just, the strong affirm;
In moveless Asia's withered womb the embrace
  Of barren suns shrivels each lifeless germ.

Down in the river-reeds the Ascetics brood
  Lulled by pure waves that whisper on the shore.
Weep, sages, weep for wisdom's widowhood!
  On the Blue Lotos Vishnu dreams no more.

Bright Hellas, virgin crowned with golden locks,
  To whom a world's love came with wreaths and
    hymns,
Lies mute for ever on her sacred rocks,
  Strown with the white Immortals' sacred limbs.

No more the live coal burns on prophet-lips!
Adonaï! on the winds thy voice is whirled;
And the bowed Nazarene, in pale eclipse,
Wails his last agony to a heedless world!

Thou whose fire-haloed brows are veiled in gloom,
Whose wandering feet the lone lake-margin trod,
All hail! The soul of man in thy sealed tomb,
O young Essene, keeps watch on his last God!

The barbarous West grows faint and fain would
drowse.
Our souls in heavy slumber crouch fordone,
Like shrubs, with cankered root and mildewed boughs,
Green for a day, and withering with the sun.

Only the wise, that keep an even soul,
Couched in the shade of secret thresholds lie,
While stormy years and peaceful seasons roll
The stream of man to vast eternity.

But we, whose soul unfed desire devours,
A prey to faith beguiled and love in vain :—
Answer, new days! Shall life again be ours?
Speak, days of old! Shall love be ours again?

Where are the golden lyres, with hyacinth wreathed,
The hymns to happy gods, the virgin choirs,
Eleusis, Delos, hopes that burned and breathed,
And holy songs that sprang from pure desires?

Where are the promised Gods, the ideal forms,
The rites in purple and in glory clad,
And cloven skies that hailed in wingèd swarms
The Ascension of white souls, serene and glad?

Sadly the Muses, scourged with bitter scorns,
  Like heavenly outcasts through our cities flee,
Too long they bleed beneath their crown of thorns,
  And sob with ceaseless sorrow like the sea!

The Eternal Evil on our heads is hurled.
  Round ulcered souls the vile age weaves her charms.
Hail, blest oblivion of this crowded world!
  Fold us, O Nature, in thy sacred arms!

In golden chlamys clothed, mysterious Dawn,
  Waken a song of love in woodlands dank!
Sun, be thy glorious veil again withdrawn!
  Calm mountain, open wide thy perfumed flank!

Majestic murmur of waves appeased and stilled,
  Deep in our careworn hearts exhale your sighs!
O forests, shed your dews from urns fulfilled!
  Stream through us, sparkling silence of the skies!

Console us for vain hopes and vanished joys:
  Our naked feet are bruised on barren roads.
From headland summits, pure of human noise,
  Waft us, O winds, towards the unknown Gods!

But if no answer wakes the vast expanse,
  Save the everlasting echo of desire,
Farewell, void wastes, in which the soul's wings glance,
  Farewell, wild visions, fringed with fading fire!

And thou, divine Death, womb and tomb of all,
  Welcome thy children to thy starry breast,
Of time and space and number disenthral
  Our souls, and from life's fever give us rest!

Dies Iræ.
(Poèmes antiques.)

Naboth's Vineyard.

In his dark chamber, on the cedarn couch,
  With cold hard eyes and pale lips quivering,
His face turned to the wall, Ahab doth crouch.

  Not tasting bread or wine Samaria's king
Broods, as in noonday heat the traveller doth,
  Wearily bending o'er a thirsty spring.

Ahab, whose heart ferments with hate's foul froth,
  Athirst the wine of wickedness to drain,
Conjures the Golden Calf and Ashtaroth.

  —'Am I a king', he asks, 'whose wrath is vain?
'By Baäl! thrice I chased thy horsemen proud,
  'Benhadad, swift athwart the Tyrian plain.

'Those of Damascus kissed the dust in crowd,
  'With sackcloth on their loins and ash-strown hair,
'Like camels low before their keepers bowed.

  'On their parched lips my sign struck dumb the prayer,
'Their blood in the high-place reddened the sods,
  'And on their warlike flesh my dogs did fare.

'My prophets are most wise; I have three Gods
  'Most mighty, of my kingdom the strong staff;
'They scourge my people with their scourging-rods.

  'And now my glory is like worthless chaff,
'My sceptre as a reed that bends and breaks
  'Before the servile crowd's insulting laugh!

'The Rock of Israël thus his vengeance slakes
'For Baäl, throned by the black terebinth,
'Beneath whose rubied brow Samaria shakes.

'Twice dyed in crimson, clothed with hyacinth,
'Like a sun, golden-red, the God doth shine
'In the vast precinct on his jasper plinth.

'But if his anger waxeth not with mine,
'My high-priests shall abolish him and place
'The Golden Calf of Ephraïm in his shrine.

'Desire consumes me in her fierce embrace ;
'By the ass's hoof and ox's horn laid low,
'Like a dead lion flouted in the face.

'I said "I will", and one dared answer "No!"
'And lives, nor my suspended falchion heeds
'And wrathful heart, swollen with shame's overflow'.—

The son of Omri thus his anger feeds
With hate, his hair dishevelled hangs awry,
And torn with furious teeth his pale lip bleeds.

Then softly towards the haggard king draws nigh
Eth-Baäl's daughter, crowned with swarthy tresses,
Whose beauty the king loves exceedingly.

Nursed in the arms of Ashtaroth's priestesses,
She darkens sun and moon with secret spells,
And curbs wild lions under her caresses.

In her dusk eyes a drowsy influence dwells,
And souls by violence hurled to endless woe
Thrill at her voice even in the lowest hells.

She nears the couch, with port superb and slow,
And speaks:—'What ails my Lord? What unblest thing
'Bends the proud cedar with the herbs below?

'Hath Baäl sent some spirit on evil wing?
'The night falls. Let my Lord rise and break bread!
'What sorrow stirs thy troubled soul, O King?'

—'Woman, I must have vengeance', Ahab said,
'For sleep I shall not taste, nor bread nor wine,
'Till Naboth's reeking blood in dust be shed.

'Hard by mine orchard grows his fertile vine,
'Now to this man the King his master saith
'It pleaseth me, exchange, or sell me thine!

'Quoth he:—"My father's field is mine till death,
'Shouldst thou against its grapes gold shekels measure
'I would not sell, even with my latest breath!

'Though thou, with Phogor's plain for land of pleasure,
'And Ramoth-Gilead, Seir, and Edom's shore,
'Gav'st me thine ivory house and hoarded treasure,

'O King, I should but love my vineyard more!"—
'Thus Naboth spake to Ahab, Omri's son,
'Calm on the smoking threshold of his door'.

Then Jezebel:—'By the Gods of Akkaron!
'Surely this people, swollen with arrogance,
'Doth boast a gentle king, to patience prone.

'When wilt thou smite the land with sword and lance?
'The wild ass, till his flanks be curbed, will rear;
'Yield to the dromedary and he doth prance'.—

—'Because the Rock of Israël I fear',
  Said Ahab :—'Naboth and Elijah trust
'In Him. The nations fall beneath His spear.

  'My pride, by Him brought low, would kiss the dust,
'As the bound heifer, towards the altar drawn,
  'Moans while the knife is sharpened for the thrust.

'Nay wait! The Gods of Beth-El and of Dan
  'To him that worships, hearkening their behest,
'Will surely grant the slaying of this man!'

  —'Rise then, O chief! eat bread and take thy rest',
Said the Zidonian, laughing bitterly ;
  'What my Lord dares not do shall whet my zest.

'To-morrow, when the sun slopes towards the sea,
  'Ere yet thy royal hand hath touched this slave,
'He dieth on Mount Shomer, slain by me.

  'Then may the Tishbite spit his spume and rave
'From Carmel unto Horeb, like a hound
  'That hungering flies before the brandished stave.

'My Lord shall say to him :—"Where hast thou found
  'My handwork in this murder, or my sign ?"—
Then Ahab smiled :—'O woman, fitly crowned,

  'I shall spill this man's blood and drink his wine!'—

La Vigne de Naboth: I.
(Poèmes barbares.)

The Black Panther.

Along the rosy cloud light steals and twinkles ;
  The East is flecked with golden filigree :
Night from her loosened necklace slowly sprinkles
  Pearl-clusters on the sea.

Clasped on the bosom of the sparkling azure
  Soft skirts of flame trail like a flowing train,
And cast on emerald blades a bright emblazure,
  Like drops of fiery rain.

The dew shines, like a sheaf of splendour shaken,
  On cinnamon leaves and lychee's purple flesh ;
Among the drowsed bamboos the wind's wings waken
  A myriad whisperings fresh.

From mounds and woods, from mossy tufts and flowers,
  In the warm air, with sudden tremors thrilled,
Fragrance bursts forth in sweet and subtile showers,
  With feverish rapture filled.

By virgin jungle-track and hidden hollow,
  Where in the morning sun smoke tangled weeds,
And where live streams their winding channels follow
  Through arches of green reeds,

Steals the black panther from her midnight prowling,
   With dawn turned to the lair in which her cubs
Among smooth shining bones, with hunger growling,
    Grovel beneath the shrubs.

Restless she slinks along, with arrowy flashes
   That scan the shadows of the drooping wood.
The bright, fresh-sprinkled crimson dew that dashes
    Her velvet skin is blood.

Behind she drags the relict of her quarry
   Torn from the stricken stag, a mangled spoil
That leaves a loathsome trail and sanguinary
    Along the moss-flowered soil.

Round her the tawny bees and light-winged dragons
   Flit fearless as she glides with supple flanks ;
And clustering foliage from a thousand flagons
    Pours fragrance on the banks.

The python, through a scarlet cactus peering,
   Slowly above the bush lifts his flat head
And curious eyes, his scaly folds uprearing
    To watch her stealthy tread.

She glides in silence into the tall bracken,
   Then plunges, lost beneath the lichened boughs :
Air burns in the vast light, earth's noises slacken,
    And wood and welkin drowse.

                      La Panthère noire.
                        (*Poèmes barbares.*)

In the Clear Sky.

In the clear sky, cloven by the lissome swallow,
Heaven's dawn, that blossoms like a blushing rose,
Sheds fragrance on green glade and leafy hollow
Whence nests of love send full-voiced songs to follow
Wings quivering where the woody heights disclose
Heaven's dawn that blossoms like a blushing rose
In the clear sky, cloven by the lissome swallow.

Drop answering drop, in golden notes rained shrill,
Live streams on the smooth gravel glance and glisten,
With showers of fleecy spray that kissing thrill
Heath-flower and thyme, iris and daffodil ;
The while young kids that wake with sunrise listen,
Live streams on the smooth gravel glance and glisten,
Drop answering drop, in golden notes rained shrill.

Through thickets where the light wind laughs and rushes,
By paths that into dreamy distance wind,
Beneath blue veils of haze dissolved in blushes
These two, while dewy dawn the soft air flushes,
Pass slowly, with linked hands and arms entwined,
By paths that into dreamy distance wind
Through thickets where the light wind laughs and rushes.

Aswoon with love's delight that fills their eyes,
They heed not how the moments swiftly vanish ;
The charm of earth, the beauty of the skies,
For them the enraptured hour immortalise,
And blissful dreams all dreams of sorrow banish.
They heed not how the moments swiftly vanish
Aswoon with love's delight that fills their eyes.

In the clear sky, cloven by the lissome swallow,
Heaven's dawn still blossoms like a blushing rose,
But they, athwart green glade and leafy hollow,
Shall thrill no more to songs of love that follow
Wings quivering where the woody heights disclose
Heaven's dawn that blossoms like a blushing rose
In the clear sky, cloven by the lissome swallow.

Dans le Ciel clair.
(Poèmes tragiques.)

The Imperishable Perfume.

When the rare Indian rose, soul of the sun,
    In crystal cup or golden urn distilled,
Hath shed its fragrant tear-drops, one by one,
    On burning sands the essence may be spilled.

Enclosëd thus, over the narrow shrine
    Rivers shall roll in vain and oceans sweep.
The sands insphere each odorous drop divine,
    And even in dust dispersed its perfume keep.

Since through this open wound no craft can cure
Thou pourest from my heart in effluence pure,
    O Love ineffable, drawn by her spells!

Her sin be shriven, my sorrow sanctified!
For, beyond mortal hours and the infinite tide,
    Even in my dust a deathless fragrance dwells.

L'impérissable Parfum.
(Poèmes tragiques.)

143

Charles Baudelaire.

Born in Paris, 1821 . . . Died near Paris, 1867.

The life and death of Charles Baudelaire is one of the most awful tragedies in the annals of literature. The fate of Chatterton and Collins, of Gilbert and Bertrand, and of so many other children of despondency and madness is pale in pathos beside the spectacle of Baudelaire, after his strangely lurid existence in Paris and Brussels, lingering in a madhouse, paralysed and speechless, until death released his suffering soul.

Charles-Pierre Baudelaire-Dufaïs belonged to a family of some social distinction. His father was a professor in the University of Paris, an accomplished scholar, and the friend of Condorcet and Cabanis. Charles Baudelaire was but a boy when his father's widow married General Aupick, afterwards French ambassador to the Porte (1850). At home he was a spoiled child, in school a rebellious subject. His precocious love of letters and his capricious temper were a source of anxiety to the family, and these faults were aggravated by his irreconcilable attitude towards the disciplinarian step-father. A violent outburst of anger at an official dinner given by the General (who was grossly insulted by the boy before his guests) determined the 'parents' to send him abroad, after a fortnight of solitary confinement in his own room. Baudelaire lived for a time in the East Indies, travelled thence to Mauritius, Bourbon and Madagascar, failed to find any attraction in commerce, and squandered his time and the

money with which he was liberally furnished. Returning
to Paris he inherited, on reaching his majority, a small
fortune (about seventy thousand francs*) and decided to
follow the literary vocation. He had learned English
when in the East, and toiled assiduously for a time
to fit himself for his chosen career. His relations
tried to introduce him into social life, but his wilful
eccentricity always frustrated their wishes. Then he
launched into the world of cafés, saloons and studios,
trod the primrose path of dalliance, ran through one
half of his little patrimony in about two years, and
was put under legal tutelage. This temporary access of
Bohemianism caused Théophile Gautier to express some
apprehension lest Baudelaire should go the way of
Petrus Borel.

Théodore de Banville says that Baudelaire had immense
erudition. Maxime Du Camp avers that he was wofully
ignorant. The two things are not incompatible, but there
is not much evidence of deep learning in Baudelaire's
literary works. He was certainly a devouring reader.
Although he had been something of a lexicomaniac from
his youth upwards his methodical habits and accurate
memory enabled him to dispense with a large library. His
criticisms shew that he had the gift of keen observation
and profound spiritual insight. In literature his predilection was for the old French poets and the poets of the
Latin decadence.

Baudelaire was a consummate connoisseur in painting
and music. In his *Salon* articles he fought the battle of

* It has been argued that because Baudelaire left some thirty or forty
thousand francs he could never have been in absolute penury. But the fact
is overlooked that he had only the revenue of this sum, which to a man of
his luxurious habits was of little account. He earned but a pittance by his
pen, and was always desperately in debt.

Eugène Delacroix. He was the first of that enlightened band of French poets who championed the cause of Richard Wagner. In 1861, when not one French composer of music had the least inkling of the essential qualities of Wagner's genius, Baudelaire declared that 'no 'musician excels him in *painting* material and spiritual 'space and depth'. Indeed the æsthetic writings of Baudelaire are full of lucid and discerning judgments, at once subtle and sober in their discrimination. He held uncompromising opinions on the artist's right of choice in subject and treatment as an essential privilege of genius; and his scorn for every concession to easy popularity or vulgar consistency was pronounced. 'The 'most sacred right of man', said he, 'is the right to con-'tradict himself'.

It was in *les Fleurs du Mal* that Charles Baudelaire threw down the gauntlet by the application of his æsthetic theories to poetry. Most of them written in 1843-1844, but not published until 1857, these poems caused a tremendous commotion. The criminal prosecution which followed their appearance embittered the poet's character, for, although he was legally acquitted and could not but rejoice at the vogue given to his verses, he resented the humiliation of having to defend from the criminal bar his claim to literary freedom. The Sapphic poems which gave the occasion of legal procedure were judiciously eliminated in the definitive edition of the *Fleurs du Mal*. It is therefore to be regretted that the moral offence should have been renewed, if indeed the erotic poems surreptitiously published in Brussels were written by Baudelaire. But it ought to be charitably remembered that he was then under an intellectual cloud, overwhelmed with debt, and riddled with cynical disgust of life. He was not instigated by any mere greed of gain,

for, as Banville truly says, the poet had 'a profound and
' absolute scorn of money '.

The decay of Baudelaire's noble mind was rapid and
ruinous. He had drained the chalice of his youth with
full lips, and freely indulged all the desires and delights
of his restless fancy. In later years the fiery fret of his
imagination turned inwards and wore him down. His
genius had been largely recognised after the notorious
trial. He was tempted into journalism, but his fastidious
taste and scrupulously slow method of composition unfitted him for the kind of toil which exhausted Théophile
Gautier. For a while he lived a life of wretched expedi-
ents in Paris, renewing his bills, dodging his creditors, and
constantly putting off the day of regular labour. Although
he knew and declared that 'inspiration is work every
' day' he had the idle disposition of a luxurious man.
He revolved in his imagination vast plans of drama and
romance which never came near to execution. His posthumous notes shew that he bitterly regretted the dissipation of his energies ; his life gives evidence that he had
not the strength of will to amend the evil of his ways.
He succumbed at last to the charms of literary lecturing,
in emulation of some successful authors in England and
America. The experiment was tried in Brussels. Disheartened by his reception he became moody and morose,
and alarmed his friends in Paris by writing insane exe-
crations of Belgium and the Belgians. His constitution
had been ravaged by debauch, by opiates, by stimulants,
and by the remorse of faculties unused or fatally misused.
He lost the power to work at anything, his speech became
slow and faltering, and the insidious disease soon culminated in a shock of paralysis, varied with spasms of
maniacal frenzy. He was brought back to Paris, where
after a year of confinement, shut off from the converse and

sympathy of mankind, unable to speak or write and with
a fixed look of haggard despair on his face, but apparently
conscious of his terrible condition, he died. Sad destiny
for a poet who was justly described by Charles Asselineau
as 'one of the most perfect, most exquisite, and best en-
' dowed men of genius' ever given to France. English
readers will remember Swinburne's magnificent threnody
beginning

> ' Shall I strew rose, or rosemary, or laurel,
> ' Brother, on this that was the veil of thee?'—

one of the finest tributes of many paid to the memory of
' this rare and extraordinary poet'.

The character of Charles Baudelaire is an unsolved
psychological problem. All that Gautier and Asselineau
and Banville and Sainte-Beuve and Du Camp have written
about him only serves to bring into relief the contradictions and complexities of this strange idiosyncrasy. He
had Bohemian instincts, but was too fastidious to be a
real Bohemian. His dandyism in dress and demeanour
often took the most fantastic forms. He was notorious
for capricious changes in his apparel, in his toilet, in his
attitudes, and even in his facial expression. His characteristic mannerism was a peculiarly deliberate emphasis
of gesture and speech.

The acknowledged portraits of Baudelaire are so dis-
similar as to beget a doubt if they represent the same
person. Gautier describes his appearance as that of 'a
' devil who had turned monk', and such he certainly seems
to be in the counterfeit presentment by Naugeot; but in
the tragic likeness by Émile Deroy (1844) he looks sad
and dreamy—a Hamlet whose brow is prematurely
' sicklied o'er with the pale cast of thought'.

Whether Baudelaire's dilettante experiences in debauch,

his ostentatious nympholepsy and the cold cynical perversity of his moral sentiments were entirely real, or in a certain measure merely affected, it would be idle to speculate. He took a malicious pleasure in 'astonishing 'fools' and loved to 'flabbergast the Philistines' (*épater les bourgeois*). Even among his intimate associates he would enunciate the most monstrous theories and argue them out with all the earnestness of grave conviction. He was deeply conscious of the cause for grief which his disordered life had given to a fond mother, and he endeavoured to make amends to her by constant affection and tenderness. He did not display the characteristic indifference of a voluptuary towards the wretched mulatto woman with whom he lived for so many years, and whose charms he has sung in strangely sensuous verse; for in his darkest days, long after she had ceased to charm his senses, he ministered to her necessities, and indeed nearly ruined himself to help her when she was sunk in misery and afflicted with an incurable disease. His petulant sallies of violence seem to have been sometimes sincere and sometimes assumed. These whimsical excesses must have been but transient, and perhaps superficial, or else his literary friends could not have left such a fascinating record of his courtesy. 'If ever the word seductiveness ' could have been applied to a human being '—says one of them—'it was to him, for he had nobility, pride, elegance, ' a beauty at once infantine and virile, the enchantment ' of a rhythmical voice and the most persuasive elo-' quence'. He was an absolute aristocrat in character as in genius. In general he was not voluble of speech, for he rather affected an English reserve of manner. He had a scrupulous love of neatness, cleanliness and order. Altogether a peculiarly sensitive, nervous and impressionable nature, prone to fantastic idealism, mystically voluptuous and madly amorous of new and strange sensations.

Baudelaire's poetical work is distinguished by its rare perfection of form. If it is insignificant in volume it is exquisite and precious in quality, and has had a larger influence on contemporary poetry in France than the work of any other author. The verse of the *Fleurs du Mal*, with its shapely line and luminous melody, has been the glass of fashion and the mould of form for Verlaine and Mallarmé and many other poets of the present time. Baudelaire's excessively fastidious taste saved him from the direct imitation of models, although he could appreciate and assimilate foreign ideas, as his prose translations of De Quincey and Edgar Allan Poe and his poetical images from Shakespeare and Gray and Longfellow clearly demonstrate. And although Victor Hugo was in the plenitude of his supremacy in 1840 there is little or no evidence of his formative influence on Baudelaire, who sedulously applied himself to the cultivation of that closely-wrought and deeply-concentrated style which in poetry marks him as a man apart. There is seldom a glimpse of sudden passion in his song, but the expression of his love for the beautiful is so intense, so super-refined and so subtle that his verse glows with a white heat, which fiercely smoulders if it never flames. In his colder and more deliberate moods there is a sculpturesque solidity and a serene beauty that is not excelled even by Landor and Rossetti at their best. Many of his lines have the curved delicacy of flesh and the firm smoothness of marble. If there is a fault in his woven harmony of words it is uniformity of tone : he thrilled a lyre of rich and splendid resonance, but of few strings. Hence the repetition of images when, as in the *Hymn to Beauty*, he exceeds his customary range.

CHARLES BAUDELAIRE

Baudelaire's tropical experience and his responsiveness to exotic sensations assisted him in giving a new colour and a new vibration to French verse. There is a matchless charm and fragrance in such lines as

'Parfum qui fait rêver aux oasis lointaines'—
(*L'Amour du Mensonge.*)

'Et trouve un goût suave au vin le plus amer'—
(*La Voix.*)

and there are hundreds like them in those intoxicating *Flowers of Evil.*

That Baudelaire's book should have been sometimes wilfully and sometimes ignorantly misunderstood is not surprising. The poet has been roughly handled by a few of the eminently sane critics of the present time, represented by Ferdinand Brunetière and Jules Lemaître. But Sainte-Beuve and Paul Bourget and Anatole France have been more tender, more sympathetic, and therefore more just in their judgments on this strange genius. Baudelaire's curious blending of religious mysticism with voluptuous emotion has seemed to many to be blasphemy and even atheism, and yet his inmost thoughts were always a passionate prayer to God for deliverance from the world, the flesh and the devil. His bold and occasionally crude analysis of diseased passion has been mistaken for an appeal to fleshly indulgence by those whose regard for the outward and visible forms of morality blinds them to the spiritual elements of human desire. It is true that such a poet as Baudelaire could have been produced only in an epoch of social corruption and decay, and that he was in many respects the morbid embodiment of the Lower Empire. But he was nevertheless a great and true poet ; and if his life was a moral failure and his life's work a moral phenomenon it is because a mysterious fatality has denied to the children of light the wisdom which is so plentifully bestowed upon the children of this world. The sinister eclipse of genius endowed with such conspicuous gifts and graces is only the more appalling if it be true that

'. . . . . not for this
' Was common clay ta'en from the common earth,
' Moulded by God, and temper'd with the tears
' Of angels to the perfect shape of man '.

Benediction.

When, by the sovran will of Powers Eternal,
  The poet passed into this weary world,
His mother, filled with fears and doubts infernal,
  Clenching her hands towards Heaven these curses
    hurled.

—'Why rather did I not within me treasure
  'A knot of serpents than this thing of scorn?
'Accursëd be the night of fleeting pleasure
  'Whence in my womb this chastisement was borne!

'Since thou hast chosen me to be the woman
  'Whose loathsome fruitfulness her husband shames,
'Who may not cast aside this birth inhuman,
  'As one that flings love-tokens to the flames,

'The hatred that on me thy vengeance launches
  'On this thwart creature I will pour in flood;
'So twist the sapling that its withered branches
  'Shall never once put forth a cankered bud!'

Regorging thus the venom of her malice,
  And misconceiving thy decrees sublime,
In deep Gehenna's gulf she fills the chalice
  Of torments destined to maternal crime.

Yet, safely sheltered by his viewless angel,
  The Childe forsaken revels in the Sun;
And all his food and drink is an evangel
  Of nectared sweets, sent by the Heavenly One.

He communes with the clouds, knows the wind's voices,
　　And on his pilgrimage enchanted sings ;
Seeing how like the wild bird he rejoices
　　The hovering Spirit weeps and folds his wings.

All those he fain would love shrink back in terror,
　　Or, boldened by his fearlessness elate,
Seek to seduce him into sin and error,
　　And flesh on him the fierceness of their hate.

In bread and wine, wherewith his soul is nourished,
　　They mix their ashes and foul spume impure ;
Lying they cast aside the things he cherished,
　　And curse the chance that made his steps their lure.

His spouse goes crying in the public places :
　　—' Since he doth choose my beauty to adore,
' Aping those ancient idols Time defaces
　　' I would regild my glory as of yore.

' Nard, balm and myrrh shall tempt till he desires me
　　' With blandishments, with dainties and with wine,
' Laughing if in a heart that so admires me
　　' I may usurp the sovranty divine !

' Until aweary of love's impious orgies,
　　' Fastening on him my fingers firm and frail,
' These claws, keen as the harpy's when she gorges,
　　' Shall in the secret of his heart prevail.

' Then, thrilled and trembling like a young bird cap-
　　　　tured,
　　' The bleeding heart shall from his breast be torn ;
' To glut his maw my wanton hound, enraptured,
　　' Shall see me fling it to the earth in scorn '.

154

CHARLES BAUDELAIRE

Heavenward, where he beholds a throne resplendent,
  The poet lifts his hands, devout and proud,
And the vast lightnings of a soul transcendent
  Veil from his gaze awhile the furious crowd :—

'Blessëd be thou, my God, that givest sorrow,
  'Sole remedy divine for things unclean,
'Whence souls robust a healing virtue borrow,
  'That tempers them for sacred joys serene!

'I know thou hast ordained in blissful regions
  'A place, a welcome in the festal bowers,
'To call the poet with thy holy Legions,
  'Thrones, Dominations, Princedoms, Virtues, Powers.

'I know that Sorrow is the strength of Heaven,
  'Gainst which in vain strive ravenous Earth and Hell,
'And that his crown must be of mysteries woven
  'Whereof all worlds and ages hold the spell.

'But not antique Palmyra's buried treasure,
  'Pearls of the sea, rare metal, precious gem,
'Though set by thine own hand could fill the measure
  'Of beauty for his radiant diadem ;

'For this thy light alone, intense and tender,
  'Flows from the primal source of effluence pure,
'Whereof all mortal eyes, though bright their splendour,
  'Are but the broken glass and glimpse obscure'.

                    Bénédiction : Spleen et Idéal.
                         (*Les Fleurs du Mal.*)

Ill Luck.

To bear so vast a load of grief
    Thy courage, Sisyphus, I crave !
    My heart against the task is brave,
But Art is long and Time is brief.

Far from Fame's proud sepulchral arches,
    Towards a graveyard lone and dumb,
    My sad heart, like a muffled drum,
Goes beating slow funereal marches.

—Full many a shrouded jewel sleeps
In dark oblivion, lost in deeps
    Unknown to pick or plummet's sound :

Full many a weeping blossom flings
Her perfume, sweet as secret things,
    In silent solitudes profound.

          Le Guignon: Spleen et Idéal.
                (Les Fleurs du Mal.)

Beauty.

My face is a marmoreal dream, O mortals !
    And on my breast all men are bruised in turn,
    So moulded that the poet's love may burn
Mute and eternal as the earth's cold portals.

Throned like a Sphinx unveiled in the blue deep,
    A heart of snow my swan-white beauty muffles ;
    I hate the line that undulates and ruffles :
And never do I laugh and never weep.

The poets, prone beneath my presence towering
  With stately port of proudest obelisks,
Worship with rites austere, their days devouring;

  For I have charms to keep their love, pure disks
That make all things more beautiful and tender:
My large eyes, radiant with eternal splendour!

La Beauté: *Spleen et Idéal.*
(*Les Fleurs du Mal.*)

Ideal Love.

No, never can these frail ephemeral creatures,
  The withered offspring of a worthless age,
These buskined limbs, these false and painted features,
  The hunger of a heart like mine assuage.

Leave to the laureate of sickly posies
  Gavarni's hospital sylphs, a simpering choir!
Vainly I seek among those pallid roses
  One blossom that allures my red desire.

Thou with my soul's abysmal dreams be blended,
Lady Macbeth, in crime superb and splendid,
  A dream of Æschylus flowered in cold eclipse

Of Northern suns! Thou, Night, inspire my passion,
Calm child of Angelo, coiling in strange fashion
  Thy large limbs moulded for a Titan's lips!

L'Idéal: *Spleen et Idéal.*
(*Les Fleurs du Mal.*)

157

Hymn to Beauty.

Be thou from Hell upsprung or Heaven descended,
　Beauty! thy look demoniac and divine
Pours good and evil things confusedly blended,
　And therefore art thou likened unto wine.

Thine eye with dawn is filled, with twilight dwindles,
　Like winds of night thou sprinklest perfumes mild;
Thy kiss, that is a spell, the child's heart kindles,
　Thy mouth, a chalice, makes the man a child.

Fallen from the stars or risen from gulfs of error,
　Fate dogs thy glamoured garments like a slave;
With wanton hands thou scatterest joy and terror,
　And rulest over all, cold as the grave.

Thou tramplest on the dead, scornful and cruel,
　Horror coils like an amulet round thine arms,
Crime on thy superb bosom is a jewel
　That dances amorously among its charms.

The dazzled moth that flies to thee, the candle,
　Shrivels and burns, blessing thy fatal flame;
The lover that dies fawning o'er thy sandal
　Fondles his tomb and breathes the adorëd name.

What if from Heaven or Hell thou com'st, immortal
　Beauty?　O sphinx-like monster, since alone
Thine eye, thy smile, thy hand opens the portal
　Of the Infinite I love and have not known.

What if from God or Satan be the evangel?
Thou my sole Queen! Witch of the velvet eyes!
Since with thy fragrance, rhythm and light, O Angel!
In a less hideous world time swiftlier flies.

Hymne à la Beauté: Spleen et Idéal.
(Les Fleurs du Mal.)

Exotic Fragrance.

When, with closed eyes in the warm autumn night,
I breathe the fragrance of thy bosom bare,
My dream unfurls a clime of loveliest air,
Drenched in the fiery sun's unclouded light.

An indolent island dowered with heaven's delight,
Trees singular and fruits of savour rare,
Men having sinewy frames robust and spare,
And women whose clear eyes are wondrous bright.

Led by thy fragrance to those shores I hail
A charmëd harbour thronged with mast and sail,
Still wearied with the quivering sea's unrest;

What time the scent of the green tamarinds
That thrills the air and fills my swelling breast
Blends with the mariners' song and the sea-winds.

Parfum exotique: Spleen et Idéal.
(Les Fleurs du Mal.)

Sonnet.

In undulant robes with nacreous sheen impearled
  She walks as in some stately saraband ;
Or like lithe snakes by sacred charmers curled
  In cadence wreathing on the slender wand.

Calm as blue wastes of sky and desert sand
That watch unmoved the sorrows of this world ;
  With slow regardless sweep as on the strand
The long swell of the woven sea-waves swirled.

Her polished orbs are like a mystic gem,
  And, while this strange and symbolled being links
  The inviolate angel and the antique sphinx,

Insphered in gold, steel, light and diadem
  The splendour of a lifeless star endows
  With clear cold majesty the barren spouse.

Spleen et Idéal: XXVIII.
(*Les Fleurs du Mal.*)

The Spiritual Dawn.

When on some wallowing soul the roseate East
  Dawns with the Ideal that awakes and gnaws,
  By vengeful working of mysterious laws
An angel rises in the drowsëd beast.

The inaccessible blue of the soul-sphere
  To him whose grovelling dream remorse doth gall
  Yawns wide as when the gulfs of space enthral.
So, heavenly Goddess, Spirit pure and clear,

Even on the reeking ruins of vile shame
  Thy rosy vision, beautiful and bright,
  For ever floats on my enlargèd sight.

Thus sunlight blackens the pale taper-flame ;
  And thus is thy victorious phantom one,
  O soul of splendour, with the immortal Sun !

L'Aube spirituelle: Spleen et Idéal.
  (*Les Fleurs du Mal.*)

Music.

Launch me, O music, whither on the soundless
    Sea my star gleams pale !
I beneath cloudy cope or rapt in boundless
    Æther set my sail ;

With breast outblown, swollen by the wind that urges
    Swelling sheets, I scale
The summit of the wave whose vexèd surges
    Night from me doth veil ;

A labouring vessel's passions in my pulses
    Thrill the shuddering sense ;
The wind that wafts, the tempest that convulses,
    O'er the gulf immense
Swing me.—Anon flat calm and clearer air
    Glass my soul's despair !

La Musique : Spleen et Idéal.
    (*Les Fleurs du Mal.*)

The Flawed Bell.

Bitter and sweet it is, in winter night,
  Hard by the flickering fire that smokes, to list
While far-off memories rise in sad slow flight,
  With chimes that echo singing through the mist.

O blessëd be the bell whose vigorous throat,
  In spite of age alert, with strength unspent,
Utters religiously his faithful note,
  Like an old warrior watching near the tent!

My soul alas! is flawed, and when despair
Would people with her songs the chill night-air
  Too oft they faint in hoarse enfeebled tones,

  As when a wounded man forgotten moans
By the red pool, beneath a heap of dead,
And dying writhes in frenzy on his bed.

La Cloche fêlée: Spleen et Idéal.
(*Les Fleurs du Mal.*)

Henry Mürger.

Born in Paris, 1822 . . . Died in Paris, 1861.

Henry Mürger, the son of a poor German tailor, was born
in one of the slums of Paris. He had no regular education,
and took the road to Bohemia from necessity rather than
choice. His first experience of life was as a notary's clerk
with a small salary. He wished to become a painter, but
his progress in art was so slow that he resolved to try
letters. His sole source of inspiration was his own
narrow experience of the world ; his greatest gift a
faculty for hard work. He would spend the whole night
over a single page of prose or verse. He had a limited
knowledge of literature, and nourished his mind by reading over and over again the few books which he possessed
—among them the poems of Victor Hugo and Alfred
de Musset, with Letourneur's hazy translation of Shakespeare's plays. With classical literature and the older
French poets he was totally unacquainted.

Mürger was the acknowledged chief of the lesser
Bohemia, in which Privat d'Anglemont, Auguste Vitu,
the witty and refined Alfred Delvau and the novelist
Champfleury* were his principal satellites. Their places
of rendezvous were the *café Momus* in *rue des Prêtres-
Saint-Germain-l'Auxerrois* and the *cénacle* of the *barrière
d'Enfer*.

By craning over the window of their poor chamber in

* Jules Fleury-Husson, afterwards Curator of the National Museum at
Sèvres, a prolific writer of novels and a recognised authority on ceramic art.

rue Vaugirard, Champfleury and Mürger could see *one* of
the trees in the garden of the Luxembourg. The furniture
at first consisted of six earthenware plates, a superannu-
ated commode, a few volumes of poetry and a Phrygian
cap, the property of Mürger. Champfleury, who was more
luxuriously endowed, contributed to their heterogeneous
plenishing two mattresses, more than a hundred books, an
armchair, two common chairs, a table and a skull. These
two Bohemians spent the most of their time in reading,
writing and smoking. Between them they had an income
of 70 francs a month, out of which they paid 300 francs
per annum for their lodging. Nearly all the payments of
this curious household were made on the first of each
month, when the joint revenue fell due, and they kept a
diary of disbursements in order to guard against extravagance. Well might Léon Gozlan parody Racine's famous
verses :—

'Aux petits des oiseaux Dieu donne leur pâture,
'Et sa bonté s'étend sur toute la nature'—

by substituting for the second line of the couplet :—

'Mais sa bonté s'arrête à la littérature'!

And yet the gaiety which these poor wretches ex-
pended on their existence was prodigious. They acted
on Voltaire's principle. 'Five or six miseries together'—
said the Geometer to the Man with Forty Crowns—'make
'a very tolerable establishment'.

When Mürger was writing his *Scènes de la Vie de Bohême*
for the *Corsaire* at eighteen francs the *feuilleton* he could
afford neither the railway-fare to go out to the country and
see nature nor the cost of a black coat to go into society and
study manners. Hence the close atmosphere in which his

characters so vividly and so intimately move ; every line
records an incident of his own sad life.   Occasionally he
had a little money—at one time he was private secretary
to some great Russian *seigneur*—and then his habits
blossomed into brief luxury, for he was always of a most
improvident disposition.   In his later days he was accustomed to fly from Paris in spring, summer and autumn
to a thatched hut which he had discovered in the forest
of Fontainebleau.   This welcome change was unhappily
of little avail.   It is true that his genius was beginning to
be recognised and that he seemed to be fairly on the road
to fame ; in earnest of which a pension had been granted
to him by Napoleon III.   Mürger had no specific ailment ;
but the poverty of his Parisian blood, drained by wasteful
excesses, by the abuse of strong coffee, and by the
generally unwholesome conditions of his life, doomed him
to premature decay.   The blight came upon him suddenly
in a loathsome disease, which caused rapid mortification
of the flesh, and was thereupon pronounced incurable.
'Bohemia', he   once   wrote, 'is   the   preface   to   the
' Academy, to the Hospital, or to the Morgue'.   In his
case it was followed by the hospital.   During his sojourn
there this Voltairean scoffer, composed religious poems
for the sisters who nursed him ; and, timid as he was in
the struggle for existence, he faced death with resignation
and even with cheerfulness.

   Like most of his fellows, Mürger wrote a good deal
which was scattered in journals and will never be collected.   He was also an active contributor to the theatre.
The *Scènes de la Vie de Bohême*, which met with little
recognition in their *feuilleton* form in 1848, had a fuller
measure of success on the stage.   The dramatised version
was studded with brilliant and touching things, for, as
Théophile Gautier said at the time, Mürger had 'that rare

' and marvellous gift of wit full of feeling . . . his laugh
' touched on tears'. The same critic signalised Mürger,
along with Balzac and Gavarni, as perhaps the most
truly Parisian artist of his epoch. He had real originality, which owed little to learning, for in that squalid strife
of his youth he had wasted the time that might have been
given to study, to experiment and to assimilation.

Scenes of Bohemian Life remains the supreme example
of pure humour in the French language, and it is perhaps
significant that it should have been contributed by an
author of Teutonic extraction. Humour, indeed, is hardly
a French characteristic. Of wit there is enough and to
spare, whether in the caustic sarcasm of *Le Neveu de
Rameau*, the shrewd irony of *Candide* or the grotesque
exaggeration of *Tartarin de Tarascon*. The jovial
humour of Rabelais, like that of Falstaff, stands alone.
Béranger's sprightly style is essentially satirical, and
Balzac falls into gross pleasantry when he essays the
humorous vein. Even the quaint spiritual humour of
Charles Nodier cannot be compared with that of Henry
Mürger, which is as spontaneous as it is captivating and
rare. And it owes little or nothing to the fescennine
fancy which runs so freely through Gallic literature :—

> ' Ah! la muse de Collé
> ' C'est la gaudriole, ô gué!'

as Béranger so genially sings.

The life of Henry Mürger is the life of the poor poet in
every age, and, whatever glamour of romance may have
been thrown over it, too often has it been one of ignoble
enjoyment and sordid misery. A few of the Bohemians
escaped from their dungeon with clean limbs and unclouded minds ; the greater number succumbed in a hopeless struggle with starvation and debauchery. Mürger

might have enfranchised himself had he possessed a
healthier body and a more ambitious mind. Sapped by
early privations, broken by youthful excess and anxiety and
toil, he died on the threshold of manhood, the most attrac-
tive and the most pathetic figure of the later Romantic
period. With him the Bohemia of the nineteenth
century disappeared. We know that the poor poet is ever
with us, but the conditions that gave his existence a local
habitation and a name have changed, and with them the
genial good-fellowship and generous emotions which
graced his forlorn lot. Where is the feast of reason and
the flow of soul? Where is the symposium of choice spirits
bound together by kindred sorrows and kindling ideals?
Where is the sparkling *Cydalise* and the pale *grisette*,
whose charms shed a consoling light on lives that knew
too little of the joy of living ; and

'Where are the snows of yester-year ? '

The Diver.

To enrich her circlet, starred with precious things,
   The queen said to the diver :—' At my sign,
' Plunge to the palace where the siren sings,
   ' And pluck me the blonde pearl beneath the brine '.

Then into the wild wave the diver springs ;
   On golden sands, where crimsoned corals shine,
Plucks the blonde pearl, and to his sovereign brings
   The treasure prisoned in its nacreous shrine.

The poet, like this diver, is a slave,
Lady, and if your smiling fancies crave
   A verse to voice abroad your beauty's spell,

Straightway he plunges into depths of thought,
Where sleeps the hoarded rhyme with gold inwrought,
   And brings the wished-for jewel in its shell.

Le Plongeur : Fantaisies.
      (*Les Nuits d'hiver.*)

1844.

Near Juliet's Balcony.

Your balcony, my lady, boasts such art
   As the fond sculptor loves to contemplate ;
Of wondrous shape, each richly-chiselled part
   A masterpiece of Art's divinest date.

An arch young Love, sharpening his wanton dart,
  Bears up the baluster, and mocks the fate
For ever threatening thence the wounded heart
  That you must cure, my lady.—Soon or late,

A hapless lover, touched with arrowy fire,
And blending with night's sighs his soul's desire,
  Will steal, like Romeo, hiding from the moon,

And scale thy balcony, Juliet, when 'tis dark,
Lingering until the hour when sings the lark,
  The parting hour, that ever comes too soon !

Au Balcon de Juliette : Fantaisies.
(Les Nuits d'hiver.)

1844.

Pygmalion.

In vain the priests of Venus long to raise
  Her image in the void Athenian shrine ;
The jealous artist, deaf to prayers or praise,
  Enamoured of his handiwork must pine.

Love's naked goddess to his love displays
  The moveless splendour of her shape divine ;
Till kneeling, lo ! beneath his ardent gaze
  In lifeless marble sudden life doth shine !

Poet ! this marvel chanced in antique years ;
The gods, long exiled from Olympian spheres,
  Grant not to thee the Cyprian sculptor's grace :

Though of thine own soul's beauty amorous grown,
Like old Pygmalion doting on the stone,
  She will not glow with life in thy embrace.

Pygmalion : Fantaisies.
(Les Nuits d'hiver.)

1844.

169

Blanche-Marie.

The virgin veil of Blanche-Marie
　　Was white as mountain-snows;
The heavenly robes no brighter be
　　That Mary's love bestows:
With flowers of silk enwoven thereon
　　She wrought so cunningly
That like a saint with garlands shone
　　The body of Blanche-Marie.

Her veil of white but once she wore,
　　When, swathed in folds thereof,
With downcast eyes she knelt before
　　The chalice of Christ's love.

The spousal veil of Blanche-Marie
　　Was black as raven's plume;
Wrought when her mother died, and she
　　Watched in the silent room;
Of willow-leaf and yew she made
　　Its sombre broidery:
The dew-drops glistering through its shade
　　Were tears of Blanche-Marie.

Her veil of black but once she wore,
　　When, dowered with love unpriced,
She stood a bride on convent-floor
　　And gave herself to Christ.

HENRY MÜRGER

The mystic veil of Blanche-Marie
　　Was woven of heavenly blue,
So fine, so clear, that you might see
　　Her pure face shining through ;
And on her veil were sprinkled stars,
　　A radiant mystery :
With lilies white and nenuphars,
　　A crown for Blanche-Marie.

The veil of mystic blue she wore
　　By God's own love was given,
That day her guardian-angel bore
　　The sinless soul to heaven.

*Les Trois Voiles de Marie Berthe.**
(Les Nuits d'hiver.)

April, 1844.

---

* A little liberty has been taken in translating this prose *ballade* into verse
form. *Blanche-Marie* and the preceding sonnets present a different aspect
of Mürger's poetical talent from the *Chanson de Mimi* or the *Chanson de
Musette,* but it would have been superfluous to translate the latter after the
specimens of Mürger's Bohemian muse which have been so delicately and
so gracefully rendered into English by Andrew Lang.

Théodore de Banville.

Born in Moulins (Allier) 1823 . . . Died in Paris, 1891.

Few better examples of a peaceful and unpretentious life, wholly devoted to letters, could be found than that of Théodore Faullain de Banville.   He was the son of a retired naval captain, who belonged to a family of country gentlemen once possessed of large estates in the departments of the Allier and the Nièvre.   It was 'the land of 'the Loire', in the midst of that beautifully-wooded country which lies between the ducal domains of the ancient families of Bourbon and Mazarin.   The lavish hospitality and Quixotic caprices of Banville's great-grandfather had ruinously impaired the family patrimony, and thus it was that Théodore de Banville was 'reduced ' to the condition of a lyric poet, so that he might break- ' fast on a sunbeam and sup on the wandering breeze and ' moonlight '.   His choice of the poetic calling needs no vindication, for even his prose gives evidence how spontaneously his thoughts crystallised themselves in lyrical form.

From an ancestral race of robust and healthy constitution Théodore de Banville inherited those characteristics of good sense, simplicity and kindliness which underlay his lyrical genius and were displayed in his daily life. His philosophy was unaffected and full of amiability. ' Give children everything they desire and allow them to ' do anything they wish, but never let them hear false ' or foolish things' was one of his axioms.   Another : ' If

' you have a piece of bread and a piece of cake, always eat
' the cake first, for you never know if you will live long
' enough to eat the bread also'. These aphorisms were
the essence of a genial disposition, which enabled its
possessor to meet with a smiling face all the troubles and
toils of existence.

Coming to Paris soon after his *pension* expired, Théodore de Banville was brought under the influence of
Count Alfred de Vigny, in whom he recognised a great
poet and a noble man. The young provincial soon rallied
to the Romantic Movement, for the simple reason that he
was always in search of 'the latest expression of Beauty',
as Baudelaire had defined it. He also knitted acquaintance
with Jules Janin, and became the advocate of Victor Hugo's
genius, which 'the prince of critics' was at that time
unwilling to acknowledge. Among Banville's more or less
intimate friends were Charles Baudelaire ; Paulin Méry,
renowned for his phenomenal memory ; that strange
heteroclite creole, Privat d'Anglemont ; Pierre Dupont
the chansonnier ; the painter Émile Deroy ; the witty
sculptor Auguste Préault ; and Félix Pyat, in whom the
love of letters was sacrificed to revolutionary zeal.

Living in a chamber which, with 'a bed, a small table
' and three volumes of verse, was infinitely well furnished '
Banville set to work in earnest, and quickly achieved
celebrity with *les Cariatides* (1842) and *les Stalactites*
(1843-45). From 1846 to 1856 he laid purely lyrical
poetry aside to compose and publish those charming
comedies which he wrote with such rare felicity. He was
a great lover of plays and players, and delighted in the
innumerable small theatres which swarmed in Paris from
1830 to 1870. Among his most successful of a dozen
comedies are *le beau Léandre* (1856) *Diane au Bois* (1863)
Gringoire (1866) and *Socrate et sa Femme* (1885) ; but in-

deed they are all instinct with poetic feeling and full of delicate beauty. His avowed object in writing these plays was to do for comedy what Victor Hugo had done for tragedy; and those to whom Beerbohm Tree's acting in the English version of *Gringoire* has revealed the possibilities of poetry on the stage (if indeed any such demonstration should be necessary after *The Tempest* and *A Midsummer Night's Dream*) will understand how diverse from that of the average playwright was Théodore de Banville's ideal of comedy. Banville resumed his lyrical work in 1866 with *les Exilés*, followed by *les Occidentales* in 1871, and other collections of verse in 1873, 1874 and 1876. His prose miscellanies were numerous and full of vitality.

As a journalist Théodore de Banville did excellent and varied work, sometimes in his own name and sometimes under the disguise of Francis Lambert or François Villon. He threw up his appointment as literary and theatrical critic in the *National* rather than keep silence on the subject of Victor Hugo; and afterwards wrote in the *Gil Blas* a series of delightful *Chroniques* which were alive with wit and fancy, if sometimes easy on the score of morals. These, however, brought him more money than he ever earned by his poetry or plays.

Perhaps the most characteristic and striking achievement of Théodore de Banville was his *Odes funambulesques*, a series of satirical poems in which he aimed at the introduction of a new comic element into French literature. In these odes the *tours de force* of rhyme, ingenious plays on words, parody and witty badinage are singular and original. They were the first and are the finest examples of refined lyrical buffoonery in French verse, but many of them cannot be translated owing to the puns, peculiar devices of verbal imitation, and allusions to contemporary personages, places of resort and popular ephemera with which they abound. So much so, that to many intelligent Parisians of the present time they are almost as obscure as the satire of Aristophanes.

Throughout his long life Théodore de Banville remained faithful to the men and the traditions of the Romantic Movement. He of all that survived, if Théophile Gautier be excepted, best understood and sympathised with the wild passion and faith of 1830, keeping unchanged his warm admiration for Louis Bertrand, Théophile Dondey, Émile Cabanon, Théophile de Ferrière, Alphonse Esquiros, and all the nigh forgotten names * of that unforgotten time! When Charles Asselineau, the high-priest of the French Renaissance, published his *Bibliographie des Romantiques* in 1866, it was Théodore de Banville who welcomed it in a famous ode, in which he thus summed up the glories of that great revival :—

The Dawn of the Romance.

To Charles Asselineau.

Hail to thee EIGHTEEN HUNDRED
AND THIRTY! Dawn that sunderëd
The night of things unborn ;
    O laughing morn!

Dawn bursting into sunlight!
Whose blended lights like one light
Renew, even in my dreams,
    Their rosy gleams.

* Among the poets of 1830-1840 there was at least one who deserved a kinder destiny. The *Roland* of Napoléon Peyrat (Napol le Pyrénéen) has more of the true Romantic colouring and flavour than any poem of the period, Victor Hugo's alone excepted.

With radiance amethystal,
Turning the clouds to crystal,
Thou breakest and the night
    Takes sudden flight.

Crowned with ambrosial garlands,
The exiled Muse from far lands
Returns with subtile art
    To touch the heart.

The Drama's web is woven
Rich-hued ; the silence cloven :
The Ode harmonious rings,
    The Sonnet sings.

Here Shakespeare shouts sonorous,
While Petrarch sighs in chorus ;
Gay Horace, clear and strong,
    Trolls out his song.

Ronsard repeats his proem
In canzonet and poem,
Swelled with the wild refrain
    Of Baïf's strain.

Lethe's dull flood beguiling,
Old Rabelais rises smiling
To dower romance with store
    Of jovial lore.

Love's rosy fire so flushes
The cheek of youth with blushes
That even the journal grows
    Ashamed of prose !

THÉODORE DE BANVILLE

Proud Architecture raises
Her pure and holy praises
In pillared arch and aisle
      That heavenward smile.

Sculpture records the features
Of saint-like loyal creatures
That white as lilies wear
      Their virtues rare.

Music on wings immortal
Lifts soul up to the portal
Whence echoes loud and long
      The heavenly song.

O converse hymeneal
Of Life with the Ideal!
Antiphony sublime
      Of Lute and Rhyme!

Hugo, with tragic presage,
Sends forth his sombre message
To great hearts desolate,
      The slaves of fate ;

To the exile, to the dreamer,
His Muse is a redeemer ;
Marion de Lorme, alas !
      And Ruy Blas :

While, lost in contemplation,
Great David's emulation
Prophetic wreathes his brow
      With laurel-bough.*

* An allusion to the celebrated bust of Victor Hugo by David d'Angers.

THÉODORE DE BANVILLE

George Sand reveals the human
Love-tremulous soul of woman ;
Musset unfolds his wings
    And weeping sings.

The whole World's Comedy dances
Round Balzac, who advances
To strip, with supreme art,
    Man's naked heart.

Barbier displays his trophies
In bright and burning strophes ;
Sainte-Beuve to lyres that ring
    Lends a new string.

Plaintive Valmore sings sobbing ;*
Her heart, with sorrow throbbing,
A bitter sigh exhales,
    As the sea wails.

Throned on her mountain-summit
Art, holding wisdom's plummet,
Gives Théophile Gautier
    A world to sway.

In days superb and sordid
Karr keeps more young love hoarded
Than Rothschild's coffers hold
    Of massive gold.

---

* Marceline-Félicité-Josèphe Desbordes-Valmore—1786-1859—an actress, singer and poetess whose sad life and lyrical talent excited the sympathetic admiration of Sainte-Beuve, Lamartine and Victor Hugo. Her poems are full of sensibility. According to Michelet she possessed, above all, 'the 'gift of tears'.

With lips enthralled and tender,
Gérard reveals the splendour
Of faëry dreams and rhymes
From Orient climes ;

Deschamps, twin harps and voices :
One on swift wings rejoices,
One groans beneath the weight
Of Romeo's fate.

Lemaître leads the captured
Melpomene enraptured,
And grand Dorval stands near,
His only peer ;

Berlioz, with storm and thunder,
Cleaves the thick clouds asunder,
And calls in lightning-glare
To Meyerbeer ;

Préault's fantastic finger
Bids trembling pathos linger,
Pale, with immortal grace,
On Sorrow's face :

Johannot's brain, o'erflowing
With fancies warm and glowing,
Leads Love in pilgrimage
Through each new page.

Fond Art is fain to hover
O'er Boulanger her lover,
And even on Nanteuil's brows
A kiss bestows,

But pours, in amplest measure,
On Delacroix her treasure
Of gems and jewelled things,
  Too rich for kings.

While Daumier wields, audacious,
The pencil large and gracious
Of Michael-Angelo,
  Lost long ago,

Gavarni thrids the traces
Of amorous nymphs and graces,
Whose charms Devéria weds
  With nobler heads!

Alas, delusive Vision!
Where is thy light Elysian?—
The days on which it shone
  Are dead and gone!

Where are they?—Singers, Sages,
That charmed the feast of ages,
Those heroes noble-souled,
  Those hearts of gold,

Brave hearts of honour zealous?—
The most lie dead.   Their fellows,
Grown gray in glory's quest,
  Now long for rest.

Their great and noble story
Is like a legend hoary
That by the hearth's pale light
  Is told at night.

THÉODORE DE BANVILLE

A clown now wears the cluster
Of jewels rare whose lustre
Once showered from souls profound
    Their radiance round.

Brave Hamlet stands dejected,
Discrowned, forlorn, neglected,
Even on the friendly shore
    Of Elsinore.

Farewell, Romance star-crownëd!
But not one link renownëd
O' the antique chain forgo,
    Asselineau!

As Homer's muse rehearses,
In skilled and sounding verses,
The galleys and their freight
    Of kings in state,

With deeds of fame refresh us!
Those volumes quaint and precious'
In Renduel's rubric rare*
    Rehearse with care;

Marshal them in their order
From border unto border,
Con page and picture well
    Back to Borel;

---

* Pierre-Eugène Renduel (1798-1874) was the principal *éditeur* of the
Romantic period. He published Victor Hugo's and Heine's earlier works;
also the celebrated translation in twenty volumes of Hoffmann's *Fantastic
Tales* by the writer known as Loewe-Weimars or Loëve-Veimars.

For thou their annals gleanest
So close that scarce the meanest
Of many names obscure
    Escapes thy lure.

So, since thy blazon names thee
Our herald and proclaims thee
Guardian of glorious rhyme
    Unto all time,

Tell us of EIGHTEEN HUNDRED
AND THIRTY, year that thunderëd
With storm and stress of fight
    And splendours bright,

A glorious revelation
On which the loud oblation
Of hoarse Thérésa's lips
    Now casts eclipse!

Thine be the tongue that clamours,
In days whereon the glamours
Of gilded gauds prevail,
    'Ye Vanquished, Hail!'

For though the fortress tumble,
Though stone by stone may crumble
Those moss-grown towers, no spell
    Can ever quell

The good old Rhineland giant,
Romantic and defiant,
Whose shattered walls environ
    A heart of iron!

L'Aube romantique.
    (*Nouvelles Odes funambulesques.*)

21 *July*, 1866.

THÉODORE DE BANVILLE

Banville's *Souvenirs* and *Esquisses* reflect the freshness and healthfulness of his intellectual life. His criticisms give evidence of an appreciative rather than a censorious attitude towards letters and art. He considered Victor Hugo and Heinrich Heine the two best poets of this century, and loved better to bestow too much praise on a minor bard than to disparage the glory of a great name. He was familiar with the entire range of French verse, but he had little or no knowledge of contemporary English literature. His own verses stamp him as the most truly lyrical of all French poets. In his return to the sources of classical inspiration he followed and developed Victor de Laprade and preluded Leconte de Lisle. He had a prodigious variety of rhymes and successfully attempted almost every form of verse. His *Sonnets*, his *Ballades*, and his *Rondels* after the fashion of Charles d'Orléans, are triumphs of fanciful learning and lyrical grace. His colouring is warm and luminous. He displays more *esprit* than humour, and in general his imagery is more copious than his ideas. He is never prosy, never pedantic and never profound ; but the elasticity and ease of his style, his felicity of illustration and his fine sense of verbal melody give wings to a verse which is always radiant and joyous.

Banville saw the sensuous rather than the spiritual side of things, and no poet was ever so little troubled with the problems of life and the mysteries of death. To him the world was full of beauty and sweetness and light. He was one of those whom the gods love, for although the days of his years were nearly three-score-and-ten he died young.

Home-Sickness.

When trivial volumes roll before my sight
    In endless panorama,
When tired Thalia travails every night
    With a new melodrama ;

When journalists dispense their Attic salt
    In columns analytic,
And with each dose in divers keys exalt
    The function of the critic ;

When pallid lecturers to flocks that faint
    Discourse on dying 'niggers',
When tawdry actresses daub all their paint
    On lank and bony figures ;

When in the market-place provincials crowd,
    Grown greedy with digestion
Of filthy lucre, and in conclave loud
    Discuss the sugar question ; *

When sorry playwrights, with mahogany gaze,
    Flatter their flimsy model,
Write Victor Hugo down, sing d'Ennery's praise,
    And in vile farces twaddle ;

* In England, to-day, the silver question.

THÉODORE DE BANVILLE

When the cold winds that haggard rhymesters haunt
    Give Pegasus the imposthume,
When shameless painters in the Salon flaunt
    Women that pose in costume;

When at Miss Prue's, between two cups of tea,
    A full-blown genius blossoms,
When queens of beauty, crowned for gallantry,
    Display their half-blown bosoms;

When between painted trees on green baize swards,
    Ogled by rake and dullard,
Dolls stuffed with cotton dance for English lords,
    And frisk their limbs flesh-coloured;

O could I, Paris (city sore decayed)
    On foot light as a leopard's
Fly far, where the woods cast a pleasant shade,
    And dwell with Vergil's shepherds!

Watch wanton kids that browse on the wild vine,
    Or, in the plain between us,
Stray with Mnasyllos whither, drowsed with wine,
    Lies jovial old Silenus;

Neath bending willows glimpse the bosom warm
    Of buxom Amaryllis,
And see the nymphs that round Alexis swarm
    Filling their laps with lilies;

On flowery swards dream, while the flight of Time
    Is lulled by murmuring waters,
Weaving a song in amœbean rhyme
    To charm Apollo's daughters;

185

Mourn Daphnis, ravished by a cruel fate,
   Or, when the dance dishevels,
Like blithe Alphesibœus imitate
   The satyrs in their revels!

Nostalgie.
(*Les Cariatides.*)

February, 1842.

Idolatry.

Heavenly rhythm, through the ages victorious,
   Whence to new days a new bard is the bringer,
Horace of yore was thy champion and glorious
     Sappho thy singer!

Bend thou, enamoured, the nymph for whose beauty
   Burns my desire, be love's pleader between us,
Though her heart, vowed to Diana's cold duty,
     Scorns me and Venus!

Since every night the fair sisters, the Graces,
   Tuning their steps to thy heavenly numbers,
Kiss her white bosom, where, wooing embraces,
     Lydia slumbers.

If in the chace, loosely clad and with tresses
   Streaming, she runs to your reeds from the meadow,
Give her, O naiads, your warmest caresses
     In the cool shadow!

Help, thou that wieldest the lyre, oh! inspire in me,
   Thou whose fleet chariot the flying winds follow,
Songs that are filled with the amorous fire in me,
     Phœbus Apollo!

Wilt thou, too, Cypris, to help me, ensnare her?
　Then will I give thee, with myrtle in blossom,
Turtle-doves white as the snow is, or fairer
　　Lily's pure bosom.

Idolâtrie.
(*Les Cariatides.*)

June, 1842.

A Love-Song.

Si je l'dis à l'alouette,
L'alouette le dira.
La violett' se double, double,
La violett' se doublera.

Who, ere daylight breaks above,
　Since I faint with love and languish,
Will to him, my soul's dear love,
　Bear the secret of my anguish?

How, my heart, when all is dark,
　Shall my secret send him warning?—
If I breathe it to the lark
　She will tell it to the morning.

Love, that in my breast doth burn,
　Thrills me with what pang he pleases:—
If the wave my secret learn
　She will tell it to the breezes.

Fear my tremulous lip turns pale,
　Sleepless pain my lid uncloses:—
If I tell the nightingale
　She will tell it to the roses.

187

How shall I beseech my love
    Respite from the woes that follow ?—
If I tell the turtle-dove
    She will tell it to the swallow.

Like a reed I bend and dream,
    Cold neglect my beauty shadows :—
If I tell the azure stream
    She will tell it to the meadows.

You that see my soul's despair,
    Wings and waves and winds of summer !—
If my glass the secret share
    She will tell each curious comer.

Yet, because I faint with love,
    You that see my swooning anguish—
Fly and find, abroad, above,
    Him for whom my soul doth languish !

               Chanson d'Amour.
                   (*Les Stalactites.*)

July, 1844.

A Boat-Song.

Et vogue la nacelle
Qui porte mes amours.

The waves on the lagoon
    Drowse and swoon ;
With breath that balm discumbers
    The zephyrs softly creep :
The ripple lulls our slumbers,
    Let us sleep !

THÉODORE DE BANVILLE

Sweet lips with melodies
  Swell the breeze,
The wind flings on their numbers
  Our kisses to the deep.
The ripple lulls our slumbers,
  Let us sleep !

In vain thy jealous lord,
  Spouse adored,
Each haunt of love encumbers ;
  This sheltered bower we keep.
The ripple lulls our slumbers,
  Let us sleep !

Ah ! while the starlight pale
  Neath her veil
Swathes us in faint penumbers
  Cling close to me and weep !
The ripple lulls our slumbers,
  Let us sleep !

What reck we if the night,
  Swift of flight,
With cloudy spindrift lumbers
  The elemental sweep !
The ripple lulls our slumbers,
  Let us sleep !

Chanson de Bateau.
(*Les Stalactites.*)

July, 1844.

The Blacksmiths.

With rhyme and chime of sounding hammer
Lo, how the smiths in song rejoice!
Rising towards the dawn their clamour
  Rings louder than the clarion's voice.

JOHN and JAMES.

See the bellowing flames that lighten
  Our foreheads by the north-wind tanned!
They glimmer through the haze and frighten
  The hungry ravens from the land.
Feast-day, fast-day, one with another,
  In fires of hell we toil and sing.

JAMES.

My brother John . . .

JOHN.

            And you my brother . . .

JAMES.

The bellows blow!

JOHN.

            The hammer swing!

JAMES.

Iron, rough as earth thy neighbour,
  In the hearth's black shadow thrown,
Ere the close of this day's labour
  On our anvil thrill and groan!

THÉODORE DE BANVILLE

JOHN.

Once obscure, through changes growing,
  Fate shall snatch thee, bright as Fame,
From the fiery furnace glowing
  In a shower of golden flame!

JAMES.

Thou shalt be the plough that burrows
  Deep in earth, whence smiling rise
Harvests fair that clothe the furrows,
  Hailed by light-winged butterflies!

JOHN.

Thou shalt be the fearless courser
  In whose flanks of flaming coal
Moves a spirit that murmurs hoarser
  Than the distant thunders roll!

JAMES.

Thou shalt be the sweeping sickle,
  Reaper of the ripened wheat
Like a living sea whose fickle
  Waves the wind doth bend and beat!

JOHN.

As the dawn from darkness rushes
  In the sun's resplendent flood,
Thou shalt be the blade that blushes
  With the crimson bloom of blood!

JAMES.

Now for justice thou descendest!
  Whether wrapped in gloom or gleam,
Sword or ploughshare, still thou blendest
  With the moving human stream!

THÉODORE DE BANVILLE

JOHN.

Thou dost wield the warrior's thunder!

JAMES.

Thou dost tear the bosom true
Of thy Mother Earth asunder!

JOHN.

Fighter thou!

JAMES.

And worker too!

Les Forgerons.
(*Les Exilés.*)

October, 1859.

The Nightingale.

See how the violets shimmer,
   With pearls of night bedewed,
Fresh drops that glance and glimmer!
   Hark! in the sombre wood
That shivers with her wings
The nightingale now sings!

O linger, half-revealing
   Thy naked charms so near:
Beneath thy window kneeling,
   Tell me thou holdest dear
Words whispered once or twice
Of yore in Paradise!

The moon unveils her splendour;
   The sea's vast bosom throbs:
The tuneful sea is tender,
   . And heaves with long-drawn sobs
Of fond desire and fear,
As I, when thou art near!

Nay, hush! Again thy lover
   Kneels near thee to adore
Those lids black lashes cover,
   Those lips that sigh once more!
O yesterday . . . those curls
My wanton touch unfurls!

O coronal! O caresses
   On locks of love forlorn!
Nymph of the golden tresses,
   Thou canst not be forsworn;
Lost angel now redeemed!—
'Twas madness! I have dreamed!

Le Rossignol.
(Améthystes.)

June, 1860.

A Starry Night.

Night throws a royal splendour
   Of diamonds on the dune.
   Her face, beneath the moon,
Like thine is pale and tender.

Thine eyes, O Sorceress! mingle
   Their heaven of cloudy hue
   With the unrelenting blue
That laves the Tyrrhene shingle.

A thousand roses blossom
Around her smiling bed,
Even as the wild-flowers shed
Their sweetness on thy bosom.

Thou knowest, O queen of wonder,
Enchanted, holy Night!
With what entranced affright
My soul is torn asunder.

O sapphire! veilless azure!
O calm! O ecstasy!
The sea is like the sky
And shines with starred emblazure.

Thy flowery lips unsealing,
To calm this wounded soul,
Breathe in a word : Be whole!
And in a kiss love's healing.

Nuit d'étoiles.

February, 1861.   (*Améthystes.*)

Herodias.

Her eyes are clear as Jordan's wave serene.
On dainty neck and ear droops pearly lustre ;
She seems more sweet than the grape's trellised cluster
And shames the wild-rose with her dusky mien.

She laughs and wantons like a scornful queen,
Baring the wondrous beauty of her bosom.
Her luscious lips are like a scarlet blossom,
And her white teeth outshine the lily's sheen.

Lo! now she comes, with charms voluptuous glowing!
A black page holds her robe of draperies flowing
That proudly sweep the floor in ample folds.

Sapphire and topaz flash and rubies ruddy
Flame on her hands : her golden charger holds
The head of John the Baptist, pale and bloody.

Hérodiade.

(*Les Princesses.*)

June, 1854.

•

Medea.

Medea, in whose heart love swells at height,
  Sings with the wave obscure ; and the swift river,
  In which her long look sees the starlight shiver,
Dimly reflects her naked beauty white.

Her wan charms spell the Phasis in its flight,
  And, as she sings, the wandering winds deliver
  Her voice, blent with the sound of lyres that quiver,
And spread her tresses like a stream of light.

Fixing her gaze on gloomy skies, aglimmer
With sanguine flame, she sings.   Her white limbs
    shimmer
Like snowy gleams athwart the dusky swards.

On sombre mountain-slopes she culls the tender
  And mystic herb whose sap fell poison hoards,
And on her bosom shines the moon's pale splendour.

Médée.

(*Les Princesses.*)

September, 1865.

Remembrance.

O Gautier! thou a sage among the sages
    With looks sublime and bland,
Even thou whose spirit lived in all the ages
    And dwelt in every land,

Thou wert a Greek indeed, now haply gazing
    With thine immortal eyes
On temples tall, harmonious profiles raising
    In pure blue gulfs of skies.

Of those soft sword-bearers thou wert the lover
    (Theirs more than sorrow's power)
For in thy dreams, whenas the sap boiled over
    Of all thy thought in flower,

Thou wert a bard, and now, to charm the leisure
    Of many stranger kings,
In heaven's high dwelling thy melodious measure
    Of swift Achilles sings.

Naught was unknown to thee.   His art unfolded
    Antique Polycletes;
And forms athletic by thy finger moulded
    The Dorian sculptor sees.

On the green swards, made glad with laughing daisies,
    Such as the Gods desire,
Theocritus now hears the herdsman's praises
    He taught thy child's clear lyre.

Loving, with Pindar, the serene dominions,
    Like fowlers loosing flight
Thou sendest forth thine Odes on eagle-pinions
    Towards the red sun's light.

And there, by Aristophanes, thou scoffest,
 With words for scourging-rods,
The impious and intolerable sophist,
 Vile scorner of the Gods.

* * * * * *

So while on earth, with tears more salt than sorrel,
 Sadly we make our moan,
Thou greetest, under wreaths of rose and laurel,
 Those once thy fellows known.

The craving of thy lips at last thou cloyest
 In feasts whereto they throng,
And, tasting things ambrosial, enjoyest
 Their converse sweet and long.

Round thee the sun makes warm with his caresses
 The laughing landscape wide,
And Helen, grave, with beautiful bright tresses,
 Sits smiling at thy side ;

She, of that chainless scourge the dreadful sender
 On kings and heroes old,
Radiant with beauty now and starry splendour
 Thou dost in heaven behold !

 Ressouvenir.
 (*Le Tombeau de Théophile Gautier.**)

November, 1872.

* Reprinted under the title *À Théophile Gautier* in the definitive edition of
les Exilés.

André Theuriet.

Born in Marly-le-Roi (Seine-et-Oise) 1833.

André Theuriet received his education in Bar-le-Duc, to which place his family belonged; and his youth was spent among the hills and woods of Western Lorraine. He afterwards studied for the law in Paris, but on taking his degree in 1857 his attention was turned to literature, and with this vocation in view he became a clerk in the offices of the Ministry of Finance. From that time his life has been almost entirely and unostentatiously devoted to letters. His long catalogue of work is composed of four volumes of verse, a multitude of novels and plays and innumerable contributions to periodical literature. He seems to have sacrificed poetry to romance, for he is better known as a novelist than as a poet.

Theuriet's first poetical effusion, *In Memoriam*, appeared in the *Revue des Deux Mondes* in 1857. *Le Chemin des Bois* was published in 1867 and crowned by the French Academy in 1868. *Le Bleu et le Noir* followed in 1873; then *le Livre de la Payse*; and the *Jardin d'automne* in 1894. As may be gathered from the titles of these volumes, André Theuriet is pre-eminently a poet of the country. He excels in the delineation of delicately-coloured scenes of rural life. His song is full of birds and flowers and the charms of idyllic love. To his delight in natural beauty he adds a contemplative melancholy which enhances the poetry of his simple pictures. The wind-swept *landes* and ruined towers of Brittany seem to have fascinated his fancy more than the ancestral fields and forests of fertile Lorraine. There is nothing of Parisian sensuality or disappointed cynicism in his healthy love of rustic enjoyment.

The poetical range of this bucolic bard is not a wide one. His latest volume of verse gives only a fuller and richer expression to the sentiment which inspired his youthful muse. In his prose tales, which have a large circle of readers, he displays the same tender and observant study of human character in humble life and dwells on the same exquisite descriptions of pastoral scenery, without intruding those voluptuous and violent elements which so many French novelists love to handle. Once or twice only has he allowed himself a little licence, but the author of *les Œillets de Kerlaz* needs no such meretricious accessories to relieve the unaffected freshness of his narrative talent.

The Song of the Willow-Weaver.

Willow wands, wicker bands,
Let your supple withies bend beneath the weaver's hands.

You shall be the cradle where the mother rocks her child,
  Soothed by lullabies of love that breathe some old
  refrain ;
Nestling in the frail couch, by happy dreams beguiled,
  When closing lips still white with milk he goes to sleep
  again,

Willow wands, wicker bands,
Let your supple withies bend beneath the weaver's hands.

You shall be the basket brimmed with berries ripe and red,
  Gathered by the girls that roam in copses clothed with
  fern ;
Fragrant on the fresh air a balmy breath is shed,
  When laughing to the homestead in the twilight they
  return.

Willow wands, wicker bands,
Let your supple withies bend beneath the weaver's hands.

You shall be the riddle in the buxom peasant's arms,
  Whence the barley beaten from the flail overflows,
While upon the threshing-floor the sparrows pounce in
  swarms,
  And skirmish for the golden grain she sprinkles as she
  goes.

ANDRÉ THEURIET

Willow wands, wicker bands,
Let your supple withies bend beneath the weaver's hands.

When the grapes in autumn grow purple on the vine,
  When the labourers on the slopes trail their weary
  limbs ;
You shall clasp with strong hoops the casks that burst
  with wine,
  Oozing through the reddened staves and bubbling at
  the brims.

Willow wands, wicker bands,
Let your supple withies bend beneath the weaver's hands.

You shall be the cage wherein the captive linnets sing,
  You shall be the treacherous weir, hidden in the reeds,
Where the nimble trout, as he darts from spring to spring,
  Prisoned in the sudden snare vainly writhes and bleeds.

Willow wands, wicker bands,
Let your supple withies bend beneath the weaver's hands.

You shall be the humble bier on which the weaver lies,
  When worn with age he falls and is laid at last to sleep,
Waiting for the grave, while the evening zephyr sighs
  Through willows on the river-bank that bend their
  heads and weep.

Willow wands, wicker bands,
Let your supple withies bend beneath the weaver's hands.

La Chanson du Vannier.
  (*Le Chemin des Bois.*)

The Kingfisher.

When from dewy dawn to night
Flames the dog-star's fiery light
  In a heaven of cloudless glow,
Let us haunt those hollow nooks
Where on rock-strown bed the brooks
  Under channelled arches flow.

There, in coverts cool as dusk,
Honeysuckle, thyme and musk
  Blossom in the fresh sweet air;
There, on green and azure wing,
Like an arrow from the string,
  Darts the glittering kingfisher.

Swift of flight he skims the stream,
Shines, and like a fading dream
  Lures the vision as he flies;
But his plume of purfled blue,
Bright with many a changing hue,
  Lingers in the dazzled eyes.

Le Martin-pêcheur: Chansons d'oiseaux.
(Jardin d'automne.)

On the Water.

The willows shiver. On the stream
The pale moon spreads her silvery beam,
  Blue gazing from the gulf of stars;
Beneath broad branches black as night
We glide along the waters, white
    With nenuphars. . . .

ANDRÉ THEURIET

The fresh cool dews of evening shed
Among the dense leaves overhead
   Melt, drop by drop, in mystic tears ;
Showered on the waves that thrill and throng
They seem to lull us with a song
      From heavenly spheres. . . .

O friends, the night serene and clear !
Laugh, yet so low we scarce can hear
   Your laughter . . . trembling lest it rouse
The sad reality of things
That in the shadow fold their wings
      And fain would drowse ! . . .

Sing ! . . . here beneath the weeping skies,
Heedless of time, with half-closed eyes,
   My thought shall flow while flows the stream,
Even as a nurse, of rest beguiled,
Fondles and soothes her weary child
      To sleep . . . and dream. . . .

Promenade sur l'eau: Paysages d'autrefois.
                (Jardin d'automne.)

Armand Silvestre.

Born in Paris, 1837.

Paul-Armand Silvestre (known also in letters as Paul Forestier) was a pupil of the *École polytechnique* in Paris, and found employment, like André Theuriet, in the offices of the Ministry of Finance. He began his literary career as a poet under the wing of the Parnassian group. His first poems were published with a commendatory preface by George Sand, and he thereupon took a prominent place among the lyrical writers of his day. The verse was rich in ideas and imagery, harmoniously moulded, and furnished from a wide knowledge of classical, legendary and mythological lore. Several collections of verse followed at intervals; notably *la Chanson des Heures* (new and enlarged edition in 1887) *les Ailes d'or* (1880) *le Pays des Roses* (1883) *le Chemin des Étoiles* (1885) *Roses d'octobre* (1890) and *l'Or des Couchants* (1892). Silvestre's models are Gautier, Banville and Baudelaire, but he has a highly-coloured voluptuous style of his own.

The turning-point in Armand Silvestre's literary life was his accession to the *Gil Blas* in 1880. Without forsaking altogether the higher walks of literature he essayed a resurrection of Rabelais in his coarser and broader vein, and revelled in that species of pleasantry which is so well characterised as *gauloiserie*. In *les Malheurs du commandant Laripète, les Farces de mon ami Jacques, Contes pantagruéliques et galants, Contes grassouillets* and *Nouvelles gaudrioles* he gave free scope to his libertine fancy and riotous humour, often lightened up with flashes of real learning and wit, and interlarded with charming descriptive passages which are worthy of a more refined environment. Silvestre has not carried this wanton gaiety into his verse, and the excellent poet of *Golden Wings* and *Starry Ways* will always find readers willing to forget the frolics of his earthy Muse.

Armand Silvestre has written a number of robust plays and *libretti*; among the latter being *Dimitri* for Victorin Joncières and *Henry VIII* for Camille Saint-Saëns. Musicians have always admired his verses because their graceful cadence lends itself so naturally to modulation and melody. He is also an eloquent orator and knows how to infuse an almost lyrical emotion into his vivid and virile speech. According to Paul Verlaine he is one of the few who have succeeded in untying the Gordian knot, that is to be a lyrical poet and live by the profession. It is not unlikely, however, that Silvestre owes his good fortune rather to Momus than to Erato.

To One by the Sea.

Lo! the new season on the meadow flings
   Her robe of purple, hyacinth and blue,
Pure in her nakedness, with sprouting wings
   That on the air a breath of jasmine strew.

She leaves a joyful furrow where she leaps;
   A sound of kisses springs beneath her tread:
Round her the broken bonds of heavy sleeps
   In the freed æther float like silken thread.

Endless enchantment, ecstasies of birth!
   On mount, in meadow, and on bosky bank
Of the blue rivers, everywhere the earth
   Feels living germs pierce through her quickened
   flank.

Hard by the barren sea, the sea whose breast
   Bears scentless flowers and trees of bitter leaf,
Thou dwellst alone, while, with the sea's unrest,
   My heart rolls at thy feet an endless grief!

À Celle qui est au bord de la Mer: IV.
(Les Ailes d'or.)

Why should I weep?

Ah! since thy loveliness brings hither
  The beauties lost in time's eclipse,
Why should I weep if roses wither?—
  Their purple laughs upon thy lips.

Since all the splendours shame doth banish
  Sole in thy splendour weave their spells,
Why should I weep if lilies vanish?—
  Their whiteness on thy forehead dwells.

Since in thy being love rekindles
  The flame that fades from evening skies,
Why should I weep if sunlight dwindles?—
  Its beam sheds brightness from thine eyes.

And since thy living soul incloses
  The soul of every dead delight,
Why should I weep for stars or roses?—
  Thou art my fragrance and my light!

                Q'importe?: *Vers pour être chantés.*
                        (*Les Ailes d'or.*)

Judith.

Her sweet and fatal name of fear and wonder
  Now like warm wine fills me with wild desires,
  Now chills me and my echoing heart inspires
With far-off terrors of the Almighty's thunder.

Breathed in vast heaven her name awakes there-
      under
  Jehovah's eagle, winged with vengeful fires,
  And in my troubled soul evokes the choirs
Of antique myths Christ smote and clove asunder.

207

I see her, flushed as if from fierce caresses,
Rise up and shake the darkness of her tresses
  Beneath the waning starlight clear and pale.

Grim as a sheeted ghost the grave delivers,
  I see her stoop and swathe in the red veil
With Holophernes' head my heart that quivers.

                Judith: Les Visions.
                  (*Le Chemin des Étoiles.*)

Sonnet.

Flowerage of lilies opening to the Dawn
  On the pale edge of Heaven's great garden-close,
  Ye whom the keen wheel of Aurora mows
Beneath her car by ruddy coursers drawn ;

Snow, whose clear ermine mantle, cold and wan,
  On granite flank of the vast mountain flows ;
  Jasmines, sweet silvery bells aswing when blows
The wind of April brushing the soft lawn ;

Pearl, whereof Venus from the foamy crest
Fashioned the milky drop that gemmed her breast,
  When cruel love forsook the sobbing sea ;

Marble, pure glory of the Parian isle,
Wherein the radiant shapes of heroes smile :
  Lo ! all your whiteness is less white than She.

              Sonnets à l'Amie: VI.
               (*Roses d'octobre.*)

A Spring Thought.

Lo! the new Year a fresh green raiment wears.
  Undulant as the light wave fringed with foam
  A misty veil floats on the emerald loam,
Fulfilling with white dreams our black despairs.
—Lo! the new Year a fresh green raiment wears.

The subtile blood of flowers throbs through the earth;
  The sweet soul of the flowers is tired of sleep,
  And in a vermeil kiss the soft skies weep,
Weaving the spell of mystical rebirth.
—The subtile blood of flowers throbs through the earth.

Glad sunlight sparkles in the clear-eyed stream
  Whose icy lid now melts to the warm breeze;
  Through tender wreathings of the lithe young trees
A thrill of verdure shoots with delicate gleam.
—Glad sunlight sparkles in the clear-eyed stream.

Smile, clear-eyed stream! Smile, rosy-blossomed lips!
  Spring, in her puissant and gracile flight,
  Sweeps with sole stroke of wing from heaven's height
Like breath accurst the shadow of day's eclipse.
—Smile, clear-eyed stream! Smile, rosy-blossomed lips!

Pensée de printemps: Paysages et Fleurs.
(Roses d'octobre.)

Nature's Reflections.

Soft on thy dusky tresses dwell
   The shadows of the twilight sphere,
A sheen, as of the pearly shell,
   Shines in the hollows of thine ear.

The lily smooths thy velvet brow,
   And on thy lips pale roses spring ;
So heaven each beauty doth endow
   With colour of some lovely thing.

Yet is there none like to thine eyes.
   They seem to mingle, glad or grave,
The changing hue of wondrous skies
   Divinely mirrored in the wave.

Each charm of thine its colour wears
   And weaves for me a spell supreme . . .
But O thine eyes, say what is theirs?
   —The colour of my dearest Dream.

Rimes légères. II.
(Roses d'octobre.)

Léon Dierx.

Born in the Island of Réunion, 1838.

Baudelaire has defined the literary character of the Creole. 'No originality, no power of conception or ex-'pression . . . women's souls, whose genius is on a level 'with their fragility and gracility of form, their velvety 'eyes that gaze without scrutinising, and their singularly 'narrow foreheads, unfriendly to labour and thought'. Leconte de Lisle was, as Baudelaire confessed, a brilliant exception to this rule ; Léon Dierx is another, though in considerably lesser degree.

Léon Dierx celebrated his literary apprenticeship by the publication of some light verse and threw in his lot with the Parnassian group of singers. Under the influence of Leconte de Lisle, his poetry thenceforth took a more solid and sober form. He has not been a voluminous writer. His first volume of *Poèmes et Poésies* (1864) contains several fine versions of Hebrew, Egyptian and Celtic legends, handled after the fashion of his great compatriot. The same vein is worked in *les Lèvres closes* (1868) but in one or two of the poems, particularly in *Lazare*, he sounds a deeper and more individual note. This volume closes with the *Chorus of the Last Men*, not unlike one of Campbell's poems in conception, but much more elaborately wrought out. And Dierx has neither the Northern poet's firm faith nor the touch of pathos which vibrates in these fine verses from *The Last Man* :—

211

'For all those trophied arts
'And triumphs that beneath thee sprang,
'Healed not a passion or a pang
'Entailed on human hearts'.

Léon Dierx supplies the want of emotion with sonorous rhymes and splendid imagery. Although his verse is modelled on that of Leconte de Lisle, he fails to achieve the firm outline and luminous colouring of the master. The peculiar characteristic which he has best reflected is a mood of melancholy discontent, alike in the contemplation of mankind and of external nature, but a certain voluptuous element of his own always wells up, and he often displays the capriciousness of a *dilettante*. He is apt to repeat his ideas and surcharge his images when he ventures on a longer flight than he is accustomed to.

In *les Amants* (1879) the tone becomes lighter again, but there is little or no lyrical buoyancy. The poet, in returning to his early love, seems to have been conscious of the effort with which he sustained the weight of his more imitative manner. He has never paralleled the perfection of *Lazare*.

In private life Léon Dierx has the reputation of a sober and restrained talker. He lives out of the whirl of Parisian literary and social life, is a pronounced republican in politics, and occupies a post in the Ministry of Public Education. He is a great friend of painters and has himself essayed their art with some success. He has also tried the drama in his *dilettante* fashion. *La Rencontre*, a short theatrical scene with two characters only—a couple of old lovers who meet again by chance at a nocturnal festival *al fresco* and who finally take leave of each other in a colloquy of elegant rhyme—was privately represented in 1875. There are some admirable lines in this play, but neither the dialogue nor the climax is dramatic.

Lazarus.

When Jesus called him, Lazarus awoke ;
  Livid, he rose erect in the cold gloom ;
  Then, shivering in the vestments of the tomb,
Fared forth, grave and alone, nor turned nor spoke.

Alone and grave thenceforth, without a word,
  He walked like one that seeks and cannot find,
  Stumbling at every step, as he were blind,
Against the things of life and earth's vile herd.

Beneath his forehead, shining deathly pale,
  No lightnings flamed from glassy eyeballs dim ;
  Even yet the eternal splendours haunted him
As though he dared not look beyond the veil.

Frail as a child and with a madman's stare
  He went.   The crowd recoiled when he drew nigh.
  None cared to question him, slow passing by
Like one that stifles in unwholesome air.

To him the murmur of dull things below
  Was vain.   Engulfed in his ineffable dream ;
  Beneath that awful secret he did seem
Aghast, in silence wandering to and fro.

Sometimes he shuddered in his cold eclipse,
  And half stretched forth his hand, as speech would
    come,
  But still the unknown word of yore was dumb,
Hushed by a viewless finger on his lips.

Then young and old in Bethany feared this man
  And fled from him.   He passed alone and grave.
  And in their veins the blood, even of the brave,
Ran cold before his visage vague and wan.

Ah! who can tell thy torment and strange pains,
  Risen from the grave, where all the world finds rest,
  To live again and trail on paths unblest
The shroud girded like sackcloth on thy reins!

Phantasmal semblance of the man that died!
  Couldst thou endure anew life's change and chance,
  O thou, doomed to bring back in speechless trance
The knowledge to a hungering world denied?

Scarce had Death yielded to the light her spoil,
  When shadow swathed thee, a mysterious ghost
  That calmly moved athwart the human host,
Knowing no more its joy, its grief, its toil.

Thy second life, passionless and profound,
  Hath left to men a memory, not a trace,
  Didst thou regain at last, in Death's embrace,
Those azure deeps that ever wrapt thee round?

How oft, when shadows filled the heavenly space,
  With tall form reared against the golden sky,
  With arms towards the Eternal raised on high,
Thou didst implore the lingering angel's grace;

How oft, thou, wandering where the rank grass grows,
  Grave and alone, in dwellings of the dead,
  Didst envy those that, on their stony bed
Once laid, should wake no more from deep repose!

Lazare.
(*Les Lèvres closes.*)

Funeral March.

(*Chorus of the Last Men.*)

The time draws nigh, foretold by ancient sages!
 The days of universal terror come!
Grown denser hour by hour the shades of ages
 Lengthen on fear-crushed brows and lips struck
 dumb.

Our days are lives of agonies and spasms!
 No more with a new dawn the East is crowned;
Like the black bronze that shuts sepulchral chasms
 The resonant soil sends forth a mournful sound.

Gross darkness round us folds her heavy curtain.
 Forlorn of look or word the skies lie furled.
Last sons of Cain! the doom of things is certain,
 Death comes for all time into the dead world.

Beneath the quenched stars and the wan sun's
 burden
 Funereal night winds her shroud wide and deep:
In Earth's cold bosom lies the sower's guerdon,
 Her turn has come to seek the eternal sleep.

Now the last gods lie dead and no laws bind us,
 Our prayers are hushed, our heroes are no more;
No hope before us shines: no light behind us
 Shall bring to birth again the dreams of yore.

Wide o'er the universe Death spreads his pinion.
 The chill hard ground rings hollow to our tread.
We vaunt not now the days of pride's dominion,
 In these, as in our veins, the sap is dead.

Men! gaze on us, in hideous ruin cowering;
    O beams that shone clear in our fathers' sight!
Our cavernous orbs, with grief and horror lowering,
    From dead to dying things turn their dull light.

O Love, thou charming phantom, earth's consoler,
    Love, whose delights deluded ages sung,
Thou hauntest not these twilights pale and polar,
    Die, ancient ghost, inspired with lying tongue!

Our tears are dry, our veins are bloodless courses,
    Our laughter douts thy fatal torch with spume;
If ever man's heart throbbed beneath thy forces,
    O Love, our empty souls are now thy tomb!

No praise, no prayer, in temples swells the chorus;
    And, even as Love, Pleasure her slave lies dead.
No light glows in the heavens, no hope before us:
    Let our wild laughter fill the gloom with dread!

Where is the pride of yore, O race that slumbers?
    Erst on your brows it cast a flaming light.
Pride struck the Gods down, reckless of their numbers,
    And died in glory, yearning for the fight.

By the last glimmering of our fires, like cattle
    That cringe with terror, huddling in vile herd,
We crouch; our limbs are shrunk, our dry bones
        rattle,
    And scarce with pulse of life our hearts are stirred.

Does any clutch for gold with shrivelled fingers?
    Or shiver in his flesh with shamed desire?
No, in our wasted souls no longing lingers,
    Nor lightens from our looks one glimpse of fire.

LÉON DIERX

Flush of crime's fever, thirst of blood fraternal,
  At least ye spoke of vigour in the strife ;
Evil, that lured man's heart with charms infernal,
  Haply with courage starred the gulf of life.

But strength and courage died in us with evil,
  No leaven in our hearts the vices own.
Triumphing o'er our souls the beast primeval
  Moans on the verge of the imminent unknown.

Honour ! who follows thee, who hears thy clarion,
  Or feels thy ferment raise his fury blind ?
Thy creeds beneath our dunghills rot like carrion.
  The phantom Reason sleeps, time out of mind.

No knell echoes in graveyards lone and hoary.
  Soundless oblivion gulfs the gods of Fame.
Who mourns them ? who remembers them, O Glory ?
  Yet none like them worshipped thy lying name.

Thou, Sun that ripened Youth, crowned Beauty's
    tresses,
  Made the woods sing and Care with laughter led,
Save for thy dismal glare and dark caresses
  We have not known thee, Sun of centuries dead !

    *   *   *   *   *   *

And thou whose beauty filled the dawn with wonder,
  Daughter of light, lover of things sublime,
Whose towering forests thrilled with tuneful thunder
  And breathed green fragrance to heaven's golden
    prime ;

217

Earth, that lies fated with man's doom to dwindle ;
Void, voiceless, ghastly as a naked skull,
Turn to thy sun again and haply kindle
New beauty at his fire, waxed cold and dull !

But may thy globe impure on his be shattered
And broadcast spill our countless bones, O world !
Lest some new earth receive their germins scattered,
Crush them, in one vast crater's ruin hurled !

Marche funèbre: Chœur des derniers Hommes.
(Les Lèvres closes.)

Villiers de l'Isle-Adam.

Born in Saint-Brieuc, 1838 . . . Died in Paris, 1889.

The glories of our birth and state
Are shadows, not substantial things.

Max Nordau, in his notable study of *Degenerescence*, has revived against the author of *Axël* the charge that he had no title to the ancient earldom of Villiers de l'Isle-Adam, the birthright of a family whose achievements are interwoven with the romance of French history as those of the family of Douglas with Scottish history. No reader of the admirable biography of the poet published by the late vicomte Robert du Pontavice de Heussey can harbour a shadow of doubt that the poet's claim to this dignity was entirely authentic. Philippe-Auguste-Mathias de Villiers de l'Isle-Adam was the son of the marquis Joseph de Villiers de l'Isle-Adam and his wife Marie-Françoise Le Nepveu de Carfort, who represented another old Breton family.

When the famous grandmaster of the Order of Malta, Philippe de Villiers de l'Isle-Adam, set out to defend Rhodes against Sultan Soliman in 1521, he left behind him not only the allegiance of an army of vassals but the revenues of a vast estate in the *Ile-de-France*. Very different was the inheritance of his poetic descendant in hapless quest of fame and fortune. The marquis Joseph had ruined himself in searching for the hidden treasures of a family tradition, amongst other fantastic speculations. The heir to this ideal wealth began in early youth to plan great romances and dramas, and so much did his parents believe in his vocation that they sold at some sacrifice their small estate, with its ruined keep, and removed to Paris.

At twenty years of age, his pocket bulging with manuscripts and his brain full of visions, the young Count burst on the circle of the Parnassians in Paris and was welcomed by Catulle Mendès, Glatigny, Coppée, Alphonse Daudet and the band of youthful men of letters who essayed to keep alive the lingering traditions of the Romantic epoch during Victor Hugo's exile. Though certainly endowed with genius, Villiers de l'Isle-Adam was eminently unfitted by temperament and training for the conditions of civilised life. Almost the only happy period of his literary existence was the beginning of his career in Paris, when he was comparatively free from the cares of daily subsistence, encouraged by some of the best men of the time and sustained by the blind faith and affection of his kindred. He was an excellent singer and pianoforte-player, and enlivened the *cénacle* with his skill, but it was not in his nature to follow any regular employment. If he had a brief access of activity, and devoted himself to literary toil, it was broken by a sudden plunge into debauchery and idleness, followed by remorse and unavailing revolt against the degradation of his genius. Neither ambition, nor self-interest, nor a sense of duty, nor the need of independence could teach him the value of time and opportunity. His parents lived in extreme poverty, and on the death of an aged aunt who helped them with her annuity they were reduced to the direst distress. From that time forth to the day of his tragic death the poet's life was one long sordid struggle with misery. Not even the pride of race interposed to save him, and he gradually assumed the very look and gait of a vagabond of the lowest class. 'This much is good in journalism', wrote Théophile Gautier, 'that it mixes you with the crowd, 'humanises you by perpetually giving you your own 'measure and preserves you from the infatuations of 'solitary pride'. Villiers would have done better to accept the veriest drudgery of daylong journalism, if only to learn the lessons of discipline and steady diligence. Every pittance earned in such a way would have had its value. . . . 'If this is not glory, at least it is bread and butter' said Rameau's dissolute nephew to Diderot. Villiers succumbed to the foul atmosphere of Paris, from which his only escape was an occasional visit to Switzerland or Germany to see Richard Wagner, for whose music he had an unbounded admiration.

Villiers had a first and last glimpse of good-fortune in 1888. He made a lucrative lecturing engagement in Brussels, his books at last began to command a sale, and he was being sought after by publishers. But while he was trying to gain a little relief from the fatigues of Paris at Nogent-sur-Marne a cruel cancerous disease suddenly declared itself in his ravaged constitution. He was taken into the retreat of the *frères de Saint-Jean de Dieu* in *rue Oudinot*, and in this charitable refuge he ended his wretched and wasted life, comforted by the friendship of two poets who had been peculiarly kind to him—Stéphane Mallarmé and Léon Dierx. On his deathbed he married a widow of humble estate, absolutely destitute of education, with whom he had lived for many years, and who had consoled his sorrows with a constant affection. Their son, Victor de Villiers de l'Isle-Adam, if he still lives, is the sole inheritor of an ancient name and of the degraded glory of a great race. The marquis Joseph and his wife, who had vainly sacrificed everything for the poet, died in 1883.

The character of Villiers de l'Isle-Adam was full of contradictions. His youth overflowed with robust gaiety and cheerfulness. He had abundant energy without the capacity for sustained effort. Although a shrewd observer of human frailties he was credulous to an extraordinary degree when his enthusiasm was awakened. His manhood was deeply tinged with that cynical bitterness which so easily surges up in the disappointed Celt. Throughout his whole life he remained an ardent Catholic, but he was deeply versed in occult lore and metaphysical philosophy. Villiers was always a most careful writer, his disordered life notwithstanding. He weighed and reweighed his sentences with the scruple of a real artist. He refused to prostitute his pen for a price, even in the days of his deepest poverty.

His first volume of poems, published, when he was little more than twenty years old, by Scheuring of Lyons, is one of the most remarkable ever written by so young a poet. There is quite a masterly case in the versification, and at times the true touch of pathos. Had the promise of these poems been fulfilled there is little doubt that Villiers would have taken his place among the foremost French poets of this century.

Much of his prose is spoiled by a flippant cynicism which should perhaps be attributed in some measure to the pernicious personal influence of Baudelaire during the early years of the Breton poet's life in Paris. But he has passages of the highest sublimity and beauty, some of them not surpassed by the masters of impassioned prose. His *Contes cruels* and *Histoires insolites* are collections of short stories, some frivolous and satirical, others full of poetical charm, with a vague groundswell of mysticism. In *Tribulat Bonhomet* he has delineated one of the types of the time, the self-seeking and purely practical man. *L'Ève future* is a pseudo-psychological romance inspired by the experiments of Edison in physical science, and suffused with a strange and disquieting irony. *Morgane* and *Axël*, superb prose poems in dramatic form, are too discursive and too transcendental for successful representation on the stage. The great name of Shakespeare has been pronounced by some French admirers of these dramas, but, in spite of the flashes of pure poetry which lighten them up, there is nothing in their artificial passion and elaborate declamation to justify such a comparison. *Axël*, his finest drama, was produced in Paris after the poet's death, but it failed to impress the Parisian public, although the literary beauty of the dialogue did not escape the perception of discerning critics. A later performance of *Elën*—a moral tragedy which may be described as an idealised version of *George Barnwell*—was greeted with general indifference and occasional laughter. These are but a small portion of the extensive dramatic, historical and metaphysical writings of Villiers. It is much to be regretted that in his effort to accomplish great things he neglected the vein of genuine lyrical poetry which was in him.

Villiers de l'Isle-Adam was 'a grandiose mystifier', says Jules Lemaître, who loves to dismiss with an epithet the writers with whom he is not in sympathy. In this case the epithet is just, but Villiers was more than that; he was a true singer, he had the supreme gift of imagination, and he was a subtle if often capricious and erratic thinker.

Discouragement.

Athwart the unclean ages whirled
　To solitary woods sublime,
Oh! had I first beheld this world
　Alone and free in Nature's prime!

When on its loveliness first seen
　Eve cast her pure blue eyes abroad ;
When all the earth was fresh and green,
　And simple Man believed in God!

When sacred accents, vibrating
　Beneath the naked sun and sky,
Rose from each new-created thing
　To hail the Lord of Life on high ;

I would have learned and lived in hope
　And loved! For, in those vanished days,
Faith wandered on the mountain-slope . . .
　But now the world has changed her ways.

Our feet, less free, less fugitive,
　Tread beaten tracks from shore to shore . . .
Alas! what is the life we live?
　—A dream of days that are no more!

Découragement: Les Préludes.
　　　　(*Premières Poésies.*)

Twilight Witchery.

Night on the great mystery showers
   Jewels from her cloud-veiled eye :   .
On the earth are many flowers,
   Many stars are in the sky.

Many a light, through sleeping shadow,
   Sparkles on the dusky bar,
Now from flowers that charm the meadow,
   Now from many a charming star.

But my night, with sombre bosom,
   Knows for charm, for light above,
One sole star and one sole blossom :
   There your beauty, here my love!

                    Éblouissement.
                        (*Poésies.*)

The Gifts.

If thou dost seek to soothe, at vesper,
   My heart that broods on secret wrong,
To move thy pities I will whisper
   The burden of some antique song.

If thou, to share my grief, dost lull thee
   With hopes deceived and dreams untrue,
For simple answer I will cull thee
   A sheaf of roses starred with dew.

If, like the flower that blooms to brighten
  The grave and death's dark exile loves,
Thy lips my soul's remorse would lighten . . .
  For offering I will bring thee doves.

Les Présents.
(Poésies.)

Confession.

Since I have lost the woods, the flower
  Of youth and the fresh April breeze . . .
Give me thy lips; their perfumed dower
  Shall be the whisper of the trees!

Since I have lost the deep sea's sadness,
  Her sobs, her restless surge, her graves . . .
Breathe but a word; its grief or gladness
  Shall be the murmur of the waves!

Since in my soul a sombre blossom
  Broods, and the suns of yore take flight . . .
O hide me in thy pallid bosom,
  And it shall be the calm of night!

L'Aveu.
(Poésies.)

Albert Glatigny.

Born in Lillebonne (Lower Normandy) 1839 * . . . Died in Sèvres, 1873.

Life's . . . a poor player.

Albert Glatigny is one of the inheritors of unfulfilled renown. 'If you like antithesis'—says Théodore de Banville—'here is one. This poor comedian, prompter ' at need, who played parts of twenty lines in vaudevilles, ' and because of his lank stature, like a dishevelled reed, ' took silent parts such as those of king and giant in ' melodrama ; this dreamer, who lodged in a garret and ' was clothed in a coat as thin as paper ; this reciter of ' nothings belonged to the aristocracy of intellect and in ' a special science of superior kind was in himself more ' learned and more accomplished than a whole Academy '.

Lillebonne is a small town with Roman remains and a Norman castle. Albert Glatigny's mother was a peasant girl. His father had been a carpenter by trade and became the village policeman. They were married when the husband was twenty-one and the wife eighteen years old. The first-fruit of this humble union was a poet. Apprenticed in early youth to a letterpress-printer in Pont-Audemer he ran away to join a company of strolling players which had passed through the place.

* The published *Extrait de naissance* of Ernest-Albert Glatigny, born at Lillebonne in 1843, must relate to some other person of the same surname. The letters of invitation to the poet's funeral give his name as Albert-Joseph-Alexandre and his age as thirty-four. The surname Glatigny is a not uncommon one in Normandy.

Glatigny's poetical education began with a volume of Ronsard's verse which he found in his father's house. A copy of Banville's *Odes funambulesques* fell into his hands at Alençon and completed the initiation. His natural aptitude was such that he blossomed all at once into a lyric artist. He had no other talent and never learned any other trade. At verse he laboured day and night ; whether he walked or drove or rested his thoughts were always shaping themselves into poetry and weaving romances. Neither cold nor hunger nor illness nor disappointment— and he knew them all—could freeze the genial current of his soul. Hence, as he modestly sang,

> These rhymes made in my wanderings
>> By chance or choice throughout the land,
> As one drinks water from the springs
>> In the warm hollow of his hand.

Glatigny came to Paris at seventeen or eighteen, became acquainted with Baudelaire, and published *les Vignes folles*, a book of exquisite verse. The poet's life in Paris was a poor one. He earned two francs a night as Third Senator in Alfred de Vigny's version of *Othello*, and furnished impromptu verse on rhymes proposed by the audience at the *Alcazar* or some other *café-chantant* on the boulevards. He was always famished and never sufficiently clad. It seems ironical to say that this poor comedian was as generous as a prince when he had anything, but it is true nevertheless. He toiled diligently for his wretched subsistence and from time to time travelled through the pleasant land of France with ambulant companies of play-actors.

During the Franco-German war Glatigny returned to his native village. His health was broken and his poverty pitiable. In 1871 he married Emma Dennie, a young girl of American parentage and French education who was also a fugitive from Paris, and who, like the poet, was a victim to consumption. Her resources were slender, but they sufficed to keep the humble household until Glatigny could earn something by means of his pen. He practised his art sedulously, and contributed political pasquinades and poems to Parisian newspapers. Then he was fortunate in getting a one-act piece played at the *Odéon*. It was *le Bois*, a jewel of poesy and fancy. His collected poems were published by Lemerre, and one of his dramas was accepted and produced in some provincial theatre. He gained the encouragement of several literary celebrities in Paris; he had sent a clever comedy, *l'Illustre Brizacier*, to the *Odéon*; and he was meditating a translation of *Cymbeline* when his health gave way. During a visit to Corsica in 1869 an officious gendarme had arrested this harmless Bohemian in the belief that he was a notorious brigand under ban of outlawry for the assassination of a magistrate. Glatigny, bound hand and foot, was thrown into a noisome dungeon infested with rats and mice and such small deer. He lay there for a week, riddled with cold and hunger, and came out crippled by rheumatism, covered with sores and almost deprived of sight. His constitution, feeble at the best, never recovered from this calamity; but the letters written during his illness are full of courage and have a note of gaiety which is pathetic. He went to Bayonne in hopes of a cure and returned to Paris only to die. A few months later his wife, who had been his good angel, followed him to the grave.

Albert Glatigny is now recognised as one of the purest and truest poets of his time in France. He was a disciple but by no means a slavish imitator of Banville, and was influenced also by Victor Hugo and Leconte de Lisle. Free from affectation, devoid of pedantry, full of fresh images and fine touches of feeling, his verse has a beauty of form and an unforced felicity which is remarkable in view of his opportunities. It is true that he laboured like an artist and that the most perfect work is that which shews the least trace of toilsome effort.

Glatigny had his brief hour of posthumous glory in the enthusiasm of some young actors who hired a room in the *faubourg Saint-Honoré*, hastily fitted it up with poor scenery and in presence of some of the choicest spirits of Paris played *l'Illustre Brizacier*, which had been refused at the *Odéon*. Such a homage in his lifetime would have been a godsend to Glatigny, for he was a man of the simplest character and his ambition was easily satisfied.

The proper epitaph for this most amiable of poets has been provided by the kindliest of critics. 'This poor 'devil'—says Anatole France—'had a good and great heart'.

Wild Vines.

Wild vines, cling close! Climb round the monument!
 Ye cannot climb too high, for even a child
May pass beneath the porch, with shoulders bent.

 Fane built too low to fear the storm-winds wild!
The pilgrim scans thy height from base to crown,
 Nor turns on thee again his glance beguiled.

And yet, ye Vines, in wanton tendrils grown,
 Climb, and with leaves enwreathe those pillars frail
Whose frieze records the names of starred renown.

 Not mine on Parian marbles to prevail;
But clay disdained of potter's hand I chose
 And wrought therein with fingers weak and pale.

I planted near the threshold a wild-rose,
 And, where the pathway winds, its fragrance shed
Is borne abroad by every breeze that blows;

 Some jasmines, also, mixed with amaranths red,
When the June sun, O Vines, appears at last,
 Their radiant colours with your leaves shall wed!

With tears a Naiad sprinkled as she passed
 Your tendrils light, that climbing seek the sun,
And pale charms in the crystal streamlet cast.

231

This is the secret lodge whence my thoughts run
In ode and song, if supple art aright
   With cadenced phrase the imperious web hath spun.

There, in the faint mysterious evening light,
   They preen their wings, like youthful seraphim,
Soon to unfurl them for victorious flight.

   And now, with the green dragon-flies that skim
And ràze the restless surface of the streams,
   They fly, perchance to dwell in regions dim.

O sobs and smiles! Children of loves and dreams!
   Where shall the wild winds waft you, O my heart?
For you what island glooms, what pleasaunce gleams?

   See! See! In swarming myriads they depart;
Cherish them, Spring, thou god of woods grown green,
   Thou that with singing rills so charmëd art!

Lo, the bold pilgrims soar to lands unseen!
   Alas! how few shall scape the stormy swell,
How few behold the heavenly shore serene!

   Yet shall no fears their fiery courage quell;
For ever floats before them, even as now,
   The infinite wonder of the luminous spell.

Thus flown so far, Muse of the lofty brow,
   With passionless face and form of fluctuant lines,
Goddess before whose sovran grace I bow,

   Let me regain my roof, clothed with wild vines!

Les Vignes folles.
(*Les Vignes folles.*)

Roses and Wine.

*Versons ces roses en ce vin
En ce bon vin versons ces roses. . . .*

Thrice-sacred Rose, lover of Venus' shrine,
Where trembling I adore her blood divine!

O Wine! how purple glows thy gushing liquor,
Imprisoned sun, with magic flames that flicker!

O Rose! Spring breathes of thee, her blossomed queen,
On thy tall stalk the shady swards between;

My lips in thy clear wave the Mænad presses,
O Wine! sprinkler of rubies on her tresses;

Thou bringest back the hopes of youth that sung,
Swathed in the fragrance from thy censers flung;

Thou givest courage, swayed with kindly forces,
The soul of one divine swells in thy sources!

For thee the nightingale, that shuns the light,
In sombre woodland swoons with love each night;

Angel! thy ruddy flagon is the giver
Of Joy and dead Beliefs that live for ever;

Thee, to refresh their unappeased desire,
The zephyrs kiss at dawn with lips of fire;

Thy hoary clusters, curled in leaves that crinkle,
Our thirsty lips with tears exuberant sprinkle;

233

The dawn, thy lovely petals to bestrew,
Turns into myriad diamond-drops the dew ;

Lyæus calls us, and the dusky leopards
Dance with the solitudes and listening shepherds ;

O Rose ! thou radiant chalice, the red wine
Tinges thy leaves delicious and divine ;

O Wine ! the light thy crystal cup encloses
Blooms with the delicate blushing of the roses.

Wed your bright hues, your blessëd perfumes wed,
O Rose and Wine, now pain and grief lie dead ;

With nuptial song, in love supreme and splendid,
O flood ! O foliage ! sense and soul are blended !

Les Roses et le Vin.
(*Les Vignes folles.*)

In the Arbour.

Green is the arbour, clothed with clematis,
   That braves the golden arrows of the sun.
Tell me that on the morrow such a kiss
   Shall yield me love again, O dearest one !

Thine eyes are blue, but in the light thereof
   There seems a change, their look is dim and cold.
Yet, though thou liest, speak to me of love,
   My heart is sad and fain would be consoled.

Sous la Tonnelle.
(*Les Flèches d'or.*)

The Night is Come.

The night is come : like moonbeams clear and bland
  Those charming eyes beneath long lashes gleam ;
  The air is delicate ; how sweet to dream
Along the sea-shore, on the soft sea-sand.

A song arises, with my heart in tune,
  A song of love thy soul exhales and breathes ;
  Sad and so sweet, towards the sky where wreaths
Of flame would seem to melt in languorous swoon.

The sea is there.   Her waves, with silvery crest,
  Lisp, soft and low, words tender as our own ;
  Here, seated at thy knees, we two alone,
Thy two hands held in mine lie sweetly pressed.

Speak no more, dream no more, but let the long
  Hours pass, and every glimmering star shine pale ;
  The wind is cool to-night, draw down thy veil ;
I feel thy bosom's tremulous pulses throng.

             Voici le Soir.
              · (*Les Flèches d'or.*)

A Winter Walk.

Her garb of snow not yet does winter wear ;
  A thin chill cloud sails shivering overhead.
The distant summit cleaves, with ridges bare,
  A dense sky looming dull and gray as lead.

A yellow leaf floats slowly through the air,
  Like a strange butterfly with wings outspread ;
As on the lone black pathway forth I fare
  The ground rings hard and clear beneath my tread.

The church, more distant, rears its pointed tower,
   Crowned with a creaking old iron weathercock
That long has borne the brunt of storm and shower.

   By this same footpath, climbing on the rock
To the poor belfry, once in summer mood
We went to pluck wild strawberries in the wood.

Menneval.
(*Les Flèches d'or.*)

Resurrection.

To-day I throw the windows of my prison
   Wide open to the sun's first radiant flood.
Rejoice! Rejoice! for now is Spring rerisen;
   From the rough bark bursts forth the rosy bud.

Hoar-headed winter dwindles to behold her,
   His furry mantle falls to the earth, and lo!
The fresh white bosom and the rosy shoulder
   And laughing virgin's eyes that glance and glow!

The gray sky turns to blue. Harmonious strophes
   Sing in my heart and whisper words of love:
My dreams array themselves in brilliant trophies,
   Coloured, like hope, with hues of heaven above.

No longer on the hearth the high flame dances,
   Nor on the wall with shadows flickering;
Home-keeping Muse, unveil thy mutinous glances,
   Forth to the fields and hail the blue-eyed Spring!

Réveil.
(*Les Flèches d'or.*)

Sully Prudhomme.

Born in Paris, 1839.

Sully Prudhomme is a finely-cultured and fastidious artist whom it would be gross flattery to describe as a great poet. He was trained in the *École polytechnique* and is well versed in science ; but his family designed him for an industrial career and obtained a place for him in the great ironworks of Le Creusot (Saône-et-Loire). He left them to turn his attention to law, but had soon to forsake his studies and go to Italy to recruit a somewhat sickly constitution. On his return to Paris, Sully Prudhomme associated himself with the Parnassians and was encouraged by Sainte-Beuve and Théophile Gautier. He published his first volume of verse—*Stances et Poèmes*— in 1866 and immediately became famous as the author of *le Vase brisé*, a little piece of twenty lines which reveals the characteristic delicacy of his craftsmanship but leaves the reader wondering why the poet ever gained so much celebrity thereby. For many years the Muse of Sully Prudhomme allowed no day to pass without a line. *Les Épreuves, les Solitudes* (1866-1872) *les vaines Tendresses, la Révolte des Fleurs, les Destins* (1872-1878) *la Justice* (1879) *le Prisme* (1886) *le Bonheur* (1888) and numerous other collections of poems gave invariable evidence of his devotion to art and his love of finished form. It was doubtless this sense of elegance and shapeliness which in 1870 caused Théophile Gautier to single him out of the group of young poets as one of exceptional promise.

Le Bonheur, the largest and most ambitious of Sully Prudhomme's poems, is a sort of French *Faust*, in which the author's avowed aim is ' simply to caress the noblest ' inspirations with a beneficent dreaminess which may ' cause us to forget awhile the silence and immorality ' of nature'. Faustus and Stella are translated to another world (very much like this one) in which they taste the pure pleasures of earthly love and speculate in fine philosophical verse, with much delicacy of moral sentiment, on the discoveries of science and the eternal problems of life and death. French poetry, that of Victor Hugo always excepted, had been running for a long time in somewhat narrow channels, and *le Bonheur* was one of the longest poems written since the middle of the century. But Sully Prudhomme has not the imaginative sweep to carry him over such a wide area. He is a thinker of no great depth or individuality and a distiller of refined emotions. Devoid of epic passion and lacking in lyrical swing, he is a master of fragile expression, daintily cold and exquisitely transparent; and he handles the thinnest texture of ideas with a feminine softness of touch. His feelings are chastened by philosophy, his timid scepticism is modified by faith and his good taste seldom gives way to excessive transports. One admirable characteristic of his verse is the healthy note of cheerfulness which runs through it. He is never rebellious, because he believes in labour and endurance. He shuns the purely voluptuous; indeed he is not ashamed to confess a lingering regard for ' the duenna ' Virtue whom so many clever men have decried'.

Sully Prudhomme is a man of grave and calm demeanour, a deliberate speaker and a model of discretion in everything. He has written amiably and elegantly on æsthetics in two volumes of prose: *l'Expression dans les Beaux-Arts* and *Réflexions sur l'Art des Vers*. It seems almost superfluous to add that he had scarcely passed his fortieth year when he was cordially welcomed into the French Academy, which Catulle Mendès and Paul Verlaine will never be permitted to enter, and which keeps the foremost French writer of to-day in the position of perpetual candidate.

Let Jules Lemaître, who is full of indulgence and even of admiration for Sully Prudhomme, sum him up:—' He ' is the least sensuous and the most precise of poets; he ' thinks and defines instead of feeling and singing '.

Where?

Souls slain by love rise not in heaven to dwell:
  There is no twilight path, no leafy screen;
  No sweetness known in that abode serene
The sweetness of earth's kisses can dispel.

Nor do they sink to everlasting hell:
  On earth love burned them with lips purpurine,
  And in the breast thrill demon claws less keen
Than cruel scorn and doubt incurable.

Then where? What griefs profound, what transports
    high,
If in the grave hearts change not, can outvie
  Griefs once endured and transports erst enjoyed?

Since life for them held heaven's delight, hell's fire,
Love's infinite fear, love's infinite desire,
  They die, even to the soul; they are destroyed.

Où vont-ils?: Amour.
(Les Épreuves.)

Saving Art.

If naught were blue save cloudless sky and sea,
  Golden save grain and roseate save roses,
  Or lovely, save when Nature's breast reposes,
No bitterness in life's delight would be.

But earth and wave and air are full of thee,
  Woman, whose love a dolorous charm discloses ;
  The spell of looks and smiles and luring poses
Lies far too deep on souls that would be free.

We love thee, knowing thence our griefs unended :
For God, that fashioned grace with solace blended,
  Made love that longs and gains no answering sigh.

Yet would I, clad with sacred art for armour,
Gaze on lips, eyes and golden hair, O charmer !
  As on ripe grain and rose and sea and sky.

L'Art sauveur: Amour.
(Les Épreuves.)

The Light of Truth.

As Christmas sees some vast Cathedral waken
  With sudden glory in the winter gloom :
The crypt, from cold sepulchral slumbers shaken,
  The redness of its iron lamps relume ;

Then higher, in the nave, where wreathing vapours
  Ascend, the darkness round its pillars thrilled
With flames that, one by one, on kindling tapers
  Tremble, and blaze from brilliant lustres spilled ;

Then the light, waxing ampler and more splendid,
  Climb the great altar, whence high chandeliers,
Of rarer craft with richer substance blended,
  Lift to the golden dome a thousand tiers ;

So the whole earth, a temple with wide porches,
  Sees light still brightening in her ancient shrines,
The flame-bearers whereof are living torches
  Of thought that trembles, palpitates and shines.

Deep dawn of life, soul of things universal,
  Reason, in ceaseless quest of broader bourne,
Rises from form to form through Time's rehearsal,
  Dark dream, pale image and clear thought in turn.

Her quenchless light, fanned by love's fiery pinion
  From age to age athwart dense shadow grows,
Smiles on man's mightiest birth and meanest minion,
  And beams and burns on ever loftier brows.

Following her lamp, whose light is sure and single,
  On each new age a brighter aureole,
In finer clay, wherewith more splendours mingle,
  The whole world travails towards the supreme soul.

But infinitely slow, as with derision,
  Drops in the hour-glass the old dust of years,
And still the eternal purpose is a vision
  That shines awhile, then fades and disappears.

Oh when shall Thought on Truth touch her deep plummet,
  Then scale the height of Heaven with wings unfurled,
And sit enthroned for ever on Life's summit,
  Star of mankind and Conscience of the world!

So many dreamers die and leave no traces!
  Oh when, in native shape and true abode,
Shall the Prince, springing from the Beast's embraces
  In man's ideal image, be as God!

· *Majora canamus. II.*
(*Le Prisme.*)

Catulle Mendès.

Born in Bordeaux, 1840.

This prolific and versatile writer is of Hebrew lineage. He has the true Jewish love of bold outlines and brilliant colours, with that sensibility to artistic impressions which often takes the place of creative power in the finer minds of his race.

Although his people were wealthy Catulle Mendès came to Paris a poor man and had to gain his own livelihood until he could convince his parents that he was fitted for a literary career. He is a man of letters to the fibres and roots of his being. His nature seems to be entirely free from that vain and irritable jealousy which is said to be the badge of all the literary tribe, and he has been a consistent friend of poets, artists and sinners.

The modern Parnassian group of poets, so notable in number and talent, began to gather round Catulle Mendès about 1860, when he founded his *cénacle* in *rue de Douai* and established the *Revue fantaisiste*. Among the contributors were Alphonse Daudet, Philoxène Boyer, Léon Cladel, Jules Claretie, Albert Glatigny, Charles Monselet and Jules Noriac (Cairon). Several of them conquered a considerable place in French literature. According to Émile Zola they spent their evenings in admiring each other. The *Revue fantaisiste* came to a sudden and violent end by the condemnation of Catulle Mendès to a fine of 500 francs and one month's imprisonment in *Sainte-Pélagie* for the publication of his reckless libertine comedy in verse, *le Roman d'une Nuit.* A few years after his return to liberty Catulle Mendès reorganised his Parnassus under the ægis of Leconte de Lisle. Thenceforth Albert Mérat, Léon Valade (the translator of Heine's *Intermezzo*) and François Coppée, with a new swarm of aspiring poets, frequented his poorly-furnished chamber in the *hôtel du Dragon bleu* in *rue Dauphiné (quartier latin).* The charming conversation of Catulle Mendès, the amiable discourse of Anatole France, the whimsical sallies of Paul Verlaine and the impassible philosophy of Louis-Xavier de Ricard gave an ever-changing delight to their symposium. The men of this interesting set differed from those of the Bohemia of Nerval and of Mürger inasmuch as most of them had some steady employment (in the government offices or elsewhere) which helped discipline, discouraged idleness and debauch, and enabled them to live independently until they could afford to give their undivided attention to literature.

Catulle Mendès is the author of several volumes of verse. His first collection, entitled *Philoméla*, was followed by *les Sérénades*, in which there are some dainty lyrics of love. His *Contes épiques* have a fine dramatic flavour and are equal to anything of their kind in the French language. He has mastered almost every variety of rondel, chanson, canzonet and sonnet form and handles his rhymes with a lyrical ease and delicacy worthy of Théodore de Banville. In his new book of poems—*la Grive des Vignes*: 1895—he exhibits this dexterity of touch in some of the most graceful and fanciful verses ever penned by a French poet.

As a writer of short stories Catulle Mendès has few rivals. His romances, not over rigid on the ground of morals, are always fresh and sprightly. He has done a good deal of work for the theatre. His latest play, in five acts, *la Reine Fiammetta*, was first produced in the *Théâtre-Libre*, and has since been refused at the *Comédie-Française*. He is a fanatical admirer of Wagner's music, and has published a remarkable study of that master's melodramas. Among other miscellaneous labours he has edited one or two collections of the *lieds* and *chansons* of France. Variegated and vivacious as his genius is, none of his work bears traces of raw haste or forced labour. He is always an artist and readily responds to every form of intellectual and emotional beauty.

The personal fascination of Catulle Mendès is legendary. He was 'beautiful as an Apollo' when he first appeared in Paris, and the excitements of a very irregular life have not destroyed his power of attraction. He is now a rich man. In 1866 he married Théophile Gautier's charming and accomplished daughter, known successively in French literature as Judith Walter, Judith Mendès and Judith Gautier. This richly-gifted couple has been long divorced.

The Curses of Hagar.

When Abraham's days a hundred years had burdened
  (So falls a ripe sheaf on the threshing-floor)
With fruit at last old Sara's womb was guerdoned,
  The Elohim having blessed her barren store.

'The word of the Most High, O Lord of Camels!
'Nine months in my enlargëd flank did rest,
'But now thy race unnumbered bursts its trammels
  'And wails in the child's cry that seeks my breast!

'A man being born of me, how canst thou cherish
  'Henceforward the strange woman's seed impure?
'She whose foul scorn o'erweening pride doth nourish,
  'Whose green eyes leering haunt the shades obscure.

'Go! with her son chase hence the Egyptian mother,
  'As one flings the seared branch with cankered bud:
'Ill brooks the fruitful spouse that such another
  'Should flaunt the opprobrium of her alien blood!

'Since still thou seest, beneath soft linen swelling,
  'Her youth in ripened orbs of rounded grace,
'Let her go hence, far from the nuptial dwelling,
  'Nor fill thine eyes with love, with shame my face!

'Surely my handmaid's fawn, the hireling creature
  'Of breasts unwithered and unwrinkled loins,
'Shares not with the man-child, born out of Nature,
  'The inheritance reserved by God's designs!'

So spake the Old Mother, moved by cruel anger,
   And, towards Beersheba's thirsty, treeless land,
Hagar, a hushed cry on her lips, with languor
   Went sadly leading Ishmaël by the hand.

Driven by the wind, dawn's shifting clouds discovered
   The star of night waned in the welkin calm,
As if o'er the wan Orient vaguely hovered
   Vast undulations of a viewless palm.

In camp the distant tents shook like a vesture ;
   On thresholds gray, with rosy vapours veiled,
Women drew back the screens with sluggish gesture
   In which the sloth of recent slumber trailed.

Light tinklings rose from flocks in fold assembled,
   Blending with song of birds, a shrill sweet strain
That in the broad-branched cedar lingering trembled
   With floating fleece of fog risen from the plain.

Then, in a sudden burst of wakening glory,
   Like a fierce lion from his lair outrun,
With golden mane ablaze and flanks all gory,
   On the red sky-line rose the splendid sun.

With murmur like an ant-hill's marching millions,
   The shining heavens beheld, alert and strong,
Forth from the hoary patriarch's blest pavilions
   Contented toil and prosperous leisure throng.

Robust beneath their load tall handmaids ambled,
   Poising, with pendant sleeves, the milk-brimmed jar ;
Among the white kids naked children gambolled :
   And these the exiled twain watched from afar.

Then Hagar :—'Woe to them that chase me !   Smiling
  ' In the fat valleys safely they sojourn,
'Whilst I, to the arid desert backward toiling,
  ' Fly like the beaten hound their foot would spurn.

'While on fresh swards, where the stream glides and
      drowses,
  ' They still shall share the loaves of honey and wheat,
' I, like an ox on the void air that browses,
  ' Shall drink my thirst, my hunger eat for meat.

' And when, on the hard sand sinking aweary,
  ' I bite the wind in one long cry of drouth,
'My son, crawling to me, wan-eyed and dreary,
  ' With ravenous kiss shall menace my pale mouth.

' O centenary chief of tribes that wander !
  ' Since want and woe must feed my banishment
' I that, with wealth of beauty and youth to squander,
  ' Curbed my wild shame and to thy pleasure bent ;

' Tremble in thy twin hopes, sire of twin races !
  ' Twixt Sara's seed and Hagar's seed this day
' Undying hate is born of thy embraces :—
  ' Sleek beasts full-fed to ravening wolves a prey !

' They shall be free, fierce and of bold endeavour
  ' Beneath the sun, these bastards of thy slave :
'From the antique crater of my flanks for ever
  ' Revenge shall roll, like lava's fiery wave.

' With looks askance thy satiate Isaacs, drooping,
  ' Shall gaze athwart the vapours of the feast,
Lest they discern out of the distance swooping
  ' Those famished horsemen of the hungry waste.

'Thence, numberless, through devastated regions,
  'My vanquished sons, proud in defeat and fears,
'And all earth's vagabonds and rebel legions,
  'Shall people with my seed the ceaseless years.

'Fear them, ye conquerors!   By fierce frenzy driven,
  'Or fiercer joy, their scorn shall rise to God!
'And man's proud temple, by their laughter riven,
  'Shall crack from base to crown its fabric broad.

'Yet, more than these, my daughters shall have power!
  'Spurned though she be that shamed thy shrivelled
    flesh,
'Because her lips were like a living flower
  'And her breast, like a lily's, firm and fresh,

'Mother august, with many-peopled bosom,
  'Boast not, too sure of his uncertain line,
'Thy first-born, like a worm in the rathe blossom,
  'But mourn, O Sara . . . daughters shall be mine!

'White women, crowned with soft and floating tresses,
  'In long loose robes, voluptuously sweet,
'That leave beneath the thrill of charmed caresses
  'A perfumed furrow filled with amorous heat.

'For love of their bare breasts, with beauty dowered,
  'And dainty bodies clothed with delicate down,
'The strongest man shall crouch, a nerveless coward,
  'The purest stoop to infamies unknown.

'Thy sons, hiding the blush of fierce carouses,
  'And jealous with regret of secret bliss,
'Shall drag to the dull couch of weeping spouses
  'Hearts drained of blood by the avenging kiss!'

Thus to the wind that flying cloud disperses,
  Her wrongs on desert skies and sands outpoured,
Tall Hagar prophesied with bitter curses ;
  Mother of harlots and the rebel horde.

And towards the distant solitudes, where Sions
  And opulent Tyres and haughty Romes should rise,
The wild gusts fled, sowing in wide defiance
  The sombre malediction of her cries.

Les Imprécations d'Agar.
(Contes épiques.)

The Mother.

When the Lord fashioned man, the Lord his God
Took not the human clay from one sole clod ;
But earth from the four corners of the world :
South, where on burning winds the sand is whirled ;
The green-leaved East ; the chill North, hoar with
      frost ;
The West, where shattered oaks and ships are tossed
In whirlwind and eclipse and earthquake gloom ;
Lest anywhere the Earth, that is man's tomb,
Should say to him, the weary traveller
With drooping head, who fain would rest in her
'Away ! what man art thou, I know thee not !'
But that his mother earth, in every spot
Where he would lay his heart, by hope beguiled,
Should say : 'Sleep in my bosom, O my child !'

La Mère.
(Contes épiques.)

The Disciple.

With hands that touched his toes the Bouddha dreamed.

Said Poorna : Like the winds are souls redeemed,
Free as north winds in sky no clouds bedim ;
Therefore, o'er rocks I'll climb, through rivers swim
To furthest tribes beneath the furthest heaven ;
That souls be comforted and sins forgiven,
Master, thy helpful creed I'll bear abroad.

—But if these tribes, answered the Son of God,
Insult thee, child beloved, what wilt thou say ?

—That with a virtuous soul endowed are they,
Since they have blinded not these lids with sand,
Nor raised, to smite me, either stone or hand.

—But if they smite thee, then, with hand or stone ?

—These folk, I'll say, to gentleness are prone,
Because their hands, thus filled with stones to fling
Against me, stave nor sword are brandishing.

—But if their steel doth reach thee ?

                              —I will say,
How soft their blows, that wound and do not slay.

—But if thou die ?

                    —Happy who cease to live !

—Go forth, said Bouddha, comfort and forgive.

                    Le Disciple.
                        (*Contes épiques.*)

Three Novelists.

Many excellent poets have succeeded in romance ; and most novelists have occasionally dropped into poetry. Walter Scott, Victor Hugo, Théophile Gautier and George Meredith are among those who have achieved greatness in both. Thackeray, Dickens, Daudet and Zola belong to the order of those who have gone through a period of poetry or thrown off verses in the course of their literary career.

Émile Zola is among the poets as Saul among the prophets. Large as the place is which he fills in French literature he is a Frenchman only by his mother. His father was an Italian of Venice and his maternal grandmother a Greek. The family had settled in Aix, and Zola was born in Paris (1840) during a visit of his parents to the capital. It was under the Provençal sun that he composed his poems and sung the virginal charms and chaste love of Nina, a different ideal from the poisonous Nana of his mature manhood. This is not the place to discuss Zola's colossal labours as novelist, dramatist and critic or as Samson Agonistes of the realistic school. He is a man of overmastering intellectual power and a fierce worker. If any one doubts the poetic faculty which he has subordinated to a cruel analysis of vice and disease, let him read *la Faute de l'abbé Mouret, une Page d'Amour*, and many scattered passages of almost lyrical beauty in that lurid epic of immorality and insanity, *les Rougon-Macquart*. Zola, like Balzac and Flaubert before him, holds the forty-first chair in the French Academy and seems likely to occupy it for a long time. But, whatever may happen, he can never wholly deserve Piron's epitaph.

Alphonse Daudet (born at Nîmes in 1840) published in 1858 a delicious little volume of poems—*Les Amoureuses* —which prove that he could have developed a lyrical style of his own. The verse is full of delicacy and fancy, often touching on pathos, and for so young a man most original. Every reader of French literature is familiar with Daudet's crisp, clean, nervous, vivid, picturesque prose, a new and charming incarnation of that incomparable language which in Nodier, in Nerval, in Mérimée and in Mürger has assumed so many fascinating forms. The novelist has not returned to his first love, unless *l'Arlésienne* may be taken as a tribute to his poetical instinct.

Fleuri-René-Albert-Guy de Maupassant was born (1850) in the *château* of Miromesnil (Seine-Inférieure). He was by choice and vocation a prose writer and became one of the masters of that sober style which was established in French literature by Flaubert. There is nothing of a purely lyrical character in his sole volume of poems, modestly entitled *Des Vers*, which was issued in 1880. He makes the wilfully forced, the fantastic and the grotesque take the place of spontaneous inspiration. His verse is always deliberately cold and calm. *La dernière Escapade* is a good example of his method. A pair of venerable lovers revisit one evening the scene of their youthful flirtations, endeavouring to redeem the delight which had been theirs in the flush of life, and are discovered in the cold dawn, their withered corpses clasped in each other's arms. Maupassant is vigorous, incisive and scrupulously faithful to human nature in his novels. The man had a fresh healthy look which belied the early collapse of his intellectual powers. He died in a private asylum at Passy, near Paris, in 1893.

My Wishes.

My wish would be . . . where uplands gleam
   When sunny May shines on the meadow,
   A little hut that throws its shadow
In the clear mirror of a stream.

A hidden nest among the myrtles,
   To which no footpaths wind their tracks ;
   A nest that all companion lacks
Save only nests of snow-white turtles.

My wish would be . . . where vision ends
   And the gray rock towers up to Heaven,
   A bosk of pines whence breathes at even
A song that with the zephyr blends ;

Far-widening thence, a chain of valleys,
   Where sportive rivers wind and stray
   And, wandering with capricious play,
Shine white across the green-leaved alleys ;

Or where dusk olive-trees that lean
   In dreams their hoary heads discover,
   Or wild vines, like a wanton lover,
Climbing along the slopes are seen.

My wish would be . . . for royal palace,
   Reached by a pathway from my door,
   A bower with roses blossomed o'er
And closed in like a wild-flower's chalice :

A mossy carpet soft and sweet,
  With lavender and thyme made gracious,
  A dainty lordship, scarce so spacious
As garden spanned by children's feet.

My wish would be . . . in that lone shelter,
  Filled with the forms my fancy weaves,
  To watch, beneath the clustering leaves,
My dreams around me float and welter.

But more than all my wish would be . . .
  And lacking that I laugh at power . . .
  A queen, to share the crown, with dower
Of golden tresses floating free ;

A queen of love whose voice is tender,
  Whose pensive brow shades liquid eyes,
  Fresh from whose tread the soft flowers rise,
Because her foot is light and slender.

Ce que je veux. (*Vers inédits.*)
ÉMILE ZOLA.

AIX : *May*, 1859.

Three Days of Vintage.

I met her one day in the harvest of vines.
Her dainty foot peeped neath the kirtle that swung,
Unconfined by the fillet her loose tresses hung :
Eyes pure as an angel's, lips rosy as wine's.

Pressed close to the arm of a lover she clung,
And the fields of Avignon they wandered among
    In the harvest of vines.

* * *

255

I met her one day in the harvest of vines.
The plains lay aslumber, the sky shed no light ;
She wandered alone, as one trembling with fright ;
And her look was like wildfire that flickers and shines.

I thrill with the vision that rose on my sight
When I saw thee, dear phantom, so frail and so white,
     In the harvest of vines.

* * *

I met her one day in the harvest of vines.
And sad in my dreams is the memory thereof.

The pall was of velvet like plumes of a dove ;
Thus an ebony casket the pale pearl enshrines.
And the nuns of Avignon bent weeping above . . .
Too heavily clustered the grapes . . . and so Love
     Reaped the harvest of vines.

Trois Jours de Vendanges. (*Les Amoureuses.*)
     ALPHONSE DAUDET.

Passionless Nature.

When man mourned his first vision flown for ever,
    Nature, less scornful than she is,
Felt her maternal breast with anguish quiver,
    And longed to blend her tears with his.
The world grew dark. No star in skies beclouded,
    On earth no flower unfurled her leaf.
The sun withdrew, the moon her beauty shrouded,
The trembling forests wrung their boughs with grief.

The luminous dusks, the dawns of bright vermilion,
    Vanished in ghastly glimmerings pale.
Winter unfurled her vaporous pavilion ;
    The plains put on their mourning veil.
Lakes washed their dusky shores with waves grown
      grayer,
    And in Our-Lady-of-the-Woods
Birds and the winds, the choir and organ-player,
Sung their first requiem in minor moods.

Sadness drew streams of woe from vast abysses ;
    In angry rage volcanoes roared ;
With speech sublime sobbed the dark precipices ;
    The weeping torrents foamed and poured.
' Fain would we share the weight of human sorrow '
    Moaned the old deaf ravines in tears . . .
Man rose, forgetful of his grief, the morrow ;
But they still wept and throbbed a thousand years.

Long the great-hearted mother drank her chalice,
    Till, shamed to shew the melting mood,
She smoothed with nimble hands her ruffled valleys
    And donned once more her flowery hood.
Then she arose, radiant in all her splendour,
    And strewed with green each slope and plain,
But knowing thence how vain her love's surrender
She cried to man : ' Ask not my tears again ! '

    .   .   .   .

As for me, if the griefs that great souls cherish
    Assail and seize my heart in turn,
If lured by woman's loveliness I perish
    With love her coldness loves to spurn ;

Or if, by death bereaved of them that love me,
    I die a thousand deaths, yet live,
O Nature! changeless smile around, above me;
    I seek no pity such as thou canst give!

Colza and wheat along the slopes may blossom,
    And barley ripen on the plain;
I will not lay my sorrows on their bosom,
    But bear in loneliness my pain.
Earth, thou shalt smile; lakes, shine upon your shingle;
    And you, ye woods, with murmurs throng;
All you may sing, nor fear lest I should mingle
My tears or curses with your sacred song!

          Nature impassible. (*Les Amoureuses.*)
            ALPHONSE DAUDET.

Desires.

The dream of one is to have wings and follow
    The soaring heights of space with clamorous cries;
With lissome fingers seize the supple swallow
    And lose himself in sombre gulfs of skies.

Another would have strength with circling shoulder
    To crush the wrestler in his close embrace;
And, not with yielding loins or blood grown colder,
    Stop, with one stroke, wild steeds in frantic chace.

What I love best is loveliness corporeal:
    I would be beautiful as gods of old;
So from my radiant limbs love immemorial
    In hearts of men a living flame should hold.

I would have women love me in wild fashion—
  Choose one to-day and with to-morrow change ;
Pleased, when I pass, to pluck the flower of passion,
  As fruits are plucked when forth the fingers range.

Each leaves upon the lips a different flavour ;
  These diverse savours bid their sweetness grow.
My fond caress would fly with wandering favour
  From dusky locks to locks of golden glow.

But most of all I love the unlooked-for meeting,
  Those ardours in the blood loosed by a glance,
The conquests of an hour, as swiftly fleeting,
  Kisses exchanged at the sole will of chance.

At daybreak I would dote on the dark charmer,
  Whose clasping arms cling close in amorous swoon ;
And, lulled at eve by the blonde siren's murmur,
  Gaze on her pale brow silvered by the moon.

Then my calm heart, that holds no haunting spectre,
  Would lightly towards a fresh chimæra haste :
Enough in these delights to sip the nectar,
  For in the dregs there lurks a bitter taste.

Désirs. (*Des Vers.*)
GUY DE MAUPASSANT.

François Coppée.

Born in Paris, 1842.

François Coppée (more properly Francis and in full Francis-Édouard-Joachim Coppée) is the most graceful and genial of living French poets. His simplicity, his purity, his exquisite sense of verbal beauty and his idyllic charm are such as must be appreciated by the lovers of fine verse in any language. He resembles Sully Prud-homme inasmuch as there is a notable absence of the voluptuous element in his poetry ; and he does not dis-dain to sing the short and simple annals of the poor.

Coppée is a typical Frenchman in aspect, in character and in culture. The name is said to be Belgian, but his parents were Parisians of humble position. François was only fifteen years of age when his father was struck down by paralysis, after which the family had a struggle for existence. He was nowise a robust child. His poetical apprenticeship began in imitating Victor Hugo, Lamar-tine and Baudelaire. His first verses were published when he was a clerk in the offices of the Ministry of War and lived quietly with his mother and sister at Montmartre. For his encouragement in literature he was indebted to Catulle Mendès, the kind genius of so many living French poets. By the good graces of the Princess Mathilde he had the appointment of assistant-librarian to the Senate, a post which he held for two years until he became librarian in the House of Molière. With such assistance to his labours in journalism he enfranchised himself from daily drudgery and was enabled to devote his talent solely to literature. He was elected to the Academy in 1884.

The earliest acknowledged poetical works of François Coppée are entitled *le Reliquaire* (1866) and *Intimités* (1868). Hardly a hundred copies of each were sold. *Poèmes modernes*, in 1869, attracted more attention and *le Passant*, a poetical comedy in verse which was played at the *Odéon* in the same year, made him comparatively famous. Like Alfred de Musset forty years earlier, he became the favourite poet of women and the idol of the younger generation of readers of verse. Some vigorous utterances after the war of 1870 culminated in that beautiful and touching appeal to humanity, *le Pater*. The manuscript was unanimously accepted by the committee of the *Comédie-Française* in January 1889 and interdicted by an official decree in December. This ridiculous ukase was inspired by the fear of a revival of the smouldering embers of the Commune. There was great indignation among literary men and Coppée himself protested in a dignified letter. He appealed to his whole life for an answer to those who would denounce him as a disturber of the public peace, but his eloquence was lost on an unimaginative Republican government.

Among the more important poetical works of François Coppée are *les Humbles, le Cahier rouge, les Récits et les Élégies* and *Contes en Vers et Poésies diverses*. He has written at least a dozen comedies and dramas, of which the most noticeable are perhaps *le Luthier de Crémone* (*Comédie-Française*: 1876) *Severo Torelli* (*Odéon*: 1883— *Comédie-Française*: 1894) and *les Jacobites* (*Odéon*: 1885). *Pour la Couronne* (*Comédie-Française*: 1895) is in all respects worthy of comparison with its predecessors and deserves a place along with the finest poetical tragedies in French literature. His prose writings are exquisitely tender and full of pathos.

As a poet Coppée is never pedantic and seldom involved. Any occasional lapse into triviality is palliated by the freshness and clearness of his harmonious style. Some of his poetry has the characteristics of so-called *vers-de-société*; but he is more at home when he touches a truer and deeper note. In his more ambitious verse his genius seems to be assimilative rather than profoundly original. His idylls are superior to anything of the kind ever written in French. A good example of his talent in poetical narration is *le Liseron*, a mediæval legend which celebrates the miraculous growth of a convolvulus round the sword of a warrior who had struck the blade into the ground and sworn to destroy a certain convent unless the weapon flowered before next day. It is charmingly and delicately unfolded and is quite different in flavour from anything else in French poetry. Coppée excels in such things, for he knows how to achieve artistic simplicity with absolute ease and felicity of expression.

François Coppée has not the genius of a great singer who sums up and expresses the profoundest emotions of his age, but he is a pure and beautiful soul.

An October Morning.

It is the dim delicious hour
    That blushes with a sudden dawn ;
Athwart the autumnal haze in shower
    The leaves fall withered on the lawn.

Slow dropping, one by one, they pass,
    Distinct to the discerning eye,
The oak-leaf, bright as burnished brass,
    The maple-leaf of sanguine dye.

Anon, the serest leaves of all
Last from the naked branches fall,
    Though yet no winter winds do blow.

A white light, sprinkled everywhere,
Swathes the earth, and the rosy air
    Is tremulous with a golden snow.

Matin d'octobre.
(Le Cahier rouge.)

Pharaoh.

Thothmes the fourth is dead ; the guardians keep
His mummy, swathed for everlasting sleep :
Thothmes is with the Gods and on the throne
Of Egypt a new Pharaoh sits, his son
Amenophis, on whose dusk brow is bound
The golden pshent that mystic snake wreathes round.
With rigid flanks, stark hands, vague eyes that seem
Lost in the wonder of some distant dream

263

And fleshy lips that wear a dull cold smile
He suffers, in the long close-columned aisle
O' the palace hieroglyphed with bird and beast,
Homage from warrior lord and Theban priest.
On brazen tripods incense smokes, and chant
And prayer arise, as the chief hierophant,
Kneeling, descants on things behind the veil.
' Hail, thrice-pure Pharaoh !   King of Chemith, hail !
' O thou, of life and light the all-kindling sun !
' Speak and forthwith thy holy will be done.
' For thee Phrah, Neph and Phtah, the guardians three,
' Bless the Nile's fertile stream from source to sea ;
' For thee the Sphinx and Cynocephalus raise
' In triumph to the dawn their clamorous praise !
' What wouldst thou, Pharaoh ?   Bid and be obeyed !
' Thine are our harvests to the slenderest blade.
' Speak and the multitude is plunged in dearth.
' Beasts of the field are thine, fruits of the earth,
' Man, woman and the wide Egyptian land.
' Wilt thou have glory ?   O puissant King, command !
' And armies huge shall rise and fleets shall swarm
' And slaughtered nations sink beneath thine arm,
' And behind thee their mightiest men of war
' Shall run, like greyhounds captive at thy car ;
' Thou shalt enlarge thy borders far and wide
' And on a thousand obelisks carve thy pride.
' If battle and its spoils thou dost disdain,
' Thine amorous soul of art and pleasure fain,
' O sovereign ! whisper but the boon it craves :
' With perfumed limbs a hundred Asian slaves
' Whose dusky nakedness pale pearls adorn
' Shall, like the radiance of a summer morn,
' With tambourines and cymbals, wreathed in flowers,
' And Orient dances charm thy weary hours.

' Wilt thou in some great monument enshrine
' Thy name imperishable and divine,
' Huge fabric before which, grown dwarf and frail,
' Lake, Labyrinth and Pyramid shall pale ;—
' A dream colossal as thy soul's wide sphere?—
' Son of the Gods ! a myriad hands shall rear
' In massy blocks innumerable domes :
' For thine, O Pharaoh ! are the twenty nomes,
' The golden-helmëd warrior, cunning scribe,
' Circumcised priest, artisan and the tribe
' Of handicraftsmen to the meanest caste ;
' Nor can thy wishes ever be too vast.
' Speak and ordain—'tis ours to do thy will !'

He ceased, and all, with drooping brow, stood still.
Then, as a deep disgust his heart imbued,
And having asked himself :—How best prelude
This reign, so fated to blaze forth and bloom?—
The young King answered slowly : 'Build my tomb !'

Le Pharaon : Récits épiques.
(*Les Récits et les Élégies.*)

The Three Birds.

I said to the ringdove that fluttered above me :
 ' Fly farther than meadows and barley-fields are
' And bring me the flower that shall woo her to love me' :
 The ringdove said only : ' Too far !'

I said to the eagle : ' I count on thy pinions ;
 ' Help, help me to ravish the fire from yon sky !
' If haply the spell be in starry dominions' :
 The eagle said only : ' Too high !'

'Devour then'—I said to the vulture that tare it—
'This heart that is full of her love, but if fate
'Hath left but one atom untouched thou shalt spare it':
The vulture said only: 'Too late!'

Les Trois Oiseaux.
(*L'Exilée.*)

Persistency.

Say what you will, do what you may,
Forgetfulness would be a hell;
Her smile sheds ever on life's way
Love's farewell.

Do what you may, say what you will,
I can but love her, though in vain;
If love be penance I would still
Bear the pain.

Say what you will, do what you may,
Though guiltless of my tears she sleep,
For her, true martyr, night and day
Must I weep.

Do what you may, say what you will,
My life lives only in her breath,
Yet would I, wearied of life's ill,
Welcome death.

Obstination.
(*L'Exilée.*)

FRANÇOIS COPPÉE

On a Tomb in Spring-Time.

The lone cross moulders in the graveyard hoary,
  But April weaves again her leafy bower;
  The redwing nestles there, and with sweet flower
A rosebush hides the sign of grief in glory.

No tear, no prayer, breathes such *memento mori*
  As sobbing nightingale and dewy shower.
  These scents, these songs, these splendours are the dower
Of Earth that thrills with Love's immortal story.

  Dead and forgotten one! whose human pride
  Dreamed, doubtless, dreams of life's eternal tide
In Paradise, where the freed spirit reposes;

  Hast thou not here to-day a lovelier doom
  If now thy soul, diffused about this tomb,
Sings with the birds, and blossoms in the roses?

Sur une Tombe au printemps.
(Contes en Vers et Poésies diverses.)

267

José-Maria de Heredia.*

Born near Santiago-de-Cuba, 1842.

This Spanish poet, whose mother was of French extraction, belongs to a family which derived its wealth from
sugar-plantations in Cuba. French by education and
election he has brought into French literature a reflex
of the ideal splendours of Spanish achievement in the
New World. Although he had the advantages of fortune,
and was somewhat fastidious in manners and dress,
Heredia became a familiar member of the new Parnassian
circle in which such diverse characters as Verlaine,
Coppée, Villiers and Mendès were gathered together in
common poverty and in a common love of letters and
art. His earliest verses appeared in the *Revue de Paris*
and he has since contributed to the *Temps*, the *Journal
des Débats* and the *Revue des Deux Mondes*.

Les Trophées, the volume in which Heredia's poems
were first collected, owed its publication to the encouragement of François Coppée and was dedicated to Leconte
de Lisle. It was issued by Alphonse Lemerre in 1893
and soon reached twelve editions. This sudden conquest
of fame preluded the Spanish poet's election to the French
Academy. He is now a prominent figure in French
literary life and an acceptable spokesman at official
celebrations.

Heredia's sonnets are the admiration and delight of
connoisseurs. They depend on none of the inner qualities

* The poet's surname, sometimes written Hérédia, should have no accents.

of emotion for their beauty, which is almost entirely outward and visible. Like rich jewelry they blaze with colour
and reflect a dazzling light. Their intrinsic splendour is
often enhanced by a fine artistic setting. The range of the
author's intellectual experience is indicated by the titles
under which each series of sonnets is grouped : *Greece and
Sicily, Rome and the Barbarians, The Middle Ages and the
Renaissance, The Orient and the Tropics* and *Nature and the
Vision.* These *Trophies* are appropriately completed by
a *Romancera* in *terza rima* and a poem on the exploits
of Pizarro—*Les Conquérants d'Or*—written in alexandrines.
On these diverse themes the poet has lavished the same
wealth of colour and the same pomp of illustration. His
descriptions are gorgeous, his decorative effects superb.
He manifests a rare mastery of original rhymes. The
verse is always finely moulded, but there is little in it
that attests thought, deep feeling or imagination.

Heredia's daughter published (anonymously) some
admirable verses in the *Revue des Deux Mondes* of 1
February, 1894. They exhibit in ample measure the
father's love of brilliant imagery and denote the same
fine pictorial instinct.

The prose works of Heredia are a wonderful French
translation of *The Veracious History of the Conquest of
New Spain* by Bernal Diaz del Castillo, and *la Nonne
alferez*, a new version of the fantastic story of that
notorious Spanish adventuress; both enriched with
critical, philological and topographical notes, which are
a tribute to the poet's ripe culture and learning.

Sunset.

The glittering furze that crowns their granite crest
  Gilds rugged summits that in twilight loom ;
  Remote, though shining still with fleecy plume,
Where the land ends heaves endless the sea's breast.

Beneath me night and silence lie. The nest
  Is hushed, on thatches curls a thin blue fume ;
  Only the Angelus, shivering through the gloom,
Blends with the murmuring Ocean's vast unrest.

Then faint, as from a deep ravine, arise
On waste and wold and down the distant cries
  Of shepherds mustering their belated clan.

Dense shadow swathes the welkin like a shroud ;
And the sun, sinking in empurpled cloud,
  Furls up the splendours of his golden fan.

Soleil Couchant : La Nature et le Rêve.
(Les Trophées.)

The Shell.

Through what cold seas, what wilderness of waves
  Unknown to man, O frail and pearly shell !
  Have tidal surges and deep underswell
Rolled thee in hollow gulfs of their green graves ?

Now, in the sun, no bitter refluence laves
   The golden-sanded bed where thou dost dwell.
   Yet from thy hollows, like a hopeless spell,
The vast voice of the sea moans in her caves.

Like thee, my soul is a sonorous prison ;
And ever weeps and wails in dirges risen
   With echoing clamours of old griefs profound :

So from its depths this heart, too full of Her,
Slow, sullen, as the sea's eternal stir,
   Groans with a thunderous and distant sound.

       La Conque: La Nature et le Rêve.
                  (*Les Trophées.*)

On a Broken Statue.

'Twas pious moss that closed those eyes forlorn.
   For vainly would they seek in this bare shrine
   The Virgin pouring forth pure milk and wine
On the famed earth within its sacred bourne.

Now tangled ivy and hops and trailing thorn
   Impleaching round this ruined form divine,
   Heedless if Pan or Faun or Hermes, twine
To weave on battered brows a wreathëd horn.

See ! the slant beam those hollow lids absorb
Relumes on the flat face each golden orb ;
   There laughs the wild vine as with ruddy lips ;

And, wondrous sign, the wind that stirs abroad,
   Leaves thrilled, and flickering shade o' the sun that dips,
Shape in the crumbled stone a living god !

      Sur un Marbre brisé: La Nature et le Rêve.
                  (*Les Trophées.*)

Stéphane Mallarmé.

Born in Paris, 1842.

He o'er-refines, the scholar's fault.

The master of the modern school of symbolist poets in France belongs to a family which has held since the Revolution an unbroken succession of important posts in the National Registration Office. Several of his more immediate ancestors had dabbled in letters. Stéphane Mallarmé was destined to the traditional career, but his predilection for English literature brought him over to this country at the age of twenty. He learned our language thoroughly, witness his translation of Poe's *Raven* and other poems into perfect French prose—'bold and beauti-' ful in its literalness'—says Jules Lemaître, who is not too tender to the *décadents* of French poetry.

On his return to Paris, Stéphane Mallarmé qualified for a preceptor's post in the provinces, and in thus accepting the daily drudgery which is necessary to a healthy development of the individual literary character he gave himself the one thing lacking in the lives of such men of genius as Villiers and Verlaine. From his obscure retreat the poet contributed to the *Parnasse contemporain* some of those exquisitely-wrought pieces which have given him a place of his own in French literature and which are acknowledged as models by the new generation of French artists in verse. Since he resumed his residence in the capital Stéphane Mallarmé has continued to lead a sequestered and studious existence. There is nothing of the vagabond Bohemian in him ; his chief recreations are stage-ballets and organ-recitals, with an occasional excursion on the Seine along the solitary boundaries of the forest of Fontainebleau.

Stéphane Mallarmé is a man of simple and unassuming character and his discourse is full of fascination. It would scarcely be believed, in face of the elaborate achievements of his maturer muse, that he had the boyish ambition to emulate Béranger as a singer of chansons. His first effusions were nevertheless inspired by the popular song. In his later poems symbol is linked to symbol so closely that it is hard to seize the sense on a superficial reading and a difficult task to translate them. Every idea has been distilled through an intellectual alembic until a degree of subtilised expression is reached which has no rival in French poetry and which seems almost alien to the natural lucidity and simplicity of the language. Hence the charge of 'obscurity' which has been levelled at Mallarmé as persistently as it was against Browning, who attained to a similarly intense concentration of poetical utterance. Curious involutions, abnormal punctuation, the employment of the absolute image instead of the metaphor and an individual vigour of expression which seems almost independent of the recognised articulation of language give character to a poetical style which is perhaps more nearly akin to that of *Sordello* than to any other type in English or French literature. This designed 'obscurity', which is the cynosure of the super-spiritual school of verse, is naturally the aversion of the common-sense critic, whose scientific analysis has stripped Baudelaire almost bare and attempted to polarise the brilliant light of Victor Hugo.

The work of Stéphane Mallarmé is somewhat scattered

S 273

abroad in unfamiliar reviews and periodicals. He has edited a reprint of Beckford's *Caliph Vathek* in the original French, with an admirable preface. He is said to be assiduously engaged on a vast scheme of poetry which has occupied his attention for fifteen years and of which some considerable fragments have already been published. Other specimens of his verse have been given to the world by Paul Verlaine and Catulle Mendès. In *Vers et Prose* there are several sonnets of exquisite workmanship and of abstruse metaphysical significance. When the poet limits himself to 'rich rhyme', for which he has an artist's love, the result approaches perfection. *L'après-midi d'un Faune* and *Hérodiade* are superb specimens of his peculiar style. *A Faun's Afternoon* opens thus :—

The Faun.

I would perpetuate those nymphs.
                     So clear
Their flesh-tint that it floats i' the atmosphere
Drowsy with tangled sleeps.
                     Were they a dream?
My doubt, night's ancient hoard, exhausts its stream
In many a subtile branch, which, left the true
Woods themselves, proves, alas, I lent my view
For triumph the ideal fault of roses!

Now think . . .
                  or if the nymphs thy fancy glozes
Body to fabulous sense a wish that lies!
Faun, this illusion bursts from the blue eyes
And cold, a spring in tears, of the most chaste:
But one all sighs, now say, doth she contrast

As day-breeze blowing in my fleece warm boon !
No! Through the immovable and languorous swoon,
Choking with heats the fresh morn in her throes,
Murmurs no stream more than my flute bestows
On the tune-sprinkled bosk ; and the sole wind
Prompt to exhale itself from reed-pipes twinned,
Ere sound disperses in an arid rain,
Is, in the smooth unwrinkled air-domain,
A visible breath serene, shaped by the sighs
Of inspiration, that regains the skies. . . . . . .

and so forth through a labyrinth of symbols bewildering
to the unaccustomed eye.

It is a notable fact that not one of the critics of this so-
called obscurity seems to have remembered that the
symbolic language of Mallarmé is nearly akin to the
metaphor of common-place speech, albeit endowed with
new and unfamiliar images. The manufacturer is forsooth
a symbolist when he '*engages* a *hand*' and the merchant
when he '*ventures* on a new *branch* of *business*'. Whether
the effect of language thus tormented out of its conventional forms is equal to the labour bestowed upon it may
nevertheless be reasonably doubted. It is perhaps a pity
that any great artist should diverge so far from that direct
simplicity of speech which is the mark of the master-
minds of humanity, but if he prefers fit audience though
few to the admiration of the general he may surely
exercise the right to choose his own way.

Flowers.

From golden avalanches of heaven's blue
  And primal snows of everlasting stars
Thou didst shape splendid chalices to strew
  This fresh young earth, virgin of woes and wars.

The tawny iris, by the rank pool's rim,
  And laurel, dear to souls on alien lawns,
Ruddy as the pure heel of seraphim
  Still blushing with the shame of trampled dawns.

Myrtle and hyacinth, glory of love's bower,
  And, fair as woman's flesh, the cruel rose,
Herodias of the garden-bed with dower
  Of bloody dew, that fierce and radiant glows.

Thine is the sobbing lily's splendour pale,
  Afloat on seas of sorrows, thence in swoon
Athwart the waning air blue vapours veil
  Dreamily wafted towards the weeping moon!

Hosannah! censers smoke and cithems sing!
  Praise, O our Father, from these dim purlieus!
Their echo, in heavenly twilights vanishing,
  Let looks entranced and shining aureoles lose!

Thou didst create, with just and subtile breath,
  These cups that charm the vials of our fate,
O Father! Flowers inwoven with balmy Death
  For weary souls by life made desolate.

Les Fleurs.
(*Vers et Prose.*)

Sonnet.*

My tomes reclosed upon the Paphian name,
  I laugh, when on sole spirit-sense emerges
  A ruin, blessed with foam of myriad surges
Beneath the hyacinth, in days of fame.

Cold with scythe-silences outstrips the flame ;
  Yet shall I ululate no hollow dirges
  If such mere virgin-sport, that earthward verges,
Balk every site of the false landscape's claim.

My hunger that no fruits of earth appease
Finds in their learnëd lack the savour of these:
  Burst, one of human flesh with fragrance blent !

Some snake, stirred by our love, I tread upon,
  Long pondering and perchance with ravishment
The burned breast of an antique amazon.

(Vers et Prose.)

* *Mes bouquins refermés sur le nom de Paphos,*
  Il m'amuse d'élire avec le seul génie
  Une ruine, par mille écumes bénie
Sous l'hyacinthe, au loin, de ses jours triomphaux.

  Coure le froid avec ses silences de faulx,
   Je n'y hululerai pas de vide nénie
   Si ce très vierge ébat au ras du sol dénie
  A tout site l'honneur du paysage faux.

  Ma faim qui d'aucuns fruits ici ne se régale
  Trouve en leur docte manque une saveur égale :
   Qu'un éclate de chair humain et parfumant !

  Le pied sur quelque guivre où notre amour tisonne,
   Je pense plus longtemps peut-être éperdûment
  A l'autre, au sein brûlé d'une antique amazone.

Paul Verlaine.

Born in Metz, 1844.

*The poet Verlaine has taken up his winter-quarters in the
Bichat Hospital (Daily Newspaper : December, 1894).*

Paul Verlaine, the only son of a military officer and
the spoiled darling of an indulgent mother, was left an
orphan when very young.   Brought up at Batignolles by
a poor widow of highly-refined character he received his
education at the *lycée Bonaparte* in Paris, associated himself with the Parnassian group, and wrote his first verses
while engaged at work in some municipal office.   On the
publication of *Poèmes saturniens*, as little noticed at the
time as Coppée's *Reliquaire*, which was issued on the same
day, he made himself known to the discerning few as a
new poet of strangely original genius.   Sainte-Beuve and
Nestor Roqueplan gave him some good counsel, but there
is no evidence that he ever took it to heart.

Verlaine had always a nomadic disposition.   When he
lived in Paris his leisure was spent in Sunday excursions
along the Seine and in the country round.   After he
broke loose from the restraints of civilised society he
travelled a good deal in England, Belgium and France ;
and perhaps no living poet has had a more intimate
acquaintance with the seamy side of life.   In his nature
the elements are unkindly mixed.   Too capricious, too
excessive and too rebellious to be schooled into the
ordered ways of men, he is a creature of impulse and
imagination ; one who throws himself into the mood of the

278

moment and follows no fixed purpose. With the countenance of a satyr and the instincts of a savage he has
lived a vagabond life from his youth upwards, oscillat-
ing between the brothel and the cabaret and tossed
from prison to hospital. And yet, with all his faults,
Verlaine is one of the most fascinating figures in contemporary literature. He is the Villon of the nineteenth
century.

Verlaine vaunts Lamartine and Baudelaire as the
greatest poets of this age, and, diverse in character as
these two singers were, he has an artistic affinity with
each. Lamartine's love of nature and large melodious
line, Baudelaire's lucid vision and closely-woven harmony,
have both had an influence on his poetical style, but he
brings into French verse a profound and powerful note of
his own. Sometimes his work is disfigured by conceits
and subtleties which are due to the wilful application of a
vicious theory of art ; too often he has stooped to sing
the perversities of passion and to disclose the morbid
imaginations of a mind diseased ; but, at his best, no
living singer can touch him in fervour and sincerity of
accent and at times he has a tone of pathos, as rare as
it is exquisite, to which there is no parallel in con-
temporaneous French poetry. He is a master of modulation and rhyme and he handles all the musical elements
of verse with consummate craft.

The theory of the artist's impassibility, which was
promulgated by Gustave Flaubert and his friend Louis
Bouilhet and eloquently preached to the Parnassians by
Louis-Xavier de Ricard, is applicable to poetry only in
the sense that it is applicable to every other form of art.
It is simply Diderot's *Paradoxe sur le Comédien* in a new
guise. Let the poet be ever so cool and deliberate in the
carving of verse his ideas, like those of the painter or the

composer, must have been conceived in the very heat and fever of the brain. Verlaine seems to imagine that the problem has been solved when he triumphantly exclaims: 'Est-elle en marbre ou non, la Vénus de Milo?'—as if such cold and hard material could be endowed with beauty unless the artist possessed the vision and the faculty divine. And in spite of theory the verse of Paul Verlaine, more often than that of any French poet of his time, thrills with true emotion and records the experience and passion of the man himself. Verlaine is also in the right sense a symbolist and impressionist, that is, he seizes quickly the essential spirit and the characteristic outline of things; and he excels in that vague appeal to the feelings which is the function of music rather than poetry. Observation and reflection have taught him more than individual study, for his classical and romantic lore seems to be derived chiefly from the works of other French poets. Yet he has used his hospital and prison leisure to extend his literary acquaintance and he tells us how he read the whole of Shakespeare's plays in the original, with English and German notes and commentaries, during an imprisonment in Brussels. He professes boundless love and admiration for Shakespeare, but in his heart of hearts he prefers Racine.

Poèmes saturniens was the first as it is the freshest and in some respects the finest of Verlaine's volumes of verse. He now affects to regard it with some disdain, as displaying too conspicuously the influence of two great models, Baudelaire and Leconte de Lisle. It appeared in 1866 and was followed two years later by *Fêtes galantes*, an entirely novel collection of tender and sensuous idylls swathed in the sentiment of the seventeenth century. *La bonne Chanson* (1870) is a pure and joyous song of the one calm period in Verlaine's life, when love led him into a sweeter atmosphere. After his marriage he was mixed up with the Commune. Thereupon he took refuge in England and lived an obscure and chequered existence for about ten years. His *Romances sans paroles* (1874) are the only poems belonging ostensibly to this period, which was probably one of wasteful excess, for in 1881 he published *Sagesse*, a volume of pious verse inspired by remorse and filled with a longing for better things than the husks that the swine do eat. *Jadis et naguère* (in 1884) was a return to his earlier ideals of the poetic art, and *Amour* (in 1888) renewed the note of *Sagesse*. His next volume, *Parallèlement*, was a palinode to this devotional access, and here the poet sang in voluptuous verse the praises of Sapphic passion. In mould and manipulation this work is worthy of Baudelaire. Since then the vitality of Verlaine's creative power has been evinced by a series of poetical effusions named *Bonheur*, *Chansons pour Elle*, *Liturgies intimes*, *Odes en Son honneur*, *Élégies*, *Invectives*, *Dédicaces* and *Dans les Limbes*; to be followed by *Varia*. Though first and always a poet, Paul Verlaine has published several works written in a peculiarly capricious and tormented form of prose, which is often relieved by picturesque description. These have evidently an autobiographical basis : *Mes Hôpitaux* and *Mes Prisons* expressly so. *Louise Leclercq* and *les Mémoires d'un Veuf* are less directly personal. *Les Poètes maudits* is a plea for several singers who have been left a little in the shade by their contemporaries. 'Pauvre Lelian' himself is in certain senses a *poète maudit*, and one of those to whom much must be forgiven because he has loved much. Among a thousand broken lights and shapes there are always glimpses of the true in his song. And in spite of all his doubts, his degradation, his despair and the vagaries of his life and language there is much invitation to sympathy in his brief testament, so full of bitter irony :—

My will. I leave nothing to the poor, because I am myself one of the poor. I believe in God.

PAUL VERLAINE.

Nothing is more curious than the attitude of the 'sensible and lucid Latin' critic towards the poetry of Paul Verlaine. Where an English reader sees beauty and hears melody, he avers that he can find only 'a vexatious medley and uncouth dissonances'. Even the verbal examples which he gives of these faults seem to be just the things of which the boldness, the vividness and the felicity would be most admired in a northern poet. Much of the contemporary criticism of France is strangely blind to the beauty of fresh forms of art. Whether the criticism proceeds from formulas established on the methods of the earlier masters of French verse or from the æsthetic ideals developed by the individual its practical result is always the same. Even when captivated by the genius of such a poet as Paul Verlaine the critic is strangely mystified by something novel or abnormal in the mode of expression. Anatole France has faced the problem with characteristic sympathy and pronounces Paul Verlaine the creator of a new art. Jules Lemaître, after a severe and sarcastic censure of the syntax, the sentiments, the symbolism and the spiritual expression of the poet's style is constrained to say that Paul Verlaine is 'a barbarian, a savage, a child . . . only this sick child has music in his soul, and on certain days he hears voices which none ever heard before him'. The truth is that in respect of those essential qualities which are among the highest in poetry Paul Verlaine is incomparably the greatest living master of French verse and perhaps one of the greatest in this century. He has given a new colour to the language of emotion and a new turn to the subtleties of ideal thought. In striving to enfranchise himself from certain narrow moulds of poetical expression he has achieved by sheer instinct the supreme triumph of the art of the nineteenth century—that subordination of conventional forms to the individual vision and voice which was the work of Turner in painting, of Wagner in music and of Carlyle in letters. So far from initiating the decadence of French verse, it is not unlikely that the impassioned and spiritual poetry of Paul Verlaine will usher in a new era and vindicate afresh the indefeasible privilege of genius.

NOTE.—A translation of *The Death of Philip the Second* is given among the selections from *Poèmes saturniens* as a single specimen of modern French realistic verse. It must not be imagined, however, that such bold and naked realism is anywise characteristic of Verlaine's style. Unlike Richepin and Rollinat, he employs it only as an occasional device. He never heaps up foul images or revels in loathsome details, and if he employs a repulsive natural fact for purposes of poetical contrast or illustration no excuse should be necessary. For as Ruskin says in (for him) an amazingly uneuphonious sentence of *Modern Painters* :—'Unideal works of art (the studious production of which is termed Realism) represent actual existing things, and *are good or bad in proportion to the perfection of the representation*'.

Resignation.

Even as a child I dreamed of thee, Light-blender,
Kohinoor! Of Persian pomp and Papal splendour,
Heliogabalus and Sardanapâl!

Beneath the golden domes my fancy haunted
Were perfumes rare and melodies enchanted
In harems built for pleasures sensual.

And now, more calm, though not with colder heart,
But knowing life and prone to melancholy,
Late have I learned to curb my youthful folly,
Yet not too much resigned to play this part.

My soul, since the sublime will not unbend,
Spurn elegance, the lees of all things human!
Still, as erewhile, I hate the pretty woman,
The facile rhyme and eke the prudent friend.

Résignation: Mélancholia.
(Poèmes saturniens.)

Weariness.

For battles of love a field of down.

Soft, soft, I pray, sweet heart that pants and presses!
Oh calm awhile those feverish ecstasies!
Even at the height of transport she is wise
Whose warmth a sister's tranquil love confesses.

Be languishing! And lull me with your sighs,
As with your slumberous looks and slow caresses;
Not the fierce clasp nor the spasm that possesses
Is worth one lingering kiss, even one that lies!

But, in your golden heart, you say, dear child,
Love blows her oliphant with longings wild! . . .
There let the gipsy trumpet in her fashion!

Lay on my brow your brow, your hand in mine,
Breathe vows, to break them with the morrow's shine,
And let us weep till dawn, O soul of passion!

Lassitude: Mélancholia.
(Poèmes saturniens.)

Anguish.

Nature, thou movst me not at all, nor fields
That nurse mankind, nor rosy echoes tender
Of Southern pastorals, nor auroral splendour,
Nor saddening calm that solemn sunset yields.

I laugh at Art, I hold man in derision,
Verse, song, Greek temples, towers whose spirals rise
Wreathed in the void of vast cathedral skies;
And good and ill to me are one vain vision.

I have no faith in God. Thought I despise
And spurn, and as for that old tale of lies,
Love, let them speak of it to me no more!

Life-wearied, fearing death; like a lost vessel,
Light plaything tossed betwixt wild surge and shore,
My soul with fate's last storm prepares to wrestle.

L'Angoisse: Mélancholia.
(Poèmes saturniens.)

An Autumn Song.

The long-drawn sighs,
Like violin-cries,
   Of autumn wailing,
Lull in my soul
The languorous shoal
   Of thoughts assailing.

Wan, as whom knells
Of funeral bells
   Bemoan and banish,
I weep upon
Days dead and gone
   With dreams that vanish ;

Then helpless swing
On the wind's wing ;
   Tossed hither and thither
As winter sweeps
From swirling heaps
   Worn leaves that wither.

Chanson d'automne: Paysages tristes.
                    (*Poèmes saturniens.*)

The Lover's Hour.

The red moon moves along the misty hill ;
   Swathed in a tremulous haze the dreaming meadow
   Drowses ; the frog croaks hoarsely in the shadow
Of green reeds, stirred when the faint zephyrs thrill ;

The marsh-flowers furl their heads, hidden in rushes ;
   In dwindling line tall poplars cleave the gloom,
   Serried and straight, and gaunt as vague ghosts loom ;
Slowly the glow-worms wander towards the bushes.

The screech-owl wakens and in noiseless flight
Winnows the swarthy air with lazy pinion ;
Dim glimmerings fill the dusky cloud-dominion :
Venus emerges pale, and lo ! the Night.

L'Heure du Berger: Paysages tristes.
(Poèmes saturniens.)

The Nightingale.

With noisy flight of birds that seek the tree
All my stirred memories swoop down on me,
Swoop down on my sere heart's once leafy pillow
Whose withered boughs, glassed like a bending
willow,
Gloom in the violet waters of Regret
That flow beneath in sullen rivulet ;
Swoop down, ere yet the breath of vaporous breezes
Risen in the dusk their clamorous sound appeases,
And in the tree it dies away, until
The moment comes when all is hushed and still,
All save thy voice, hymning the Absent Lover,
All save thy voice—O tremulous sighs that hover !—
Sweet bird, soul of my First Love, ever young,
And singing as on the first day she sung ;
And now beneath a moon whose sorrowing splendour
Waxes in solemn sadness, wan and tender,
The mournful night, heavy with summer heat,
Full of dim shadows, full of silence sweet,
Lulls in blue air, wherethrough a soft wind shivers,
The bird that weeps and the worn tree that quivers.

Le Rossignol: Paysages tristes.
(Poèmes saturniens.)

The Death of Philip the Second.

The red September sunset bathes in blood
　The sullen plain, the sharp sierra-rims
And drowsy mists that in the distance brood.

　On smooth sands the Guadarrama o'erbrims
Her restless wave, reflecting here and there
　Dwarf olive-trees that writhe their shrivelled limbs.

The ravenous hawks, in high flight angular,
　Cleave the dun sky and from the dusky west
Their hoarse cry grates athwart the spacious air.

　Uprising to the stars, with granite breast
And brutal pile of towers octagonal,
　The proud Escorial rears her lordly crest.

Pierced with funereal windows the square wall
　Stands sheer and white, with no device endowed
Save grille and crown carved at like interval.*

　With clamours, rude as uncouth howlings loud
When, armed with axe and spade, the shepherd fells
　A bear whose cries of anguish echoing crowd,

Rolling as on the rocks a torrent swells
　Her waves, then sinks in murmurings long and deep,
Drearily on the night air clang the bells.

---

* In the original—'grils sculptés qu'alternent des couronnes'—apparently the *portcullis* and *crown* of heraldic blazon, as borne by John of Gaunt and his descendants the Nevills of Abergavenny.

Through the hushed palace-courts, where shadows sleep
—So winds a sacred serpent's tortuous trail—
White-kirtled friars in slow procession creep,

By rule monastic ranked, like spectres pale,
    Barefoot, with girdled loins, taper in hand,
Chaunting with awful voice a psalm of wail.

Who then lies dying? Why this ghostly band,
This pavement strown with straw? Whose doom deplores
    That cross, long-veiled as Roman rites demand?

The room is vast and sombre. The wide doors,
    Enamelled ebony, on their hinges turn
Noiseless, with locks oiled smooth as polished floors.

A vague gleam, sad as twilight thoughts that yearn,
Is filtered tremulous through the curtain-folds
    From panes whereon the fires of sunset burn,

And, caught in angles on the corniced moulds,
    Casts flickering on the roof, with shade embrowned,
A halo faint as some strange picture holds.

In the wan gloom, transparent and profound,
Clusters of men and women move dismayed
    With furtive feet, like lynxes stealing round.

From lords and dames, in splendid garb arrayed,
    A changeful symphony of colour flows
In velvet, frieze, silk, damask and brocade.

And piercing the dense shade, that deeper grows,
From brazen breastplates fitful lightnings glance
    On guards ranged cunningly in ordered rows.

A black-stoled leech, with viperine countenance,
  Bends o'er a bed ; his hands caress his thighs,
As one that on a volume pores in trance.

  Cloth-of-gold curtains drape in rigid guise
An ebon daïs, studded with the shine,
  From point to point, of cold hard diamond eyes.

A gaunt old man, on the bed stretched supine,
  Kisses and counts the beads between his frail
Long fingers, curled like tendrils of the vine.

  His throat sends forth a shrill and hollow wail,
First of death's agonies on life impinged,—
  And his foul lips a fearful stench exhale.

In his beard, as with blighted amaranth tinged,
  Through his white hair, streaked with a ruddier glow,
Beneath his yellowing lawn, with rich lace fringed,

  Quick, cruel, hungry, swarming to and fro
To suck their sallow victim's blood unclean,
  The lice in serried squadrons come and go.

This is the King, writhing in pangs obscene.
  Philip the Second, King of Spain—All Hail !—
The Austrian eagle cowering seeks her screen

  And mighty shields, on panels glimmering pale,
Shine, and on many a flag once borne in fight
  The black bird's wings, thrilled vaguely, droop and
    quail.

The doors unfold . . . A flood of dazzling light
  Bursts suddenly, unfurls, and soon is spread
Along the ample chamber broad and bright.

With looks sublime, beneath the torch-fires red,
Ten monks march in, then halt and pause in prayer.
One walks apart and stalks with stony tread

Towards the King's couch.   He is tall, young and spare,
And the fierce transports of religion burn
In his dark orbs that through long lashes glare.

His footstep, weighty as the law and stern,
Upon the tapestried floor imperious rings.
Now to the King his eyes, cast downward, turn.

And each, in passing, an awed gesture flings,
Kneels, and thrice smites the bosom with clenched
hand ;
For he it is that Holy Unction brings.

With grave respect the leech aloof doth stand;
The body's doctor, sooth, in such a case,
Must to the soul's physician yield command.

And, as the fray draws nigh, the King's shrunk face,
Furrowed with pain, reflects a calmer mood :
So comes Religion, big with hopes of grace !

The monk, in whose now lifted looks a broad
Light of reproach and pardon blended dwells,
Stands, herald of the just decrees of God.

Drearily on the night air clang the bells.

* * * * * *

Confession follows.   On his flank half turned
The King, with muffled voice in low appeal,
Whispers of blood and flames, Jews racked and burned.

'Wouldst thou, perchance, repent thee of thy zeal?
' To burn the Jews was love and charity.
' So doing thou didst thy very faith reveal '.

And with arms crossed, head raised in ecstasy,
    The Father seems, in proud petrific force,
The sculptured soul of Papal cruelty.

    Then gathering breath, in broken accents hoarse,
Painfully, as though his thoughts from deepest glooms
    Plucked shred by shred a dolorous remorse,

The King, while ghastly in the torchlight looms
    His haggard face and wan and faded brow,
Gasps 'Flanders'—'Alba'—'torments'—'deaths and
    tombs'.

    —'The Flemings, to the church rebellious, thou
' Didst justly punish and that glory won,
    ' O King, now vainly wouldst thou disavow.

'Pursue'—and the King murmured of his son,
    Don Carlos, and two tears ran down his cheek
That quivered, clinging grimly to the bone.

    —'Thou dost deplore this deed!—its praise I speak—
' Doubtless the Infanta, tainted with the schism
    ' Of English birth, was guiltier far than weak,

' That would have dragged Spain down to the abysm,
    ' Scrupling not to conspire—O craft accursed !—
' Against his Sire, hallowed with Crown and Chrism '.—

Soon as the monk those sacred words rehearsed
Whereby is given remission of our sin,
    He took the host, with hands that trembled first,

And set it on the King's tongue.   Then all din
  Was hushed, and every soul, in anguish bowed,
Prayed pale and speechless, and none knows therein

  If with true prayer or treacherous prayed the crowd.
—How tell the thoughts obscure that brooded deep
  Beneath this silence like a friendly cloud?—

Now shriven the King, plunged anew as in sleep
  Mid ample pillows, with beatitude
Of Absolution won, seemed fain to steep

  His soul in the clear light of trust renewed,
That broke into a smile of strange delight,
  With fever half, and half with faith imbued.

And while around pressed duke and earl and knight,
  Whose mournful eyes peered into sombre deeps,
The King's soul to the conquered heavens took flight.

  Then in the dead man's breast, with furious leaps,
The weird death-rattle sounded once or twice,
  —So through a ruin the wild whirlwind sweeps—

And from a thousand holes, sprung in a trice
  Like clammy serpents from their foul abode,
On the cold corpse worms mingled with the lice.

  King Philip was at the right hand of God.

La Mort de Philippe II.
(Poèmes saturniens.)

A Song at Sunrise.

Before the flood of day prevails,
  O pale star of morning prime!
  —A thousand quails
Are singing, singing in the thyme.—

Turn on me thy lingering spark,
  Me whose eyes are filled with love;
  —Lo! the lark
Flutters in the heavens above.—

Turn thy look, bathed in the bright
  Blue splendour of the shimmering morn;
  —What delight
Dwells in fields of yellow corn!—

Till my thought shines through and through
  Sweetest dreams . . . so far, so far!
  —O the dew
On every blade of grass a star!

Sweetest dreams that dower the chaste
  Slumbers of my dearest one . . .
  —Haste, oh haste,
For yonder comes the golden sun!

                    (*La bonne Chanson: V.*)

The Art of Poetry.

Oh music above everything !
And therefore take for choice the Uneven ;
Nothing that clogs or chains the wing
  In vague and vaporous flight to Heaven !

Yet choose your words from the vocal throng
  Not too easily apprehended :
Nothing more dear than the gray song
  In which the Cloudy and Clear lie blended.

Such is the tremulous flush of noon,
  So through the veil bright eyes shoot lustre,
Such is the autumn sky aswoon
  With stars that swim in a hazy cluster !

Tone we must have and all else scorn ;
  Only shade, no colour, no splendour :
O tone ! the tender sole love-blender
Of dream with dream and flute with horn !

Far from the murderous Epigram fly,
  From cruel Wit and unclean Laughter,
That bring the tears to Heaven's blue eye . . .
  Stale garlic from the kitchen-rafter !

Take Eloquence and wring his neck !
  Right it is, when the Muses revel,
To keep these frolicsome jades in check,
  Lest unawares they run to the devil !

PAUL VERLAINE

Oh who can tell the wrongs of Rhyme?
   What deaf child was the first to chink it,
Tinsel that rings, to the true-gold-chime,
   Hollow and false as a twopenny trinket?

Oh music ever and evermore!
   So let your verse take wings and follow
The soul that seeks, on a sunnier shore,
   Fresh climes, fresh loves, like the flying swallow.

So let your Muse, in the morning prime,
   Fling to the cool crisp wind her fetters,
Flowered with the fragrance of mint and thyme . . .
   And all the rest is . . . only Letters!

Art poétique.
(Jadis et naguère.)

Paul Déroulède.

Born in Paris, 1846.

Paul Déroulède is the son of a lawyer, and a nephew of the dramatist Émile Augier. He received a good education and was nursed in strong national sentiments. This fiery soldier, versifier and politician has lived a stormy life. After being trained for the law he travelled over a great part of Europe in his youth and fought heroically in the war of 1870. Taken prisoner at Sedan, he escaped, offered his services to Gambetta, served under General Chanzy on the Loire, and was badly wounded at a barricade during the Commune. He has been an active member of the Chamber of Deputies.

It is impossible not to admire the fine chivalrous character of Paul Déroulède. Full of courage, uncompromising in speech and direct in action; he is also an idealist with more zeal than discretion and is easily led away by enthusiasm. When General Boulanger on his black charger pranced into popularity Paul Déroulède was one of those who welcomed the sham Cæsar. He founded the Patriots' League and a militant journal—*Le Drapeau*—to propagate his opinions. He is a great advocate of physical regeneration and no man has done more than he, by precept and example and in speech and pamphlet, to revive ideals of national duty and devotion in France.

Paul Déroulède is the author of a novel and three spirited dramas, but his best work has been the lyrical celebration of the soldier and the peasant. He is by no means a great singer, yet he has a note of his own and touches a chord which is perhaps not so dormant in French life as some superficial observers would like to believe. His books of songs are called *Chants du Soldat* (two collections . . . 1872 and 1875), *Chants du Paysan, Marches et Sonneries* and *Refrains militaires*. They are exceedingly popular, especially the earlier ones. In 1894 the French Academy awarded the *prix Jean Reynaud* of 10,000 francs to the singer of these patriotic songs, although he had announced his 'resolute refusal' of the proposed honour.

PAUL DÉROULÈDE

The Marseillaise.

Have pity on yourselves and cease that song ;
In silence, when the hour comes, march along
Like vanquished heroes whose undaunted breath
Whispers one word : ' Revenge !'—or haply ' Death !'

Yet hear the accursëd story and be stirred :
Or if your ears in bygone days have heard
On many a trembling tongue the twice-told tale
'Tis well ; ŋo need drive home the hammered nail !

You love, no doubt you love, our people's hymn ?
You love its sacred rage, its transports grim :
And, like proud sons, you feel in its song-fires
The quenchless spirit of your puissant sires.
Its rousing voice recalls our flag unfurled,
Floating to the four corners of the world,
Nations struck dumb and kings that looked askance ;
You think of that?   Our great and glorious France !
Think of this too, the day of our defeat,
Sedan—a name that with bowed heads you greet—
Frenchmen, remember in that surge of woes,
When conquered France surrendered to her foes,
When in crushed souls our soldiers bore unmanned
The mangled ghost of the poor fatherland,
When all was lost and leaving the fought field
Our troops, disarmed, were forced at last to yield—
O unforgotten blow !   O worst of evil days !
Loud from the Prussian trumpets shrilled the Marseil-
    laise !

La Marseillaise.
(Chants du Soldat.)

299

Credo.

I trust in God.   The time is vile and troubled.
  A breath of blasphemy blows souls aflame ;
When wealth with honour plays the stakes are doubled ;
  Sin knows no punishment and vice no shame.

I trust in God.   Faith has gone out of fashion.
  The priest is hounded down, the cross undone.
A Christian is the butt of scornful passion ;
  Every man claims his rights, his duties none.

I trust in God.   Nor fails my fervent prayer,
  Though evil-doers boast their triumphs blind !
Let Dante's hell hold circles of despair,
  My heart, that enters, leaves not hope behind !

I trust in God.   France, sunk in degradation,
  Is sick at heart and bears the oppressor's rod ;
But though in deadly sleep lies the Great Nation
  The wakening hour will come.   I trust in God.

Credo.
(*Chants du Paysan.*)

Maurice Rollinat.

Born in Châteauroux (Indre) 1846.

If Maurice Rollinat is not one of the greatest poets of his time he has at least a style so individual and so vigorous as to command attention. The publication of *les Névroses* (1883) disclosed to connoisseurs in verse a geniuś of powerful character, prone to a peculiarly morbid and even funereal realism. Rollinat himself, with his expressive and fascinating features, was for a season the object of a fashionable hero-worship. Possessed of the rare faculty of reciting verse, he thrilled and captivated with the creations of his sombre muse the literary *dilettanti* and sensitive fair ones of the *salons* of Paris. *Les Névroses* is a sinister study of all that is horrible and ghastly in life and death. Paul Verlaine regards it as a vulgarisation of the Satanic element in art —Baudelaire brought within the range of the general reader—but he does scanty justice to the vital force and originality of Rollinat's poetic temperament and to the masterly artistic treatment of a daring realism which he himself has not disdained to handle on occasion.

A previous volume of Rollinat's verse—*Dans les Brandes* —was in its own way quite as worthy of admiration. These poems and rondels of the Berry landscape (so dear to George Sand) were exquisitely sung, with their quaint rhymes and dainty devices. Two other volumes—*l'Abîme* in 1886 and *la Nature* in 1892—displayed afresh the ingenuity of Rollinat's lyrical gift without adding much to the range of his earlier works. They might, indeed, be regarded as exercises and variations on the themes already employed in his verse.

Maurice Rollinat has a fine eye for nature, a rich fancy and a large vocabulary. Even in *les Névroses* there are episodes of idyllic beauty and lyric grace. Although he is not endowed with the imagination that assimilates the external to human moods and aspirations, he has given a distinctly new chord to the French lyre, and along with Verlaine, Richepin and Moréas he must be acknowledged as one of the notable poets of these later days.

Like so many other French artists, musicians and men of letters, Maurice Rollinat is a lawyer's son. He formerly held an appointment in the Prefecture of the Seine. For the last two years he has lived the life of a hermit at Fresselines (Creuze) and his appearances in public have been few and far between.

The Poppy Ravine.

Deep in a wild lone hollow hid,
Where never comes the light-foot kid,
Nor cornflower opens her blue lid
     In dusky coppice ;
Far from the track the mule's hoof makes,
Far from the noise that echo wakes,
In desert silence dreams and shakes
     A bloom of poppies.

But there the sleepy lizards crawl
Round loathsome pools funereal
In which heaven's shadows when they fall
     Their darkness sully ;
Between stark sprays of heather grim
And boxwood bushes cold and dim
That crowding creep along the rim
     Of the red gully.

The sky, like coloured windows dight,
Sheds only here a crenelled light
Above their clustered coral bright
     That so bewitches ;
Yet on the rocks and marsh below
They cast a fresh and ruddy glow,
Like those that in the valleys blow
     And woodland ditches.

They rustle in the thin light air
When signs of change the seasons wear
And forth the wandering breezes fare,
      Their temples brushing ;
And fling about in furious mood,
Beneath the north-wind wild and rude,
As one might see a stream of blood
      Rippling and rushing.

In vain the sullen cloud that lowers
From upland slopes and ridgy towers
The splendour of these flaunting flowers
      In shade would smother ;
The dragon-flies, on nimble wing,
Above their beauty vibrating,
Turn two by two in ceaseless ring
      One round another.

Razed by the birds in warbling flight
And touched by starry glimmerings white
· They flourish in the cool of night
      And noonday swelter ;
And, crowned with radiant diadem,
Like fireflies tremble on their stem,
As though the furrow fostered them
      And gave them shelter.

Their brightness, like a furnace-fire,
Makes glad the willow and the briar,
The snake that coils its drowsy spire,
      The shrub's bare bosom ;
The sombre crags, though shorn of sun,
Loom not so dark, look not so dun,
Because their shadow leans upon
      That blaze of blossom.

There scarlet glitters, crimson glows ;
The purple stream from crime that flows,
The ruby and the blood-red rose
        Shine in their chalice ;
And so, when the soft foliage feels
The warmth that from the noontide steals,
It is the swarming cochineal's
        Resplendent palace.

           Le Ravin des Coquelicots.
               (*Les Névroses.*)

The Chamber.

This room of mine my soul resembles ;
   So sleep and death seem even as one :
No flame in the dull fireplace trembles !
   On the dull window shines no sun !

A melancholy pattern covers
   The gray walls of the sombre room,
And where the green blind's shadow hovers
   It flecks, like verdigris, their gloom.

Above my pillow gazes ever
   A Christ, with innocent looks unblamed,
Who seems in the dense shade to shiver,
   As of his nakedness ashamed.

My fate has a funereal fellow,
   For on the chimney-mantel lies
A broken skull, worn smooth and yellow,
   That haunts me with his hollow eyes.

MAURICE ROLLINAT

In heavy folds the ancient curtain
  Clings round my bedstead like a pall ;
Fantastic creeping things uncertain
  Athwart the ceiling dance and crawl.

When on my clock the hour comes knelling
  It fills me with a wild dismay ;
Each loud pulsation, strangely swelling,
  Lingers and slowly dies away.

The angel of my buried passion
  Comes nightly, swathed in sable cloke,
And wails a dirge in ghostly fashion,
  With tears that blind and sobs that choke.

Books, pictures, flowers seem phantoms risen
  With poisonous airs from deepest hell,
And, like a shroud that wraps this prison,
  Horror, that loves me, comes to dwell.

Sad chamber where, with mocking curses,
  Care keeps her vigil day and night,
Along thy wall I write these verses
  And love thee for thy black delight ;

For as the gulf the torrent pleases,
  And dear is darkness to the owl,
So thou dost charm my soul's diseases
  Because thou art so like my soul !

La Chambre: Les Spectres.
(Les Névroses.)

The Song of the Speckled Partridge.

The song the speckled partridge sings,
  Or shrill cicala sad and sweet,
  From furrows rising comes to greet
My soul that loves melodious things.

Through the blue air it thrills and rings,
  Blended with whirr of winglets fleet ;
The song the speckled partridge sings,
  Or shrill cicala sad and sweet.

In vain would weary thought with stings
  Assail me in this fresh retreat
  Where, shielded from the noonday heat,
Comes wafted on the wind's soft wings
The song the speckled partridge sings.

La Chanson de la Perdrix grise.
(*Dans les Brandes.*)

Jean Richepin.

Born in Médéah (Algeria) 1849.

Jean Richepin is the son of a military surgeon and was educated at the Normal College (*École normale supérieure*) in Paris. He had a hard struggle to gain his place in literature and published several works before a little play —*l'Étoile*—brought him into notice. It was written in collaboration with André Gill and produced (1873) in a small theatre which has since been demolished, the *École-Lyrique* in *rue de la Tour-d'Auvergne*, a street haunted with memories of Chateaubriand, Béranger and Victor Hugo and inhabited in later days by Francisque Sarcey, critic-in-chief of the great school of common-sense.

Richepin's first real renown was due to the *Chanson des Gueux* in 1876. This volume of bold and violent verse in praise of vagabondage revealed a new poet, and brought him also before the bench of criminal law. He was fined 500 francs and costs and sent to prison for thirty days. Some of the pieces to which Justice took exception have been suppressed in the definitive edition of his work. In the new issue of 1891 Richepin claims for this volume of verse 'a superb and healthy immorality' and declares that the popular indecency of proper terms and the designation of things by their actual names never corrupted anybody.

The *Song of the Beggars* was followed by a series of notable novels and plays, all giving evidence of a frankly original if sometimes riotous and uncontrolled genius.

308

La Glu (1881) *Miarka* and *Nana-Sahib* (1883) and *le Flibustier* (1888) mark the principal points of his progress. *Par le Glaive*, a tragedy played at the *Comédie-Française* in 1892, is a masterpiece of impassioned declamation. *Vers la Joie*, a satirical comedy in verse, which was produced at the same theatre in 1894, has an idiomatic vigour of expression and an atmosphere of idealism which, for a French play, are almost Elizabethan.

Les Blasphèmes burst on the literary world in 1884. It had been the poet's work between twenty and thirty years of age and was intended to form part of a large scheme of daring and aggressive verse. Richepin boldly declared his *Blasphemies* to be 'the Bible of Atheism'. In his magnificent invective he was sometimes like Ajax defying the lightning; sometimes more like the Gallic cock on his dunghill crowing defiance to the Almighty. But the everlasting revolt against authority has seldom been clothed in such sonorous and splendid language. The verse is full of novel rhymes and vivid images, and abounds in bold neologisms borrowed from the popular speech, in which Richepin is an adept. The recollection of *Songs before Sunrise* would have dulled the effect of such a book in this country, but it was the first outburst of the kind in France. Its insolent bravado is a thorn in the side of the decadent poets, with their pale colours and delicate lines. ' This bitter wine', said the author, 'is not for the cream-licking palates of children, but for strong stomachs and powerful brains'.

There is no reason to doubt the sincerity of the *Blasphemies*. Richepin carried on a long campaign in the *Gil Blas* in defence of his literary methods. He had pursued his robust course across storms and scandals and passions and protests; even at the cost of' some friendships which were dear to him. But there is a visible abatement

of the fever-heat in his later works. *La Mer* (1886) is a
superb song of the sea in all its changes and caprices.
Mes Paradis (1893) is a volume of comparatively calm
and reflective verse, and here again the poet vindicates his
claim to be regarded as a virtuoso in harmony and rhyme.
He confesses that this work is very different in execution
from what he conceived it when he was 'burned with the
fever of pride and drunk with the wine of youth'. It has
not the rough sweep and dazzling colour of his earlier
verse, yet he shows by an occasional coarse phrase that
he retains his love of startling effects.

It is a strange paradox that Richepin, with his consummate mastery of the vernacular and his love for brilliant
and brutal images, should of all contemporary poets be
the one who is most akin to the French classics in pre-
cision of sense and distinctness of form. 'He is one of
those rare writers'—says Jules Lemaître—'to whom you
can listen always with a feeling of entire security; you
are sure, at least, that he will not sin against grammar
nor against syntax nor against the genius of the language'.
This opinion is perfectly true in relation to the fact that
many of Richepin's lines are as bald as anything Voltaire
ever wrote, but it is also beyond a doubt that his finest
verse is modelled more on Victor Hugo's than on that of
any older poet. What other than the Romantic influence
could have inspired such a line as

'L'ululant hallali que clangorent les cors'

in *Mes Paradis.*

Whether Richepin in his sober period will send forth
any new verse equal to *les Blasphèmes* is doubtful. These
fiery poets, when they cool down, are apt to become
extinct volcanoes.

The Death of the Gods.

See! brothers, weak and weary have I striven
    Against the Almighty Ones clothed round with fear ;
Glorying in impious pride my pledge was given,
    And, having ransacked Heaven, lo, I am here!

When I snuffed out the Gods, as one erases
    A word, they thundered not nor reasoned why :
You, therefore, shall lift up your prostrate faces
    And gaze on these great corpses where they lie.

You, searching Heaven, void as a pauper's fingers,
    Shall scorn the phantoms that no more bewitch,
And, free to pluck from hope the flower that lingers,
    Shall cast your terrors in the wayside ditch.

You shall tear down the veils of fraud and wonder,
    Finding no Lord beyond Life's utmost bars,
And watch in brooding space, now cloven asunder,
    Beneath the wing of Chance burst forth the Stars.

For you the Force of Things in wide dispersal
    Streams, as a shoreless, soundless ocean flows,
In endless whirlpools of life universal,
    The whence and why whereof no mortal knows.

You, knowing your own souls lost in infinite numbers,
    Even as a dewdrop plunged in the deep stream,
Shall judge the Gods, those nightmares of man's slumbers,
    In life's vast All as shadows of a dream.

Tranquil, as with a conqueror's calm elation,
  Deceived no more by priests' and preachers' arts,
In this warm coign o' the world's blest habitation
  You shall repose in peace your ransomed hearts.

Good shall be yours, though mixed with evil measure,
  Even as the nursling, the poor vagrant's child
That sucks her breast, closes his eyes in pleasure,
  Heedless of wrinkled teats and skin defiled.

Cleansing your souls of every vague desire,
  Your love, on wives' and mothers' flowery lips,
Shall soon forget youth's kiss of frenzied fire
  On shadowy bosoms lost in dim eclipse.

By simple craving that like comfort pleases,
  Renewed at ease and with each morning fresh ;
By hope drawn nigh, that small endeavour seizes,
  Your spirits shall live free in the freed flesh.

Longings fulfilled and solace for all sadness
  Shall be your blissful lot, your wonted fare,
So shall ye drink the wine of holiest gladness
  In boundless Beauty and Love that all may share.

No longer shall your hearts dread pale-eyed Sorrow,
  Misshapen Will, Remorse with choking curse ;
Living like children careless of the morrow,
  Cradled on Nature's knees, your loving nurse.

Faith's agonies, the barren vows of ages,
  Fantastic superstitions, cruel deeds,
Gospels, Korans, Vedas, those lying pages,
  The time-worn wreckage of Beliefs and Creeds,

JEAN RICHEPIN

Like carrion vultures, hoarse and fierce and savage,
  That hovered on your hearts six thousand years
And with your bleeding flesh glutted their ravage,
  Fouling the air in mockery of your fears,

Baffled and blinded by the morning glory
  And shrieking in the sun's remorseless light,
Shall whirl in confused flock, haggard and hoary,
  As in their dismal swarm the birds of night.

And when at last, with clouds and darkness blended,
  They speed their flight, like a funereal knell
Their ghosts shall hear your laughter vast and splendid
  Exultant from earth's shivering bosom swell.

Then comes the end. Climbing on fanes forsaken
  Wild vines shall hide the doors, like grass on graves ;
Dead idol and dead priest no more shall waken,
  Oblivion rolls them under her slow waves.

Alone lost legends live in hearts of lovers
  That wander in the woods of old romance,
Charmed by an echoing voice, that vaguely hovers,
  To linger there awhile in mystic trance.

Even they, losing the names dark generations
  Gave to those bloody spectres, when day comes,
Shall hear their echoes, hushed to faint vibrations,
  Die like the muffled roll of distant drums.

Then, when those names that filled the world's loud clarion
  Sink like the memory of a vanished clan,
Man's pride shall spring, a rose from gods grown carrion,
  For earth has one sole God, and he is Man !

La Mort des Dieux.
(Les Blasphèmes.)

The Wanderer.

When wandering on my waggon through the earth
  I halted first and gazed on these abodes,
A city held within its antique girth
  Towers, temples, workshops, palaces and gods.
And when, curious as one that homeless plods,
  I cried : ' Whence rose this city's golden prime ? '
An answer came, in measured periods :—
  ' Our city stands established from all time '.

      Full five thousand years had flown
      Ere I wandered there alone.

Towers, temples, palaces, gods, all were gone.
No vestige there.   With sunlit jewels red
The hard green blades of grass like javelins shone.
A poor old shepherd, grossly garmented,
Sole on the plain stood munching his brown bread ;
Now, when I sought to know how many days
On this new pasture flocks had strayed and fed,
With scornful look the shepherd spake :—' Always '.

      Full five thousand years had flown
      Ere I wandered there alone.

The plain was changed into a gloomy wood.
Through broad arcades lithe creepers in the breeze
Swung, like wreathed serpents in their knotty brood,
And, tall as masts, above those sombre seas

Of foliage towered the trunks of giant trees.
Then to the huntsman through the green leaves whirled
I called : 'When did these woods first clothe the leas?'—
'Yon oaks'—quoth he—'are older than the world!'

Full five thousand years had flown
Ere I wandered there alone.

The sea, the vast sea, in her winding-sheet
Had shrouded the fresh sward and woodland wide.
A bark, on whose frail bulwarks the waves beat,
Swayed in the twilight winds from side to side.
I hailed the boatman :—'Tell me when the tide
First swallowed thus earth's fields and forests green':—
'You jest!'—said he, and then more grave replied :—
'Since the sea was the sea, here hath it been'.

Full five thousand years had flown
Ere I wandered there alone.

Where once light billows tossed their silvery plume,
Before me stretched a golden-furrowed strand—
The desert! Not a tree rose through the gloom :
Sand here, sand there, and nothing else save sand.
And while I looked askance on that bare land,
The Arab, as he checked his camel's pace,
Spoke :—'Since life sprang on earth by Heaven's com-
    mand
This waste has lain, eternal as our race'.

Full five thousand years had flown
Ere I wandered there alone.

And lo! once more a city's stately form,
With walls, towers, temples, palaces and gods
Rose, boiling like a spring with life aswarm.
Then with loud voice I asked those insolent crowds :
'Where are the golden sands, green swards, blue floods,
And haughty walls of yore?'—'Thus'—said a wight—
'Were, are and ever shall be, these abodes':
And in that Arya's face I laughed outright.

Years shall flow as years have flown
Ere I wander there alone.

Le Bohémien : La Chanson du Sang.
(*Les Blasphèmes.*)

The Hun.

Fly swift, my furious courser!
  German and Goth and Frank
  And Gaul and Roman rank
  Roll back beneath thy flank.
Before my fiery courser,
      Ha! Ha!
The old world reels and quivers
Like mist the tempest shivers.
      Attila!
      Attila!

JEAN RICHEPIN

Gallop full-blown and breathless!
   I fly before the sun,
   From naked uplands dun
   By wild winds whirled and spun:
They breed the whirlwind breathless,
      Ha! Ha!
That round my swift flight whistles
Light fleece from shaken thistles.
      Attila!
      Attila!

I plunge through limitless spaces
   And leaping hill and dale
   Swoop on those purlieus pale
   Where horseless legions quail:
I revel in boundless spaces,
      Ha! Ha!
Nor halt my flying eagles,
Swift in the chase as beagles.
      Attila!
      Attila!

With gallop proud and splendid
   I pass, like hounds in cry,
   And where my chargers fly
   Wide-strown the corpses lie:
My swords are swift and splendid,
      Ha! Ha!
The land with slain they scatter,
As flails the red sheaves shatter.
      Attila!
      Attila!

Le Hun: La Chanson du Sang.
          (*Les Blasphèmes.*)

Ballade of the Swallow.

The swallow, bird of stale romances
    And trivial tag of tinkling rhyme,
Is regent of heaven's vast expanses.
    But though she skims, in flight sublime,
    A thousand worlds of Space and Time,
With sweep of wandering wings that follow
    The far track of the season's prime,
She owns one only nest, the swallow.

Here, there and everywhere she glances . . .
    ' She tumbles like a madcap mime ! '
' How light-o'-love she darts and dances
    From Eden-bower to Niebelheim ! ' . . .
    So worms and snails say, in their slime.
Be like her, libertines that wallow
    In coverts of connubial crime ;
She owns one only nest, the swallow.

No doubt, when the chill tide advances
    And soft fleece falls in snow and rime
Or hail that stings like little lances,
    The swallow flies our wintry clime.
    But, back from lands of flowering thyme,
Faithful she seeks the same old hollow
    Beneath bare eaves of straw and lime :
She owns one only nest, the swallow.

ENVOY.

Prince, leave your loves of diverse chime
    And choose one lodge, like bright Apollo,
For rest from the day's weary climb.
    She owns one only nest, the swallow.

                    Ballade de l'Hirondelle.
                          (Mes Paradis.)

Hervé-Noël Le Breton.

Born in Nantes, 1851.

Leiz ar kalon ag arok.

The name of this Breton poet * is almost if not altogether unknown in Parisian literary circles. He is descended from a purely Celtic family; not one of those, like Villiers de l'Isle-Adam, which became Breton by early territorial acquisition or matrimonial alliance, but one of the ancient and authentic Armorican race. The Le Bretons were irretrievably ruined in the Vendean struggle for Catholicism and Royalty. Since fighting was their only vocation and the ranks of the Republican armies were closed against them they fell into the deepest poverty. The present representative of the family had a close acquaintance with chill penury in his youth. To a defective education he willingly attributes his 'profound and deplorable ignorance' of classical literature and the exact sciences. Like most modern Frenchmen he was

---

* The other Breton poets of this century, among whom may be named Auguste Brizeux, Hippolyte Lucas, Tristan Corbière and Charles Le Goffic, have not found a place in this collection. Nor has space been provided for the Provençal group of poets, notably Frédéric Mistral, Téodor Aubanel, and Félis Gras; the Parisian chansonniers Béranger, Dupont and Désaugiers; Marceline Desbordes-Valmore, Delphine Gay-Girardin, Amable Tastu, Louisa Siefert and the singing-women of the nineteenth century; Auguste Lacaussade (who belonged, like Leconte de Lisle and Léon Dierx, to the island of Bourbon or la Réunion); also Alfred de Vigny, Émile and Antony Deschamps, Victor de Laprade, Joseph Autran, Auguste Vacquerie, Joséphin Soulary, Albert Mérat, Léon Valade and many other remarkable poets.

nourished on Voltairean and Revolutionary ideas, to which his traditional beliefs have so far succumbed that his political predilection is 'a Republic governed by an absolute aristocrat' and his religious creed 'an unaggressive Atheism, tempered by a profound belief in the Divine'.

Le Breton's natural inclination to literature was frustrated in youth by the premature death of his father and the claims of a resourceless household, aggravated by his own early marriage. He was compelled to turn his attention to commerce and is now engaged in some branch of the cotton-trade in Rouen. It is understood that he seeks consolation in the unobtrusive culture of *belles-lettres*. The poet for whom he professes most admiration is Leconte de Lisle. Whether his own final renunciation of the literary career is due to a preference for the flesh-pots of Egypt, to a lack of ambition or to a justifiable distrust of his equipment and power cannot be determined. His only answer to the remonstrance of an indiscreet correspondent was the rejoinder of Naaman : Are not Abanah and Pharpar, rivers of Damascus, better than all the waters of Israel?

A few of Le Breton's prose compositions, and those of little importance, have appeared in the leading journal of the province in which he lives. *Rêves et Symboles* is an unpublished volume of experiments in verse, mostly written during that space of existence between boyhood and manhood, which has been described by Keats, when 'the soul is in a ferment, the character undecided, the way of life uncertain, the ambition thick-sighted'. The specimens which have been translated for this collection were procured with some difficulty, but Le Breton's note is a little different from that of other French writers of the present period, and for that reason, if for no other, one or two of his poems may not be out of place here.

Sic itur ad Astra.

I pity not the man whose years
 Are spent in sore and ceaseless toil,
Even though his bitter bread with tears
 Be wrung from a rebellious soil.

Nor him whose vigils shorn of sleep
 And days forlorn of gladness find
Still labouring, brave of heart, to reap
 The larger harvest of the mind.

For work alone can quench and quell
 All feverish doubts, all fierce desires ;
And idleness is instant hell
 Kindling on earth her penal fires.

The luminous souls that look with calm
 Consummate from their supreme height
Won not the halo and the palm
 In dreamful purlieus of delight.

The splendour of the rainbow dwells
 Not in the clear but on the cloud ;
And Virtue less in cloistered cells
 Than with the conflict and the crowd.

Labour can lull, with soothing breath,
 Sorrow and shame and pain to sleep ;
Outstrip swift Time, laugh at dull Death,
 And over gulfed Oblivion leap.

Work, therefore, if no dawn should come
To break against these prison-bars;
Though Truth be dark and Fate be dumb . . .
For so they climb that reach the stars!

Vers les Étoiles.
(Rêves et Symboles.)

The Burden of Lost Souls.

I.

This was our sin.   When Hope, with wings enchanted
And shining aureole,
Hung on the blossomed steps of Youth and haunted
The chancel of the soul;

When we whose lips haply had blown the bugle
That cheers the wavering line,
And solaced those to whom the world was frugal
Of Love, the food divine;

Whose hands had strength to smite men's chains asunder
And heal the poor man's wrong,
Whose breath was blended with the chords that thunder
Along the aisles of song;

Whose eyes had seen and hailed the Light of Ages,
In cloudiest heavens a star,
Whose ears had heard, on ringing wheels, the stages
Of Freedom's trophied car :—

We turned, rebellious children, to the clamour
And tumult of the world;
We gave our souls in fee for Circe's glamour
And white limbs lightly whirled;

322

HERVÉ-NOËL LE BRETON

We drank deep draughts of Moloch's unclean liquor
    Even to the dregs of shame,
And blinded by the golden lights that flicker
    From Mammon's altar-flame

We burned strange incense, bowed before his idol
    Whose eucharist is fire,
And on the neck of passion loosed the bridle
    Of fierce and wild desire :—

Till now in our own hearts the ashy embers
    Of Love lie smouldering,
And scarce our Autumn chill and bare remembers
    The glory of the Spring ;

While faith, that in the mire was fain to wallow,
    Returns at last to find
The cold fanes desolate, the niches hollow,
    The windows dim and blind,

And, strown with ruins round, the shattered relic
    Of unregardful youth,
Where shapes of beauty once, with tongues angelic,
    Whispered the runes of Truth.

II.

This is our doom.   To walk for ever and ever
    The wilderness unblest,
To weary soul and sense in vain endeavour
    And find no coign of rest ;

To feel the pulse of speech and passion thronging
    On lips for ever dumb,
To gaze on parchëd skies relentless, longing
    For clouds that will not come ;

Thirsty, to drink of loathsome waters crawling
  With nameless things obscene,
To feel the dews from heaven like fire-drops falling,
  And neither shade nor screen ;

To fill from springs illusive riddled vessels,
  Like the Danaïdes,
To grapple with the wind that whirls and wrestles,
  Knowing no lapse of ease ;

To weave fantastic webs that shrink and crumble
  Before they leave the loom,
To build with travail aëry towers that tumble
  And temples like the tomb ;

To watch the stately pomp and proud procession
  Of splendid shapes and things,
And pine in silent solitary session
  Because we have no wings ;

To woo from confused sleep forlorn the dismal
  Oblivion of despair ;
To seek in sudden glimpse of dreams abysmal
  Sights beautiful and rare,

And waking, wild with terror, see the vision
  Cancelled in swift eclipse,
Mocked by the pallid phantoms of derision,
  With spectral eyes and lips ;

To turn in endless circles round these purlieus
  With troops of spirits pale,
Whose everlasting song is like the curlew's,
  One ceaseless, changeless wail.

III.

This is our prayer to God, the Lord and Giver
        Of Life.   If it be well,
Do Thou from penance all too long deliver
        Our souls, immured in Hell ;

If in the flush of fever, in the twilight
        Of doubt and dwindling hopes,
Thee we denied, nor saw the dawn of Thy light
        That glimmered on the slopes,

Remember not the sins of youth that wandered
        In sinful ways apart,
Cast wide the gifts of heaven and rashly squandered
        The treasures of the heart ;

Though bitter be the wage and hard the guerdon
        Of wasted fire and force,
Make not too heavy for our souls the burden
        Of sorrowful Remorse :

Forgive Thy children !   Send sweet Peace, Thine
    angel,
        With anodyne and balm,
To soothe our anguish with the blest evangel
        Of everlasting calm !

Let one pale gleam of consolation linger
        On her starred coronal :
Carve not the judgment with Thy fiery finger
        Along the darkened wall.

Or if indeed our sin·hath been too grievous
   For pardon, even of Thee,
Plunge us in Lethe's pool profound. There leave us,
   And let us cease to be.

          La Plainte des Damnés.
             (Rêves et Symboles.)

A Poet's Grave.

This humble grave is holy ground,
   For here a poet lies,
Far from the turmoiled city's sound
   Beneath the unruffled skies.

Across the still campagna comes
   The murmur of the sea,
And round the crimson clover hums
   The golden-girdled bee.

Fit place of rest for one whose soul
   Fed most on silent things,
And let the world's vext surges roll
   In tidal thunderings.

Cold are the pulses once fulfilled
   With living blood and breath ;
The heart that all men's sorrows thrilled
   Moulders in dusty death.

What is earth's fame or blame to him
   Who lies in dreamless sleep ?
He heeds not if love's light grow dim
   And midnight shades are deep.

Yet, ere I take my lonely way
  Athwart the thickening gloom,
Sadly my reverent thoughts shall lay
  This tribute on the tomb;

For I, too, hear behind me tread
  The inexorable years
That soon shall lay me where the dead
  Lie voiceless.—Hence these tears!

Le Tombeau du Poète.
(Rêves et Symboles.)

Hymn to Sleep.

Sommeil! consolateur du monde.

Keeper of the keys of Heaven,
Lingering near the starry Seven!
Guardian of the gates of Hell,
Hushed beneath thy drowsy spell!
    Fold thy wings and come to me,
    Sleep! thou soul's euthanasy.

When the pilgrim of strange lore
Haunts thy pale phantasmal shore,
Dreams and absolution grant,
Priestess thou and hierophant!
    Fold thy wings and come to me,
    Sleep! thou soul's euthanasy.

327

Builder of eternal towers!
Weaver of enchanted bowers!
Thou dost forge the fighter's arms,
Thee the lover woos for charms:
    Fold thy wings and come to me
    Sleep! thou soul's euthanasy.

Thou dost soothe the virgin's fears,
Thou dost stanch the widow's tears,
Smooth the wrinkled brows of Care,
Still the cries of wild Despair:
    Fold thy wings and come to me,
    Sleep! thou soul's euthanasy.

Healer of the sores of shame!
Cleanser of the unholy flame!
Thou dost breathe beatitude
On the evil and the good:
    Fold thy wings and come to me,
    Sleep! thou soul's euthanasy.

When the cup that Pleasure sips
Turns to wormwood on the lips;
When Remorse, with venomed mesh,
Frets and tears the writhing flesh:
    Fold thy wings and come to me,
    Sleep! thou soul's euthanasy.

Queller of the storms of Fate!
Quencher of the fires of Hate!
In thy peaceful bosom furled
Lies the turmoil of the world:
    Fold thy wings and come to me,
    Sleep! thou soul's euthanasy.

Calm as noon's abysmal blue,
Soundless as the falling dew,
Soft as snow with fleecy plumes,
Sweet as curling incense-fumes :
    Fold thy wings and come to me,
    Sleep ! thou soul's euthanasy.

Keeper of the keys of Heaven !
(Cease your vigil, starry Seven)
Guardian of the gates of Hell !
(Loosen not the drowsëd spell)
    Fold thy wings and come to me
    Sleep ! thou soul's euthanasy.

Hymne au Sommeil.
(*Rêves et Symboles.*)

Arthur Rimbaud.

Born in Charleville (Ardennes) 1854 . . . Died in Marseilles, 1891.

Fantastic beauty ; such as lurks
In some wild Poet, when he works
Without a conscience or an aim.

The indiscriminating eulogy of a few indiscreet admirers need not blind anyone to the real merits of this remarkable poet. Arthur Rimbaud was of respectable parentage and received a good middle-class education. He developed a precocious faculty for making verse, along with a certain bizarre fashion of looking at men and morals. Thrown too early into the whirlpool of Parisian excitement he led a dissipated life in the company of Paul Verlaine, and in his visits to Belgium, England and Germany gave the rein to his wandering disposition. When he was in Brussels with Paul Verlaine in 1873 a drunken quarrel between the two vagabond poets had a well-nigh tragical climax. There was a pistol-shot and a wild pursuit through the streets, followed by the arrest of Paul Verlaine, who was sent to prison for two years. There is a characteristic and incoherent record of this episode in the elder poet's personal reminiscences.

Rimbaud's *Saison en Enfer* appeared at Brussels in 1873 and attracted scant attention. *Les Illuminations,* another volume of obscure prose interlarded with capricious verse (with a brief preface by Paul Verlaine) was published in 1886. These pieces were composed between

1873 and 1875. They may be read as a psychical autobio-
graphy burdened with the regret of a wasted youth.
Other poems by Rimbaud, giving glimpses of real genius
and singularly original in their eccentricity, have been
published here and there, *e.g.* in the *Poètes maudits* of
Paul Verlaine. They shew a fine sense of melody, which
is sometimes squandered on fantastic and grotesque themes.
Now and then the verse is moulded by a master-hand.

Arthur Rimbaud seems to have continued his aimless
career, but the history of his peregrinations is somewhat
obscure. After visiting Russia, he travelled towards Asia
Minor to assist in some official excavations or explora-
tions. It was rumoured that he had taken refuge in one
of the monasteries of Lebanon and his death was prematurely announced from time to time. On his return to
France he died in the public hospital of Marseilles, where
he had submitted to a surgical operation for tumour on
the knee.

It is doubtful if Arthur Rimbaud could have conquered
an important place in French literature, although with
severe labour and discipline he might have produced some
durable work. He had a vast command of uncommon
imagery and a strange power of associating alien ideas.
His phrases are often extremely felicitous, but he loves
to spoil the harmony of his picture by the deliberate
violence of a monstrous climax. He blends flashes of
spiritual imagination with the crudest strokes of realism.
Sometimes he reminds the reader of Robert Browning or
Walt Whitman; again he paints with the fidelity of a
Flemish master. His genius bordered on madness, and
so far as can be judged from his fugitive fragments he
represents a sort of anarchism in the poetic art.

Love and Labour.

Four on the clock of a summer morn.
  The sleep of Love still overpowers.
An odour, of festal evenings born,
  Evaporates from the bowers.

In the world's vast workshop, ere the sun
  Hesperidéan islands leaves,
The Carpenter, to work begun,
  Is astir—in his shirt-sleeves—.

In virgin Wastes, with moss o'ergrown,
  His craft he calmly plies
On precious panels, which the town
  Will dabble with false skies.

O charm of the Labourers led in file
  When a king in Babylon rose supreme!
Venus! leave thy Lovers awhile
  With souls in a crownëd dream!

Queen of the Shepherds, bring
  To the husbandmen barley-bree,
Their strength in peace replenishing
  Before the bath in the noonday sea!

(Une Saison en Enfer.)

ARTHUR RIMBAUD

Wasted Youth.

Far from the birds and the herds and the meadows,
Kneeling I drank in the heather, aswoon
With a tender caress of the hazel-tree shadows
In the haze of a genial and green afternoon.

What could I drink from this young river welling—
Voiceless elms, flowerless swards, skies cloud-accurst!—
Drink in these green gourds, so far from my dwelling?
But some golden liquor that kindles the thirst.

Sinister signboard to swing on a tavern!
Storm in the welkin changed noon into night;
Then were black islands, dark creek and dull cavern,
Stark poles and bare columns athwart the blue light.

The wave from the woodland the virgin sands swallowed,
God's wind paved the pools with ice to the brink;
'Twas gold-diver's, pearl-fisher's luck I had followed
For, fancy, I never bethought me to drink!

(Les Illuminations.)

The Vowels.*

Black A, white E, red I, green U, blue O,
Vowels that echo like remote carillions:
A, sheen of black-haired corselet on winged millions
Round cruel stenches buzzing to and fro;

Gulfs of gloom.   E, clear vapours and pavilions,
White kings, thrilled blossoms, spears of frozen snow;
I, purples, blood-dews, crimson lips aglow
With shame of rosy limbs on languorous pillions:

U, spheres, divine vibrations of green surges,
Calm of meads sown with beeves, æthereal verges,
Calm wreathed on furrowed foreheads of the wise;

O, supreme clarion shrilling forth strange clamours,
Silences cloven of worlds and angels, glamours;
Omega, O the beam of Her blue eyes!

Les Voyelles.
(*Poèmes inédits.*)

---

* Those who wish to understand the occult significance of this sonnet may interpret for themselves the following sentence from René Ghil's luminous *Traité du Verbe* (Bruxelles: Edmond Deman: 1888):—

' *& inſtrumentation plus haut qu'idiome & que muſique & que peinture*
' *que, lumineuſe et ſonnante & diſante, elle eſt à la fois, & inſtrumenta-*
' *tion idéale, authentique! en ſavamment hors du haſard uſuel des*
' *gloſſaires éliſant les mots où le plus je multiplie la voyelle là inſtru-*
' *mentalement déſirée, en raiſon qu'elle s'authentique de la loi même qui*
' *divulgue que va à ſe ſavoir en ſe penſant, la matière: quand, en effet,*
' *fatalement et eſſentiellement, & quant à ſes ſonorités! la parole eſt liée à*
' *l'idée, & qu'ainſi, logiques & ſans haſards, & à élire, ſont les mots*
' *ſeulement, dont ont même valeur idéale le ſens vulgaire & la ſonorité'.*
—O Voltaire!

Jean Moréas.

Born in Athens, 1856.

The roll of French poets in this century, as in the last, ends with a Greek. But André Chénier was only half a Greek and Jean Moréas is purely Hellenic. And if Chénier helped to give a new impulse to true and natural poetry Moréas has also the ambition to be a reformer, more, perchance, in material than in spiritual things. He has adopted most of the modern innovations in French verse and introduced several of his own. Among them are a deliberate disregard of the regular cæsura and likewise of the enlacement of masculine and feminine rhymes ; a violation of the rules which forbid rhyme between singular and plural and masculine and feminine words of similar sound ; a frequent use of assonances instead of pure consonances ; and the bold elision of the vowel before a consonant. Moréas is also addicted to the employment of lines of irregular length and verse of mixed rhythms. Whatever the permanent influence of such experiments may be, they have at least demonstrated that French verse can be successfully freed from the verbal limitations which custom has imposed upon it. Zola, who sympathises with these efforts to give 'more freedom and more music' to French verse, thinks that the new movement may give birth to a Malherbe who will thence initiate 'a true poetical Renaissance'.

Jean Moréas is a scrupulous and accomplished artist.

He differs from Jules Laforgue* inasmuch as he has always something to say and does not depend for his effects on the violence of incongruous symbols and startling neologisms. Much of his verse is novel, romantic and picturesque. Many of his forms are singularly felicitous. Although the leaders of the new school have helped to mould him, he is thoroughly impregnated with archaism and has borrowed from Villon, Ronsard and other old poets many charming and expressive words which should never have been allowed to become obsolete; indeed, the influence of the sixteenth-century singers is manifest in most of his work. It may be that his research after rare and choice words is sometimes carried to excess and even gives an air of labour to his lyrical style. But he is modern in his substitution of spiritual impressions for clearly-defined outlines, and this lends a vagueness to his verse without destroying its archaic character. Hence it is true, as Anatole France says, that 'he is one of the seven stars of the new Pléiade and also the Ronsard of symbolism'.

Jean Moréas is said to be descended from two Greek heroes; one the naval commander (*navargue*) Tombazis and the other Papadiamantopoulos, a name for ever associated with Missolonghi. But he has made Paris his home and given himself to the serious study of letters.

---

* Jules Laforgue, author of *les Complaintes* (1885) *l'Imitation de Notre-Dame la Lune* (1886) and some rhapsodical prose essays, died in 1887 at twenty-seven years of age. He had a wonderful gift of rhyme, melody and metaphor, and, like Arthur Rimbaud, the power of sudden poetical illumination without any coherent purpose. One of his crazes was the creation of hybrid compounds, such as *sexciproques, sangsuelles, hymniclames, voluptés*. In his lucid intervals of inspiration he could throw off such a couplet as

' Où vont les gants d'avril, et les rames d'antan ?
' L'âme des hérons fous sanglote sur l'étang '.

336

JEAN MORÉAS

He was educated at Marseilles, the old Greek colony in France. His principal volumes of poetry are *les Syrtes* (1883-1884) written under the influence of Paul Verlaine *les Cantilènes* (1886) in which his imitation of Stéphane Mallarmé is more marked, and *le Pélerin passionné* (1891) a work in which he has given himself up almost wholly to mediæval attractions. All these volumes are published by Léon Vanier, the famous '*éditeur* of the moderns'.

* * *

The leaves from the woodland
That whirl on the breeze,
Blown far on the headland,
The leaves from the woodland
That whirl on the breeze,
Will they ever come back
To clothe . . . the same trees?

The waves of the streamlet
That sparkles and pours
In the shade of the hamlet,
The waves of the streamlet
That sparkles and pours,
Will they ever come back
To bathe . . . the same shores?

Conte d'Amour. XI.
(*Les Syrtes.*)

Little Blue Bird.

Little blue bird, with time-coloured wings,
    That sings, and sings:
To soothe with tenderness hearts that are torn
And scourged by the lashes of Scorn.

Little blue bird, with time-coloured wings,
    That sings, and sings:
To renew as with force, to refresh as with fire,
    The languorous limbs of Desire.

Little blue bird, with time-coloured wings,
    That sings, and sings:
To breathe new life into Hopes that lie dead,
    And banish the phantoms of Dread.

Little blue bird, with time-coloured wings,
Long have I sought thee by rivers and springs,
Long have I sought thee on mountain and plain,
    In vain, in vain!

Oisillon bleu.
(*Les Syrtes.*)

Sweets to the Sweet.

*   *   *   *   *   *

III.

Bastion shadow,
Reddened where flickering lamplight looms,
    Lakes profound, dense-frondaged glooms
When Hecate's chariot leaves the meadow,
    Raven plumes
That love the gibbet, ebon braid
    With gems arrayed;
Ye are not the tresses of my Lady.

339

Nor you, O sheaves of golden grain,
    Shimmering star,
Tawny sunsets, splendorous dawns
    That gild the lawns ;
Refinëd gold, your pride is vain,
    And vain your symbols are !

Fragrant fraughtage of triremes
    From Araby, how sweet meseems
The glorious auburn tresses of my Lady.
    Be they pleachëd and dispread
    In simple fillets on her head,
Or curtained loose when she doth languish,
    Yielding to a lover's anguish.

IV.

To crown her head I fain would bring
Flowers all unnamed of lips that sing.

Lavender, marjoram, marigold red,
And the rose that breathed on lutes enchanted ;
White flower-de-luce by Perdita vaunted
    For sweet Prince Florizel's bed ;
Pink, pale primrose, iris, orris,
And all the treasure of buxom Chloris :
    Poor would the sheaf be, garlanded
        To crown her head.

*   *   *   *   *   *

VII.

Sooth, he had none like you to sing,
The King
Whose song was of woman more bitter than death.

For, pressed on your lips of languor,
All is sweet, and sweet the breath
Of your lips, love, even in anger.
And you, are not you
In sweetness the true
Month of Mary, sweet Virgin,
If your look brings the burgeon
To bloom in my pale-coloured soul!

Étrennes de Doulce.
(*Le Pélerin passionné.*)

Index.

343

INDEX

345

INDEX

.

www.ingramcontent.com/pod-product-compliance
Lightning Source LLC
Chambersburg PA
CBHW021529110726
47902CB00004B/802